The year is 1953. Sigurbjörn Helgason the architect yearns to create a cathedral echoing the shapes of the landscape, the arc of a seabird's wing, the hollows of a cliff-face cave. Yet his current project, plagued by doubt and debt, is for the first franchised department store in Reykjavík. His eleven-year-old son, Tóti, cycles up and down the steep streets of the town, reluctantly having taken a summer job delivering meat for Trough Butchers. Sigurbjörn's older son, Helgi, a national football star, longs to play in the English League. The family can celebrate as the leases on the shop space are finally taken up, but a single seemingly random act, an assault on the young boy in the unfinished shell of the store, will destroy each of them. Obsessions, dreams and memories lead, inevitably, to violence.

SHAD THAMES BOOKS

Also in this series:

Páll Valsson (ed.) Brushstrokes of Blue
(Greyhound Press)

Einar Már Gudmundsson Epilogue of the Raindrops
(Greyhound Press)

Thor Vilhjálmsson Justice Undone
(Mare's Nest)

Einar Már Gudmundsson Angels of the Universe
(Mare's Nest)

Frída Á. Sigurdardóttir Night Watch
(Mare's Nest)

Forthcoming from Mare's Nest:

Gudbergur Bergsson The Swan
Matthías Johannessen New and Selected Poems

For details of Mare's Nest books, please see pages 291–4.

Trolls' Cathedral

Trolls' Cathedral

Ólafur Gunnarsson

Translated from the Icelandic
by David McDuff and Jill Burrows

MARE'S NEST

Published in 1996
in the Shad Thames series
by Mare's Nest Publishing
49 Norland Square London W11 4PZ

Trolls' Cathedral
Ólafur Gunnarsson

Copyright © Ólafur Gunnarsson 1992
Translation copyright © David McDuff, Jill Burrows 1996

Cover image: Gaudí – Sagrada Familia Cathedral, Barcelona
Original cover design by Börkur Arnarson
Typeset by Agnesi Text Hadleigh Suffolk
Printed and bound by Antony Rowe Ltd Chippenham Wiltshire

ISBN 1 899197 30 3

Tröllakirkja was originally published in Iceland by Forlagid,
Reykjavík, 1992. This translation is published by agreement with
Forlagid, to whom the publishers are grateful.

This publication has been facilitated by the generous participation
of the Icelandic Embassy, London.

This book is published with the financial assistance of the Arts
Council of England.

Dedicated to the memory of
Alfred Flóki (1938–1987)

The Icelandic troll is a large, malevolent creature.
It is a shape-changer, nocturnal and cannibalistic.
If caught in daylight it will turn into a rock.

SUMMER

I

1

For Sigurbjörn Helgason the architect the worst embarrassment imaginable was to be seen in public improperly dressed. Come winter and come summer, whenever the weather was fine, he would take long walks with his son Thórarinn. Father and son were very close, and it made people smile to see them, out walking together, wearing their smartest clothes, deep in conversation.

'Whose side are you on, Mother's or mine?' Thórarinn asked.

'Give it a rest, lad,' said his father.

It was a mild evening early in June 1953 and they were heading north across Skólavörduholt. Sigurbjörn was wearing a black tweed overcoat. He had a peaked cap over his thick hair. His cheeks were coarse and scarred. He was tall, and walked with his head held high. A broad, black bow-tie was knotted beneath his chin.

His eye was caught by a man in a ragged, flapping anorak sitting on a bench under the statue of Leif Eiríksson, the great medieval navigator. He looked at the man's paunch and stocky thighs with distaste. The man was wearing large rubber boots. His legs were splayed and his blue jeans had frayed in the wash. He turned his face away from the father and son and looked towards Frakkastígur. His cheeks were flabby and his face wore a dazed expression.

A new green Dodge drove slowly by. As the boy gawped at the car, his father looked across to the bare mound of sand and grass and the stony slope where the chancel of Hallgrímskirkja stood, under its temporary roof. All construction work had stopped. For years Sigurbjörn Helgason had worked on designs for the Gothic church to be built on Skólavörduhæd and at this point on his walks with his son he was in the habit of stopping and visualizing the completed church.

3

Suddenly he remembered a long-forgotten sketch. As a first-year architecture student in Copenhagen, purely for his own pleasure, he had drawn up plans for a cathedral on a hill. He squinted up at the sky and grimaced as he saw that very idea take shape before him.

Now he turned back and glanced once more at the man sitting under the statue. Now he was leaning forward, glowering at the father and son. His expression took Sigurbjörn aback. He looked behind him, expecting to find the object of the man's animosity, but there was no one there. Why was the chap in the anorak looking at them like that? Had he noticed Sigurbjörn sizing him up? Was there something wrong with Thórarinn? He looked at his son.

Thórarinn Sigurbjarnarson was nearly twelve years old. He was wearing a light-green double-breasted coat, a light-brown peaked cap and shiny black patent-leather shoes, just like his father's. His prominent forehead gave his face a stubborn look. His eyes were blue, his face broad and the light glinted in his cropped red hair. He was short for his age and thickset. His schoolfriends, sensing a remoteness about him, sometimes called him 'Sir Professor'. Sigurbjörn stole another glance at the stranger, who was now sitting right on the edge of the bench, staring at the two of them, open-mouthed and intense. He seemed angry.

Thórarinn broke the silence: 'Father, do you think they could make cars run on atomic energy?'

For a moment Sigurbjörn did not answer. He felt like asking the ruffian what he wanted. Had they met before? Then suddenly he was very angry. He took a step towards the bench, the other man's eyes still on him. 'Excuse me,' he said. 'Do we know each other?'

'Not as far as I know.'

'Is there something you want?'

The man shook his head.

'Then why the hell are you staring at us?'

The stranger looked him up and down. 'You can't have everything your own way,' he said, spitting the words out. 'You don't make the rules.'

Sigurbjörn moved closer, more aggressive, clenching his fists. The man scrambled to his feet and shuffled off like a startled horse,

4

covering his head with the hood of his anorak, muttering to himself.

'What was all that about?' Thórarinn asked.

Sigurbjörn took a moment to recover from his surge of violence. 'We have every bit as much right to be here as that tramp, Tóti,' replied his father. 'There's something odd about that chap.'

'You are on my side, aren't you, Father? I'm counting on you.'

'On your side?' Sigurbjörn, without thinking, reached for his son's hand.

'Get off!' snapped Thórarinn angrily. 'We don't hold hands any more. I'm nearly twelve.'

'Not until the autumn,' said his father, absent-mindedly unbuttoning his coat. He was keeping one eye on the stranger, who looked as if he was about to take something out of his pocket.

'I'm sure it'll be best for everyone if I'm allowed to make up my own mind,' said the boy, with great aplomb. 'Come on, let's go.'

'I know what you're saying, Tóti, but I'm on your mother's side in this,' said Sigurbjörn, and he strode off with his hands thrust deep in his pockets, staring down at the pavement with his bulging eyes. 'Let's leave it and talk about it later.'

They walked to the corner and looked down the steep slope of Frakkastígur. In the calm bay below Mount Esja a white, five-masted schooner lay off the point at Engey, its reflection sharp on the surface of the sea. The sun was setting. The sailing ship gleamed in the evening light, but the steep cliffs of the mountain were now in shadow. Involuntarily, Sigurbjörn turned to look back: the man was once more sitting on the bench staring like a zombie towards Hnitbjörg. The hood of his anorak was still up, and he was chewing on a matchstick.

Father and son set off down Frakkastígur.

2

Sigurbjörn's father had built the first house on the stony hill to the south of the Hnitbjörg, the Einar Jónsson Art Museum, in the summer of 1924, number 1a Sjafnargata. Sigurbjörn was then sixteen years old, and had helped with the building. One evening in late summer after Sigurbjörn had put in a long, hard day, the sculptor Einar Jónsson came and offered him three krónur an hour to work the clay for a few afternoons.

A plank was balanced across two wooden barrels, and there he stood. He had never known anything so hard, even though his hands were large and he was a strong lad. He thought the sculptor's model, a black-haired woman who wore a white smock, had an even worse time of it: she began work first thing in the morning and was scarcely allowed to move until the evening.

One day the model got down from the dais and walked about the studio, stretched, did some knee-bends, and then disappeared into the house to visit the sculptor's wife. Sigurbjörn was enjoying his coffee and a pastry by the plank. The sculptor was standing a little way away, staring at his work. He had just lifted his cup of coffee to his lips when suddenly he let both cup and saucer fall to the ground and rushed at the statue, scraping at it with a small trowel.

'Huh!' Sigurbjörn laughed his hollow, mirthless laugh at the memory.

'What's so funny?' asked Thórarinn.

'I was thinking of the time Einar Jónsson dropped his coffee.'

'There's something I've never asked you about that.'

'What?'

'What did his wife say?'

'What do you think she said, Tóti? In the old days women knew their place,' Sigurbjörn said, morosely.

'He wouldn't have got away with that sort of behaviour with Mother,' said Thórarinn.

'You're not far wrong there, Tóti,' said his father.

'I don't know how many times you've told me that story,' said the boy, gloomily.

They crossed Laugavegur in silence and walked down to the corner of Frakkastígur and Hverfisgata.

'Shall we drop in on Grandfather and Grandmother?' asked the boy.

'No,' said Sigurbjörn, obstinately. 'I'm not in the mood.'

However, they did walk a short way east along Hverfisgata until Sigurbjörn could see the home of his parents-in-law on Vitatorg. They lived in a green, two-storey wooden house with a yellow brick chimney and a jet-black roof. The house, somewhat in need of repair, stood on the corner of the square facing Bjarnaborg. The old man had divided the ground floor into two, and rented both halves to doctors. Beneath the west gable there was a well-tended kitchen garden screened by a picket fence. There were redcurrants and a little clump of old rowan trees.

'Grandfather will never let you build there,' said the boy.

'Whatever makes you think that?' Sigurbjörn gave his son a sharp look.

'Mother and I dropped in the other day. She wants you to find a site somewhere else. Grandfather says he is far too old to move now. He says the rent the doctors pay him is like a pension. Grandfather says you'll go bankrupt and he'll never see a single króna and mother will be left destitute. That's what Grandfather says will happen.'

'The old boy can see into the future now, can he? After all, it's not as if he'll have to move far. He owns flats all over town. And he'll get valuable floor-space instead.'

'Grandfather says it's impossible to build a house in such a short time. There's no question of him letting you have the site. He says that no one is interested in this new way of trading. It's just a lot of stupid nonsense. And he ought to know, he's kept a shop for half a century.'

'Half a century too long!' said Sigurbjörn, angrily. 'Nobody ever visits that run-down hole of a shop. The only people who go there are a few old women after black-market ham. He doesn't know anything. I'm the one who knows how to build houses.'

'Grandfather says . . .'

'Yes, "Grandfather says", "Grandfather says". Don't be cheeky, Thórarinn. You don't have to repeat everything the old goat tells you. I'm used to handling workmen. If they'll give me the site I'll have the place built in two or three months and then they'll be fighting for floor-space.'

'Is anyone interested in it?'

'I haven't really gone into all that yet.' Sigurbjörn grew expansive. 'But this is a good old house. There's no rot in it. It's as good as new.'

Sigurbjörn could hear the old man's voice in the boy's mouth.

'Let's turn back now,' he said, staying his son with a hand across the boy's chest. 'I don't want your grandfather to catch us sniffing about.'

'Is there a good reason for pulling down a place like this when it's as good as new? Why don't you build somewhere out of town?' asked Thórarinn.

'Because of the asphalt streets. People don't want to drive through a lot of mud when they go shopping.'

Sigurbjörn was keeping a wary eye on the windows of the house and on the edge of the front steps. The door was hidden from view round the corner.

'I'd come.'

'Yes, perhaps you would. But what good is one boy in a whole department store, however keen he is?'

'I think it'll be a shame if Grandfather's house gets pulled down,' said Thórarinn, gloomily.

'Don't talk about things you don't understand, lad. You know full well the house isn't going to be pulled down. It'll be moved as it stands. There's a man in Selfoss who'll be keen to buy it . . .'

Sigurbjörn put his index finger to his lips and signalled to Thórarinn to keep quiet; his father-in-law was on the front steps. Geir Sveinsson was in his eighties but he was still slim and spry. His hair was black on top and grey at the temples, and his face was as brown as if he had been lying in a peat-bog for centuries. He smoked a long-stemmed pipe which rarely left his mouth. The old man was watching a car moving east along Hverfisgata. Sigurbjörn took hold of the boy's arm and whispered, 'Come on, Thórarinn, quick. Don't look round, we don't want him to see us.'

The day had been unusually warm, and there had been a lot of people about, but now the streets were nearly deserted. As they walked towards the city centre, a gentle breeze blew up, the evening sun shone on the corrugated-iron roofs and its reflection flashed in windows here and there. A car or two passed lazily by, clanking over a manhole cover. Sigurbjörn held his son's hand, whether he liked it or not, and crossed over into the cool shadow on the other side.

'I wouldn't want to get involved in the building business,' said the boy.

'All you want to do is fritter your time away,' said his disgruntled father. He was thinking about what the boy had told him, and he was trying not to let it annoy him. 'So the old devil's not going to let me have the site,' he thought. 'I thought he would do anything for his daughter.' Out loud he said, 'Don't come moaning to me about your mother.'

They walked briskly, with their heads down, until there in front of them was the National Theatre. Sigurbjörn pointed. 'Look!'

'Are you going to be on my side or mother's?' asked the boy.

'Leave it, Thórarinn.'

'What was it like for you when you were my age? Did you have to go out to work? No! You just ran Grandfather's errands for him.'

'Yes, and a fine summer holiday that was!' said his father, bitterly. 'On my feet from morning till night. That's one hell of a job, errand boy in a wholesale business. Can't you find something like that?'

'Maybe. If I wanted. But that doesn't count as work, running errands for your own father.'

'I always had to knock on the door before I went into your grand-father's room,' said Sigurbjörn Helgason, looking as though it was the greatest hardship in the world. 'Three light taps, one two three.' He mimed knocking on an imaginary door. 'How would you have liked that, son?'

'I won't go out to work,' the boy muttered. 'I won't change my mind, whatever anyone says.'

'It's not as though you had to earn your keep, Thórarinn,' said his father, and his shoulders heaved as he moved his hands in his pockets. 'You'll soon be a young man. Twelve years old! Of course, you won't have to pay for your board and lodging, but everyone must work. That is how life is. Besides, doing nothing is damned boring. There's no pleasure in it.'

Sigurbjörn quickened his step.

'So I'm twelve all of a sudden, am I?' said Thórarinn, almost breaking into a run to keep up. 'Well, well! There's the National Theatre. Iceland's most beautiful building. Architect: Sigurbjörn Helgason.'

'Don't be mean to your aged father,' said Sigurbjörn, and stopped. 'You know I didn't design the National Theatre. But I did do all the costings . . . and I did a great many working sketches and dealt with all the tenders.' Sigurbjörn dug his hands deeper into his pockets and looked up at the National Theatre and said, 'You're all the same, you all think I don't know what I'm doing.'

'I'm sorry,' Thórarinn said sadly, with his eyes on the pavement. 'I just can't see myself taking a job this summer.'

At Arnarhóll they sat beneath the statue of Ingólfur Arnarson, the city's first settler. The sun was an orange-red disc above Snæfellsjökull; it was possible to look straight at it. Sigurbjörn scanned the windows of Government House. 'Shall we go up and see if there's anyone at the City Architect's, perhaps get invited in for a coffee?'

'No, let's go somewhere else.'

'Öldugata, then?'

'No, Gudbrandur teases me.'

'You don't want to let him upset you. Tease him back.'

'It's no use, Father. He talks so fast and laughs at his own jokes and then the others laugh too, and I feel so stupid. I can never get a word in.'

'You are far more intelligent than Gudbrandur, Tóti,' Sigurbjörn said firmly.

'Oh, I'm not so sure about that.'

'What did you get for Icelandic composition this spring?'

'Ninety-six per cent,' said the boy proudly.

'I don't say that book learning is all that counts in life, but there you are!' Sigurbjörn prodded him with a large finger.

'It was my idea that was so good,' said Thórarinn. 'We were allowed to do what we liked. I had just read *Of Mice and Men* by John Steinbeck and I had the brilliant idea of writing a new ending to the story, letting Lenny live and George and him get the farm. But dreams never quite come true: they couldn't find any bunnies for Lenny anywhere, so the story ends with him sitting out on the veranda looking sadly at the creeping clover and cuddling a porcupine.'

'Damned fine work,' said the father, and the boy tried to conceal his pleasure. 'Just between you and me, Tóti, I have big ideas for the future of Reykjavík.' Sigurbjörn waxed grandiose. 'They've talked about roofing over Laugavegur or some other street, but I'd like to put a roof over the whole city, son.' His hand described a vast arc and he said, with an air of importance, 'I want to build a glass dome over Reykjavík. It's not possible at present with the technical know-how at our disposal, but one day, Tóti . . .'

'Over the whole . . . ?' Thórarinn gaped at him.

'Then the city would have a tropical climate.' Sigurbjörn raised his voice. 'Palm trees and tropical plants would grow in backyards. The climate here would be quite different, people's faces wouldn't freeze in the north wind every time they went out to get milk or fish in the wintertime, and the womenfolk could just reach out of the window and pick bananas. It would be like in the Golden Age.'

'And peaches,' said Thórarinn. Peaches were his favourite fruit.

'Yes, and raisins and plums, too, if you like.' Sigurbjörn was laughing.

'Oh, it's only a joke.' Thórarinn was disappointed.

'No, of course it isn't. I'm serious. First, you'd need to build an enormous Great Wall of China round the city for the dome to rest on.'

'But what about the rainwater? Wouldn't you need gutters running round the whole dome, and a conduit leading out to sea?'

'No,' said Sigurbjörn after considering this idea. 'The conduit could flow into Lake Tjörnin, and the water could fall from a great height. Then, whenever it rained, we could have a waterfall in the city. It could be called "The Thunderer".'

'A rain waterfall,' said Thórarinn. 'That would be wonderful.'

Sigurbjörn stretched his arms out along the back of the bench and looked up at the sky. Then he frowned, and said, 'I suppose you might as well stay at home this summer, Thórarinn, if that's what you really want.' He glanced at his son and saw his features brighten under the broad forehead.

'That's great,' said the boy, after a long pause. 'I've a lot to do this summer. We're going to make the world's biggest catapult, me and my friend Bragi, it will be as tall as a man and we'll be able to fire it all the way to Videy. Do you think you could help us to get materials for it, Father?'

'I expect so. Good grief! That's a catapult and a half. You'd be able to fire all the way across the bay and straight into the jaws of Snæfellsjökull.'

A ship's siren sounded. A foreign cargo vessel with a large, sooty smokestack had docked in the harbour; the warehouse on the quayside jutted out against the side of the ship. Sigurbjörn sprang to his feet and they walked down the hill to the kiosk where he bought a bag of gobstoppers and offered one to his son. A bus came along Kalkofnsvegur, drove around the small transformer and stopped. A group of people was waiting beside another bus with its engine running. Sigurbjörn told his son that the transformer was art nouveau in style and put a red gobstopper in his mouth. As they crossed Hverfisgata and walked along Lækjargata, a cool breeze was blowing off Lake Tjörnin and the terns hovered, crying. The cathedral clock struck nine. Father and son turned up Bókhlöðustígur.

'This must be the steepest street in town,' puffed Thórarinn.

'Frakkastígur is a damned sight worse,' said his father.

'No, there you can have a breather at the crossroads, but it's uphill all the way here.'

'You ought to go to San Francisco,' said his father. 'It's uphill there all day long. They wouldn't even notice a gradient like this.'

'One day we'll go there,' said Thórarinn. 'You promised.'

The boy couldn't wait to look in a particular shop window on Skólavördustígur, but his father was fond of the old corrugated-iron houses in Thingholt, and wanted to walk slowly. On the corner of Spítalastígur and Grundarstígur the architect stopped and stared at a decrepit single-storey wooden house where the corrugated iron was rusted through. It was empty and ripe for demolition. All the windows in the basement were broken.

'Do you see this nasty little hovel, son,' he boomed at the boy. 'There was a time when this house was a fine sight. Probably imported from Norway. About 1908, I'd say. But it's had it, Thórarinn.' Sigurbjörn loomed over his son. 'Do you think it's a shame to pull down houses like this and build new ones?'

'Grandfather's house is in a bit better state than this one,' said the boy.

'Yes, yes, yes. And with some effort a lot of things here could probably be fixed up. This is caused by years of neglect.' Sigurbjörn cast a professional eye over the central support and the windows, went up the front steps where the cement had begun to crumble away revealing the pebbles, then grasped the door handle. The paintwork of the door was red and scratched, blue showed through here and there. The house was not locked. There was a strong smell of damp. Sigurbjörn called loudly, 'Hallo, hallo, is there anyone at home?' Thórarinn looked around him, anxious.

'Let's have a look at it.'

'Oh no, I don't like doing things like this.'

'Oh, come on.'

'No, I don't want to, Father.'

'Well, you're some chip off the old block. Huh!' laughed his father. The laughter was coarse. Sigurbjörn stayed in the house a good while and then came slowly over to the window, in order to examine the windowsill. The boy waited outside. Then his father came back down the steps and cast his eye over the façade. 'It would be fun to take down a house like this. The windows are two-by-four, son. Oak! I cut off a shaving with my pocket knife. You could probably get it free if you offered to take it away. There's prime wood in this house,' he said, affectionately. 'The oak in the frames is probably as good as new. They've not used a single metal nail; they're all wood. It's terrible to see good timber like this go to waste. I'd like to see your brothers here with a crowbar working up a good sweat.'

Thórarinn imagined Ragnar and Helgi hard at work and then remembered his sister. 'Yes, and Vilborg as well,' he said. 'It's almost enough to put you off wanting to be an architect.'

His father smiled, exposing his large, irregular teeth with their gold fillings. His smile sat oddly on him, and did not suit his face. It was as though he had it on loan from someone else. Even his family found it unpleasant.

They reached Skólavördustígur, where there was a toyshop in a small wooden building. In the window a dark-blue Hawker Hurricane fighter plane was suspended on strings, the exhaust vents visible in its nose. The fighter plane was impressive enough to attract even the older man's attention.

'It runs on petrol,' said his son.

Sigurbjörn came close, read the price tag and suggested his son should put money by in a savings account until he had enough to buy it.

'If you weren't too lazy to work this summer, you could earn enough to get it.'

'But can't you give it to me?'

'Isn't it your birthday soon?'

'In the autumn!' The boy thought it impossible to wait that long.

'Stop it, Thórarinn. You've been going on and on all evening about what you want. Give it a rest, and let me think.'

Thórarinn smiled almost imperceptibly.

On Skólavörduhæd Sigurbjörn remembered the man in the hooded anorak, but he was nowhere to be seen. The architect stopped as he usually did to look at the hill and then up at the sky, and see in his mind's eye the church that was to be built there.

3

As they walked down Njardargata Thórarinn was pretending to be a member of the Kikuyu tribe. Palm trees grew in alleys and gardens and a long-tailed parrot fluttered across the street. From all points of the compass through the humid air came the sounds of the jungle. He was a bearer for a white architect who had emigrated from Britain with his family and now lived in the lap of luxury in a large white house in Kenya. He was working in the household as an errand boy, but that was only a cover. In reality he was one of the leaders of the Mau-Mau, the militant secret society. Soon there would be all-out war. He had taken note of all the most important distinguishing features of the man he had been told to spy on. He put his hand on the garden gate and looked at the white man. Aged forty-five. Wears a peaked cap and bow tie. He would have been better off with a solar topee. A very strange man, to put it mildly. A lot of scars on his cheeks. Narrow shoulders. Staring, really quite murderous eyes. A very dangerous man.

'Why are you staring at me like that, Tóti?'

'Oh, just . . .'

'Just what?'

Thórarinn opened the gate and they walked up the garden path.

The house was on the corner at the top of a steep slope. Along the path Sigurbjörn's father had planted rowan saplings. They were too close and after thirty years of growth they shaded the path completely in summer. One colossal rowan obscured the parlour window. A hand rake and a small trowel lay in a flowerbed.

Sunneva had seen them, and the front door was open. 'Meet anybody interesting?' she asked.

'Not unless you count your father,' replied Sigurbjörn.

'What's the news with him?'

'We only just caught a glimpse of Grandfather. We didn't speak to him,' said Thórarinn.

Sigurbjörn untied his black silk scarf and laid it on the wooden shelf over the radiator. Sunneva took their coats and Thórarinn's cap. Sigurbjörn warmed his hands at the radiator. He seemed preoccupied with something. Sunneva wondered what the matter was now. Sigurbjörn took his comb from his jacket pocket and smoothed his hair back from his temples, but a moment later it sprang back away from its natural centre parting.

'See anyone else?'

'Yes – there was some damned lout sitting up on the hill, staring at us,' said Sigurbjörn.

'And what a fabulous sight he must have seen.'

'He was pretty odd himself,' said Thórarinn.

'And what did this man want, Sigurbjörn?'

'Damned if I know.'

'Have you come across him before?'

Sigurbjörn opened his copy of *Vísir*. He was sitting on the sofa, and looked up from the newspaper as if a thought had suddenly struck him. 'And what have you been up to this evening, woman?' He wanted to change the subject.

'Working in the garden.' She tried to sound casual. 'Oh, by the way, Tóti, about that summer job. There's an advertisement in *Vísir*. A butcher's shop is looking for an errand boy. Why don't you go down there first thing in the morning, so you can be standing outside when they open?'

Thórarinn walked away from them into the dining room; his cheeks were flushed. He looked back at his father who was loosening his bow tie with one hand, stretching his neck. 'I'm not going to take a job,' the boy shouted. 'Father said.'

'Well, I never! Is this true, Sigurbjörn?' She stared at her husband.

'I think the boy deserves it.' Sigurbjörn shrugged his shoulders and buried himself in his newspaper.

'There, you hear, you hear?' The boy was screaming now.

'Well,' said his mother, 'don't expect me to clean up after you and that gang of boys you trail in and out of the house all day long.'

'I'm not going to take any damned bloody job. I won't go! I won't do it! Father, you promised.'

'Listen, Thórarinn,' said his mother, sternly. 'I won't have language like that in my house.'

'I did promise the boy he could do what he wanted this summer.' Sigurbjörn put on his most masterful voice and gave his wife a meaningful look.

'Well then, I'll just move out.' She stamped her foot. 'I'll go and live somewhere else. Do you want to be a layabout all your life, Thórarinn?'

'Can't we discuss this calmly, woman?' muttered Sigurbjörn.

'It's out of the question for the child to hang around here at home all summer. It's out of the question.'

A spiral staircase led up from the dining room. Vilborg, the couple's only daughter, was standing on the second step. Her friend was hovering two steps further up. Vilborg was like her father. Her features were long, her hair was mousy and she had a serious manner. She had inherited his fingers and three weeks earlier she had been very proud when she started piano lessons and the teacher praised her fine piano hands. Now she stepped down on to the parlour floor, leaned against the bannister and put one foot in front of the other, pointed her toe, looked with superior contempt at her brother, and used the sing-song taunt she had long since devised solely in order to infuriate him: 'Heigh-ho, heigh-ho!'

Her friend, a frequent guest in the house, was called Gudbjörg. She was plump and the belt of her jeans cut into her stomach. Her face was freckled and more often than not her mouth was stained with liquorice or some other sweet. She was frantically trying to make sense of the conversation.

'Father, you promised!'

'Calm down, Thórarinn.'

'Are you going to betray me?' shouted the boy, taking refuge in attitude-striking. He was well on the way to losing control completely. He sensed it was all up and that a temper tantrum was his only hope. 'Are you going to let Mother tell us what to do?' he shouted.

'I'd rather stick to what's already been agreed,' said Sigurbjörn.

'Stop it, Tóti, behave yourself,' said Vilborg.

'Stay out of this!' screamed the boy.

'I'm certainly not going to stay out of it,' she said quietly. 'Sjafnargata is my home too. I think you ought to do something this summer. It's not good for you to hang about here all the time. You've gone awfully red, Tóti.'

'Don't come the grown-up with me. You never do anything yourself. You gave up your piano lessons after two weeks. "Piano hands", ha!'

Sunneva was firm. 'You haven't got the job yet.'

'And I'm not going to take it, and I won't take it, no matter what you say,' sang Thórarinn.

'I'm going to be nanny for Gudbrandur and Ingiridur this summer,' said Vilborg, haughtily. 'I think it'll be unbearable if you're going to be hanging around at home. It's not good for you to do nothing.'

'Shut up, bossy-boots. Get out of here and take Fat Gudbjörg with you.'

'Shut up yourself, fatty.'

'Be polite, son,' said Sigurbjörn, sharply. 'Be polite.'

'Yes, Thórarinn, we'd like you to be polite to our visitor,' said his sister. Gudbjörg had gone as red as a peony.

'"We"!' shouted the boy. 'You're all against me. You're all *traitors.*' He struck a dramatic pose right in front of his mother and glowered at her with such theatrical hatred that he began to shake. He had seen this done in films and noticed how effective it was.

'Oh, for goodness' sake, child, stop it,' said Sunneva.

'He's always like this, Mother,' said Vilborg. 'It's quite impossible to live in the same house as this child.'

'Grandfather would never have done this to you,' said Thórarinn, now facing his father, his lower lip trembling and his hair damp with sweat.

Sigurbjörn Helgason did not answer. He got to his feet, folded the newspaper, and opened the door to the staircase that led down to the basement. As he was going downstairs, he heard his son yell: 'We're not poor! I don't need to go out to work!' He did not hear Sunneva's reply.

Sigurbjörn had set up a drawing office two years earlier when he had left his post at the City Architect's office in a fit of pique. His father, Helgi Vésteinsson, had run his import–export business from the same basement. Helgi had been circumspect in his business dealings, and did not want to been seen giving himself airs by having an office in town. Near the door hung a framed photograph dating from the summer Helgi had spent in a department store in Canada. On the left there were two photographs of models of Hallgrímskirkja together in the same frame, one with a tower, the other with wings extending from the base of the tower. These wings were to house a parish hall and an office. There had been a public debate about which of the proposed models should be built. Sigurbjörn was a keen supporter of the wings. They had been his own idea, though it had been attributed to the City Architect, as was only natural when a mere assistant came up with a suggestion.

The trunk of the rowan tree filled one window, making the basement dark. The other window looked out on to the gravel area by the house; sometimes water stood there in puddles long after it had rained. The walls inside never got damp; this was a well-built house. Sigurbjörn sat down at his father's enormous writing desk. He was fond of it. It was resonant with the memory of Helgi Vésteinsson the import–export merchant: suit, stiff-pressed shirt and cufflinks. A smell of cigars. Schnapps . . . Helgi had been fond of schnapps in his coffee. Sigurbjörn could hear his father saying in his nasal drawl, 'When I worked at Eaton's, Sibbi, there was trading on five floors. And a medical clinic and pensions. He looked after his people well, old Eaton.' There was a heavy ashtray on the desk, and a green blotter with a glass roller on top. To the right, against the wall, stood the drawing board. Against the wall on the left was a bookcase containing hundreds of books and periodicals collected by the architect.

He turned the pages of the newspaper and found the butcher's shop advertisement. *Quick, keen boy wanted for delivery work. Ability to ride a bike desirable.* He heard his wife and son arguing. He could not make out the words, only the rise and fall of the voices, and Thórarinn pursuing his mother about the house. Sigurbjörn closed the newspaper and tetchily spread out a design on the desk. 'Sigurbjörn Helgason – Architect's Office'. The name sounded elegant. The design was for a six-storey department store on Vitatorg.

He had had little to do over the winter. One day he had looked over towards the door at the old picture: there was no building like the Eaton Department Store in Reykjavík. The Reykjavík Department Store. As the name had formed in his mind, his hand had begun to draw.

He knew of a man in Selfoss who wanted to buy the wooden house on Vitatorg. Sigurbjörn was looking forward to having an excavator clear the flat rock site, putting up a corrugated-iron fence and bringing in an air compressor and dynamite, smiths, plumbers, cement-layers and electricians, linoleum-fitters and painters. He needed to gauge the depth of the topsoil, but he hesitated to go and scrabble about in his mother-in-law's kitchen garden with a shovel. During his years at the National Theatre he had got to know dozens of craftsmen when dealing with the contracts. He felt he knew how to handle workmen. But he could not talk his father-in-law round. It was years since they had spoken a friendly word to each other. Old Geir kept a grocer's shop on Hverfisgata, Geir Sveinsson Provisions. How anyone could ever bring himself to buy a packet of coffee there was a mystery to his son-in-law. Sunneva had had to go abroad when she became pregnant with Ragnar. The old boy had hated the child's father. 'If you want to be the greatest man on earth, then you should have a daughter,' said Sigurbjörn loudly. 'But if you want to be the most stupid one, then try to hold on to her when she wants to go her own way.'

After Sunneva and Sigurbjörn had got married, Geir kept saying, year after year, that Ámundi, Ragnar's father, was everything a young man should be.

Sigurbjörn had gone to see Geir, and suggested the idea to him. 'A department store! Whatever for, Sigurbjörn?'

'People will want to shop in a building where they can get everything all at once.'

'Has anyone reserved space with you?'

'Not yet. They will.'

'Well, I'm not so sure about that,' said Geir, without interest.

'No, but I am.'

'And what will you give for the square? Do you realize I'm the only man in Reykjavík to own a whole square, and that it was a pure stroke of luck I managed to buy it?' said Geir, brightening. 'The City Council tried to block the sale, said it had the first right of purchase. But I beat them to it by getting the papers stamped and the bailiff's seal on it sharpish.' The old man was moist-eyed with happiness at the memory.

'Half the ground floor, seven hundred square metres – that's what you'll get, Father-in-law.'

'No,' the old man snapped, shaking his head. 'I have no use for it.'

'You'll get rent on it.'

'I've got that already.' The old man was not going to be done down.

'Just wait till they see the moving staircase taking people up to the second floor.'

'Moving what?' Geir leaned forward, put a hand to his ear and looked at Sigurbjörn with steel-grey eyes in his burnished-leather face.

'A moving staircase running on electricity. People step on to it at the bottom and it whisks them upstairs all by itself.' Sigurbjörn made a gesture with his arm to demonstrate the whisking process.

'I say, that would be rather splendid,' said Geir Sveinsson, admiringly. He had a weakness for technical innovations, had owned one of the first lorries in the country, and it had once occurred to him when he was shovelling sand that it would be a good idea to make a machine that would tilt the back of the lorry so that the sand would run off by itself. Not long afterwards the same thing had occurred to someone else overseas.

'I'd like to go on a staircase like that,' shouted Rósa, Sunneva's mother, from the kitchen.

'Well, that's a surprise,' Geir had snorted.

It's lucky that Sunneva ran away to Copenhagen when she got pregnant, otherwise I would never have met her, thought Sigurbjörn, letting his mind wander. He had been at a party in a large flat on Gammel Kongevej just after he had returned to Denmark. He had walked down a long corridor looking for the toilet. He opened a door and found a man and a woman lying naked on a mattress on the floor. The man was asleep and had his back turned to the woman; his shoulders were broad and his neck thick. Outside the window streetlamps were shining like an angled light in a gallery above an old painting. The woman raised herself on one elbow and they looked straight into each other's eyes. He closed the door.

The door opened. He had not heard them come downstairs. Sunneva was standing in the doorway in her long blue skirt and white blouse, her red hair lying uncombed over her shoulders. 'Sigurbjörn, did you mean it about Thórarinn staying at home this summer?'

'I haven't quite decided yet, Sunna,' the architect muttered, without looking up, running his hand over the plans. The eaves were horizontal. It made the house very grand to have stone wave-patterns on it, like seagulls' wings in flight. It was a masterly touch.

'Here you sit giggling in the basement. Have you gone mad, Sigurbjörn? I'm not having the boy hanging around the house all summer. I'll go crazy.'

'Sweetest model, let me smile.' He deepened his voice, and looked up. They were both remembering that first moment in the flat on Gammel Kongevej.

'Don't call me that, you bugger.' There was a warmth in her voice.

Thórarinn stood behind his mother in desperation. His father could hardly bear the look in his son's eyes. It would not do to keep wife and son in suspense much longer.

4

Thórarinn turned his face to the wall. They had lost. Father had betrayed him. Earlier his mother had come storming into his room and ordered him to get up. A smell of pancakes was wafting through the door, making him restless. He began to wonder what was going to happen. It was long past eleven. He was just dozing off when Sunneva appeared in the doorway again, with her coat on. 'Now get up, Tóti, and go and talk to the man at the shop, or I'll drag you out of bed by the scruff of your neck.'

He sat up and swung his feet round to the floor. His mood was dark with melancholy and fear. 'And what am I to say to this shopkeeper?'

'There's nothing to be frightened of, child. Just tell him who you are. If you don't get yourself over there by midday, you won't have a chance to talk to him before one o'clock.'

He began to look for his socks. They were not within reach, and he scoured the floor for them. He heard his mother slam the front door and listened to her footsteps going down the front path. Then he flopped back on to his bed again leaving his legs dangling over the side. 'Father betrayed me,' he said to himself. He could scarcely believe it.

He had nowhere to turn to. It was hard having to go and talk to the man at the shop. But staying at home and being nagged was worse. Thórarinn knew his mother inside out. 'If I don't go now she'll only drag me down there later.' Slowly he got out of bed.

He put his clothes on, brushed his teeth and went out. Tell him who I am! Who am I? I am the son of Sigurbjörn Helgason who runs the Sigurbjörn Helgason Architect's Office. He once worked for the City Architect. I am twelve years old. You have been advertising for an errand boy.

He took a shortcut over Skólavörduholt. I am the son of Sigurbjörn Helgason who runs the architect's office of the same name. He once worked for the City Architect and helped to design the National Theatre. No, that was too long. He should confine himself to his name, the City Architect's office and his age.

The butcher's shop was on the ground floor of a grey stone house. Above the windows and doors large blue letters announced TROUGH BUTCHER'S. Two sheep gazed longingly at the generous selection of titbits in a clumsily painted wooden trough.

It was almost noon, and the shop was full to bursting with people who had come to buy hot food. He saw that he would have to wait, hesitated before going in, and mentally rehearsed his speech about his origins again.

Hjálmur the storekeeper was large and loud and had come through into the shop to help the two woman assistants at this busy time of day. The older woman was short and very thin, with one eyelid drooping like a pirate's. She was chewing her false teeth absent-mindedly. The other was tall and elegant, with pale yellow hair and fiery red lips, like a woman from the cabaret. Was there a circus at the back of the house? Bears jumping through fire? She held up a lamb chop. Hjálmur was dashing about. Beneath his white coat, which was grubby around the waist, he was wearing a suit. He waved a fork and a spoon in the air and directed the women to and fro serving the customers. The older one took it in good part, but the younger one tended to bridle and bristle. 'There are people waiting, my dears,' said Hjálmur. 'There are people waiting.'

He picked up a small, white, waxed box and broke it open. Then he waited, hovering above steel trays containing a variety of delicacies. 'Yes, and what can I do for you, my friend? Beef stew? Eh? Hamburger? Speak up. Yes, hamburger it shall be.'

Dozens of hamburgers sat in the congealing brown sauce and shimmering gravy. The people hung about the shop a little afraid of this giant storekeeper who spoke more loudly than anyone else dared to and did not hear a thing that was said to him. The rubbery salt meat lingered in a dish. There was a round steel tray with a heap of mashed turnip. Another with a creamy white sauce. 'Do you want gravy?' Meatballs with mashed potato and red cabbage. Boiled lamb. Sour whale. Boiled sheep's head. Fried fish. The best fried fish in town. And the remoulade sauce he made himself: a steel tray piled high with a mixture as yellow as the sun. And now Hjálmur broke open yet another small waxed box with fingers that were blue with cold in spite of the sunny summer's day, deftly threw square pieces of fish into it, went to the potato dish and chucked in two or three potatoes, added a spoonful of remoulade, put the lid on, and pulled a length of wrapping paper off the roll. 'Next, yes, what can I do for you, friend? Speak up.'

Awestruck, Thórarinn timidly watched all this, wondering whether he should dare to speak to the great man: I am the son of the architect Sigurbjörn Helgason. My brother Helgi is the best footballer in the country. I came because of the advertisement in *Vísir*. He turned round and looked at the pane of glass in the door. The glass behind the handle was opaque from the scratches made over the years by the rings on people's fingers. Ought he to run away? He must regain control of the beating of his heart.

Gradually the crowd of people in the shop thinned out, and Hjálmur returned to the back room. Ought he to mention Grandfather Geir? No, no, Grandfather was not really very popular; it might make things worse. The best thing would be not to get the job. But his mother would simply get him work at the harbour instead. He knew that.

'Yes, what can I do for you?'

'I want to talk to the proprietor,' he mumbled.

'What did you say?' asked the tall woman, sharply. 'I can hardly hear you.'

Thórarinn was startled. 'I want to talk to the proprietor,' he shouted, nervously. The woman accepted this, and disappeared into the back room. Thórarinn's heart was galloping at full tilt. The elder woman had her hair tied up in a kerchief as she mopped the floor. She leaned on the mop, made her false teeth wobble and looked at him curiously.

The fair-haired woman came back and asked, 'What do you want with the proprietor?'

'You've been advertising for an errand boy.'

'And who are you?'

'I'm called Thórarinn. My father's name is Sigurbjörn Helgason. He's nearly twelve. He runs a draughtsman's office but once worked for the City Architect.'

There must have been something seriously wrong with this speech. The big woman had to support herself on the shop counter and the small woman glanced at him, a smile on her face. Thórarinn stared at the gleaming white tiles on the floor. 'Well, he must have started early to have such a fine, big son,' laughed the big woman.

Hjálmur came sailing out, looking distracted. His hair was long and tousled. The curls that were pale grey as they erupted from his forehead were almost black near the top of his head. His eyes were blue and watery. There was a mesh of blue veins in his cheeks. A considerable double chin spilled over his white collar. The tip of his nose was purple. 'This lad here wants to talk to you,' said the fair-haired woman.

'Yes, what can I do for you, my boy?' asked Hjálmur.

Thórarinn was not going to let himself slip up this time. His mood had hardened, and he was angry. His heart had stopped galloping and had regained its natural rhythm. 'Well, I came because of the delivery job you were advertising.'

'You're far too small.'

'Size and strength do not always walk hand in hand.'

'Yes, that's true, my boy,' said Hjálmur, spreading his arms. 'I like that! That is how young boys ought to be, able to stick up for themselves. Come through here and talk to me.'

In the inner room there was a band-saw. On the floor there was a salt-meat barrel with two flat stones on its lid. An open doorway led through to a small room. There was a telephone, and bills hanging in bundles from the wall. In this cubicle there was a sofa with a blue-checked woollen rug on it. On the sofa a man sat still as a statue, holding the back of his hand in front of him. He had a thin trail of snuff on it, kept his hand still, and waited. 'I'm coming, Gútti, don't worry,' Hjálmur called, and ambled out. Thórarinn saw an open freezer and several stiff carcases of lamb with their legs apart. The backyard was bathed in sunlight. 'Come here, my friend,' said Hjálmur.

In the courtyard stood an errand boy's bicycle, freshly painted black. Here and there the older layers beneath showed through the thick, enamel paint on the heavy frame. At the front of the bicycle there was a carrier for the deliveries. The bicycle had a lamp, a bell, and a registration number, as though it was trying to be taken for a motor car: RE 213. TROUGH BUTCHER'S, it said in fancy lettering on the plywood board below the handlebars. Thórarinn pulled the bicycle away from the wall. It was as heavy as lead. 'What does the E in the number stand for?'

'Errand boy, so no one will think you're driving a government minister's car. Is it too heavy for you?'

'No, it's fine.'

'Well, well, that's a relief. Get on, let me see.'

Thórarinn clambered on to the seat, gripped the handlebars and began to pedal. The bicycle lumbered off. 'It's a bit stiff, but I can manage it.'

Hjálmur looked on doubtfully. 'Go once round the yard.'

Thórarinn cycled around him in the narrow yard. Hjálmur stood with his hands on his hips, leaning backwards, watching him. As the boy went faster, the bicycle became easier to ride. 'It's absolutely fine,' he said, and put his foot to the ground as a brake.

Hjálmur pursed his pink lips thoughtfully. Thórarinn looked at the dustbins behind him. There were some four of them against the outside wall, all battered and mistreated. It was as though a sick troll had staggered against them, aimed to vomit into them and missed. A noxious smell rose from the bins. He had never seen dustbins like these before, and found himself thinking of his mother. What would she say to such filth?

'I don't know,' said the old man, absent-mindedly.

'No one knows what wonders he may achieve until he is put to the test,' said Thórarinn. He had no idea where he had got this proverb from, perhaps from a radio play. He had a vague notion it might go down well here.

'That is absolutely correct!' said the businessman, opening a large palm and striking it with a clenched fist. 'You're hired! It's no small area that you'll have to look after, my boy. Do you know where Sóleyjargata is?'

'Yes. Of course,' said Thórarinn, eagerly.

'And Bókhlödustígur?'

'Yes, it's the steepest street in the town.'

'I'm not so sure about that. Frakkastígur is worse.'

'And Fjölnisvegur.'

'I know it like the back of my hand.'

'And Gunnarsbraut?' Hjálmur looked at him searchingly.

'Right down near the swimming baths.'

'Well, that's just about it. You'll find out, my boy. You'll find out. And what did you say your name was?'

'Thórarinn Sigurbjarnarson.'

'And which Sigurbjörn would that be?'

'Sigurbjörn Helgason the architect who now runs an office under his own name, but used to work for the City Architect and designed the National Theatre. When do I start?'

'Start? Right now, my boy. Half the city is waiting. The fine ladies are sitting as hungry as she-wolves all across Reykjavík.' Hjálmur shuffled through the shop with Thórarinn back to the women. 'This is young Thórarinn. He is going to be our assistant for the summer,' he said.

'Welcome to your post, Mr City Architect,' said the fair-haired woman, her eyes twinkling at Thórarinn. Her name was Ragna.

5

Her courage almost failed her as she stood and surveyed the front door of her girlhood home. She saw a curtain twitch in Bjarnaborg. It did not fall back at once, but rested a moment on a single finger. She was certain that some old crone had recognized her, seen the plate of pancakes, and put two and two together as to the purpose of her visit.

She was going to make a final attempt to acquire the site.

The covered staircase at the back was a sorry sight. The corrugated iron had rusted under the nails and there were brown trickles all the way down to the lowest crossbeam. She stopped part way up the stairs. Her mother heard her, and opened the kitchen door.

Geir was up and about, pottering around in his slippers. The pipe dangled in its usual position, hanging out of the corner of his mouth where it had made a permanent indentation on his lower lip. His daughter was looking at the kitchen sink. There was no washing-up for her to hide behind. Her mother was about to make coffee. She had developed a waddle. Either it was the result of a broken hip or Rósa had grown so fat with the years that her bulk obliged her to walk like that. Sunneva's heart beat faster as she raised the napkin from the dish.

'Well, look at this,' said her mother, quite astonished. 'Pancakes! Your father'll be pleased. Geir!' she called into the living room, where he had strolled. 'Geir, come and see what your daughter has brought you.'

'Is he in a bad mood?'

'He's always grumbling about the used-car showroom, Sunneva. They came to an agreement with him about using the square, but now people park outside the house,' said Rósa, sadly. 'I don't understand how your father can let the whole thing upset him so much.' She sighed.

Geir made them wait in the kitchen. For weeks on end he had been tortured by doubts about whether he should sell the house and the ground or not. Rósa was having difficulty with the stairs. The time had come to move. What if she were to break her hip again, or fell and died as a result? Who would take care of the house? Sunneva would not be able to come every day and cook. Geir owned a flat at Vídimelur and had long been intending to move into it. It would be grand living on the ground floor. They would not have to hobble up and down the stairs. This old hovel was about to fall down. He had consulted an estate agent about whether there was money in property. Was his son- in-law likely to make a profit? The man had simply laughed and said 'my dear Geir', then laughed again and pointed out that there was no sign of all those millions yet awhile.

'Does anyone want to buy space there? No, damn it,' said Geir doubtfully, looking lost and childlike, and trying to read the expression on the man's face.

The estate agent moved his head from side to side. 'Isn't it the way of the future, my dear Geir? That's the way they do it abroad. That much I do know.'

'And how do people pay in a store like that? All at the same cash till at the exit?' The old man was getting irritated.

'No, I think they get one each.' And he laughed.

'Yes, that's what I imagined,' said Geir.

Geir could not bear the thought of anyone but himself making a profit from the site. The house had stood there ever since the Year of Our Lord 1904. It was a good house, he thought suddenly. As a young trawlerman he had rented a room in it when it was newly built. Sigurbjörn had offered him half of the ground floor, room enough for four shops.

'I'm not interested,' replied Geir. 'I have traded on my own premises in Hverfisgata all my life.'

The other man was quick to reply, 'Yes, but you can rent out three of them, Father-in-law.'

Father-in-law! Well, so what. The damned boy was trying to flatter me, he thought. He had thought the offer a decent one at first. But this plan to put in an electric staircase to whisk people upwards! Ha! He was a slippery customer, all right. He was going to get shot of the ground floor, because not a living soul would spend any time there. They would all be crazy to get on the moving staircase and would buy everything they wanted upstairs. Do you think I don't see through your little scheme, my lad? Then the rascal had laughed, showing a row of big teeth, and then, sounding so hoarse you would think he was speaking from his guts, he had offered him half the basement as well. The damned scoundrel was so sharp he'd cut himself. Was there that much money in it? Let's wait and see what happens. Nine hundred square metres. What am I going to do with such a big store, anyway? People would be worn out tramping around it. Geir waved him away with his hand. 'No, my dear friend, you're making a big mistake. You ought to build a place with a lot of small flats in it. That's the kind of place people want to buy.'

'I know my profession,' the other man had growled. 'I know all there is to know about buildings!'

Ha! 'No, my dear friend, you damned well don't know all there is to know about buildings.'

'Oh, I think I do, Geir! I was educated abroad.'

'Yes, yes, many a man has been educated abroad and come back with nothing in his head but air. This grand store of yours might be all very well abroad, but it won't do here on Hverfisgata. And what will I do with my assistant Freysteinn if everyone is going to grab what they want off the shelves for themselves?'

'The devil if I know,' the son-in-law had replied, furious, and had grabbed his plans, turned on his heel and stormed out.

Geir had not reckoned on allowing the damned scoundrel use profane language to him. And now she had arrived. And with pancakes! There was no peace in the house. The old man snorted.

Geir appeared in the kitchen doorway and looked sulkily at the dish of pancakes. He was wearing a singlet, and his arms were white and stringy. 'Humph, pancakes!' He put his braces in his pockets.

'Yes, your favourite.' Rósa raised her voice.

'Oh, is that so? You don't have to shout at me. These women! In the old days we men used to let them feel the back of our hands.'

'Sit down, my dear, and take a fritter. He's young at heart,' she giggled to Sunneva, waddled to the sink and began to wash the coffee-strainer.

Geir reached out for a pancake before the coffee arrived at the table. He shovelled sugar on it and bit it in half. Rósa poured coffee into his cup. He sipped it through his teeth and then boomed savagely, 'I want the whole of the ground floor and half the basement as well.'

Sunneva was flabbergasted. Her mother stood at the kitchen sink, aglow with well-being and neutrality.

'The whole of the ground floor, Father? Fifteen hundred square metres?'

'Yes,' the old man yapped. 'Any less and this will be the most expensive pancake I have eaten in all my born days.' He stuffed the other half into his mouth.

'What do you think about it, Mother?' Sunneva looked at her mother, wide-eyed.

'I don't understand these things, Sunneva.'

'Humph. You'll all go bankrupt.'

'And what will you do with a whole floor, Father?'

'I won't do anything with it,' said Geir, firmly. 'Your mother will own it when I pass away, and that could well be any day now. Then she can rent it out to support herself. We're living on rent income now, as you know. And have done for many years.' He looked up, honesty itself. 'The shop doesn't make anything. I only keep it open because I don't know what to do about my assistant Freysteinn. Anyway, you're letting me have by the far the worst floor in the building.'

'It's the best floor, Father,' she said, blushing.

'Bah, I'm not as daft as you think.' Geir grinned. 'Not a soul will buy anything there. The moving staircase will take everyone straight upstairs.' The old man half smiled at his daughter as if he expected the look on her face to confirm his suspicion. 'Do you think I can't see what you're up to?'

'What are you talking about, Father?'

'Oh, this electric staircase that's supposed to be so terribly dandy.'

'People will only use it if they need to, Father. And there'll be another staircase beside it to take them down again.'

'Don't you try to tell me anything.' Geir made a defensive gesture with his hand. 'You've all studied from the same book. And there's another thing. If I have to let this house go for next to nothing and you get the site – and I am informed that it is very valuable and one of the best sites in town – then I want collateral from you.' His eyes were steely grey.

'Collateral!' Sunneva looked speechlessly at her mother, who was looking out at Mount Esja.

'The view from the kitchen window here has always been so fine,' said Rósa. 'I dread the day someone builds something to block it.'

'Collateral!' said Sunneva. 'I don't like the sound of that. Are you with him on this, Mother?'

'No, but I do like the sound of it,' said Geir with heavy emphasis, and reached for another pancake.

'I shall have to discuss this with Sigurbjörn.' Sunneva blew the hair away from her cheek. 'And see what he has to say.'

'Yes, do.' The old man seemed to have lost all interest the matter.

At the mention of Sigurbjörn, Rósa sat down. 'I have always thought Sigurbjörn was so handsome,' she said, smiling.

'Handsome is as handsome does,' muttered Geir, adding, 'I've never thought of him as particularly good-looking. You should have married Ámundi the plumber. Now there was a reliable man with a steady income.'

'Ámundi? I wasn't even sweet on him.'

'Yes, well, there's no need to look so shocked, madam,' said Geir, roughly. 'Why did you have a child by him, then?'

'Because I was a young girl and didn't know what I was doing.'

'The leopard doesn't change his spots,' said Geir. 'The pair of you still don't know what you're doing.'

'If you're talking about my husband,' said Sunneva, 'he knows very well what he's doing.'

'That's a good one,' her father snorted.

'Will you have some more fritters?' asked Rósa.

'But you've no capital,' said Geir. 'I don't see how a large store can be built without capital.'

'We've got capital and, anyway, we'll get a loan. Firms will sell building materials on account. People will buy space and put up the money in advance.'

'Put up the money in advance! The devil if they'll put up the money in advance. Loans and advances have to be repaid, woman.'

'Sunneva, dear, won't you have any more fritters?'

'Oh, for goodness' sake, Mother, do stop calling them fritters. They're pancakes. I'm beginning to feel sick.'

'Nína over in Bjarnaborg made some good pancakes with rice-milk porridge the other day and took them to a friend of hers and she scoffed the whole plateful. When she'd swallowed the last of them, she said, "That was very good and now I've eaten so much I'm fit to be judged by the Lord, but I'm very glad that they weren't made from old rice-milk porridge, because then I'd bring them all up, every last one." "Well, but they *were* made from old rice-milk porridge," said Nína. And do you know what? The woman ran through to the toilet and sicked up the whole damned lot.' Rósa slapped the palms of her hands on her hips. If something amused her, there was no hiding it.

'Well, that's something I can understand,' said Geir. 'Pancakes womenfolk make from old rice-milk porridge are disgusting.'

His daughter longed to say, 'But you've just eaten some, dear.' Instead, she kept quiet. Her father might change his mind, and then God only knew how many months it would take to persuade him again.

'Well, I'll talk it over with Sigurbjörn.'

'Very well,' he said, reluctantly.

Sunneva got to her feet and looked at Mount Esja through the window. A rusty foreign cargo ship lay at anchor. On the bows of the vessel was painted MARITA SCHELLING HAMBURG. Further out there was a five-masted training ship. 'There will soon be a lot of expensive repairs to do here, Father. So I'm not sure that it's all that bad.'

'I have lived in this house nearly all my life, Sunneva, and I haven't had any trouble with it up till now. And I can probably make do with it until my time comes. Don't you lot worry about that. This house'll see me out. When I'm gone you'll fight over it and grab it all anyway.'

'The whole of the ground floor and half of the basement? Is that what you want?'

'Yes, and a note of guarantee or a mortgage on Sjafnargata.'

'And what do you say to that, Mother?' Without meaning to, Sunneva was beginning to sound like a little girl.

Her mother stood up. 'Shall I wash up the fritter plate, dear? Then you can take it home with you.'

'No, it can wait. What do you say?'

'I'll just vote Liberal, like your father. That is what I've always done.'

6

When Sunneva got home she took off her coat and sat down at her usual end at the parlour table. She looked at the gigantic branch outside the window. She had asked Sigurbjörn over and over to cut down one of the large trees. Preferably the rowan. After ten years of argument he had given in and felled one of them, but it had been the beautiful tree further out on the lawn, the laburnum. She missed its bright dangling clusters. The rowan obscured the grey façade, making it impossible to paint the house. Thórarinn dreamed of the house being white.

'I don't want this wretched department store,' muttered the woman. 'I don't want it.'

She had shown no interest whenever Sigurbjörn had wanted to consult her about the plans during the winter, and had been startled when he told her where he wanted to erect the building.

Marry Ámundi! She had got pregnant when she was eighteen. Mother didn't give me any help at the time, she thought. Any more than she had done this morning. She looked angrily at the gloomy parlour and saw before her the Café Skindbuksen in Copenhagen, a narrow, dark cave with its habitual clientele of drunks and bohemians. She had worked there as a waitress all one summer after travelling alone to Denmark and giving birth to her first child. The kitchen was in an outhouse at the back and a draught of cool air wafted through the café when the door to the courtyard was open. Sometimes there was nothing to do early in the morning. Then she would sit at a table at the back of the café, listening to the chefs going about their business and gazing out of the door until her eyes were dazzled by the sun, or until the bleating of the old woman who carried the trays to the counter for the waiters to serve at the tables made her jump. One of the waiters was called Christian and she had immediately fallen for him, because he was irresistible.

Sigurbjörn came into the tavern early one day in his long black overcoat, spotted her and pretended to look anywhere but at her. She was standing at the counter, and recognized him at once. He was the one who had seen her naked. He sat down at the 'deacons' table' and snapped his fingers. Christian asked her to attend to the customer. She went over to him and asked, 'Are you an Icelander?'

'Yes,' he said, surprised. 'Can you tell?'

'I know that stupid look,' she said, coldly. 'We Icelanders don't have any manners. Snapping your fingers. That's the way you call a dog.'

He laughed loudly and Christian looked at them. 'I don't like that fellow,' Christian had said as she put beer and bread on a tray. 'They call him Rasputin.'

'Wasn't he a Russian priest?' she asked.

'No, a Russian con man, and he was murdered. Be careful. He's a drunk and good at getting other people to pay for him. He's too lazy to chase the girls. I've seen him with whores.'

'So you're studying theology?' she asked as she put the beer and schnapps down on Sigurbjörn's table.

'No.' He looked shocked.

'I think you look like a priest.'

'I was never called to the priesthood,' he said, and gave her a serious look. His eyes were sharp, dark brown and hypnotic. 'I'm studying architecture. As a boy I was always drawing. My brother was a theologian, but he's dead now. But tell me about yourself.' The deep voice had put a spell on her. He was slow of speech, and she thought that was nice in a man.

The old woman brought a plate of Skipperlafs stew from the kitchen. He seldom ate anything at the tavern apart from this peppery hash of meat and potatoes garnished with bay leaves and with a knob of butter on it, as tradition dictated. Years later, his sons acquired a taste for it. He made her sit down at his table. She thought he was beautiful in his ugliness. The first time they slept together he was drunk and whispered a Danish girl's name in her ear.

He sat in the tavern in the evenings and sometimes for whole days at a time. He made her give him credit, and then had trouble paying. She fell in love with his clothes and his education, with his air of doomed recklessness and his elegance. She was so alone, and knew few Icelanders. He was so griefstricken over the death of his brother and so much in need of comfort. Later he was going to return to Iceland to build lots of large houses. He could explain in detail to her how church towers and cupolas were constructed. It seemed there were few things he did not know. What days they were! Wine in tall glasses, snails in garlic butter, freshly baked bread, a table under a thick mass of leaves. She fell pregnant.

She ran her finger along the parlour table. They had bought it together at an antique shop on Islandsbryggen. How often he had sat dead drunk at the end of the table, mourning for his brother. 'Oh, Jóhannes, Jóhannes! What do you think it's like to be nineteen years old and to know that your brother is dying in Germany and not be able to do anything about it? What do you think it's like? No one understands that.'

She could hardly bear to see him cry. 'Sigurbjörn. The man is dead. I know what it is to be alone. What do you think it was like for me to have my child alone? I was utterly alone. They drove me away. Mama did not stand by me. I hardly understood the language here.' He looked at her uncomprehendingly. Then he stretched out a large hand, took hold of hers and squeezed it.

Sigurbjörn had worked for several architects. They were lucky, and managed to rent a place on Østerbrogade. Sometimes now she missed that flat – the ceilings on Østerbrogade had been higher than they were on Sjafnargata and the rooms had been enormous. They got married and she sent her mother the wedding photograph. Ragnar was in the photo. Curly fair hair and a white lace cravat. There was just one shadow over everything. Sigurbjörn could not accept another man's child.

He persuaded her to send Ragnar back home to Ámundi's parents in Iceland. And now he has got me to wheedle the site out of my father, she thought, and felt angry.

Sigurbjörn was a good provider. He liked to haggle for meat and vegetables in the market, and had salt fish sent to him from home. They used to throw great parties that got a bit out of hand, and the master of the house tended to slip away without warning and go and drink in taverns, dreaming of the palaces he would build in Iceland.

They spent an Easter holiday at home in Iceland and stayed longer than they had intended. Denmark was invaded by the Germans, so they could not get back to Copenhagen. They lived in a small rented flat. When Helgi was nearly nine, she fell pregnant with Vilborg. It was an accident. She took Ragnar back after six years in the country. She lived in constant fear of bumping into his father whenever she strolled into town with the family. How relieved she was when she heard that Ámundi had moved to Canada.

Her love became less passionate as the years passed. Strange, she thought, that they could not agree about one little town square, even though they had so many things in common. The point came when she had definitely decided to leave Sigurbjörn. Then he had got into a terrible fight in Vetrargardurinn, had injured a man badly and ended up in gaol. There had been a suit for damages and a lot of talk in the newspapers. To her great astonishment he gave up drinking completely and bought his mother's share in the house on Sjafnargata and his dead brother was never mentioned again. Thórarinn was the child of their reconciliation.

Sunneva heard a rustling sound. A thrush was sitting on the branch. She could see it clearly in the reflection in the gun cupboard. Sigurbjörn is a genius at getting his own way and then making it look as though he were doing someone else a favour, she thought. Perhaps he really did want the boy to work this summer. Was I too hard on him? The young like to be left alone to play. I ran away from my father and mother. Why didn't I leave him? I went to Copenhagen alone when I was eighteen. I'm used to looking after myself.

Christian saw at once what a two-faced bastard he was, she thought. Christian had had such a beautiful body. He had been such a wonderful lover. It had been so good to sit astride him and feel the silky blond hairs of his firm stomach curling between her fingers.

7

Sunneva covered the table with a white cloth and put a rose in a glass vase. She laid the table with the royal porcelain, its dun-coloured enamel cracked with age, on the blue rims girls with parasols walking near the palace at Dyrehavsbakken, deer grazing. Sigurbjörn's father had bought the crockery at an auction after the Danish royal visit in 1921.

In the evening she sat between Thórarinn and Ragnar. 'Well, wasn't I right to tell you to go down there?' she asked Thórarinn.

He was telling them all about his visit to the shop for the second time, but he did not mention the slip he'd made over Sigurbjörn's age. At the climax of the story he looked at the shopkeeper boldly and declared, 'No one knows what wonders he may achieve until he is put to the test.' And Hjálmur struck his palm with his fist and replied, 'You're hired.'

'Heigh-ho, heigh-ho,' Vilborg sighed in irritation, and looked at her mother.

The master of the house sat hunched over his plate. The reflection of the rowan branch in the gun cupboard had grown darker, the stem of the rose seemed to grow larger in the water. In the Kjarval painting there was a fissured rock and milk-white water. Art galleries had often made offers for the picture, which Sigurbjörn had bought shortly after their return to Iceland.

Sunneva rested her elbow on the table, laid her cheek on her hand and looked at her husband. The knife and fork looked awkward in his large hands. It's good that I didn't leave him, she thought. Why didn't I go? She looked at her older sons. They were like the sun and moon, Ragnar bright and broad-faced, his face like an open book, his nose small. Helgi had inherited the curve in his mother's nose and his father's mouth and chin. He looked like a red-haired Turk. Old Sigurlaug, Sigurbjörn's mother, sat between the brothers, a weathered and bony figurehead in an tasselled bonnet.

'Is your department store going to cover the whole of Vitatorg, Father?' asked Ragnar. 'It'll be enormous.'

'Well, I am used to taking on major projects,' mumbled Sigurbjörn. 'The City Architect's office didn't design potato sheds.'

'This will be the biggest building ever built in Iceland,' Thórarinn informed the family.

'Oh, is that so, Tóti?' said Helgi, doubtfully. 'What about Austurbær School?'

'Bah,' said Thórarinn. 'It doesn't count. It's a school. Father built the National Theatre.'

'No, I didn't, not all on my own,' said Sigurbjörn.

'But it was your idea to add wings to the tower of Hallgrímskirkja,' said Vilborg.

'Yes, and your grandfather invented the dump truck,' laughed Helgi.

'Are you going to build a house, Sigurbjörn?' asked the old woman, a bit hoarse with age.

'Yes, Mother,' Sigurbjörn said loudly, and smiled. 'I'm going to put up a little shack this summer.'

'And where are you going to get the money for this building, Sigurbjörn?' asked the old woman.

'I'll get help from somewhere.' Sigurbjörn scowled at Helgi, and Sunneva guessed that he had been to see Helgi at the bank earlier in the day.

'Here's my best girl.' Helgi glanced at his mother, embraced his grandmother, kissed her on the cheek and pulled Ragnar towards them. 'Don't we make a pretty picture, the three of us together?' The brothers turned their heads to the old woman and she waved them away. 'I've often thought it's such a thousand pities we're blood relatives, Grandmother,' flirted Helgi.

'Oh, be quiet, boy,' she said.

Sigurbjörn looked at them. No one but Helgi had ever been allowed to treat his mother like that.

On the table there were two fried meatballs and a bit of mashed potato in a bowl left from the meal. Thórarinn hastily transferred both meatballs over to his plate. 'I've had six already.'

'Eight, you mean,' said Sigurlaug.

'Mother, tell him not to be so greedy,' Vilborg hissed.

'Yes, Tóti,' said his mother, absent-mindedly. 'You're not the only one. Ragnar, have you had enough?'

'Yes,' said Ragnar, irritated.

'Mother, why don't you just put a bib on Ragnar and feed him?' laughed Helgi.

'Now poor Granny will go on Tóti's Black List,' whispered Vilborg.

'When I was a girl we had good food and plenty of it, steaks on high days and holidays, enough for us to invite guests to join us,' thundered the old woman. 'We young folk sometimes went riding. I was always a great one for the horses.'

'Yes, I well remember you taking Jörp for a gallop, Mother,' Sigurbjörn smiled. 'That mare could certainly move.'

Sigurlaug grunted her agreement. 'She was a thoroughbred.' The old woman bared her teeth without the smile reaching her eyes.

Sunneva looked quickly at her husband, who usually had all the animation of a fossil in his mother's presence. 'What's he planning now?' she thought. 'To mortgage the old woman's flat to pay off his debts?' She got to her feet and tried to lift the sash window. It was stuck and she jerked it open.

To her surprise it was rather misty in the garden. Patches of moss on the garden wall made her feel anxious. Damn the old woman, she thought. Was she trying to make out I'm stingy with food?

She could never forget her mother-in-law's words when Sigurbjörn showed her the picture of Sunneva Geirsdóttir and her son. 'Well, Sigurbjörn. So that's little Ragnar. Someone's taken that bit of bother off your hands.' Sigurbjörn told her of his mother's comment, his face ash-grey, and his whole body shaking with a terrible anger.

'You don't need to make that face,' said Thórarinn to his sister, as he ladled cream on to his fruit. 'We're not eating just because of my news. It's because Father got the site as well.' Thórarinn was confident that there was more to come. His father would have bought the aeroplane to make up for betraying him and it would be presented to him after dinner.

'And when will the old house be moved, Father?' asked Ragnar.

'I think your grandfather is setting his terms awfully high,' growled Sigurbjörn. 'I shall have to think about it. I won't just accept anything he suggests.'

'He rang me at the bank today terribly worried about some kind of electric staircase,' Helgi grinned. 'What's all that about?'

'I think Father is going a bit funny in the head,' Sunneva sighed, closing the window. 'I could offer him the second or the third floor.'

'Oh, there's no point chopping and changing any more,' said Sigurbjörn.

'You don't think much of all this, do you, Granny?' said Helgi, giving his grandmother a slight nudge.

The old woman grunted her agreement.

'Tóti, tell us about getting the job,' said Vilborg, sarcastically.

Thórarinn did not recognize the gibe and began to tell them the story for the third time.

When he was about to say, 'No man knows what wonders he may achieve until he is put to the test', she got in before him and imitated his voice. 'You should have put it like this: "Will you give me money for that plane with the motor?"'

'Mother, will you tell her to stop?'

'Mother and Father can't just give you anything you take a fancy to,' said Vilborg.

'Where's your girl, Ragnar?' Sigurlaug shouted.

'It's two years since we split up, for heaven's sake.'

'Yes, what am I thinking of. That's a pity, she was such a fine figure of a girl.'

Sigurbjörn picked up his spoon and tapped the bowl with it.

'Don't break the bowl, you bugger,' said Sunneva.

'Oh, Mother, let Father speak,' Vilborg chimed in.

'What's going on?' wondered Thórarinn, his eyes darting this way and that. 'Will I get the aeroplane now?'

'When I was a lad growing up here in Sjafnargata,' growled Sigurbjörn, 'it wasn't done to splash your money about, as seems to be the fashion today even in the best families.'

Grandmother grunted again.

'But we got good presents, and I do not wish to see that tradition discontinued,' he added.

'I was against this,' said Sunneva. 'This wasn't bought with my consent.'

'Calm down, woman,' said Sigurbjörn. 'Shooting you is not on the agenda.' He fetched an oblong parcel from the kitchen and handed it to his stepson.

Ragnar took the parcel in both hands.

'Look how red Ragnar's gone,' said Vilborg.

'Open the parcel, Ragnar,' said Helgi. 'We can't wait to see what it is.'

Ragnar put the package down on the table. His lumpy fingers had trouble untying the knots. One of them unravelled and the other he slipped off. He was left holding a green bag tied at one end.

'A fishing rod,' said Thórarinn, glumly. 'How nice.'

'No, mate, you know better than that.'

'Well, what is it then?' asked Thórarinn, alarmed. 'Not another gun?'

'Tóti, dear,' said his sister. 'Your voice is shaking.'

Ragnar pulled a new shotgun out of the bag, a pump-action model with a dark brown stock. He brought it up to his cheek for a second and aimed at the chandelier. Sunneva raised both hands to her face, narrowed her eyes and said, 'Now don't you start any shooting in here, boy.'

'What a lot we'll save,' said Vilborg. 'Now they can both shoot grouse for Christmas dinner.'

'Yes, or geese.' Ragnar turned round. He was bull-necked and built like an athlete. He aimed at everything in the sitting room: the sofa, the coffee table and the pictures on the walls. The stock gleamed at his shoulder.

'You're frightening me, Ragnar. Put the gun down,' said Sunneva.

'What a weapon!' he said, beaming.

'It's a hand-made Browning,' said Sigurbjörn proudly. 'Exactly the same as Helgi's.'

'Be it thrice accursed,' said Grandmother.

'Well, you're not exactly broke, Father,' said Ragnar.

Thórarinn jumped to his feet. He ran upstairs and slammed the door of his room behind him.

'Did you see that?' Vilborg looked from one to the other. 'The tears were actually spurting out of his eyes. That boy is crazy.' She shuddered. 'Oooh, I can't stand this.'

Ragnar looked at them all in embarrassment.

Helgi got to his feet. 'I'll go up and talk to him.'

'No, you don't, leave him alone,' said Sunneva.

'This was too much on top of the Hawker Hurricane business,' said her husband, thoughtfully.

Helgi knocked gently at the door. 'Go away,' came a shout from inside.

'Tóti, it's Helgi.'

'Well, what do you want?'

'Let me in, mate, let's talk.'

After some time Thórarinn opened the door. He sat down on the bed and stared at the floor, his cheeks crimson, his hair wet with sweat. Helgi sat down beside him and put his elbows on his knees and clasped his hands together as if in prayer. Unconsciously his younger brother did the same. Thórarinn had often been bitterly jealous of Helgi's fine nose. The curve on Helgi's nose made him look like a bird of prey.

'Tóti, Ragnar is twenty-six now. You mustn't feel bad just because Father's given him a gun. I got mine last year. Ragnar had to wait five years. Father only remembered about it on my birthday.'

'It's not just that,' said the boy, his eyes round. 'I had to dash upstairs to give the goldfish some food. And when I got up from the table I hurt my hand.' He looked at his palm. 'That's why I started crying. It doesn't make any difference to me if Ragnar gets a gun.'

Helgi looked at the goldfish tank on the blue-painted chest of drawers. He could see his namesake, Helgi the goldfish, swimming all alone and not looking exactly underfed. He had been christened Helgi when Helgi the footballer had scored a hat trick against Fram. Thórarinn would not let any of the local kids remain in ignorance of those famous goals. Helgi the goldfish had twice killed a shoal of guppies. The water had gone brown with over-generous feeding. Helgi sniffed the foul-smelling liquid. 'You're killing the fish like this, mate. He's getting far too much to eat.'

'I'm going to sell him,' said Thórarinn, sadly. 'A boy up in Hlídar wants to buy him off me.'

'What? You're going to sell my namesake?' asked Helgi, scandalized.

'I'll give him someone else's name before I sell him,' said Thórarinn. 'At least he doesn't work in a bank like you,' he added.

Thórarinn pretended to be asleep when Sunneva opened the door a few hours later. Outraged anger burned within his breast. Others got presents, but he had to slave. Time passed. He heard talking at the front door and the car starting. Helgi was going home with Grandmother. He heard a door open directly below him and knew that his father was going down into the basement. His father had hurt him, Thórarinn, the most. Gradually the house grew quiet. Vilborg stood in the doorway and said, 'I know you're awake.' He did not answer. He looked at the alarm clock on the writing desk. It said half past ten. At midnight he was still lying awake. He got up on his knees and looked out. The mist had got thicker. A thrush was playing a clarinet outside the window. The rowan trunk rose from the ground and its branches, as thick as pipes, reached higher than the roof of the house. In many places there was a greenish glimmer on the bark. Some of the buds were not yet fully open. By the tree there was a dovecote. He could stand upright in it. Sigurbjörn had made the dovecote the previous spring, but Thórarinn had taken a violent dislike to the doves when the father bird had eaten a baby chick as soon as it came out of the egg. He tapped on the window to scare away the thrush. But it was no use. The trees were full of them. He fell asleep to the sound of birdsong.

8

'I dreamt I was out on a big lake, Lake Thingvöllur, I think it was. I was going to cast for trout. The bloody rowing boat was taking in water. I was baling out for all I was worth, but the water kept seeping in.' Sigurbjörn looked at his wife as if he were sharing a confidence. 'The strange thing was that all the seats in the boat were taken by these ghastly people chatting away and ignoring what was happening.'

'And who were these people?' asked Sunneva. They were sitting in the kitchen, drinking their morning coffee.

'I have no idea, woman.'

'Were they your family, perhaps?'

'No. Where did you get that idea from, woman?' he said, flabbergasted. 'Do you think I don't know my own family? Anyway, I don't take any notice of bloody nonsense like that.' He got to his feet, remembering that his wife often dreamed of things that came true and was quite good at intepreting dreams. He went out on to the steps and inspected the weather: a small cloud had covered the sun and cast a shadow on the garden, bringing out the midges. 'He didn't think there was much chance of the bank helping to sort out my affairs, my boy Helgi,' thought Sigurbjörn, bitterly. 'And the lad doesn't pay anything towards his keep and eats more than the rest of us.' He sat down on the steps.

Helgi had sat with his father in the entrance hall of the bank and told him that he would not be able to raise a mortgage. Sigurbjörn had thought he would ask his mother to give her name as security on a loan so he could pay off the most pressing of his debts, but he hadn't dared ask her. 'I'm bankrupt,' he muttered angrily. 'No one will give me any help with money. I can't build a thing. This is a farce. We'll lose the house, everything! I'm finished.' He was overwhelmed by despair and it took him quite a while to pull himself together.

Sunneva came out of the front door and opened an oblong box. 'Look what I bought as a christening present yesterday,' she said, and pulled off the cottonwool. The handle was made of silver, the bowl of gold. 'Don't you think it's fine? It's better than spending money on shotguns.'

'It's splendid, Sunna,' he replied.

Things had not gone well for Sigurbjörn after he had set up his own business. Fewer people came to have their architectural plans drawn up than he had hoped. Some had not liked the plans he had done for them. He was considered inflexible and eccentric. He had taken promissory notes. Changed the notes into letters of credit and mortgaged the house. Sometimes he woke early in the morning when the others were asleep and was scarcely awake before he remembered the mountain of debt he was in. He felt his family didn't care about the worries he had trying to support them. He looked over the garden wall. There he could see the bright red roof of their car, a 1949 Plymouth station-wagon. They had bought it new. 'Straight from the crate,' Thórarinn was fond of saying. Sigurbjörn looked downcast. He realized he was toying with the idea of selling the car. What would Tóti say then? He heard his wife calling to Vilborg, 'Tell Tóti to get up this instant. We're going to the christening party.'

The children squabbled violently all the way to Eyrarbakki. Vilborg was going to stay there, and they would be leaving her behind. Thórarinn did not reckon much to her summer job. Their mother kept telling them to be quiet. Their father was deep in thought and did not say a word. The car held the road well and the chrome on the bonnet gleamed in the sun. There was a mist over Mount Vifilsfell. Spring had come late and there was still quite a lot of snow on the pale-blue mountain. At Sandskeid there were some people standing by a glider.

'Father, stop, let's go and look at the gliders,' said Thórarinn.

'We haven't really got time for that,' said his mother.

'The boy and I won't be a moment,' said Sigurbjörn, and turned off the road and down a sandy lane. He parked a short distance from the people standing in a crowd looking up at the sky. Vilborg waited in the car with her mother. A glider was high in the sky. It looked like a solitary gnat. It described a long arc, then it could suddenly be seen clearly silhouetted against a snowdrift on the mountain slope, and then it sharpened its angle of approach and sailed down towards the airstrip, where a warm breeze was keeping the windsock well away from its pole. While the glider was still some way off, Thórarinn could see that there were two people on board. The passenger was sitting behind the pilot. The glider landed. It was little more than an iron bar and a wing, with the seats welded on to a central column. The passenger was a fair-haired woman. When they took off her goggles, she was convulsed, foaming at the mouth, and the people seized her hands and tried to hold them still. 'There, there, dear.' The crowd was silent and embarrassed. The woman was howling like an animal.

47

'What's going on?' Sigurbjörn whispered to a man he did not know. 'Has she got epilepsy?'

'She wanted to go up. It was her first flight,' the man replied, and did not seem to want to prolong the conversation.

Father and son stood for a while and looked at the woman who could not stop howling. The men were trying to lift her out of the seat.

'We'd better go, Thórarinn,' muttered Sigurbjörn.

The boy told Vilborg and his mother what had happened in great detail, until his father's patience snapped. 'There is one thing that you will have to learn in this life, Tóti,' he said. 'There are some things a man has to have the sense to keep his trap shut about.'

'Why can't I talk about it?' asked Thórarinn. 'You should have seen her eyes.'

'Father is trying to explain it to you. There are some things one has to have the sense to keep quiet about,' said Vilborg.

'Well, we're not going to talk any more about that poor frightened woman now,' said Sunneva. 'It's getting on your father's nerves. And please don't on any account mention it to Gudbrandur and Ingirídur when we get to their place east of the mountain. It's not a suitable topic for conversation at a christening party.'

'Oh, Mother, what do you take me for?' asked Vilborg.

They bought flowers and a geyser-baked loaf in Hveragerdi. Their journey then took them to Selfoss, where Sigurbjörn had a brief appointment. The man was plump and came out on to the front steps to talk to Sigurbjörn. Thórarinn watched from the car. His father seemed to be laughing too loudly.

'The old gannet's still interested in buying the house,' said Sigurbjörn, excited, when he was back behind the steering wheel.

'What house?'

'The house on Vitatorg, of course, woman. Your childhood home.'

They drove across open country where the grass was golden. The houses at Eyrarbakki appeared through a heat haze. The wind cut across the meadow like a scythe. The haze lifted and the village rose out of the plain. The silhouette of Litla-Hraun State Prison loomed into view. Sigurbjörn drove slowly down the main street, looking for the house where Gudbrandur and Ingirídur lived. He was looking forward to seeing it and recognized it at once from the description: a small, single-storey wooden house with a tall chimney. 'He said the corrugated iron was a little rusty,' he snorted. 'That was a bit of an understatement on Brandsi's part. The damned hovel is brown with rust. The fellow needs to replace all the ironwork. This is not the wonderful bargain he said it was.' Sunneva looked at her husband with a wry smile. Gudbrandur had married four years earlier and it was no longer automatic for him to take Sigurbjörn's advice about anything. They turned a corner and drove along a road that ended in a grey sand-dune. The beach was not visible because of the ridge of sand, but a flight of seagulls indicated the high-water mark. They parked next to a wire-netting fence. Sigurbjörn got out and put his hand on a post to test its firmness. The wood was quite secure. The grass had woven itself in and out of the netting near the ground, and new couch grass was shooting up out of the grey tangles of last year's growth. A rectangular plot had been freshly cleared in the garden. He studied the house from behind. There was one large window and another smaller one.

Gudbrandur came out to greet them. When Vilborg was on the point of handing him the flowers, he said, 'No, give them to Inga.'

Ingirídur was standing on the steps. She was holding her little boy against her shoulder, patting him on the back.

Thórarinn thought his mother was big and tall by comparison. Ingirídur had once kissed him on the lips. He had thought that cool touch a thousand times better than his mother's kiss, and the feeling had made him ashamed. He followed the women inside and looked round for magazines or books. Ingirídur sat down and took the child from her shoulder. He was a chubby boy and put his hands out in surprise, like an egg-collector scaling a rockface feeling a sudden give in the rope. Sunneva sat down on a stool and tickled the child under the chin.

On a table below the living-room window stood a cone-shaped almond cake, filled to the brim with confectionery. Ingirídur had put the bouquet of roses in a glass vase. Thórarinn counted five pale-blue saucers with their coffee cups turned upside-down. Two glasses, bottles of Coca-Cola next to them, and two straws lay neatly side by side on the white tablecloth. They were not expecting many people. The cake was studded with Mackintosh chocolates. His mouth began to water and he sat down on a chair and reached for the copies of *Home* and *Family Journal* from the pile of magazines.

He saw his father and Gudbrandur appear at the parlour window. His father had put on his peaked cap. He was pushing something into the timber round the window, and Gudbrandur was watching him. A gust of wind caught the house, making it creak, but Gudbrandur's thick curly hair scarcely moved. His cheeks were bluish and he had prominent cheekbones. Thórarinn thought it strange that Ingirídur should have wanted to marry such a country bumpkin. In the winter he had seen an Italian film and tried to pay her a compliment. 'You're like an Italian woman.'

'Oh?' she had replied coolly. 'Are they different from other women?'

'Yes,' he had stammered, blushing red. 'They are pretty like you and have little black spots on their cheeks.'

'Is that so?' she had said, even more coolly.

Gudbrandur saw him and grinned at him through the window. Thórarinn hunched over his magazine.

Little María, who was two, clung jealously to her mother. Sunneva took the child who was about to be christened into her arms so that Ingirídur could tend to her daughter and her nanny.

'Vilborg, I wonder if you would take María out in her pushchair for a bit?' said Ingirídur. She turned to Sunneva. 'She will keep wandering off. If I so much as let her out of my sight, she's away. It's as if she's got an appointment at the other end of the world. She got nearly all the way from Öldugata down to Lake Tjörnin the other day, and when I asked what she was going to eat and drink in the wilderness she said, "Puddle-water, and the ducks will give me bread." Oh Lord, I was so frightened.' Ingirídur put a hand to her breast.

Vilborg was tending to María after a fashion, and Thórarinn looked on, happy. He was delighted to be getting rid of his sister.

Gudbrandur and his father came in. 'You should have a fine old time in this place, Brandsi,' said Sigurbjörn. They were striding about the floor, and Sigurbjörn was talking loudly and laughing a great deal. They opened a door, and heard water leaking in the toilet. 'There's a bit of rot in the floor by the shower here,' said Gudbrandur. 'But it's nothing to worry about.'

'I think it's fine, Brandsi,' said Sigurbjörn. 'Sixty thousand, eh? A real knock-down price, my friend. And the ironwork's not so bad, either.' Sigurbjörn looked over the floorboards and up to the ceiling and placed a large hand on a crossbeam. Thórarinn saw beads of sweat on his father's brow. He waited for a crack from Gudbrandur.

'Well, that's it, then,' said Gudbrandur with one eye on Ingiridur, and seemed to want to stop talking about houses.

'When are the guests coming?' boomed Sigurbjörn.

'They're here.' Gudbrandur grimaced, as though a fierce storm was raging around him.

'Oh!' Sigurbjörn and Sunneva both looked surprised. 'Hardly the largest christening party in the world, is it?'

'Quality not quantity, Sunneva, my dear,' said Gudbrandur.

Ingiridur got to her feet, took the child in her arms and went into the kitchen, which was one step down from the parquet floor. Thórarinn became aware that Gudbrandur was watching him. 'Is he going to start on me now?' wondered the boy, and felt his thighs were exploding with fat. 'I don't like almond cake,' he said loudly.

Sunneva threw up her hands. 'Tóti, you mustn't say such things!'

'Somehow I knew you would say that,' said Ingiridur. 'And that's why I baked a chocolate cake, too.'

'All the boy wants is to look at the mole on the wife's face,' said Gudbrandur, sniggering.

Thórarinn flung down the magazine in a flash, and shouted, 'I never wanted to come here, damn and blast it!' He ran out. Vilborg was putting María into the pushchair in the hallway.

'Tóti, come back here at once,' called Sunneva.

'Gudbrandur, why do you have to say things like that?' said Ingiridur, angrily.

Thórarinn went out to the car. They had the best car in town, him and his father. He looked through the window. The speedometer said it could do a hundred miles an hour. There was a yellow-and-white stain on the bonnet. The seagulls of Eyrarbakki had shat on the car. They deserved to be killed. There were dandelions here and there in the grass in the garden. He could hear the roar of the surf. Bluebottles buzzed near the house wall in the sun and lunged at the large windowpane. He walked to the end of the road towards the sea. There were small shells in the sand. He walked to the top of the ridge of sand in the warm breeze and found the sea spread out before him. A seagull glided above the seaweed and the sand changed colour as the waves moved to and fro. The black-backed gull let the wind carry it home again then made another circuit just for the sheer joy of it. A great swarm of sandpipers rose in a cloud and settled down again when the great bird had passed over. The boy watched for a while. He lay down on his back in order to regain his composure. Clouds moved across the sun. He heard footsteps. His sister was chanting 'Heigh-ho, heigh-ho!' before he had time to turn round.

'Give it a rest, stupid!' the boy shouted.

'Scared you, did I? You must come in now, Tóti, everyone's waiting for you. Father went to look for you, he was absolutely furious. You shouldn't let people tease you like that. You can't catch me, idiot!'

He jumped to his feet. They ran in through the open door. He had his hands on her when they both crashed together against the wall in the hallway. The priest had arrived: a young church spire with a tuft of blond hair. The grown-ups looked very solemn. María buried her face in her mother's skirt. Sunneva told the children to be quiet. Sigurbjörn gave them a sharp look. The people moved over to the table. The priest had brought hymn books with him and handed them out. The little boy covered himself with his hands and looked quizzically up at the crossbeams. He had been dressed up in a long, gauzy christening gown. The priest led the singing: 'O gentle Jesus, we bring to you this child'. Thórarinn thought his mother was singing rather too loudly. Fortunately almost nothing could be heard of Sigurbjörn. 'Who will hold the child for baptism?' asked the priest.

'I was thinking of asking you to do it, Sigurbjörn,' said Ingirídur.

Thórarinn looked at Gudbrandur in surprise. He had never before seen him almost purple in the face. The priest performed the christening ritual, the child listened with old-mannish wonder, Sigurbjörn shifted his feet like a wooden marionette with the boy in his arms.

'And have the parents agreed on a name?' asked the priest.

Gudbrandur looked anxiously at his wife. 'You say it, Inga.'

'Sigurbjörn,' said Ingirídur, softly.

Thórarinn looked at his father. Sigurbjörn Helgason's face looked like raw salt meat and the scars on it were as black as tar. The child began to cry and turned a purply red. 'There, there,' said his mother, stroking him on the cheek.

'Try to relax, sir, then he'll calm down,' said the priest to Sigurbjörn in a fatherly tone, and put a hand on his wrist. 'And wait a moment before you bring him for baptism.'

The children looked at one another and giggled. Sunneva nudged her daughter, and Sigurbjörn frowned at his son. Beside the bowl of water a candle was burning. There was a Bible on the table. A flicker of light on a ceiling beam quietened the boy and held his attention. The priest took some water in the palm of his hand, and the hair on the child's head turned black with the wetness. The priest said, 'I name thee Sigurbjörn. In the name of God the Father, God the Son and God the Holy Spirit.'

Next came the laying on of hands and the prayer of intercession. Then a hymn was sung: 'May God your guide and Saviour be, that worldly things not harm you'. After the hymn there was a great commotion and a rustling of the women's dresses. Sunneva, looking flushed, kissed her husband and said, 'Congratulations, my love. Now let me have your namesake.' She took the boy from his arms.

Sigurbjörn looked bewildered and gazed at his namesake in the arms of his wife. Sigurbjörn Gudbrandsson looked at Sunneva in wonder.

Ingirídur fetched the chocolate cake. The grown-ups seemed

somehow awkward. The priest directed the conversation, which was mostly about the local fisheries and terrible storms. Sigurbjörn the Younger fell asleep in his mother's arms. The top of the almond cake had gone and there were some chocolates lying on the tablecloth. When Thórarinn saw that Gudbrandur had other things to think about, his appetite returned. He ate about a quarter of the cake, until his mother prodded his shoulder, and said angrily, 'Do you want to burst, child?' Then he put some of the chocolates in his pocket and went out into the sun to eat them in peace. He was thinking about the rigid woman foaming at the mouth and wondered why one had to keep quiet about such terrible fear.

9

Little Maria had fallen asleep and it was quarter past eight when the priest said goodbye. 'Brandsi, how about us going out for a bit and walking off all those sweets?' said Sigurbjörn.

Gudbrandur lent him a sweater and an anorak, put on an old over-coat and pulled a green woollen hat over his head. Sigurbjörn put on his peaked cap.

'You look just like Gvendur Dúllari and Símon Dalaskáld, the famous tramps,' said Sunneva, and clapped her hands, laughing.

'Do you mean that?' asked Gudbrandur, sounding surprised. You could never tell when he might take something the wrong way. He put on his 'hurt' voice. 'We don't look that bad, do we, Sunna?'

'No, I was only joking, Gudbrandur.'

'She knows rags can't disguise a man's nobility,' said Sigurbjörn, and laughed. 'Don't take it to heart, Brandsi.'

During the christening, it had been raining gently, and the gravel on the street was dark. Children were throwing a ball over a house. The two men walked steadily on. At last Gudbrandur broke the silence.

'How's your mother?'

'She's as hard as nails and never stops going on about the Word of the Lord and the importance of good manners,' said Sigurbjörn. 'But she's nothing compared to that old witch you called a mother. How long is it now since she died?'

'Getting on for three years. What a kerfuffle Mama could make in the store in the old days. People were terrified to shop there.'

'The age of the Vikings had nothing on her,' said Sigurbjörn.

They walked some distance in silence and at last Sigurbjörn said, 'Brandsi, you're the best carpenter I've ever known. There's no one to touch you when it comes to working with wood. And good building timber is not easy to come by, as we both know.' He looked at Gudbrandur and said, as if sharing a confidence, 'I've seen those damned amateurs mangling good timber – mahogany, teak, even Oregon pine.'

Gudbrandur was silent for a moment, then he said, 'I'm a carpenter, and I wouldn't want to slander my own, Sigurbjörn, but the truth is I've seen bad workmanship too.'

They walked to the end of Eyrargata and up Búdarstígur to the old Danish trading posts. As they came out into the open there was a little rain in the sea breeze. They sheltered in the lee of one of the warehouses.

'They're going to pull them all down this summer,' said Gudbrandur.

Sigurbjörn looked up at the wall. 'They're remarkable. Lefolii built them.'

'But who could afford the repairs, Sigurbjörn?'

'You could take it on in your spare time.' Sigurbjörn's large fingers caressed the vertical boarding, exposed when the corrugated iron had been ripped away. 'It's a crime to pull these houses down. The wood's dry. It's nowhere near rotten.'

'The kids run in and out. It's dangerous for them.'

'Can't the windows be boarded up? You could do it a bit at a time, two or three hours a day. You haven't got anything better to do.'

The broken windows were some way up the walls of the building. Sigurbjörn stood on tiptoe, but found he could still not see in. He jumped awkwardly. Gudbrandur stood with his legs apart, made a foot-hold of his hands and waited, hunched over. 'Up you go then.'

'Forget it, Gudbrandur, you can't take my weight.'

'Yes, I can, come on.'

Sigurbjörn put his booted foot into Gudbrandur's locked hands. Gudbrandur heaved him up, straightening his back, puffing with the exertion. Sigurbjörn was shaking all over, and scarcely had a second in which to take a look. His hands flailed in midair and suddenly he grasped at Gudbrandur's bristly hair. Gudbrandur raised a mocking eyebrow. 'Well, did you see anything?'

'A pile of mangled corrugated iron. Damn it, what a weakling you are.'

'Weakling? You were shaking.'

'I'm only fourteen stone.'

Gudbrandur sized him up. 'Nearer sixteen.'

'Then let me give you a lift up.'

Gudbrandur chose to ignore Sigurbjörn as he stood waiting, hunched over.

'Corrugated iron is the correct sheeting material for this country,' said Sigurbjörn, straightening up again. 'Nothing else will stand up to the damned south-easterlies.'

They walked out to the shore, where the grey-white waves were breaking. The wind tugged at the lyme grass on the sand-dunes.

'You'll see my daughter doesn't come to any harm, won't you?'

'We'll look after her.'

'How old is that girl of Ingirídur's?'

'She's going on seventeen.'

'Well, she'll soon be ready for a man, eh?'

They crunched small crabs and mussels under their boots and clogs. Gudbrandur flipped over a crab with his toe. The shell was empty, but even so the claws clenched. Sunbleached logs of driftwood were slowly rotting, half submerged in the sand. Seaweed had spread over one of them, giving it the look of a giant crab. A flock of terns wheeled above in a screaming tempest. One or two detached themselves from the group, flew towards the men, reconnoitring above their heads, then changed direction, still shrieking. The men snatched up sticks to defend themselves.

'They're laying their eggs at the moment,' said Gudbrandur,

'They're crazy.' He broke into a bandy-legged run, his coat flapping about his feet. Sigurbjörn followed after him with comical splay-footed leaps. The terns followed, but then disappeared back among their sisters, uninterested in the capering townsmen. Everything fell into a dead calm.

'Now would be a good moment for a drop of something strong,' said Gudbrandur, as he sat down in the shelter of the grassy ridge, facing the yellow-brown sand of the shore. Sigurbjörn settled himself down beside him, panting. 'How long is it since you had a drink?'

'Quite a few years now, nearly ten – more.' Sigurbjörn leaned back on the ridge and pulled his peaked cap forward over his forehead. 'It did me no good, Brandsi,' he added.

They lay silent, side by side, listening to the howling of the storm. Sigurbjörn had had it in mind to ask for a loan so he could pay off something towards his grocery bill and scrape by till the end of the month, but the christening had put paid to that idea. He scarcely had enough cash to buy petrol for the journey home. It's all over, he thought. The easterly gale whipped up the dry sand from beneath its covering layer of darker, wet sand, and blew it in their faces.

Gudbrandur had come into a considerable fortune. His mother had run a hardware shop in the centre of town, living in a large flat on the fourth floor. Gudbrandur had closed the shop down when his mother died and now rented the place out. He and Sigurbjörn had got to know one another when the British troops moved out of the National Theatre in the autumn of 1944 and the restoration work had begun.

'How's the practice going?' asked Gudbrandur.

'It's damned nearly not going at all,' sighed Sigurbjörn. 'There's no demand for quality. People think they can do their own designs and just throw up any old damned cowshed without applying for the proper permits. There's less money in architecture than there is in frying pans.'

'I can't picture you selling teacups to old ladies.'

Sigurbjörn cleared his throat. Gudbrandur heard the sound. He opened one eye and saw that Sigurbjörn had his hands clasped behind his head. He did the same and felt a pebble dig painfully into the back of his hand. He brushed it away and lay there for some time letting his mind wander. He found himself thinking about the National Theatre. The building was nearly completed, with most people stopping work that day. The City Architect had been talking quietly to Sigurbjörn. Gudbrandur had hung around and followed them up on to the stage. Sigurbjörn had stood with his hands behind his back gazing up at the freshly painted ceiling as though he were seeing before him the fairy-tale castle the City Architect was describing. 'This idea of Sigurbjörn's for a big department store in Reykjavík is not a bad one at all,' Gudbrandur thought. 'Once it's up and running, it might even turn out to be a real goldmine.'

Gudbrandur sat up, plucked a blade of grass and put it in his mouth. Below them the waters of the estuary broke out into the open sea, the gale lashed the grass, the light was grey and eerie. He toyed with the blade of grass with his tongue and said, 'Let me come in on it with you.'

'In on what?'

'This new venture of yours.'

'Are you serious, Gudbrandur?' mumbled Sigurbjörn, astounded.

'Of course.'

'But you have a good, steady job!'

'It's the same year in year out. I'm nearly fifty now. Men don't last for ever in my line of business. Most of them have had it by the time they're my age.'

'You do realize, don't you, that everyone says I'm a man who's no good with money?'

'But are you any worse than anyone else?'

Sigurbjörn thought for a while with his eyes closed and chewed on a blade of grass. Gudbrandur looked at his face but his expression was giving nothing away. 'Well, I won't say I'm exactly in trouble, but the business isn't really on a firm financial footing just now, I can tell you that, Brandsi.'

'No, but it could be,' said Gudbrandur. 'You deal with the plans and argue with the workmen. I'll stick to what I know best.'

'And you do it so well.' Sigurbjörn raised himself on one arm and opened his eyes. 'You saw the designs. I'm not talking small change. I'm talking millions, my friend.'

'But a department store like that would really be a big step forward, Sigurbjörn. In the foyer you could have one of those palm courtyards of yours and goldfish in a pond and maybe a monkey in a cage for the kids. That kind of thing pulls people in.'

'Damn it, it would be just dandy to see a monkey jumping around guzzling bananas,' Sigurbjörn said, approvingly. He drew up one foot and stubbed his heel in the sand. He looked down at the estuary where the glistening river divided, like a many-fingered hand. 'We'll have to risk everything on it.'

'Mortgage our houses?' asked Gudbrandur.

'A lot more than that. Your mother's old dump of a shop, as well.'

'But that's a four-storey stone house in Austurstræti. The most expensive part of the town centre. Is it really worth the risk?'

'You bet, Gudbrandur. If everything is to go according to plan.'

'But I'm already guaranteeing your bank loan.'

'Yes, I know. But do you want to see me go bankrupt? Then you won't see a króna.' Sigurbjörn laughed.

'I'll have to get Inga's agreement,' said Gudbrandur, after some hesitation.

'I shouldn't bother,' scoffed Sigurbjörn. 'Women are so damned cautious when it comes to money. They grip their purses so tight their knuckles turn white.'

'And where are you going to build it?'

'On the site of my father-in-law's house.' Sigurbjörn lay back again.

'You're still thinking of Vitatorg?'

'Yes.'

'And what are you going to do with the old man?'

'The old miser can move into one of his own flats. He's got flats all over town and he swears he hasn't.'

'And what does he want in exchange for the square?'

'A whole floor. The better part of two thousand square metres and half the basement.'

'That's far too much, man. Tell him I've come in on the deal. That

59

tin shack of his is a complete ruin. I know a bit about houses.'

'So do I, Brandsi, but I don't know if it's worth the risk. He's as stubborn as hell. Vitatorg is one hell of a site, and there are five whole floors left. We might make something out of them for ourselves if we each keep a floor. But how would you feel about reporting to me in my basement, having me as a boss?'

'You need to get out of that basement,' said Gudbrandur. 'It's healthier to go into town to work. All you're doing is frightening your family. This will be our firm. I can also put up some office space for the deal. I've got a whole factory building I own jointly with my wife.'

'You lay a paw on a lady, and she lays some property in your lap,' laughed Sigurbjörn.

He knew the building, a rectangular stone box, SKALLGRÍMUR MECHANICAL WORKSHOP it said in black, worn letters on the dark red front, the windows black as the backs of mirrors. The workshop had gone bankrupt. That was not a good omen. He had not planned on becoming a full-time contractor. He just wanted to put up a single building and get himself out of this limitless debt. He allowed the misunderstanding to pass without correction, and sat up stiffly.

'Well, what's your verdict?' Gudbrandur asked.

'Can you put up some cash? That's important, of course.'

'How about two hundred and fifty thousand?'

'I'll have to think the matter over, old chum, and discuss it with my wife, just like you.' Sigurbjörn rolled over on to his knees, sprang to his feet and pulled Gudbrandur up. They walked down to the Ölfusá estuary, where the course of the river had cut sandbanks as high as the height of a man.

'Look at the sandbanks, Gudbrandur.' Sigurbjörn raised both hands in the air. 'They're like snowdrifts honed by the wind. Anyone building a church in a place like this should take those shapes as his guide. Look! Don't you think such a building would look good over there where the terns are?' Sigurbjörn pointed up at the grassy mounds of the breeding area and spread out his arms, paced the sand and moulded a church in the air with his hands. 'And the roof would look like a sea-lashed rock.'

Gudbrandur thought of mentioning a church by Le Corbusier, Notre-Dame-du-Haut, which was at that very moment under construction on a grassy hill in France. He had seen a picture of it in the weekly magazine *Fálkinn*. Instead he said drily, 'Yes, that would be a fine piece of cement-work. But perhaps we ought to keep our ideas more down to earth.'

'But that was always the intention. Don't worry, Brandsi.' Sigurbjörn clapped Gudbrandur on the back. 'I'm not saying that our deal won't work out, I'm not planning to deny you a partnership, my friend. But I need to give the matter some thought. You must understand that. Well, I'm frozen, let's be getting home.'

The terns were none the wiser for their journey over the sand earlier that evening.

Three evenings later, father and son went for a walk. Sigurbjörn had a meeting with Hallbjörn the crane operator. The streets were wet with rain.

'I think you're stupid setting up a company with shareholders,' said Thórarinn.

'And why is that?' Sigurbjörn's eyes were scouring the pavement.

'They'll just tell you what to do all the time.'

'Oh, and who will tell me what to do, Tóti, my lad?' Sigurbjörn was strolling along with his hands behind his back, his face clouded. Both were wearing their best clothes.

'Well, Gudbrandur and Ingirídur, of course.'

'I'll make sure I have a majority share in the business,' said Sigurbjörn, morosely. 'Anyway, what's new in the land of meatballs and stews?'

'Nothing,' said the boy, sullenly.

'It's not so easy to boss me about,' said Sigurbjörn. 'Your mother and your older brothers will be in the business too. We'll run an architect's office together when you're older, Tóti, my lad. That'll be our firm.'

They had to wait a long time for Hallbjörn. He walked up Hverfisgata from the town and looked up at the house from afar, but not at father and son, fussing and cursing. Then he described a circle round Grandfather's house like a badly wounded bear laying siege to a man in a tree. Thórarinn had seen him before. He always looked as if he had come straight from the swimming baths. He looked at Grandfather's house as though he had an old score to settle with it.

'This is going to be a bitch of a job, Sigurbjörn. Old shacks like this ought to be pulled down. This is old Geir's house, isn't it?' Hallbjörn felt in his breast pocket for a cigarette. He was wearing a white shirt and an ancient black suit.

'Yes, yes,' said Sigurbjörn.

'I've seen the old boy with a pipe in his mouth clambering up the side of the house on a rotten ladder with a can of paint.' Hallbjörn looked at the house and rolled the cigarette between his fingers. 'He's always been too stingy to do any proper repairs. It's all make do and mend.' Hallbjörn offered a cigarette to Sigurbjörn. Sigurbjörn refused it. 'But that's the way those old boys think. They don't think like we do today.' Hallbjörn lit his cigarette with a lighter and inhaled the smoke with great relish. 'He's still alive, isn't he?'

'Yes, he's gone to live in the west end of town. He's moving into a flat he owns out on Melar.'

'It's a wonder he didn't fall off the ladder and kill himself long ago.' Hallbjörn looked at the side of the house.

'Well, better men than him have been lost,' Sigurbjörn said sharply.

Hallbjörn raised his eyebrows and said at last, 'He'll just hold on to his pipe for dear life.'

'Are cheap jokes your speciality?' asked Thórarinn.

'Listen to the lad,' said Hallbjörn with admiration, and looked the boy up and down. 'You're quite a fellow, Sigurbjörn. If you're not building the National Theatre you're off fathering children and moving houses all over town. Is this yours?'

Thórarinn eventually realized that 'this' was himself.

'Yes.' Sigurbjörn was rather short with Hallbjörn, because they had not yet reached an agreement.

'Bloody good clothes the boy has.'

Sigurbjörn looked fondly at his son, who had taken off his cap, and rumpled his hair.

'This is going to be a bitch of a job.' Hallbjörn turned towards the house again.

'Oh, you've known worse, Hallbjörn, old chap,' muttered Sigurbjörn. 'How much do you want for taking the damned shack away?'

They walked round to the side of the plot facing the sea and paused by the fence. There were some abandoned cars dotted about the square.

'And what do you want done with the vegetation?' asked Hallbjörn. He had not answered the question.

'That's nothing to do with me, my friend.'

'Can't my brother take care of it? He has a summerhouse out of town. He's got trees growing out of his arse.' Hallbjörn flung the cigarette into a puddle. 'And where are we going to put the crane? On the Bjarnaborg side? Close Hverfisgata for a whole day? What a way to earn a living. It's a bitch of a job. And who's going to keep the crowds away from the house while we're lifting it? The police? They're not likely to be too keen, I can tell you.'

10

The small used-car showroom on Vitatorg is deserted, its window black as a silent spot in a broad and fast-flowing mountain stream. Where the house once stood its foundations now gape; wooden debris and rafters lie around making it look as though a war has been fought on the street corner. There is an old washing-machine under the wooden debris and small pieces of concrete on the white enamel. A pile of iron radiators. The old man stands looking at all this, with a rueful expression on his face. However could I have let that woman Sunneva trick me like this? Look at what they've done with those radiators! And the biggest of the beams could be kept and re-used. I doubt they would have been thrown out before the war. The woman said the washing-machine was no use. Sheer nonsense. She just wanted a new model. Yesterday morning Geir had called over two boys who were playing and given them each an apple. The damned bloody boys had kicked them about outside the shop. In the old days we'd've sooner used our teeth on them, not our feet, wouldn't we? He cursed.

In the plot the rowan trees waited anxiously. One of them was half dead. Some idiot wanted the other, but wasn't going to pay for it. He dug a deep hole around it and showed up at Vitatorg with a strong rope and a truck. Some half-baked idiot, he seemed to be. What kind of folk are they, anyway, who go around digging up trees? A bunch of fools?

'What is the man going to do with the trees, Grandfather?' asked Thórarinn.

'Humph,' said the old man, and made no reply.

'How do you like it in the west end of town?'

'Oh, it's sheer hell, Tóti.'

'The tree will die,' said the boy.

'Well, you're a chip off the old block, my little king, my fine lad,' said Geir to his daughter's son. 'Don't you like it with old Hjálmur?'

'I'm on that bike from morning till night,' said Thórarinn, with feeling.

'Does he sell that much?' asked Geir, sounding anxious.

'Yes, I'm kept busy, serving the customers,' said Thórarinn.

'And where is your father?'

'At home in the basement with Gudbrandur. They're looking at the plans. Gudbrandur wants to make changes to the building.'

'What sort of changes, Tóti?' The old man took the ancient pipe out of his mouth.

'He wants it to be smaller. He doesn't see why they have to build another National Theatre, he says. But Father doesn't want anything changed.' The lad waved a hand. 'Father says there is no question of it being smaller. It's all settled. He's not going to build any chicken coop and won't let anyone tell him what to do.'

'Chicken coop!' The old man snorted. Well, he's got a fine idea of himself, all right, he thought. And now they want me as a shareholder in the company. Some company that'll turn out to be.

The tree maniac was busying himself around the truck and the excavator. He took off his jacket to reveal a white shirt and a woollen waistcoat. He had his two sons helping him. They were hanging about the site. The older son was obviously the lazy one, surly-looking. Their father rushed out into the dirt in his best shoes and started to attack the trench with an insane, manic passion, but he soon grew tired and gave the shovel to the older son. The older son met everything his father said with the same words: 'Yes, OK, old man!'

They tied the rope to the larger tree. The man with the excavator was in a foul mood. Clearing its throat, the excavator raised its arm. The rope slid roughly up the bark of the tree, scraping it, exposing yellow wood. The excavator driver was talking so loudly to himself inside his cab that they could hear what he was saying: 'Bloody madness.'

The truck driver had his pipe in his mouth. He took out a rubber inner tyre from under his seat. 'I think it might be an idea to wrap this round the trunk.'

At this, the lazy lad's face contorted. He looked glumly at the truck driver and ambled towards the tree. The knot was hard as iron. The excavator driver put on his sunglasses and gazed out towards the sea, his face as impassive as a death-mask. The sea was dead calm, there were midges on the square and the weather was mild. He had put in the lowest bid for clearing the earth away from the cliff. Damn Sigurbjörn, who had said nothing about helping people move trees.

They managed to unpick the knot with an awl, and wrapped the inner tyre around the tree trunk. Geir said the only sensible thing to do would be to tie a bowline knot. Thórarinn eagerly endorsed his grandfather's advice. The excavator raised its great strong arm and the tree shook its mass of leaves in fright. The excavator gave a sudden lurch, a gleaming steel arm with a thin skin of oil slid out of a red shaft. The tree rose to its feet and clutched desperately at the earth with all its thick roots. The excavator belched black fumes and made a low grumbling sound.

Old Geir shook his head. The older lad stood on the side of the trench and looked on in irritation and boredom.

'Jump down, Einar,' cried the tree specialist. The younger son looked eagerly at his father and did not know what was expected of him. 'Take the sharp shovel, boy, and cut the roots.'

'Humph,' Geir was heard to say at the side of the trench. He had learned as much about growing trees from his wife's rummaging among the rowan and rhubarb to know that the tree's days were numbered. That cheered him up. The younger son jumped down and made a feeble effort at hacking at the roots. 'Are you waiting for the shovel to do that on its own?' the father shouted, jumped down, grabbed the shovel and chopped frantically at the black, hairy hoses that were slippery with wetness. The sharp side of the shovel jumped away, and at last yellow wounds gleamed where he was hacking. The excavator tugged at the tree. The rubber tubing moved slowly along the tree trunk, the thick rope slipped off it, bark came loose and the rope caught in a hollow beneath a strong branch. The tree fell over and the roots snapped with a crack. 'It's coming loose!' The tree specialist attacked the main root like a man insane, his hair wet with sweat and his cheeks quivering. The truck driver handed a saw down into the trench.

Someone had to get down on all fours. The tree specialist looked at the saw as though he wasn't sure what to do with it. He looked up at his elder son and said sternly, 'Are you sick, boy?'

'Sick?'

'I mean, are you ready to take to your bed? Can't you understand plain language, Magnús?'

'OK, old man,' the lad said heavily, waved the midges away, got sullenly down into the trench, crouched on all fours, and sawed. He was strong and efficient. The roots snapped one after another. He sawed clean through the main root and the tree came slowly up on to the grassy bank. They hauled it up on to the back of the truck. The flatbed had been so hammered by big rocks that the iron struts were visible through it. The truck swayed this way and that. The truck driver came running over and slipped a tyre on top of the driver's cab.

He was very quick and nimble in spite of his enormous paunch and leaped up on to the flatbed and down from it again. The big root lay in the back of the truck and the leafy end of the tree was spread all over the driver's cab.

A shaggy dog with a lolling tongue was waiting behind the truck window. A group of children from Bjarnaborg wanted to give him the bone from a leg of lamb. The truck driver let the dog out, told the children it was the heaviest dog in the land and proved his point by picking it up in his arms and carrying it around the truck. 'He's a big animal,' he said. 'And he hates Icelandic sheepdogs.' The children stood and stared. 'A sheepdog used to tease him when he was a puppy, and when he sees an Icelandic sheepdog, he'll just bite straight through its neck. He's so quick about it that you don't see anything till it's all over. He's killed three of them this year.'

The dog took the bone in his mouth. Then he put it on the ground and spent a while looking around for an Icelandic sheepdog. The children kept their distance.

'What are you building here?' the truck driver asked Geir.

'I'm not building anything, my friend,' answered Geir.

'There's to be a department store over the whole of the square,' said Thórarinn.

'Oh, a big department store! And where will people put their cars?'

'The car park will be on top of the basement at the back of the building. You'll drive in from Hverfisgata through a tunnel.'

'Ah, won't that be marvellous,' said the truck driver, clambered up on to the flatbed, secured the tree, and then drove away with the heaviest dog in Iceland sitting in the front seat.

Thórarinn pointed to the half-dead tree. 'But what will happen to that one?'

'It's no good, we'll leave it,' said the lazy son. Both his knees were caked in dirt.

'Things would have turned out better if the settlers had taken good care of the forests for those who were to inherit the land,' said Thórarinn. The lazy lad looked at him and snorted from sheer boredom.

The tree specialist cleaned his shoes in the grass and thanked Geir with a handshake.

Geir took his pipe out of his mouth, and a distant look came to his eyes. 'It'll be dead as a doornail by next spring.'

The excavator put a strong paw down into the earth and dug the soil away from beneath the half-dead rowan. It pushed the tree up with its fingernails and moved it stiffly about with the side of its hand. Then it rolled towards the foundations and began to push at them gently. The big stones separated from the concrete and fell on to the rubble. Part of the fence was still standing, and two enormous black holes gaped in the lawn.

II

1

When Ragnar and Helgi were small, there used to be a handsome woman standing out on the lawn. She hugged a telescope and a ship's log in her arms, and her dark-blue gown cascaded in generous folds down into the earth. She was a figurehead from a schooner. By about the time Thórarinn was born she had rotted up to her neck, so Sigurbjörn sawed off her head and threw away her body.

Sigurbjörn woke his son, prodding him in the shoulder with a large finger. From the passage Thórarinn could see Sunneva asleep with her hair spread about the pillow and a plump arm lying on the quilt. Sigurbjörn cooked oatmeal porridge, an inedible glutinous mass, and laid the table. He ate a whole bowl himself out of sheer stubbornness.

Thórarinn sat in the car all the way to Vitatorg. An air compressor could be heard barking in the distance. They went in through the corner gate. The foundations were deep now, a corrugated-iron fence stood round the top of the ledged rockface, and the thick sheets of steel used to contain the fragmented rock during dynamiting shook as though someone was turning over underneath them.

At Hjálmur's the day's work was well under way. Thórarinn carefully planned the best cycle routes round town. He sped down Laufásvegur, past all the plain, functional houses, up Hellusund, stopped, took the package off the rear carrier and knocked at a door.

Now what was the architectural style here? In the garden there was a shack-like annexe with large windows: was this the horrible Californian style that Sigurbjörn had so often condemned, his brows knotted with disapproval? Or was it the geometrical-austere style? A curtain was raised and a woman's sad face looked him over. The curtain fell.

He heard some footsteps, and the sad-looking woman opened the door. She seemed to be very frightened of something. Perhaps of him. This called for gallantry, and before Thórarinn knew what he was saying, he found himself addressing the woman in a relentlessly formal manner: 'Do you wish me to carry the package in for you, madam? Simply telephone at once should you require anything else. We are constantly at the service of our customers.'

The woman came out to the steps and peeped into the bag. 'Oh, I've forgotten the turnips.' She looked furtively up and down the street. 'He'll murder me. You'll have to go back for them.'

She gave him her heartfelt thanks when he returned.

'Think nothing of it.' From the hallway he could see into the kitchen. In it sat a large man with short fair hair, eating in silence. The man looked at him coldly. He had bags under his eyes.

Thórarinn thought the house smelt bad.

He asked Ragna about the couple. 'She's some seaman's wife, that's all I know, Tóti. There's terrible goings-on in some of those places. I would never dare lend money to people like that.'

'Everyone has to eat, my dear,' said Hjálmur, loudly. 'She has always paid her bills.'

After dinner, Thórarinn lay down on the floor and looked at the carved grandfather clock that Geir and Rósa had given their daughter and son-in-law on their wedding day. Sigurbjörn opened the glass door in order to adjust the heavy iron weights. A bird of paradise spread its tail over the wooden casing of the clock. At the bottom of the clockface were the letters 'SS' and the year, '1932'. Helgi said that the letters stood not for Sigurbjörn and Sunneva but for 'Southern Slaughterers'. The clock struck nine, and bang on the hour Geir and Rósa arrived, as they had said they would, for coffee. Thórarinn was going with them up to Korpúlfsstadir to plant potatoes.

Sunneva got out the best crockery. The coffee cups had a picture of a knight on horseback and his squire in a forest. There was a castle on a grassy hill with a bugler in a tower on the saucers. Sigurbjörn was ready with the first of the documents relating to the foundation of the new company for his parents-in-law to sign. The company was to be called 'Enterprise'.

'And why is it to be a company with shareholders, Sigurbjörn?' asked Geir.

'In case it goes bankrupt, Father-in-law.'

'In case it goes bankrupt!' Geir stopped gnawing his sugarcube.

'If that were to happen,' Sigurbjörn smiled, 'they couldn't take proceedings against us for a larger amount than the amount of capital stated in the document. Eighty thousand krónur.'

'Well, you think of everything!' snorted Geir.

Sunneva and her older sons had already signed their names. So had Ingirídur and Gudbrandur. Grandmother Rósa signed, but Grandfather pretended he could not see where to put his scrawl. Hot Christmas cake fell under the knife like a house of cards. Sigurbjörn Helgason, director of Enterprise, stuffed a piece of it into his mouth, past his massive, horse-like teeth. He was not to know that his name had now appeared on Thórarinn's Black List for the very first time.

Grandfather said a reluctant yes to everything that Sigurbjörn asked of him, and looked angrily at the gun cupboard. 'Keeping weapons in the house like that.' He understood nothing at all of the plans for the Reykjavík Department Store, whichever way up they were shown him, but admired the grandfather clock and winked at Thórarinn and said, 'That's a damned good clock you've got there. How much did you pay for it?'

'Grandfather, can you drive me up to Hlídar?' asked Thórarinn.

'Now just let your grandfather and grandmother drink their coffee in peace. It's not all that often they come here,' said Sunneva.

'Oh well, we're going to shove some potatoes into the ground anyway. Ach, it's already too late to plant this year.'

'The spring was so dreadfully cold,' said Grandmother Rósa, politely.

'And what are you going to do up at Hlídar, little king?' asked Geir.

'Take my goldfish tank there,' said Thórarinn, frowning fiercely at the nickname.

'All right then, get it quickly.'

Thórarinn fetched the goldfish tank and was first to get down to the old Morris Geir's friends at the shop called the 'Roy Rolls'. Geir had painted the car black himself. 'Well, we're pretty old, Tóti, this car and me, so we suit each other.' Geir fished the keys out of his jacket pocket. He started up the 'Roy Rolls'. They found it difficult to hear each other above the noise of the engine.

'This is the sort of car criminals drive in the movies,' said Thórarinn, darkly. He settled himself in the back of the car, wearing his rubber boots and with the goldfish tank on his lap. He had changed the water, but there was still a bad smell coming from the tank.

'What did you say, Tóti?' shouted Geir.

'Nothing.'

'What was he saying?' Geir asked Grandmother Rósa.

'He was saying that we looked so good all three of us together in the car,' said Rósa.

'No, he was talking about some shady dealings.' Geir turned out on to Hringbraut.

'I was saying that the car reminded me of a hoodlums' car,' Thórarinn screamed.

'Oh, på den måde,' said the old man, resorting to Danish. 'But where are you taking that poor sod of a fish? It's making a terrible stink.'

Helgi the goldfish floated belly up on the swaying surface of the clear water. A catfish moved about the bottom, performing its duty. It was the last occupant to survive there in reasonable health.

'Wouldn't it have been better to make this goldfish a shareholder in your father's firm, so he could go bankrupt instead of me?' Geir's eyes twinkled at his grandson in the driving mirror.

Geir Sveinsson never drove faster than twenty-five miles an hour. 'Yes, yes, be quiet, you devil,' he said whenever anyone honked at him in irritation. He put out a knitted fist towards a surprised man who overtook them on Miklubraut.

'They go at such a speed,' said Grandmother Rósa.

The buyer of pet fish was willing to pay fifteen krónur for the catfish, but would not give anything for Helgi. 'He's half dead, man.

Don't you see the way he's lying on his side and scarcely moving his tail?' The goldfish tank was carried inside under the surly glare of the master of the house. They agreed that the buyer would look after the fish and pay something later if Helgi's health improved.

'And what did you get in hard cash?' Geir asked.

'Not one króna for the big fish.'

'Well, just be glad you're rid of him, Thórarinn. He's off your hands now.'

At Korpúlfsstadir Geir took half a bag of seed out of the boot, got into his wellingtons and, cursing, pulled on a woollen sweater. 'I'm ashamed to be seen in a sweater,' he said. 'When did Hannes Hafstein, the cabinet minister, ever allow himself to be seen in a sweater? You should have been with me, Tóti, when the farmers came to protest against the telephone in 1905. You should have seen the look he gave them from the steps of the Cabinet Office.'

Thórarinn stumbled around in the waterlogged soil with the heavy fork. The earth was blue with nitrate fertilizer from the year before. Grandmother Rósa waited in the car. It was late in the evening now and there was drizzle and the sky above the bays was grey. Grandfather put his hands on his hips and made ridges of earth with the toes of his boots. His vile temper had flushed colour into his face. He had put on a leather pilot's helmet, so that only his blue cheeks and reddening nose were visible. 'Well, that's the last time I'm planting potatoes, I'll tell you that, Tóti. They'll have to kill me first.'

They had a cup of coffee in the car, and then Grandmother Rósa got out, wrapped in layer upon layer of garments and with a headscarf tied under her chin. Grandfather made evenly spaced holes in the ridges, and she followed him, dropping a potato in each hole and brushing earth over it. Her eyes twinkled at her grandson.

Thórarinn could hear his parents as he reached the gate. He crept home along the path. Listened on the steps. Peeped in the window. His father sat on the sofa staring straight ahead, pretending to read a newspaper. Sunneva went from room to room in a white blouse and dark-red skirt with her hair flying behind her. Thórarinn walked in through the porch. 'We're practically in the poorhouse, and you go sneaking away with the post every morning,' Sunneva was shouting. 'No one wants to put money into this building of yours. What do you think it costs to advertise in *Morgunbladid* day after day? We've become the laughing-stock of the town. I had to lie to the men who came to disconnect the electricity this morning. I told them my poor old father was lying paralysed in bed upstairs.'

Sigurbjörn muttered something. Thórarinn appeared in the doorway of the parlour.

'Where are we going to move to when they sell the roof from over our heads? To your mother's? And do you think I don't know when you can't sleep? And that poor wretched fool Gudbrandur. He's going to lose everything, isn't he? He's so green he lets you mortgage all his property. I don't know how you have the heart to swindle him like that.'

Sigurbjörn was getting angry. 'Are you calling me incompetent, in front of the boy?' he asked in a fury. Thórarinn started to go upstairs.

'Where's the raincoat I bought you last spring?'

'We left it at Eyrarbakki. I told you. Brandsi will bring it to town when he gets the chance.'

'Go up to your room this instant, Thórarinn, and don't let me see you down here,' said the mother, turning her anger on the boy.

'Father didn't like the raincoat,' said Thórarinn.

'I can hardly look Gudbrandur's wife in the face,' shouted Sunneva. 'She's no fool. They have children just like we do, don't they? And they're feeding your daughter.'

Thórarinn went into his room without closing the door. Sigurbjörn thundered back at her, 'Maybe Brandsi is fond of me. That's more than you can say of some people. Why don't you go and lie down, woman, and have a nice quiet rest?'

'And you have no scruples about taking advantage of him.'

'Calm down, woman, you'll wake the boy up.'

'I'm damned if I'll calm down. Do you really imagine he's asleep?'

'Don't go on, Sunna dear, I'm doing this for my family.'

'For your family? Lord help us!'

Thórarinn heard the front door bang and his father's footsteps disappearing into the distance. The garden gate clanged. He heard his mother sobbing.

That night Thórarinn could not sleep. At the Einar Jónsson Art Museum there was a bas-relief he could not get out of his head. It was called *Pangs of Conscience* and showed a rough, coarse face, the nostrils dilated, the teeth large and the gums exposed. A man crouched on the head, forcing the eyelids apart, while another put his toe on the breastbone and whispered into the ear, 'The Black List! The Black List!'

The Black List was kept hidden in the top drawer of his chest-of-drawers. On the front cover of the book there was a skull and crossbones. At the bottom were the words, 'This book may not be opened, on pain of death, without the permission of its owner, Thórarinn Sigurbjarnarson.'

He crept softly out of bed and fetched the Black List.

Enemies of the State
1   Gudbrandur Jónsson (can never leave me in peace)
2   Vilborg Sigurbjarnardóttir (hateful ever since I first came
       to consciousness)
3   Grandmother Sigurlaug (because of the meatballs)
4   Sigurbjörn Helgason

Sigurbjörn's crime was so terrible that the boy could hardly enter it on the list, and he hadn't had the heart to put his father higher than fourth. Now it occurred to him to add Ragna at the shop to the list. She was forever calling him 'Mr City Architect'. He put her fourth and entered his father's name below hers, writing: 'Public Enemy No. 5. His crime is treason, and now I have got a job for the summer.' He made a great effort to be honest with the Black List and with himself, tore out the page, and wrote it all out again, putting his father in second place where he really belonged. Thórarinn felt his heart thumping.

He went back to bed again, fell asleep, and dreamed. Poor Sunneva had died. She lay in her coffin in her bridal dress with two small skeletons in her arms. One of them was a monkey's; the other was his own. He woke up suddenly, and kept himself from falling back to sleep for a while to free himself from his tangled dreams. Outside the night was light as day, the summer solstice.

He awoke to the lively sound of birdsong on the roof and in the trees as the sun rose. He had been dreaming about potatoes. He knew that the weather would be good. 'Perhaps they'll take all my wages from the shop off me,' he thought anxiously. Suddenly his mother was standing in the doorway. 'I've slept like a log all night,' said Thórarinn, sitting up and stretching as he had seen a good boy do in a film at the cinema. His mother looked at him thoughtfully. She cooked the porridge in dead silence. Sigurbjörn was still asleep.

He put his shoes on and opened the front door. A spider tried to run from the steps into the safety of the undergrowth, but did not make it. The garden was awake. There was a rustling, and he saw a thrush's tail high in a tree among the leaves. A wagtail with a blade of grass in its beak whisked its tail on the garden path and looked at him. Under the trees the sun filtering through the leaves turned the grass into an exotic fabric. A cat stood there, holding a front paw in the air and watching the birds closely. The day was going to be warm. The doors of the dovecote were open, and Thórarinn closed them. There was a film of dew on the car parked in the street. Once Father and he had driven along the Keflavík road and touched ninety-seven miles an hour. That was a secret between them. The car lay on the roadway like a stone. Were they going to sell it? They had lost the car, the house, everything. 'Where are we going to live?' he thought, aghast. 'And what are we supposed to eat?'

'Good morning, Mr City Architect. You're late,' said Ragna, when he arrived at the shop. 'Hjálmur's waiting in the office. He's spitting feathers.' Thórarinn looked at his wristwatch. It was two minutes to nine, what was all the fuss about? What was she wearing under that white smock? The other day he had dreamed that she was sitting completely naked on a rug on the lawn, and had smiled when he peeped at her from the balcony. And only yesterday she had asked, 'Hey, Mr City Architect, do you want to get engaged to me?'

Hjálmur sat crouched over pen and paper in his little office with his spectacles on the end of his nose. 'Have you ever heard the like, Tóti?' He picked up a newspaper, held it at some distance from his eyes, gave it a tug to smooth out the folds, and read aloud: '"Morning deliveries to your home. No one offers better service. Tómas's Butcher's." But just listen, my good chap, to what is going in tomorrow's paper! "All-day deliveries! Trough Butcher's. There's no comparison! Hjálmur Jónsson, Meat Merchant." That's the way to handle these monkeys, Tóti. That's what being in business is all about. On that cycle, my lad, off with you.' Hjálmur rocketed up from the table.

A dented corrugated-iron fence with a door divided the space at the back of the house from the street. The key hung on a nail inside the office. Thórarinn opened the door, lifted the bicycle over the doorstep, wheeled it round the corner of Barónsstígur and jerked it up on to its iron stand. He arranged the packages in an orange crate on the front carrier and zipped through the traffic on Laugavegur, standing up on the pedals, and turned up Frakkastígur, but he had to push the bicycle for the last bit of the way to the corner. He free-wheeled down Njardargata, glancing quickly towards his home, which was hidden behind the trees.

When he reached the shop shortly before noon, there was another message for him. 'Hjálmur wants to talk to you, Mr City Architect. You forgot to lock the door.'

The old man was sitting gloomily in his office, rummaging through his papers. 'You forgot to lock the back door, Tóti. You must always go through the shop and lock the back entrance when you have taken the cycle out, my good chap. How many times have I told you that?'

'Yes. I know.'

Nína came through the doorway chewing her false teeth.

'Nína was here alone, and someone stole a side of beef from under her nose.' The old man gesticulated with his hands.

'But couldn't she do anything?'

Nína leaned against the doorpost, pulled a face, shrugged her shoulders and grinned. 'They were that quick I couldn't do anything. I tried to run up Barónstígur, but my legs have been so bad lately.'

'Yes, yes, my good woman,' said Hjálmur, impatiently.

'The speed of them.' She made a movement with her hands to demonstrate the speed. 'The carcase dangling between them. The big one was completely bald.'

'And couldn't you get anyone to take up the chase for you, my good woman?'

'No, they just took to their heels and got clean away. There wasn't a living soul in the street, and I couldn't leave the shop unattended. Think if the cash till had been robbed, too.' She looked at them both with an expression of horror, as if to bring home to them the serious-ness of the situation. 'They were gone round the corner of Grettis-gata . . . like arrows.' She raised a hand and whistled as she re-created their flight with one finger. 'The bald one tried to slam the door shut after him. He was missing three fingers from one hand.'

'Go and serve the customers now, my good woman.' Hjálmur sat leafing through his order book. He wetted his thumb. Thórarinn was longing to be off and out. 'What does a side of beef cost?'

'Nearly seven hundred krónur, Tóti.'

'That's a month's wages!'

'I'm afraid I'll have to take it out of your money, Tóti,' said Hjálmur, more in sorrow than in anger. 'You have to learn your lesson. It just goes to show.' He turned towards the boy. 'Us old chaps have to think of everything. People simply don't care when it's not their own shop.'

'I'm very sorry. Do I really have to pay for it? But what about Nína? Isn't it partly her fault?'

'There's one thing you can do, Tóti. Go up Grettisgata and look in the alleys and backyards there. And behind rubbish bins. Like a policeman. If those fellows were winos, they were going to sell the meat for hard cash. They won't have got far. Chaps like that don't have any staying power. You'll probably find the beef behind a rubbish bin somewhere.

The street was full of the morning's many sounds. A painter stood on a ladder outside the swimming baths. You work with your bare hands and your wages disappear almost as soon as you get them, thought Thórarinn. You have nothing to show at the end of each month. He was sweating with vexation. If I see those fellows, I'll sock them one. Men were laying pavement slabs on Barónstígur. A boy with a wheelbarrow was pouring cement between the pavement and the gutter. Water trickled off the edge of the piece of the plywood on which he was stirring the mixture with a shovel between trips. Thórarinn could not bring himself to ask if they had seen men running with a side of beef. He looked in the backyards of the houses, walked down dank underpasses, peeped behind dustbins with buttercups in a circle around them, but nowhere was there a leg of beef to be seen. Washing gleamed on lines and children played ball. A woman stood out on the steps. A low fence screened off her bit of land and there was a circular flowerbed with pieces of lava around it in the grass. Red tulips shivered in the breeze. The woman was stirring a bowl so hard that her large, fleshy arm was quivering. 'Yes, good day, I'm from Trough Butcher's. Have you seen half a bull anywhere, lady?'

'No, I haven't, boy. Was it dressed to go out?'

'What? No, a side of beef was stolen this morning while I was out.' The woman's joke irritated Thórarinn. 'There were two thieves. The big one was bald and had three fingers missing.'

'No, I'm afraid not, my lad. No meat wandering about here.'

He went from back alley to back alley: cooing pigeons on rusted gutter pipes, low garages, the backs of the houses looking sad. He leaned his back against a burning hot corrugated-iron fence, closed his eyes, and smelt the pungent odour of angelica. I took this job so I could buy an aeroplane, he thought. Damn it! He stamped his foot in despair.

It was almost three o'clock when he at last gave up. Hjálmur was out front in the shop in his most jovial mood, but Thórarinn was still depressed.

'Oh, come on, Tóti. Don't take it to heart. What's a side of beef between friends?'

'He's such a lovely man.' Nína gazed fondly at Hjálmur.

'A lot,' said the boy, sadly.

'No, it isn't. Just remember to lock up next time, there's a good chap.'

'You don't have to remind me.' Thórarinn thought there were few things worse than being called 'a good chap' all day long.

3

Yellow timber work has now risen above the scaffolding at Vitatorg; hammers are clashing and banging; cement spews out of the wheelbarrows and hardens to form the first floor; the basement is finished, and it gives one a strange feeling to stand in the underground driveway, peep in through one of the large gaps in the basement wall and see the stone supports holding up the floor. Gudbrandur has arrived with his band of men and eased a temporary shelter for the builders down off a lorry on to the corner by the gate. The first department store in the country on its way up into the sky. Sigurbjörn is finding it difficult to sleep and is off his food.

On the pavement the boy leans on the bicycle and looks across the street. Something must be done! No one is buying any floor-space. Everything was all so much better when Father sat in the basement drawing up plans. If only Thórarinn could turn the calendar back from July to May, and have Grandfather's house sitting back on its original foundations.

The cranes suddenly snap the cables taut, and the house crawls forward away from its foundations. The whole of the street is shaking. The weight of the house grinds a grey and bone-dry dust on to the pavement. Pigeons rise up from the roof flapping their wings. Beams appear, and a floor brown with age but not rotten at all. Everyone is holding his breath. Then the house tips forward, turns through sixty degrees in the cables' embrace, swings backwards, and comes to rest hanging not quite straight in the grip of the cranes, an enormous steel cradle sagging beneath it. Then it settles very gently on the transporter, and applause spreads down the pavement and from window to window all along Bjarnaborg. 'Did you see the cradle?' says the short fellow from Selfoss who is the new owner of the house. 'As soft as marzipan.' Grandfather's house drifts out along Hverfis-gata and away to the east with one police car in front of it and another following behind. In a window a chandelier can be seen swinging to and fro. One of the doctors has not thought it worth the trouble of removing it from the waiting room. 'Well, farewell and adieu.' Old Geir snatches off his headgear and makes a deep bow.

Thórarinn had been allowed to stop work half an hour earlier than usual. Directly opposite the toyshop in a basement there was a sports shop. He had sometimes stopped outside it to look at the handballs and footballs. Sprinting shoes in the window, soccer boots on shelves, shot-puts and discuses, javelins leaning against a wall. He summoned up his courage and went down the steps.

A plump girl with long hair was serving behind the counter. She had sometimes glanced at him when he was looking in the window. But then he had really had his eyes on the aeroplane on the other side of the street. That fat girl there knew him. Strange how girls who served in shops were always plump. It was because they had such easy lives. Inside the shop there was a good, warm smell of leather.

'Good afternoon.'

'Er, yes, good afternoon.'

'Can I help you with anything?' She leaned her hands on the table so that her breasts bulged under the fluffy sweater.

'I was thinking of buying a sports bag.'

'And what sort of bag did you have in mind?'

'Well, it'll have to be a pretty good one. It's for my brother.'

'The bags are over here.' She pointed up at the shelf. He waited anxiously for her to ask who his brother was.

'Do you want to see one?'

'That blue one there.' She put the bag on the glass counter.

'My brother's name is Helgi Sigurbjarnarson. Perhaps you've heard of him?'

'Yes, of course I have.' She smiled prettily.

'He's abroad just now.' Thórarinn blushed. 'With the national team. I'm going to give him the bag when he comes home.'

'Oh, how nice of you.'

'Or maybe I should give him boots.' He looked around.

'Do you know his size?'

'Do you own the shop?' asked Thórarinn.

'No, Father does.'

'Is he here?'

'No, he'll be in first thing tomorrow morning.'

'Oh well. I'll come back then.'

'Was it something particular?' She smiled gently. There was a gold ring on her plump finger .

Thórarinn thought a moment. 'I can tell you what it's about. My father is building a giant department store. You could buy floor-space in it. We've started selling the space already. The commercial advantages are obvious. There are shops on every floor. Say someone wants to buy a watch for a birthday present. But he realizes he can't. Watches are too expensive. So he walks into your shop and buys a handball instead. He would never have done that if your shop hadn't been right opposite the jeweller's. Will you tell your father about it?'

'I promise.'

He looked in next morning. Talking to the girl's father was like talking to a statue. He was not interested in space in the Reykjavík Department Store. He had had the basement shop on Skólavördustígur for a long time and he owned the building himself. 'I'm sure your father's idea is a clever one, but that's about it. Yes, what's his name?'

'Sigurbjörn Helgason.'

'Yes, I've heard the name. Isn't old Geir your grandfather? Tell the old boy to move to this new store. The front of that little hovel of his is practically falling into the street. What's the name of that wizened old goat he's got working in his shop? Freysteinn?'

Now Thórarinn was getting angry. He hurried out. As he was wheeling his bicycle past the window he saw that they were both looking at him, laughing. He put his hand to his head and found his hair was damp with sweat. They were idiots. They had no sense of progress. Hjálmur must surely be a better bet. He decided to tell him about the whole matter once the midday rush was over.

Back at Trough Butcher's, Hjálmur opened his eyes wide and his hair stood on end. 'Eh?' he shouted. 'What are you saying, Tóti my lad? I'm to move out of my shop? Eh? I've had this shop all my life!'

Thórarinn was stubborn. 'But times have changed, Hjálmur. Get in on it right from the start! Haven't you seen the building? It's to be called the Reykjavík Department Store. The estate agents have copies of the plans. I could bring them to you for you to see, if you like.'

'It's a fine name, Tóti. A fine name, and you're a clever lad. But I'm too old for that sort of thing. What do you think the old women out front would make of it? Old Nína. Do you think I could get her to move, eh?'

'You could have the ground floor, and everyone who came into the store would start by buying things in your shop.' Thórarinn wished he would stop shouting.

'Ragna!' Hjálmur bawled to the front of the shop.

Ragna came in through the door, leaned against the doorjamb and crossed her arms beneath her breasts. 'Tóti here is saying that we've got to sell the shop and buy space in his father's new building.'

'I think he's absolutely right.'

Thórarinn's cheeks burned.

'What, is everyone taking sides against an old man?'

'I'm sure it's how things are going to be in the future,' she said. She leaned her head to one side and looked grave and thoughtful. 'Big shops like that, all under one roof. People have so much to do nowadays they haven't got time to go first to the fishmonger's and then to the butcher's, and then to the baker's, and then to the dairy, and then to the grocer's, paying separately in every shop. They'd rather get everything in one basket and pay at the door when they've finished doing their shopping. I sailed to Edinburgh with the *Gullfoss* last year and saw a place like that there.'

'Well, I'm damned if I know,' said Hjálmur.

'Should I talk to Father about it, perhaps?' asked Thórarinn, nearly bursting with enthusiasm.

Footsteps could be heard in the shop. Nína called for help.

'Should I mention it?' Thórarinn found to his annoyance that his voice was trembling.

'I'm damned if I know, Tóti. I just don't know.'

When Hjálmur saw the boy's disappointment, he opened a drawer and said, 'It's payday today.' He banged a 500-króna note on the table.

'But that's too soon. And what about the side of beef?'

'We'll discuss that later, shrimp.'

'But don't you want to buy any space at all?'

'No, Tóti, no. I like my shop. Let's not talk about it any more, son.' He looked at his watch. 'I have to go to the slaughterers and fetch a lamb carcase.'

'You're a bit old to be making trips like that every day.'

'Yes, you're damned right about that.'

'The slaughterers are in the next street along from the Reykjavík Department Store. It'd be no distance at all to walk.'

'You know what, Tóti?' Hjálmur turned his head and squinted at the boy. His fat, bloated double chin did not move. 'You should be a salesman. You could sell horseshit to the stables.'

'Will you think about it? The bailiff is practically knocking at our door.'

'I'll think about it. I'll think about it. No,' the old man shouted suddenly and waved both arms in the air. 'I won't think about it. But, Tóti, you're a dear boy. I should have had a son like you. Then I would have bought up every floor of the Reykjavík Department Store and let you run it and then I could sit by the fireside, twiddling my thumbs. Your father ought to be proud to have such a fine, brave son.'

'There's not much money in it,' muttered Thórarinn, disconsolately.

4

Eyrarbakki
19 August 1953

Mrs Sunneva Geirsdóttir
Sjafnargata 1a
Reykjavík

Dear Mother,

It's high time I wrote to you. I've been very busy here at Eyrarbakki. At first I found the sound of the sea strange, and sometimes it kept me awake. Thank you for your letter and the letter you enclosed. I was never really worried that I wouldn't be able to get into the Women's College.

Both of the children wake up here quite happily at seven. Even on Sundays. If the weather is not too bad I play with María outside. I am now world champion at making mudpies, so there is not a buttercup or a dandelion to be seen in the whole of Eyrarbakki. I go on 'Tours of Eyrargata' with Young Sigurbjörn whatever the weather, and you can tell Father that he can be proud of his namesake. You can also tell him that by now I am quite familiar with the way the houses, which, I am told, are remarkable, are built in this town. (Though I have difficulty in seeing what is so remarkable about them. Don't tell him that.) Gudbrandur thinks that his son Sigurbjörn will be City Architect one day, but if you ask me he looks more like a carpenter. Gudbrandur and Ingirídur are both very kind to me. Ingirídur says it's a shame I haven't done ballet classes. Her elder daughter came here the other day. She slept in the parlour and snored all night through her nose and then denied it in the morning. I couldn't sleep a wink and kept thinking about my bed at home in Sjafnargata. I miss you a lot. One only appreciates what good parents one has when one is away from home. My dear mother, I love you and my father and my brothers too. But please see that Tóti doesn't spend all day nosing about in my room. He often looks in my drawers and cupboards and makes everything grubby with his fingers and then tries to make it all right by saying he was looking for something that's his. But of course none of the things in my cupboards are his. I would never want to have his rubbish in my room. Well, I can't spend much longer writing this. The 'Tours of Eyrargata' wait for no woman. I have made friends with a few children here and am best friends with a girl called Rós. I expect I shall be in town in the next day or so. When I grow up I am not going to get married. Your loving daughter.

Vilborg

She did not only seal the envelope, she stuck the flap down with sticky tape. Then she could be certain it wouldn't be opened in the mail – or by Thórarinn. If he tore it open now he wouldn't be able to deny it. She took the letter down to the post office. Sometimes the streets were deserted even in the middle of the day.

She had met Rós one day when she was out with the pram. Rós was a year older, tall and thin, with long pigtails, the eldest of five children. Her father had been drowned at sea three years earlier. The family lived in one of the houses on Eyrargata, and Vilborg had assumed it was a summer cottage. When Rós said they lived there all year round, she couldn't believe it. She told Rós all about Sjafnargata, about the expensive grandfather clock that Grandfather and Grandmother had given her parents as a wedding present and that had cost more than a house in Eyrarbakki, about the thick carpet with the heraldic pattern on it and her mother's cupboard containing all her precious things which no one was allowed to touch; she described the laburnum whose seeds were poisonous and which had been cut down. She longed for home and her homesickness made it seem all the more wonderful. Rós could not prove her wrong. She had seen for herself the big red new Plymouth 'straight from the crate'. Their friendship could not take the strain of all these marvels. Rós had shouted at her, calling her a liar and a braggart. They had not spoken to each other for a week.

Vilborg dropped in to see her on her way back from the post office. She could hear Ingiríður indoors. Rós came out. These past few days it made no difference what story Vilborg told, Rós could always go one better. Hadn't she noticed that building at the end of the village? 'That's Litla-Hraun Prison. There's a farmer there who's closely related to my mother. He ate his own children.'

'You're making it up.'

'No, cross my heart. His wife left him and he went crazy. They used to live out at Hreppar. When none of the children turned up at school for the autumn term inquiries were made and the terrible crime was discovered. People visiting the farm thought they remembered it seeming awfully deserted over the summer, but the farmer said his children were staying with relatives in Reykjavík. Haven't you ever heard him screaming in the prison at night? His bad conscience keeps him awake. He made a few of his children into salt meat and fried some in a pan. Try going up there late at night. Or listen when everyone in the village is asleep.'

'But I've often lain awake for a long time, and heard nothing.'

'Then your hearing isn't very good.'

'Funny! We buy all the papers at home.'

'Do you think that such a terrible case would get into the papers? Are you loopy, or what?'

'Shall we sneak off home and put on aromatic balsam?' said Vilborg.

'And what might that be?'

'Don't you know what aromatic balsam is?'

'Yes, it's stuff you put on your cheeks.'

'No, you just put a little blob on your wrists and a tiny bit behind your ears.'

She hardly dared to open the jars standing on the glass shelf in the bathroom. There was eau-de-cologne, lipstick, face cream and talcum powder. Sometimes she unscrewed lids and tops, and inhaled. Now she invited her friend in. If they kept an eye on the kitchen window, they could see if anyone was coming. All these beautiful smells belonged to Ingiríður who had a large black curl on her forehead and a deep, resonant voice and bought *True* and *Eros* and smoked all day long and had bright red fingernails and had dresses in the chest-of-drawers in her bedroom and earrings in a little box that snapped open if you pressed the lid down. Vilborg opened the jar of aromatic balsam and put some on her wrists as though it was something she did every day. Rós touched the cream with the tip of her finger, smelt it and did the same. Vilborg pulled one of Ingiríður's dresses over her head. She only dared to do it with Rós standing by the window and looking to see if anyone was coming. The dress was too long and she tripped over the hem. Rós tried on another, and it suited her.

'A curl on your forehead like Ingiríður has is called a kiss curl,' said Vilborg. She had seen Ingiríður use a hair grip to make the curl. Vilborg opened the black box and showed the earrings to her friend. Two pearls with golden chains lay in a velvet case. Rós hit on the idea of wetting a lock of hair and curling it around her index finger. She pressed the wet hair against her forehead and then leaned against the doorjamb for a long time. Vilborg tried it too, but both attempts at kiss curls failed.

'Do you know who Rasputin was?' asked Vilborg.

'No.'

'He was a thousand times worse than the farmer out in Hreppar.'

'That isn't possible,' said Rós, smugly.

'Yes, it is. He ruled all Russia by pulling strings, hypnotized people, made the war go badly and slept with all the aristocratic women at the Tsar's court.'

'What's so terrible about that?'

'What?'

'Sleeping with women! My cousin's pregnant.'

'He wanted to be alone with girls of our age and sleep with them, too.'

'Girls of our age?' They looked at each other shyly in the dresses, Rós with her mouth half open, touching her top lip with the tip of her tongue.

'Do you want to see a picture of him?' said Vilborg. 'I read about it in *True*.' She found the magazine in Ingiríður's pile and they both looked at Rasputin. 'Do you see how horribly ugly he is?' said Vilborg.

'He's disgusting,' said Rós.

'They tried to kill him but nothing worked, not poisoned wine, nor poisoned cakes, nor bullets, nor beatings. He crawled away screaming revenge on his murderers. There was blood everywhere. They threw him into the river. When they fished him out and the surgeons cut him open they found water in his lungs. That proves he drowned and it wasn't the poison and the stabbings that killed him.'

'Ugh, that's awful,' said Rósa. 'He must have suffered terribly.'

'Well, men like that sometimes get murdered,' said Vilborg.

They heard the pram graze the outside wall. Ingiríður had come home with a bag of groceries from Laugabúd. They took off the dresses in a great flurry of activity and only just managed to get them back into the drawer in time.

Ingiríður breastfed Sigurbjörn. Rós went home but María played on the parlour floor. Sigurbjörn burped and was put back out in the pram. Sometimes he lay awake for a long time, watching the iron-grey clouds sailing across the sky and gripping his quilt in his little fists. While the children were asleep they talked woman to woman. Ingiríður sealed the lamb chops in the frying pan, boiled them quickly in water and then added a whole pint of cream to the stew. 'My mother was always so mean with the cream that I promised myself that if I ever got married I would always have enough cream,' she said.

'I don't think Tóti would mind being your son.'

'"More milk, Mummy!"' said Ingiríður, mimicking Thórarinn. 'Oh, I can't bear it when boys get all fat and go wailing after their mothers all the time.'

'Nor me. Isn't it odd being married to . . .'

'To what?'

'Oh, nothing.'

'To such an old man?'

'I didn't say that.'

'I'm crazy about him,' said Ingirídur.

'Do you think Gudbrandur's handsome, then?'

'Yes, and don't look so surprised. He's very handsome.' They both giggled.

'He's a real man, too,' said Ingirídur, after some reflection. 'Lay the table.'

'How did you meet?'

'He came to the Outpatients' Clinic. I was working there one summer before we moved to the west end of town and I starting working at Landakot Hospital. He had a broken leg. He'd been at a topping-out party. That's how it began.'

'What happened then?'

'Well, he turned up one day and invited me out for a meal. That was when he could hobble around again. God, he was so ridiculous, with his hat in his hands and his face all red. No, not red, bright purple! And I said, "If you're trying to invite me out for a meal, Gudbrandur, I'll be glad to come." "Thank you," he said and bowed as if I were the Queen of England.' Ingirídur laughed. 'So out we went and I ate so much he was quite shocked. I thought he would never speak to me again. And do you know what I said when he asked me to marry him?'

'No.' Vilborg waited in anticipation.

'Yes, if you don't have sweaty feet.'

'Why was that?'

'I used to wash my father's socks when I was a girl and I swore then never to marry a man with sweaty feet.'

Vilborg looked at her adoringly out of the corner of her eye and said, 'When I grow up I want to marry a carpenter and fill the refrigerator with cream and have a child first just like you did.'

'I don't recommend it.'

'What?'

'The last thing you said.'

'Was he handsome?' asked Vilborg.

'Who?'

'The man you had your first child with?'

'Oh, I don't remember now. It's such a long time ago. I've forgotten all about him. He was a terrible bore. I do remember that.'

'Don't you think Gudbrandur's and Father's department store will be wonderful?'

'Oh God, I've no idea.'

'I wouldn't have wanted to be in Rasputin's power.'

'The things you think of, child. Have you been peeking at my magazines?'

'Yes,' said Vilborg in a low voice.

The conversation came to a halt. In the silence they heard Young Sigurbjörn crying outside in his pram. He must have been crying for quite a while. He was almost inconsolable.

'Oh, this place'll be the death of me,' snapped Ingirídur. She put the pan on the table, sat down and dandled the little boy on her knee. 'Men think it's a great idea to buy a house for the summer and then they can't be bothered to stay there themselves.'

Gudbrandur did not arrive from Reykjavík until late in the evening. They were pouring concrete in the new building while the daylight lasted. He sat alone with his large, bony back at the kitchen table and ate the lamb chops in silence, his eyes twinkling at Vilborg. He got to his feet. She knew what was coming next. She had not mentioned in her letter how hurt she'd been the first time Gudbrandur had mimicked Sigurbjörn. He did it almost every evening and he was very good at it. Sometimes she had not been able to stop herself laughing and had then felt guilty. Gudbrandur stomped about the parlour floor, roaring, 'It's damn fine the way the cliffs lean down to the sea, Brandsi. It means we'll have less blasting to do. That was a stroke of luck, my friend.'

Now he stood on tiptoe and made wave-like shapes with his hands.

'Father wants the eaves to look like gulls' wings or waves,' shouted Vilborg. By now she was quite good at guessing.

Gudbrandur shaded his eyes and gazed towards the kitchen. Vilborg couldn't guess what her father was supposed to be doing now to save her life. Then Gudbrandur said in a dark voice, 'Look at Mount Esja, my friend. Do you know what I have always dreamt of building? A row of skyscrapers along the whole length of the mountain with the façade entirely of glass. A kind of Icelandic New York. Don't you think the light would explode towards Reykjavík whenever the sun came out? It would be like the raging anger of the Lord, Brandsi. All we'd need in town then would be the prophet Jeremiah himself.' And Gudbrandur laughed Sigurbjörn's distinctive laugh.

'I want to move to town, Gudbrandur,' said Ingirídur.

'Well then, and so we shall, Inga, my dear,' he said. He walked through the parlour, staring at the floor, from time to time bending down to pick up some small invisible object. At last Vilborg understood. Sigurbjörn was picking up nails from the gravel outside the new building.

When it was quiet again she opened the window above her bed and listened for screams from Litla-Hraun. She could not hear the cannibal for the sound of the sea. She got dressed and walked anxiously along Eyrargata, looking across at Litla-Hraun. It was the dead of night and the houses seemed deserted and abandoned in the summer twilight. A curlew was weeping. She hurried home and went back to bed. Then she said the Lord's Prayer and some other prayers that Grandmother Sigurlaug had taught her and asked God to forgive all the malefactors of the world.

5

Before they left the house, Gudbrandur took out the main fuse and Vilborg brought in the washing from the line. Eyrarbakki looked like a ghost town in the soft morning rain. María dragged her doll's pram outside. It rested in the sand, lopsided. One wheel had come off. 'Dolly's pwam bwoken,' she said.

'Is that right, Mæja, my dear?' said her father. He got down on one knee and examined his handiwork. 'Old Brandsi'll fix it, won't he?'

He put the toy pram on top of the pile of tools in the back of his van. Vilborg handed him a papier-mâché box with a few odds and ends from the refrigerator.

As they turned towards the Ölfusár river, a tourist standing in the rain by the bridge took a photograph of them.

'He's up early,' said Ingirídur.

'Why are they taking photographs of people?' said Gudbrandur tetchily. 'It's stupid.'

'They want to show their relatives back home what it's like here,' said Vilborg. 'Maybe someone in Australia will see that picture.'

'Icelanders must look like kangaroos to them,' said Gudbrandur.

'Speak for yourself,' said Ingirídur.

'Well, you're always carrying the boy around on your stomach, Inga. It wouldn't surprise me to find you hopping round town one of these days,' said Gudbrandur, grinning at his wife.

'Stop it, Gudbrandur,' said Ingirídur sharply.

At Kambarnir the sky cleared and Ingólfsfjall rose above the clouds in a misty blue light.

'Look at the Vestmann Islands,' said Gudbrandur. 'They stick up out of the sea like the teeth on a machine saw.'

He was worrying about the glass for the windows on one floor of the department store. He had got the measurements wrong and none of it fitted. 'But I'm not the only one to make mistakes,' he said. 'You can't imagine how highly Sigurbjörn thought of the man he hired to clear the building. He couldn't believe how much stuff the man could shift. Then we found out the damn fool had chucked all the rubble down the lift shaft. We thought we'd never get rid of it.' Gudbrandur turned to Ingirídur and explained, 'Cement and stuff. It reached up to the fourth floor. We had to use a winch to clear the rubbish away.'

'Doesn't anyone keep an eye on the men?' asked Ingirídur.

'Of course, Inga, but who would expect something like that?'

He put his foot down as they approached Reykjavík. 'Don't tell Father I've come to town,' said Vilborg when they got there. 'It's supposed to be a surprise.'

Gudbrandur carried little Mæja inside. She hated the smell of the car and had fallen asleep as they passed Ingólfsfjall. Sigurbjörn was put outside in the pram straightaway and his father went off to work on the Reykjavík Department Store. Ingirídur found a silvery cardboard box and an old photograph album full of pictures of famous ballet dancers she wanted to show her nanny. The box contained a great treasure, a pair of old ballet shoes. Vilborg put them on and tried to stand *sur la pointe*.

'You were made to be a ballet dancer, child.'

'Did you dance yourself?'

'No, I was far too fat and clumsy.'

'You're not fat.'

'Vilborg.'

'Yes?'

'There is something I need to speak you about.'

'What?' The girl felt anxious. Ingirídur was giving her such a hurt look.

'I can't find my earrings.'

'I don't know anything about them.'

'I know you've been going through my things. I could smell perfume on you when I came in. If you've taken them, just give them back to me, sweetheart. I used to pinch things myself when I was a girl. I'm rather fond of those earrings. They were a present from Mother.'

Vilborg's cheeks were burning. 'I haven't stolen anything,' she said. 'Are you calling me a thief?' She quickly took off the ballet shoes.

'No, I'm not, sweetheart,' said Ingirídur, thoughtfully. 'It must be the other girl then.' The album lay open on the table. Vaslav Nijinsky hovered above the stage.

A yellow statue of a lion on a metal base stood on the sideboard in the parlour. Gudbrandur usually put the post under its belly. Ingirídur picked up the letters curiously and quickly flicked through them. 'The number of times I've asked Gudbrandur to bring the post out to us. These are all bills,' she said in surprise, reading a letter written on thin rustling paper with a letterhead that Vilborg could see from the underside. The letter was not very long. Ingirídur reddened and brushed her hair away from her cheek. She said, absent-mindedly, 'I know you're telling me the truth, Vilborg, dear.' She sat down with the letter and the bills in order to study them more carefully. 'But I just can't bring myself to mention it to Rós's mother,' she said, deep in thought. 'Let's just forget about it.' She put the envelopes away.

As Vilborg walked south along Fríkirkjuvegur a short-sighted swan on Lake Tjörnin looked at her like a head teacher handing out exam papers. She stood for a long time gazing at the Women's College.

She knocked on the door, her heart racing. This time Sunneva Geirsdóttir would surely faint. It was Thórarinn who opened the door. 'Oh,' he said, and his face fell when he saw his sister.

'Tóti, you don't need to drop dead just because I've come home.'

'Oh, shut up. Father's down at the building site and Mother's not back yet.'

'And what are you doing at home? Have you given up your job?'

'I've got a day off.' He did not open the door completely. 'I had to go to the dentist.'

Thórarinn had got thinner, and Sjafnargata seemed strange to her, like Reykjavík itself.

Thórarinn watched every flicker of his sister's face. 'Will you be in town long?' he asked her with hope in his heart.

'My dear Tóti, I've only just come through the door.'

She sat down at the telephone and rang her friend Gudbjörg. 'Hello, this is Vilborg. I've just arrived from the country. I got paid; I've got seven hundred krónur. Let's meet at Stebbi's shop. What, you're too busy!' She sighed. 'What a homecoming. Heigh-ho!'

'You got seven hundred krónur?' asked Thórarinn, suddenly interested.

Vilborg studied him and sat down at the parlour table. 'No, fourteen,' she lied. 'I just didn't want Gudbjörg to know, that's all.'

'It's a lot more than I get at the shop!'

'Yes, Gudbrandur and Ingirídur are so well off.'

'How was your stay?'

'Wonderful, Tóti, and the food was incredible.' She went over to the window. 'For example, yesterday evening we went to Hotel Tryggvaskáli for about the twentieth time this summer. I ordered lamb chops in cream sauce, they were simply delicious. Ingirídur doesn't like cooking, so Gudbrandur usually takes us out to eat.' Vilborg leaned her forehead on the window pane. Through the leaves she could see the tree stump on the lawn.

Reykjavík is a city of rowan trees. They grow straight as arrows and fair of limb; they are crippled and tormented by arthritis; they live in the shadows at the backs of houses like discontented ogres; they grow in beds shy and small with a few young leaves; they crouch over garages with verdigris and moss on their bark and mope with age; they lean away from the façades of houses and block the light in parlours; they rest their elbows on garden walls and stretch their crooked, leafy fingers out towards the faces of passers-by. The city of rowan trees was strange after such a long absence. 'Perhaps I'll be a poet one day,' thought the girl. 'Rowan, my rowan, were you glad when the laburnum in the garden fell to the axe?'

She heard a door bang. Thórarinn had dashed out. From Skólavör-duhæd he saw the sun shining through a break in the clouds on the rough sea below Mount Esja. He bought the sports bag. He could not remember when Helgi's birthday was. The fat girl in the shop smiled happily. He walked back up to the corner, sweaty and morose. The wind buffeted the tall grass in Vatnsmýri and the Big Wheel at the Tivoli was turning. His mother had come home.

'What are you going to do with a bag like that?' asked Sunneva.

'Give it to Helgi for his birthday.'

'But that's not until March next year.'

'Yes, but he needs a good bag, doesn't he?'

'He has two of them already, and he's probably bought another in Norway.'

'But they lost 4–1. I wanted to give him a present to make up for it. He promised to buy something for me.'

Vilborg's friend Gudbjörg examined the bag. 'It seems to be very good quality,' she said, feeling the material.

'When were you paid, Tóti?' asked Vilborg.

'Today.'

'How much?'

'Five hundred krónur.'

'Well, this bag cost far too much. Nearly all your wages,' said Sunneva, looking at the price tag.

Thórarinn was sweating.

'Ugh, Mother. He's been reckoning on Helgi giving him something more expensive in exchange.'

'What's all this?' said Sunneva. 'I shall go and talk to the people at the shop and get them to take it back.'

'No, never!' shouted the boy. 'Never! Don't you dare!'

In view of her brother's bad behaviour, Vilborg decided not to burden her mother with the news that she stood accused of theft. When Sigurbjörn came home and took her in his arms and she noticed the similarity between him and the Russian priest, a lump came to her throat. Nothing bad must ever happen to her father. If it did, she wouldn't want to go on living.

6

Every now and then a car sped past Bjarnaborg in the late evening sun. It was getting on for nine. Gudbrandur was sitting in the workmen's shelter. Through the open door he could see the gate at the corner and a bundle of iron rods for the reinforced concrete. He was alone on the work site. They'd been asking about their money. 'You'll have to speak to Sigurbjörn,' he'd said. And at home his wife was mad as could be.

She had found the papers and he was putting off going home. Sigurbjörn had not paid out a single króna. The big loan, outstanding even from before the time Enterprise had been thought of, was with a lawyer who was now demanding payment. And the loan they had taken out at the beginning of the building work was also in default. And Sigurbjörn had bought a lot of the household provisions in his name, without Gudbrandur's knowledge. Gudbrandur had put all the letters and final demands under the lion, and of course his wife had stumbled across them, and gone berserk. A few people had come to look over the building but no one had booked any space yet. One client had just left; Gudbrandur had walked round the store with him. And now it was late August. The Reykjavík Department Store stood on the corner in all its concrete glory. 'I've done my bit,' thought Gudbrandur, 'as master builder.'

'That man has no respect for you,' Ingirídur had said that lunchtime. 'Why does he live on your credit? Why can't he pay his own way? This bill here.' She thrust a sheet of paper into his face. 'It's for groceries.'

'I don't think he can manage any more.' Gudbrandur examined the bill. 'This is for coffee and pastries in the shelter,' he lied.

'Don't the men bring their own food with them? Do you have to provide it? He hasn't paid a single króna off the old mortgage.' Ingirídur leaned across the table. A heavy lock of her dark hair fell over the famous birthmark. 'What did he say when you tackled him about it?'

'I haven't asked him about it, Inga.'

'You've still not mentioned it?'

'It seems to me Sigurbjörn has enough on his plate already.'

'Is he not to be bothered with mundane things like money? Who is he, Lord God Almighty?'

'Don't go on like that.'

'Are you afraid of that great lump?'

'No, Inga, I'm not afraid of him.'

'Then talk to him about it.'

'I will, girl.'

'Sigurbjörn isn't all he seems. He's no friend to you,' she said.

'Of course he's my friend.' Gudbrandur had got up from the table and banged the front door shut behind him.

He looked at the clock: it was twenty-five minutes past eight. He moved his foot across the sand on the linoleum and his shoe touched an awl. He kicked the tool away and unscrewed the lid of the thermos flask. The coffee had gone cold. On the table lay a pair of work gloves and a half-eaten bun on a torn brown paper bag. He clasped his hands together and stared at his knuckles. Why did I get involved in all this without thinking it through first? And then to get the window measurements all wrong! I was doing fine. And now our nice peaceful life has evaporated into thin air. Suddenly he felt a craving for alcohol and was filled with uncharitable thoughts towards his friend. The entrance to the shelter grew dark.

'How terribly sad you look, Brandsi.'

Gudbrandur looked up. Sigurbjörn was carrying a portfolio under his arm. He was kitted out like an English lord.

'Where have you been?'

'I was at the bank and I had a meeting with the estate agent.'

'What did he have to say?'

'It's bad.' Sigurbjörn sat down. 'He wants the advertising bill paid before I've sold any floor-space. The full forty thousand krónur. He's a cheeky bastard and he's a drunk,' said Sigurbjörn angrily. 'I remember that idiot Gunnar Rafn crawling around a coal yard down by the docks in the old days, blind drunk. I once lent him five hundred krónur, and he still hasn't paid me back. He never warned me how much it would cost to put an advertisement with a photograph in the newspapers.'

'Really? And you didn't ask?'

'I trusted him, Gudbrandur.'

'That's been the downfall of many a man.'

'Has someone been taking advantage of you, my friend?' asked Sigurbjörn, studying Gudbrandur. He hadn't taken off his peaked cap and the sympathy in his expression was genuine. Gudbrandur leaned back on the bench and looked at some old rags hanging up on a nail. The workmen's shelter was lined with brown lacquered pinewood. A girl with long blond hair crouched on one knee on a sunny yellow beach holding out her breasts with her hands; behind her was an enormous car tyre. The whole picture was set into the armpit of the rubber Michelin Man, raising his arm in delight at both woman and tyre. The date was 20 August 1953.

'What am I supposed to tell the men, Sigurbjörn?'

'What men?'

'The carpenters, Sigurbjörn, the men who work here. We must pay their wages. They haven't been paid for three weeks now and we're doing them out of their topping-out party. They're threatening to hold a demonstration,' laughed Gudbrandur.

Sigurbjörn joined in the laughter. 'Don't worry, Brandsi. It's all settled.'

'Have you sold some space, then?'

'Sold? Sold? That's all you ever ask about.' Sigurbjörn opened his portfolio. 'Not yet,' he said. He took out a document and laid it on the table.

'What's that?'

'That's the good news. We're raising a loan.'

'A loan – where from? Not the bank?'

'Not the same bank. A different one. Helgi sorted this one out for me at the Fisheries Bank.'

Gudbrandur pulled the loan agreement towards him. It was for eight hundred thousand krónur. The security for the loan was Gudbrandur Jónsson's house on Öldugata.

'This is the house on Öldugata.'

'Yes.'

'I can't sign this.'

Sigurbjörn looked angrily round the shelter as though he were surveying a large crowd of people, seeking out someone who had done him some wrong. Then he looked sharply at Gudbrandur and fell silent. At last he asked, 'Why not?'

'Because my wife won't let me.'

Laughter rang round the shelter. 'You're joking, Gudbrandur.'

'I'm not joking. She found the bills.'

'What bills?'

'You haven't paid any of them, man. The old loan is being called in by the lawyers and the new one is in default at the bank.'

'Oh yes, the lawyers, they're crooks,' said Sigurbjörn darkly. 'They all ought to be put on an old trawler and sunk off Hornbanki. But that's why I'm doing this, Brandsi. To make a clean sweep of it all in one go.'

'If I sign this I won't have a króna to my name.'

'But that's what we agreed right at the start, Gudbrandur.' Sigurbjörn stared across the table, and Gudbrandur looked back at him, remembering that Ingiríður had accused him of being afraid of Sigurbjörn. He looked away in order to give himself a moment to think. He looked towards the gate. Its shadow had moved and now fell across the gravel rutted by footprints and wheel tracks. An iron pike stood at the gatepost by the netting. 'I can't sign any more papers until I've talked it over with my wife,' he said, looking at Sigurbjörn.

'One of the most stupid things a man can do is to get a woman involved in his finances,' said Sigurbjörn icily. 'Don't you remember me telling you that when we were over at Ölfusá estuary? It was quite a business getting Helgi to agree to this and arrange it all.'

'I'm sorry.'

'Well, we'll have to stop the work. I can't raise another króna anywhere.'

'You'll have to manage some other way.'

'But aren't we joint owners? Isn't that how you wanted the papers made out? Aren't we equal shareholders in Enterprise?' asked Sigurbjörn, angrily.

'Yes, we are.'

'Then we should stand together like brothers. I'm doing this for us both.'

'Very well,' said Gudbrandur, and he got to his feet. 'I'll drop in and see you this evening, but first I must talk to Ingiríður. I can't do anything without her agreement. I don't want do anything that'll jeopardize my marriage, as you can imagine.'

He made as if to lock up. Sigurbjörn went outside. The store towered above them, the scaffolding reaching upwards. 'It's good to have got the concrete mixed and poured,' said Gudbrandur and looked up into the blue sky. A seagull flew off, and disappeared over the building. 'Just imagine what it was like when it had to be mixed by hand. When I was at Austurbær School you had to carry the cement up in buckets one at a time. What a business that was. The hoist was a handy invention.'

'Make sure you lock everything up, and look in at Sjafnargata this evening,' said Sigurbjörn, not paying any attention to Gudbrandur's chatter.

'I said I would, didn't I?'

Gudbrandur closed the spring lock on the workmen's shelter, walked out through the gate and looked up at the department store. I have never worked harder than this, he thought. This was no summer. He felt uneasy, looked away from the building and remembered the summer he had worked at a whaling station. They had dragged the giant creatures up on to the cement platform to cut them up. The hump-backed whale was the most terrible-looking of them all. The red squid flowed out of the harpoon gash like grass seed from a sack. Sometimes there were deep marks at the jaw and scars on the carcase. The wounds were made by killer whales. They attacked the big whale in shoals. But the mark on the jaw almost as deep as the bone was caused by octopuses. They settle on the head, try to block up the blow-hole, clench their slimy tentacles around the head, and grip tight. But the hump-backed whale knows how to deal with them. It dives down nearly a mile deep, and the octopus bursts.

7

Ingirídur barely acknowledged him when Gudbrandur asked about the children. Her daughter had called in. She was now taller than Ingirídur. She was looking at her stepfather curiously. Judging from her expression, she had been told what was going on. Ingirídur was moving from room to room, tidying up. 'I'm going out to the garage, Inga,' Gudbrandur heard himself say, but she took no notice.

Gudbrandur had converted his garage into a workshop. He had built a timber wall where the garage door had been and had put in a long window and a small door. On the windowsill there were some old jamjars containing lacquer. The brown liquid had congealed in thick dribbles on the outside of the jars. Nails and screws were kept in Mackintosh sweet boxes. There was a green plane surrounded by a heap of wood shavings on the floor. He had recently bought both a circular saw and a bandsaw. Assorted timber offcuts had been neatly stacked against a wall. Sometimes Gudbrandur worked at his carpentry late into the evening.

A framed diploma on the wall bore witness to the dampness of the workshop:

Certificate
The undersigned examination committee in Reykjavík
hereby declares:
Gudbrandur Jónsson, born 3 March 1910 at Njardvík
in the county of Gullbringa,
has in the year 1934 passed the examination in carpentry
for which he was required to construct a lacquered mirror cabinet;
and that the design and carpentry of the same were adjudged
executed with excellence.
He has completed his course of instruction and is now fully qualified
to work independently as a carpenter.
This certificate is issued and signed in confirmation thereof
with our names and that of the master carpenter.

Gudbrandur took María's doll's pram and put it on the planing bench. The axle had snapped in two and was not worth gluing back together. He dug out the remains of the wood with a chisel, found another rod that fitted, applied some wood glue to it, screwed it in place and fixed the wheels. It did not take long. He waited for Ingirídur's daughter to go, so that he could bring up the subject of the new loan.

He felt bad about mortgaging the house on Öldugata. He had sold three floors of his mother's house on Austurstræti in order to raise the money to buy this stone house – two floors and a basement and not one króna owing on it, designed in 1936 by Einar Erlendsson,

Sigurbjörn's colleague at the City Architect's office. Gudbrandur stood at his workbench with his arms crossed, worrying. The window had begun to grow dark. He heard a car, probably the girl going off back to her father. She was so pretty now, so like her mother.

He leaned forward to check, but found it was Sigurbjörn and his family at the gate. Couldn't the man wait? He heard Ingirídur greeting them and Sigurbjörn asking in his deep voice, 'Is Brandsi at home?' He leaned back so he would not be seen through the window but then the footsteps came closer and Ingirídur's daughter opened the door. 'Mother would like you to come in for a minute.'

'Just coming, Anna.'

'I'll say goodbye then.' She kissed him on the cheek.

He locked the garage door and inhaled the scent of trees and grass in the garden. In the house next door a woman could be seen through the window washing the dishes. She had become his companion without realizing it. He had been expecting the sound of people talking, but there was silence inside the house. Ingirídur was in the kitchen. Sunneva, Sigurbjörn and Thórarinn sat in silence in the parlour as though they were in a doctor's waiting room.

'Good evening, Brandsi,' said Sigurbjörn. The portfolio lay in front of him on the table.

'Can I get you anything?' offered Gudbrandur.

Thórarinn was turning the pages of a newspaper, and did not look up.

'There's coffee brewing,' said Sunneva.

'I meant something stronger?'

'You know very well I never touch the stuff,' said Sigurbjörn.

'Nothing for me, Gudbrandur.' Sunneva looked round. Everything was old and worn, like the room of some famous historical figure in a museum. There were heavy curtains on wooden rings, frills on the arms of the old chairs, two tall candlesticks on a sideboard. A large photograph of Gudbrandur's mother drew the eye like an altar painting in a church. The table was small; they sat close together. The furniture's so drab, thought Sunneva.

Gudbrandur got a bottle of whisky from the cupboard and poured himself a drink, topping it up with water from the kitchen tap.

Ingirídur glanced at the tumbler. Gudbrandur took a large swig. She saw his hand was shaking. She put cups, a cream jug and a sugar bowl on a tray. 'Aren't you going to use the best crockery, Inga?' he asked.

'Take that through.'

Gudbrandur put the tray on the table, sat down in an armchair, fiddled with the frill and looked at Thórarinn's soft, round profile. 'How are you, my boy?'

'Fine, thanks,' Thórarinn said timidly in a deep voice without looking up from the paper.

'Do they let you taste the sausages?' Gudbrandur laughed.

'We get men from your building site coming in all the time.'

Thórarinn became morose.

'Won't you take your coat off, Sunna?' said Gudbrandur, and looked quickly at his friend.

'Mother bought that coat today,' said Thórarinn. 'And I got some jeans.'

'Jeans are not proper clothes,' boomed Sigurbjörn. 'I can't think why you want to go around dressed in rags.'

'I want to look posh,' said the boy.

Gudbrandur got to his feet and took the new white coat. Under it Sunneva was wearing a dress. She went over to the door leading to the next room in order to have a look round. Ingirídur brought in the coffee, slammed it down, and sat opposite Sigurbjörn. He looked at her angrily. She looked straight at him, and Sigurbjörn dropped his eyes. He prodded the papers in the portfolio with his index finger and placed the loan agreement on the table. Gudbrandur drained the contents of his glass and moved over to them.

'Father bought new shoes and a coat today,' Thórarinn said from behind the newspaper.

'I've had enough of this.' Ingirídur stood up. 'You're using our property as collateral to finance your building, you buy expensive clothes for yourself and your family and order groceries on Gudbrandur's account. Don't you realize we're nearly bankrupt?'

'I can't go around bollock naked, can I?' said Sigurbjörn. 'Mind what you say.'

'I'll say what I damn well think. You're cheating Gudbrandur out of every króna we have. This department store is sheer madness.'

Gudbrandur looked from one to the other. Finally he turned to his wife, raised his glass and said in a loud, clear voice, 'The Reykjavík Department Store is an excellent building. I ought to know. I'm a carpenter. Will you have a drop, Inga?'

'You always think everyone is stealing from you,' said Thórarinn. 'She said Vilborg stole her earrings at Eyrarbakki.' He looked at his mother.

Sunneva raised her eyebrows and looked at Ingirídur with an almost kindly curiosity.

'Yes, they went missing.' Ingirídur stood there with her arms crossed.

'You think Vilborg took them?'

'I'm not saying that. I just asked her.'

'Sigurbjörn, are you just going to sit there?'

'This is the first I've heard about it.' Sigurbjörn fiddled with the loan agreement.

'Now I understand why Vilborg was so bitter when she came home,' said Sunneva, getting up. 'Sigurbjörn! Give them back the seven hundred krónur they paid Vilborg,' she said quietly.

'She said she got fourteen hundred.' Thórarinn exhaled deeply. 'That's Vilborg all over.'

'I haven't got any cash just at present,' said Sigurbjörn.

'That was a damn fine goal Helgi scored against France,' said Gudbrandur. 'I was listening to the match on the wireless.'

Thórarinn perked up. 'It was in all the newspapers today. Did you see the pictures of him? I was dying with excitement. They only lost 3–1. No one would have believed it.'

'Inga,' said Gudbrandur. 'I'm going to have to put my name to a little loan. We can't halt the construction work now.'

'You're an idiot,' hissed Ingirídur. 'You're not signing anything in this house.'

Sigurbjörn had not touched his coffee. Now he took the loan agreement, crumpled it up in both hands and flung it on to the table.

'You can go to the devil, the pair of you. Come on, let's go, Sunneva,' he said. 'Come on, Thórarinn.'

Gudbrandur followed them out to the front steps. 'It's all right, Sigurbjörn, take the papers. I'll sign for this damned loan tomorrow morning.'

Sigurbjörn glowered at the window in the house next door where the woman was still working in her kitchen. Outside it had grown dark and the wind stirred the trees. Gudbrandur took the briefcase from him and tried to smooth the document as best he could, stuffed it into the portfolio and pushed it into Sigurbjörn's hands. 'Don't pay any attention to the women,' he said. 'As for the earrings. They were only glass. I ought to know, I gave them to her. Take your wife and boy home, and then let's go down to Ánanaust to look round the building I want to convert into offices.'

'You'd better watch it, the pair of you, Gudbrandur, even if you did name your son for me,' said Sigurbjörn, his voice shaking with anger.

'What do you mean?'

Sigurbjörn walked to the car and Gudbrandur watched him go.

8

Sigurbjörn rushed out on to Lækjartorg, leaving the car door open. A bus sounded its horn. Sunneva moved across to the driving seat. Thórarinn called through the open window, 'Father, can I come with you?'

'No, Tóti,' Sigurbjörn shouted loudly. 'You're not dressed for it.'

Sunneva drove away and the bus drew up at its stop. Sigurbjörn strode up Hverfisgata. He opened the gate into Vitatorg and sat down in the workmen's shelter. He laid both arms on the table and rested his head on them. Then he leaned against the wall and fell asleep sitting up. He woke to the grey light of dawn. As his problems came back to him, he looked around the shelter in despair.

He went outside and looked the building. How many million

krónur would it take to finish the job? On the first floor a cold morning wind was blowing through the interior. A cement-spattered wooden ladder led up to the roof from the sixth floor. He went up the ladder. The work at the top of the building was well in hand. The beams were in place, and a section of the roof had been nailed down. He stood in a space between the beams and looked out to sea. It was very windy in the sound, the breakers were tumbling over each other, dark clouds were scudding eastward over the horizon, but down between Akrafjall and Mount Esja a glistening fog was pouring into the sea like an avalanche, driving the long, white waves before it all the way to Skúlagata. To the west a black-backed gull was sitting on the corner of a house looking out to sea.

He took a walk down by the sea while he tried to decide what he should do. He picked his way between the puddles towards the Höfdi House, the house on the cliff. He had not been there for a long time and wanted to take a look at the elegant wooden mansion the French had built shortly after the turn of the century. Many of the windows were broken and over large areas the white paint was flaking off the walls. How ramshackle this beautiful old building had become. The unbroken windows reminded him of black tarns. He climbed the steps. The house was clearly deserted. The entrance hall stood open to the elements. Sigurbjörn was so overcome by the dilapidation that he could not bring himself to go in.

On the side facing the sea a cliff jutted out, above the gravel road to Laugarnes, which disappeared into the tangle of old Nissen huts left from the war. He stood beneath the cliff. Above Kjalarnes there were heavy clouds and the rain was falling like a muslin scarf. There were a great many stones on the beach, the seaweed clinging to them wearily, making it look as if women's heads wet with rain had been scattered across the shore.

He shivered. Before him he saw an image of his father at his writing desk, a cigar between his fingers. 'You don't want to take up architecture, my dear Sibbi,' snuffled Helgi Vésteinsson. 'Take over the firm from me. Then you'll be able to afford to eat and keep yourself warm. Listen to what your father tells you. Icelanders are too

108

mean to pay anyone to design their houses. Anyway, it's not necessary.'

What would Father say if he knew I was letting Sjafnargata slip through my fingers? thought Sigurbjörn. I'm at my wits' end. Eider ducks were swimming along the shore, keeping one eye on the land. Sometimes the flock vanished, but then they reappeared on the crest of a wave. He put his hands into his pockets, leaned his back against the cliff and closed his eyes. Damn Brandsi, treating me like that. I ought to have the bloody glass taken to his house and dumped in his garden. He thought about the poet Einar Benediktsson, who had once owned the Höfdi House. There was still no dam at Dettifoss. What had happened to the Titan Hydroelectric Company, which was to have made so many people's fortunes? Now the house stood deserted and decaying. A length of guttering was dangling down in the wind, beating in a gentle rhythm against the wall. Perhaps Benediktsson himself had sometimes stood here unseen beneath the cliff to get some peace and quiet.

His face was wet with drizzle. No one was buying any floor-space. The day before Sigurbjörn had lost patience and spoken to potential clients himself, offering them floor-space at a discount. They had expressed their doubts that a large department store was quite what Iceland needed at this stage. Were they making fun of him? 'No, I chose the best career for myself and I've never regretted it,' he said out loud.

He heard the rattle of a stone and opened his eyes. Some distance away there was a man standing in the street. He was short and fat and was holding a bag. When he saw Sigurbjörn move, he walked towards him, smiling. 'Thank God, you're alive,' he said and he laughed. 'I can't tell you how relieved I am. I got a dreadful fright when I saw you so still underneath the cliff like that and your face looked so worn and heavy. I said to myself, "You'd better say a little prayer, Rúnar, because you're walking right into the arms of the ghost of Höfdi himself."'

After a moment's silence Sigurbjörn asked, 'Did you think he'd wandered out into the wasteland for a breath of fresh air?'

'Yes, it did rather cross my mind.'

The man stared at Sigurbjörn with a twinkle in his eyes. Sigurbjörn looked at him without smiling. 'Were you scared?'

'Not really,' said the man. 'But I'd have got a fright if you'd taken off your cap and your head had come off with it.'

'Well, look,' Sigurbjörn said with a smile, 'it's all right.' He lifted his cap and then put it back on his head again.

'Do you have anything to do with the Höfdi House?' asked the man, looking at the building. 'I was told that someone was planning to turn it into a jam factory.'

'No, I'm afraid not.' Sigurbjörn too looked up at the Hofdi House. 'It's a shame to see the state it's in. A jam factory, you say? It'll ruin him, poor man, like everything else in this town. And where are you off to, friend?'

'I'm a debt collector. In my job it's best to be up and about early.'

'And how's the debt-collecting business?' asked Sigurbjörn.

'In a bad way, I'm afraid.' The debt collector rocked to and fro. 'People and their money are not easily parted.'

'They want things all right, but when it comes to settling up, it's a different story,' said Sigurbjörn, scowling.

'Icelanders have no idea how to handle money,' said the debt collector, taking a pinch of snuff. 'Will you take some snuff with me?'

'Not for me, thank you.'

'Well, I'll say my goodbyes, then.'

'Yes, goodbye, friend.'

When the debt collector was some distance off, he turned round and gave the architect an evil smile.

'Oh, he'll have known who I am, all right, damn him,' muttered Sigurbjörn. 'Lord, is there no peace in this land?' He sat down on a boulder and thought about old times. He had once prayed to the Lord, passionately and vehemently, begging him to spare his brother's life. That had been a long time ago. One spring evening as a young man he had walked to the Hofdi House for an appointment with the physician Matthías Einarsson. Matthías was a doctor at the French Hospital and a friend of his father's. He had tended Jóhannes.

Sigurbjörn knew what kind of man the doctor was as Helgi Vésteinsson's voice grew deep with respect whenever his name was mentioned. The doctor had magnificent apartments in the Höfdi House. Sigurbjörn was invited into the parlour by a little girl. The rooms were large and the ceilings high, an oil lamp made of burnished copper hung from the ceiling, the cupola was white. A great deal of money had been lavished on the household furnishings, to the young Sigurbjörn's delight. A gentle breeze wafted through an open window. The sea was dead calm and sparkled in the evening sun. He waited alone for a while, very nervous. At last Matthías came into the room. He was a big man and known for not taking any nonsense from anyone. That's good, Sigurbjörn had thought, he won't beat about the bush. Sigurbjörn rose to his feet at the sound of the doctor's footsteps and greeted him with a handshake. 'I have come here about my brother, Jóhannes. As you know, he is abroad at present and very ill.'

Matthías explained his brother's condition to him. There was no hope.

Sigurbjörn arrived in Oslo one evening in September 1927, took an attic room at the Bible School and looked out over the lights of the city.

'The brother of Jóhannes Helgason? We were all very upset when we heard of his death. Are you a theologian too? Are you going to study for the priesthood?'

At half past six the students were woken by a bell. Sigurbjörn had more of an appetite at breakfast than Jóhannes, one of the teachers remarked with a smile. After breakfast there was a communal hour of prayer. Sigurbjörn found it hard to get down on his knees and pray.

He was anxious to meet Professor Hart. He knew how highly Jóhannes had regarded him. One morning, walking in the Palace Garden, he had seen Hart at a distance and recognized him from a picture. He introduced himself.

'Jóhannes Helgason's brother? When I got the news I was dreadfully shocked. Your brother was an unusual young man. Very unusual.'

They had sat in a warm parlour that early spring day. Term was over and Professor Hart had invited Sigurbjörn to his home. A white porcelain stove reached up to the ceiling. The glowing coal was shielded by coloured glass, lighting up the parlour. Sigurbjörn silently admired the broad floorboards. During the winter he had acquainted himself with selected passages from the Old and New Testaments, read ecclesiastical and apostolic history, and studied Norwegian. His marks were good. After the meal coffee was served.

'Helgason, I am planning a Nordic Christian Student Conference in Iceland,' said Hart. 'I need your help to organize it. Please stay here until the summer. At the beginning of July there will be a conference near Stockholm.' The professor had a widow's peak and a way of gazing into the middle distance whenever he said anything.

'I'm travelling through Europe,' replied Sigurbjörn.

'With what purpose?'

'Looking at buildings.'

'Are you interested in architecture?'

'Yes, I want to be a carpenter. That's how I've spent my summers at home in Iceland.'

'That is good. The Saviour himself made practical things out of wood,' said Hart. 'Then you must come next summer. The conference will be held in Norway then. If you come three days early, you will be able to see all the preparations.'

'I'm afraid that will probably not be possible. I doubt I could afford to come.'

'Then pray to God to provide for your journey, Helgason. Start a prayer circle in Iceland. "They have no wine," said the mother of Jesus at Cana. We must tell the Lord what it is we lack. That is how one should pray.'

'As it happens, I have been praying,' said Sigurbjörn, rubbing his large hands together.

'"Let the dead bury the dead," saith the Lord. Have you travelled much outside the city?'

'No.'

'Stay here tonight and come with me to Holmenkollen. You must see something of Norway, man. Tomorrow is the Christian Council, but first we will go to church together.'

Sigurbjörn looked down at his shoes. He lifted his right toe and stared at the instep. 'My boots are in a bad way.'

'What's the matter with you, young man?' said the preacher, quick to anger. 'I've worn ordinary walking shoes on worse ground than that. I'll lend you some shoes.' He fetched a pair of enormous work shoes and put them beside Sigurbjörn's chair. He also lent him a pair of thick socks. In the morning Sigurbjörn had to ask for another pair of socks, and then at last the shoes fitted.

The service was at eleven in the morning. The church was cruciform and Sigurbjörn picked up a small notebook and scrawled down a description: 'High arched stained-glass windows with variously shaped panes. Two rows of pews, the pews slightly curved and the backs arched and comfortable to lean against. Chancel north facing, elevated with steps. Gradines with an open space in the middle. On the dais a low pulpit. The altar with a red velvet cloth, gold fringe. Above it an image of Christ with outstretched arms. A white marble image. Two large chairs on either side of the altar, high-backed. No altar candles.'

He felt rather hot. In the floor there was a grating, through which warm air was rising. He quietly pulled off the work shoes and thick socks, and put the soles of his bare feet on top of the warmth and ran his fingers over the grating. It was a neatly made heating system. A woman on his right was staring at him, so he looked up and began to listen.

Hart thundered, '"And his disciples asked him, saying, Master, who did sin, this man, or his parents, that he was born blind? Jesus answered, Neither hath this man sinned, nor his parents: but that the works of God should be made manifest in him. When he had thus spoken, he spat on the ground, and made clay of the spittle, and he anointed the eyes of the blind man with the clay. And said unto him, Go, wash in the pool of Siloam, (which is, by intepretation, Sent.) He went his way therefore, and washed, and came seeing. Therefore said they unto him, How were thine eyes opened?"'

Professor Hart looked sharply about the church.

'"And Jesus said, For judgment I am come into this world, that they which see not might see; and that they which see might be made blind. And some of the Pharisees which were with him heard these words, and said unto him, Are we blind also? Jesus said unto them, If ye were blind, ye should have no sin: but now ye say, We see: therefore your sin remaineth."'

'I have been asked to look after a young Icelandic friend,' said Hart, refusing the offer of coffee after the service. 'We are going to take a walk around the wood.' Silver-birch trunks, blotched white, huddled together. A crow flew through the branches, cawing. Sigurbjörn dug his hands into his coat pockets. 'I don't think I can have anything to do with a prayer circle or with anything else,' he said.

'Why not?'

'I don't really know, somehow it isn't me. On the streets of Reykjavík a man needs a strong faith and, to tell you the truth, it was my mother who sent me here.'

'Are you just going to put your tail between your legs like a dog? I doubt that you were forced to come here, and the streets are the same the world over.'

They went to a small restaurant. The rounded hills towards the city were wooded and he could see small lakes in the sunshine. They ate in silence and were both somewhat angry. During the meal Hart asked out of the blue, 'Have you read Rousseau, young man?'

'No, who is he?'

'Jean-Jacques Rousseau. He was a Frenchman.'

'Was he a priest?'

'No, but I think you would get the spiritual sustenance you are seeking from a reading of his works.'

Many years later Sigurbjörn came across Rousseau's *Confessions*, opened the book and read on the first page: 'But I am made unlike anyone I have ever met; I will even venture to say that I am like no one in the whole world.'

The Council began at three o'clock. Hart gave the opening

address. Sigurbjörn was in no mood to listen, and looked out of the window. Withered fields. Black trees. April just around the next hill. A workman in a coarse worsted sweater and high boots was drawing a plough across a winter-worn field. A crow rose cawing above the furrow. Sigurbjörn wanted to go to Copenhagen to have a drink, go and meet a girl – several girls – eat rissoles and fried eggs at Café Parnasse, buy a train ticket to Italy and look at buildings, go home to Iceland and get back to his carpentry.

The Deacon, Finn Martinsen, a large-boned and grave-looking man, responded to Hart's address. 'I am grateful to the Lord for the prophet he has sent us in Professor Hart,' said Martinsen. 'But when the prophet discusses public affairs, then I am not alone in having the feeling that he looks more to his villa in Vestre Aker than to the reality of life.' The Deacon paused for breath, but then began again with renewed force. 'Hart considers that the war in Europe was the work of God. God's punishment for man's sin. But there are others who think that the Evil One had a hand in it.'

Professor Hart stormed up to the rostrum. 'I find this argument hurtful. Is there anything in my private life of such a nature that it should gag my mouth so that I may not plainly express my views and convictions? As for my house, it simply makes it possible for me to live in less expensive accommodation than any of my friends in Oslo. May I ask Deacon Martinsen and our highly respected guests: What would be gained if I were to move into the city and pay a higher rent? No, this is offensive, and I would ask the Moderator to see that the newspapers do not get hold of this. And as for the notion that evil has come from God . . .'

'I am ashamed to be sitting here today,' said Martinsen from the pulpit. 'Had I known how lazy the Norwegian priesthood had grown, I would have become a cobbler. Blessed are they who have enough to eat each day and simply rely on what the Lord provides.'

Hart: 'The Deacon's mention of the cobbler's trade puts me in mind of Lev Tolstoy, who wanted to sell all his possessions and give the money to the poor and become a cobbler, but his wife put a stop to that.'

'What are you insinuating, you oaf?' shouted Martinsen from the auditorium.

Sigurbjörn put his head in his hands to hide his mirth. Every time he tried to stop laughing, he would just about manage to get himself under control when some fresh aspect of the meeting would set him off again. By his side sat a young theologian. A specialist in God, thought Sigurbjörn, and laughed. How absurd. Why don't they hide their heads in shame? He tried to make himself look serious by thinking sad thoughts, and then he saw his brother Jóhannes on his deathbed. German students had arranged for the coffin to be shipped to Iceland and sent the family a photograph taken in his room at the hospital. There was a bunch of flowers in a vase on the bedside table. His face was so grey and pale that his hair seemed browner than it had been while he was alive. Sigurbjörn felt a touch on his shoulder. It was the young theologian.

'I'm sorry. Is there something the matter?'

'Yes,' replied the Icelander, turning to him with tears of laughter running down his cheeks. 'I have just realized that I am in the wrong place. I don't believe in Jesus Christ.'

On the seaward side of Skúlagata the light caught a puddle that had settled among the broken paving stones. It was long past five. The sewers must have disgorged a decent quantity of titbits. A gaggle of gulls was battling it out above the waves, clipping each other's heads with their wings. A car drove slowly by and the driver stared keenly at Sigurbjörn. The timber used to mould the concrete lay in a pile in the car park. There was quite a lot of discarded timber blocking the underground entrance to the stores. The back of the building looked dreadful in the early morning light. There were jagged ridges where the concrete had seeped between the wooden boards holding it in place as it hardened. He walked along the wooden pavement by Hverfisgata. A pile of sand had been dumped in the entrance. A concrete mixer was standing there, and Sigurbjörn looked at it for a good long while. It would be the easiest thing in the world to steal it. A few grains of dry sand blew in his face. At last he said out loud,

'They couldn't be bothered to drag it inside when it was time to knock off. Well, let it all go to the devil. I'm not going to crawl any more for those arseholes. As far as I'm concerned all the bankers and lawyers in Reykjavík can go to hell. I'll start up again somewhere else,' he thought. 'On my own. I'll go abroad and get a well-paid job in an architect's office.'

He walked home. From Skólavörduhæd he could see a passenger plane coming in to land at Reykjavík Airport, it was one of the 'Faxes', and it sank slowly out of sight behind the roofs of the houses.

Everyone at home was asleep. He flicked through the newspapers. *Spegill* had been delivered. On the front cover there was a skilfully drawn cartoon by Tryggvi Thórhallsson. Two men were standing in front of a parody of the National Theatre. One was sharp-nosed and stupid-looking with a drip on the end of his nose, obviously up from the country. The other was a citizen of Reykjavík, to judge by his plump cheeks. Both men were in tuxedos and battered old hats, drawn in profile. The citizen of Reykjavík was instructing the man from the country: 'No, this isn't the National Theatre. This is our new department store, but they are just as broke.' Some way off a tall man with black lines in his cheeks and a blindfold over his eyes stood turning the handle of a barrel organ. On his shoulder sat a cheerful-looking monkey holding a tin box. The monkey had Gudbrandur's features.

9

The estate agent's office was at the far end of Bankastræti. A steep, narrow staircase led to a frosted-glass door. 'Did you see *Spegill*?' asked Gunnar Rafn as Sigurbjörn came in. 'Good publicity.'

'Good publicity?'

'Yes, and it didn't cost a penny.' Gunnar Rafn's round face looked up from his papers. He was perpetually sweating. 'Why are you looking at me like that? Don't you think it's a good joke?'

'Oh yes, very funny.' And Sigurbjörn laughed his hollow laugh.

He picked up a grubby telephone book and turned its pages idly.

The purpose of his visit was to suggest that they should drop the asking price of the floor-space.

Gunnar Rafn put out his cigarette, got to his feet and opened the window. The noise from the street grew louder and the smoke in the room dispersed.

'It's a great pity the expenditure on advertising was allowed to get so high, Gunnar,' muttered Sigurbjörn.

'Listen, he's just about to commit himself.' Gunnar Rafn saw himself as the bringer of glad tidings.

'Who?'

'Ingvar Hjálmarsson from Akureyri. He came back to me again yesterday. He's decided to buy a mansion on Ránargata from Haraldur in Kirkjustræti, against all my advice.' Gunnar Rafn lit another cigarette and put his elbows on the desk. 'But he hasn't been able to find the right location for his shop, and that's where we come in, Sigurbjörn.'

'I knew it would only be a question of time before people started to buy,' Sigurbjörn muttered at last.

'He said he would be here at ten o'clock sharp, and he will, he's a man of his word.'

It was ten minutes to ten, and at two minutes to there was the sound of heavy steps at the foot of the staircase, shoes grinding sand into the linoleum. A handsome man with bushy eyebrows came through the door. He was wearing a thick jacket in spite of the warm weather. 'Ingvar Hjálmarsson.'

The man offered his hand, and Sigurbjörn got up and introduced himself.

'Sit down, gentlemen,' said Gunnar Rafn.

'I've been looking at the building,' said Ingvar Hjálmarsson. 'And I like it very much. First I went over the designs with a fine toothcomb, and then I spoke to your colleague yesterday evening. They were still working, and he showed me all over the building. I've actually worked in a department store abroad and this one is perfect for my needs. A very well-made building in all respects. I would have preferred to buy it outright, but there we are.' He laughed.

'That is what I have been trying to tell people,' said Gunnar Rafn. 'But your average Icelander is slow on the uptake.'

'Old Brandsi's been slaving on that building like an ox,' said Sigurbjörn.

'Weren't you a colleague of Gudjón Samúelsson, the City Architect?'

Sigurbjörn nodded.

'I knew him personally. I was involved with the church at Akureyri. I was on the parish council. He often mentioned you.'

'So it's settled then, the matter under discussion?' asked Gunnar Rafn.

'Of course,' said the man from Akureyri with a smile.

'The whole of the second floor, Ingvar, and the third?' Gunnar waited.

'Yes,' said Ingvar Hjálmarsson. 'And an office on the sixth floor, the corner on the east side facing the sea, like I told you yesterday.'

'Yes, yes, it's all here.' Gunnar Rafn rummaged around in the designs.

'I've just been to the bank and it's all signed and sealed,' said Ingvar Hjálmarsson. 'I will pay 70 per cent on signature of the contract later today. And the balance in six months. Do you agree?' He looked at Sigurbjörn.

'That will be 1.8 million on signature,' said Gunnar Rafn, also looking at Sigurbjörn.

Sigurbjörn Helgason leaned forward in his chair and laughed. It was a laughter he could contain no more than he could contain the madness in his eyes, and the two men looked at him in amazement.

'Yes, yes,' he said at last, still laughing. 'I agree. You bet.' He brought his large clenched fist down on to the table.

'Then I will have the contract drawn up, and it will be ready for your signatures this afternoon,' said Gunnar Rafn.

Both men nodded.

'This construction of yours has gone like lightning,' said Ingvar Hjálmarsson, adding, 'A lot of people thought we were crazy when we laid foundations in frozen soil up north and poured concrete in the worst of the winter and turfed it over. No one believed it would work.

But it did work, and the herring factory was fully operational by the autumn.'

'That took some guts,' said Sigurbjörn, red in the face. 'You'd've lost everything in a quick thaw.'

He sat for a while in Gunnar Rafn's office after Ingvar Hjálmarsson had gone. 'This will be a big help to me, won't it?'

'You bet it will,' said Gunnar Rafn. 'I'll phone this through to *Morgunbladid* right away.' He scribbled down some words and read out, '"Space in the new store is selling fast. Be a shareholder in the turnover of the Reykjavík Department Store!" How does that sound?'

'Marvellous! Tell me, Gunnar, who is this fellow Ingvar Hjálmarsson? He certainly made a good impression on me!'

'He's stinking rich, Sigurbjörn. Stinking rich. A herring king! Went bankrupt a few years ago but doesn't intend to have his fingers burnt again. Wants to put his money into property and low-risk ventures.'

He sat for a long time on a pile of timber in the sun outside the store. It was humming with activity. They were putting the finishing touches to the roof; a lorry with a hoist on the back stood with its bonnet in the gateway, and a container of concrete was on its way up into the sky. Two men peered down from the edge of the roof. One of them dropped a length of timber on to a pile and watched it fall. A man was pulling nails out of some timber by the workmen's shelter. 'Where is Gudbrandur?'

'In the shelter.'

The door was open. He caught a rear view of his friend, curly-haired and broad-shouldered, fixing a blade in a plane. 'We're over the worst of it, my friend,' said Sigurbjörn, standing in the doorway. 'Two floors sold.'

'Are you surprised?' Gudbrandur looked up in wonder.

'Yes, I am rather. I had begun to think that I was going to go bankrupt. That we both were.'

Gudbrandur stared at him and said, after a silence, 'Do you mean that, Sigurbjörn?'

'Yes, I really do mean it, Gudbrandur.'

'I never doubted for a moment that it would all be sold,' said Gudbrandur. 'Do you think I would have put everything I owned into it otherwise?'

'I say, what's the matter with these wives of ours?' asked Sigurbjörn.

Gudbrandur tapped the wooden bracket with his hammer, making the blade fast. 'Don't pay any attention to them.' He examined the plane at both ends. 'They're crazy,' he said with great finality. Then he added, smiling broadly, 'Did you see *Spegill* yesterday? Damn the bastards!'

III

1

Almost every day, Thórarinn struggled to ride up Bókhlöðustígur. The bicycle wobbled, his thighs and calves were like lead, he gasped for air, his feet hurt, his heart thumped, the stone wall of the Grammar School turned a dazzling white, the red of the houses turned a deep red and the green of the house at the top of the hill turned a violent green. He leaned forward but the pedals did not move. He dismounted and looked up towards the corner of the street. Nevertheless muscles were appearing where there had never been muscles before.

He padlocked the cycle outside the Fisheries' Bank and went inside to see Helgi. He had often dropped in on him during the summer. Sometimes Helgi would treat him to a hot dog.

Helgi sat there at his cashier's desk as if he was the richest man in the world with at least a million krónur in the till. He took time off with his younger brother and bought them both hot dogs with all the trimmings at the 'Best Place in Town'. Thórarinn tried not to let people see how proud he was, but he still couldn't stop looking at them to gauge their reactions. Everyone must recognize his companion. The best centre forward in all of Scandinavia, if not beyond.

The goal against the French had come in the seventh minute of the game. That immensely powerful player, Helgi Sigurbjarnason, scored with a 'back scissors' that had taken the goalkeeper completely by surprise; he had no idea where the ball had come from – it said in *Visir*. They strolled down to the harbour with their hot dogs and pints of milk. The *Gullfoss* lay at anchor in the fine weather, with its snow-white upper deck and the blue stripe round its funnel. Two years earlier Helgi, Ragnar and Snjólaug had gone on a Christmas cruise to Amsterdam, Copenhagen and Leith.

'Funny,' said Thórarinn. 'I think the hot dogs at the stadium taste better.'

'Yes, that's true,' said Helgi. 'They have their own special flavour.'

'How was the buffet on the *Gullfoss*?' asked Thórarinn, looking at the ship.

'Wonderful. Ragnar and I were stuffing ourselves all day long.'

'Was there any trouble between you and Raggi?'

'No, why do you say that?'

'Oh, it was just a thought. Because of Snjóka?'

'No, there was no trouble between me and Ragnar, Tóti,' said Helgi, irritated. 'It wasn't my fault their engagement got broken off. She just found herself another boyfriend, that's all.' Helgi dropped the empty milk bottle on the worn wood of the pier and said, 'Watch!' He balanced the bottle on his toe and then flipped it into the water between the ship and the pier without it touching the coal-black stern.

'I've got muscles in my legs I didn't know I had,' said Thórarinn. 'I think I'll start training with you at the stadium. I might as well get some use out of my new sports bag.' Thórarinn had decided not to give the sports bag to Helgi when Helgi had put a pair of socks on the arm of the sofa as a present the evening he came home with the national team.

'Yes, why don't you come out to the stadium, and you can start kicking the ball around,' said Helgi. 'Kicking hard runs in the family. Scoring a goal is the best sensation in the world. The best thing of all was hearing the silence in the stadium when I hammered the ball into the back of the French net. Come out to the stadium. You have the right build for it. I was much fatter than you when I was a boy. I'll teach you everything I know.'

'Maybe putting the shot is more up my street,' said Thórarinn, doubtfully.

'Nonsense, you can do anything you want.' Helgi said. He put his arm round the boy's shoulders and led him away from the harbour. 'I've never known a boy as tough as you. You're tougher than I am, and that's saying a lot. Let's be getting back to the bank now.'

Thórarinn unlocked the bicycle and gritted his teeth as he cycled along Lækjargata. He wiped everything from his mind except this one thought: to cycle up Bókhlödustígur without stopping. The stretch up to Laufásvegur was easy, but after that the going got harder. When he was about halfway up and within sight of Midstræti, the bicycle started to wobble under him. There was still a good way to go before he reached Thingholtstræti. He would have to turn into Midstræti, the topmost side street, twenty yards from the corner! Helgi said I could do anything! He stood up in the saddle, put all his weight into the pedals and gripped the handlebars. A man in a large black hat walked in front of the bicycle. He had some urgent business with the boy. His handshake was soft as silk. He was pink in the face. 'My God, but you're out of puff,' said the man. His bloodshot eyes looked furtively this way and that, as if he should have been somewhere else.

'I'm not fit enough. I'm trying to cycle right up the street in one go.'

'Tut, tut, tut,' said the man. 'I've never heard the like. You ought to find it easy, a big lad like you. Running. That's the thing. Builds up your speed.' The man in the large hat started running on the spot.

'My brother is Helgi Sigurbjarnarson. He's a member of the national football team. He scored Iceland's only goal against France the other day,' said Thórarinn. The man had never heard of Helgi, nor of Sigurbjörn either. He said not much news had reached him for nearly twenty years. 'I've been drinking. Could you manage a little money for food?'

Thórarinn put his hand in his pocket and found a two-króna piece. It was all he had. The man pocketed it without a word. 'My grandfather's name was Helgi Vésteinsson,' said Thórarinn, already bitterly regretting the loss of his coin.

'My name is Gústaf, and I'm a Reykjavíker born and bred,' said the man with the hat. 'And I knew him well, your grandfather. I was standing in the chemist's one day and he came up to me with a bottle of whisky in his pocket.' The drunk peered around self- importantly. 'He liked a drink, like many a good man. He said to me: "Gústaf, let's go down to the sea together and look at Mount Esja. I'll give you a shot of whisky and if you can recite 'Dettifoss' by Einar Benediktsson you can have the whole bottle ."'

The story was beginning to bore Thórarinn. Gústaf put on a superior air and looked around him as though he were gazing out across the calm surface of the sea that fine afternoon when he had sat on a weathered stone, drinking with Helgi Vésteinsson. 'We sat down on the stone and I began to recite the poem. Your grandfather stopped me almost at once.' Gústaf waved his arm. '"No, Gústi, no. You're not reciting it properly. I'll do it." "Very well, Helgi, old chap," I said. "Very well. I'm sorry I didn't get it right."' Gústaf looked crestfallen, as though Thórarinn's grandfather were standing disapprovingly before them in the street. 'Then your grandfather recited the poem. When that was done, he said, "Gústaf! You can have the bottle all the same."'

'I've got to go,' said Thórarinn.

Gústaf chose to ignore this and instead danced around on his toes with his fists up like a boxer. 'Hrafn Jónsson once challenged me to a fight behind locked doors. He was our finest heavyweight in his day. Only a minute into the first round I sent him crashing to the floor with an uppercut. A boxer can never tell where the blow that'll knock him out is coming from.' Gústaf put his clenched fist against Thórarinn's chin. 'He went down like a shop dummy falling over. But not before he'd made a mess of my bottom lip.'

Gústaf pointed to a pale scar as proof. 'I agreed to keep quiet about it. I said: "Hrafn."' Gústaf laid a soft hand on the back of Thórarinn's, where it rested on the handlebars. Three of the fingers on Gústaf's hand were missing. 'I said, "Hrafn, you don't need to worry about this getting out. It will be our little secret." And now, whenever I pop my head into his shop he says, "Do you remember, Gústi, when you knocked me down?" "How can I forget it, my dear Hrafn?" "You

125

could never do it again, Gústi," he says. "Hrafn, old chap! You can believe what you want. It's no skin off my nose. The fact is I no longer box, noble sport though it is. But I take off my hat to you as a sportsman, my dear Hrafn."' Gústaf took off his hat and bowed deeply to Thórarinn. He was completely bald.

'I've got to go now.' Thórarinn's heart was beating so hard his chest hurt.

'Have you got ten krónur?'

'I've just given you some money.'

'What money? You didn't give me anything,' said the drunk angrily. Thórarinn pushed the bicycle up to Thingholtsstræti. Gústaf, unsteady on his feet, watched him go. 'Can't you give me a little something?' he shouted, surprised and angry. 'Anything at all?'

He stood in the middle of Bókhlödustígur with his bald pate gleaming in the sun.

'I've done more than enough for you, you bloody beef thief,' shouted Thórarinn.

Instead of freewheeling down Amtmannsstigur, he pedalled for all he was worth with the wind roaring against his cheeks. He swung round into Lækjargata, parked his cycle in Pósthússtraeti and rushed into the police station.

Sigurbjörn's and Thórarinn's strolls together had grown less frequent over the summer, but this evening they took a short walk into town. Sigurbjörn had on a long overcoat and a peaked cap. The boy was wearing jeans and his new sweater. The father was not very pleased about his son's appearance. He wanted him to wear something on his head.

They walked for some time without saying a word. Redcurrant bushes hung over the garden walls, their branches heavy with over-ripe berries. 'Yesterday I nearly managed to cycle right the way up Bókhlödustígur without stopping,' said Thórarinn. 'But that meat thief Gústi the Finger started pestering me.'

'San Francisco is full of streets like that,' said Sigurbjörn.

'I gave him some money because he said he knew Grandfather

Helgi. He said he'd once run into him when he was out for a walk with a bottle of brennivín.'

'Father never went out drinking brennivín,' said Sigurbjörn.

'The police wouldn't do anything about it. They just laughed at me. They thought it was stupid. I ran to Helgi at the bank and asked him to come with me and talk to the cops but he didn't want to. He said they were right, the meat would have been cooked and eaten long ago and nothing could be proved. Do you think that's fair, Father? And Ragna at the shop said she was going to stop calling me "Mr City Architect". Now she says my name's "Tóti the Cop".'

'Oh, let me go and talk to them,' muttered Sigurbjörn crossly, trying to keep a distance between himself and his son. At last Thórarinn realized that his father was embarrassed by the sweater and jeans. They walked home through the empty streets, both feeling aggrieved.

2

Towards the end of September the light changed, became transparent. The grass in the gardens withered and then shone white and yellow as the wind moved through it. Autumn was closing in; there was frost at nights and the puddles were covered with a thin film of ice in the mornings. Thórarinn liked trying to lift the sheets of ice, but they were too thin to stay in one piece. 'Tóti, telephone,' Sunneva shouted from the steps.

'Are you coming out to the country to pick potatoes with us, Tóti?' It was Grandfather Geir.

'No, I was going to go to the match at the stadium with Helgi.'

'Take my advice, give it up, boy,' said the old man. 'The last time I went to Melavöllur Stadium was in 1912, and I've never been since. The sound of their shins snapping when they broke each other's legs was so loud you could hear it a mile off. Helgi will get killed one of these days. Football's a disgusting business.'

'I'll come and see you when the match is over, Grandfather,' said Thórarinn.

The weather that Saturday was suitable neither for football nor for potato-picking. The stadium was as grey as a photograph in an old newspaper. The footballers slithered across a mixture of clay and sand glistening white in the wet. Helgi ran determinedly backwards and forwards, his hair rainsodden, the biggest leg muscles in town on public view. A man sat in the terraces with a newspaper over his head, shouting repeatedly, '*A la batterie, français! Biscuit!*'

Helgi got the better of a defender and the goalkeeper and fired off a terrific shot but it hit the crossbar.

'What's the matter, trouble at home, you bloody failure?' shouted the French speaker. Beside him sat his friend, a fat man with a pale, rabbit-like face. They were sharing a bottle of whisky between them.

'There are some internationals next summer, Helgi,' the rabbit shouted feebly. 'Don't bother to show up.'

Helgi glared up angrily at the enclosure and terraces. He was in a bad mood when he came out of the changing room. A girl was waiting, nervously shifting her weight from foot to foot. 'Who was that idiot who kept shouting *à la batterie* all through the game?'

She shook her head.

'Just a man,' Thórarinn replied.

'Men like that should be taught a lesson. Who was it scored the goal against the French the other day?'

'You did,' said his younger brother.

'Are you coming home with us, Tóti?' asked Helgi.

'No, I'm going with Grandfather and Grandmother to pick potatoes.'

'Not the potatoes again. Heaven help us!' said the elder brother. And he set off east along Hringbraut with the girl.

'Did Helgi split the legs of those bastards asunder as I prophesied he would?' asked Geir Sveinsson as he opened the door for his grandson. Grandmother Rosa had put on her wellingtons.

'No, but his team lost 3–1.'

'Of course they lost,' snorted Geir.

It was always strange to see Grandfather and Grandmother in such a large, modern flat. At the head of Grandfather's bed, where he was in the habit of resting his head, the paint had faded. A biography of Abraham Lincoln lay on the bedside table. Grandfather read a page or two of it every night before he went to sleep. Both Ragnar and Helgi could swear that the book had been there when they were children.

On the parlour table stood a steel tape-recorder. Geir Sveinsson was fond of such novelties. He started the tape-recorder and let Thórarinn listen to a recording made early that spring.

'Tóti, my fine fellow,' said the tape-recorder.

'Yes, Grandfather.'

'Are you going to come with Grandmother and me to help us move into that bloody Vídimelur place tomorrow?'

'I would if I could.'

'And what's stopping you?'

'I've got to run errands for old Hjálmur at the Trough.'

'I bet you have. You go from Danish pastries at your mother's to hamburgers at old Hjálmur's. Come and help your old grandfather so he won't have a heart attack carrying out the radiogram . . .'

'Geir, I'm waiting,' said Rósa, putting on her headscarf.

The old man drove along Hverfisgata to see if his shop was all right and to take a quiet look at the Reykjavík Department Store. The windows had been glazed. 'Oh, Geir, I feel so uneasy whenever I pass this place,' said Grandmother.

'I'm not surprised,' said Grandfather Geir. 'We should never have been so stupid as to let the house go.'

'I caught the meat thief, Grandfather.'

'Yes, so your mother told me on the telephone. Quite tough, aren't you? And the police wouldn't help you? Lazy bastards.'

The potato leaves had fallen, exposing bare stems standing wretchedly in rows, looking like trees after a forest fire. The potatoes came rolling up under the fork and Rósa and Tóti gathered them in a metal basin. Geir whispered to the boy, 'Thank God it's not raining, Tóti, while we're getting the little devils up. Your grandmother didn't do anything about them until it began to freeze.' Grandfather huffed and puffed. 'She couldn't care less about the potatoes. She wants the crop to go bad. She only plants them out of sheer cussedness. Her only aim is to make my life a mortal plague. You think I'm an old fool, Tóti, but I'm not nearly as much of a fool as you think. Just you wait until you have a wife of your own and are my age. Then you'll change your tune, my lad.'

He thought he was speaking softly, but Grandmother Rósa heard every word, and she gave Thórarinn her famous twinkle.

A rotten herring had been thrown on the ground in the distant neighbouring garden. The seagulls swarmed in the air above it in a greedy cloud. One of them stood motionless, like a stuffed seabird in a museum. The boy had a feeling that it had its eye on him. The others were gorging themselves.

Geir and Rósa sent Thórarinn home with half a sack of potatoes for his pains. Some of them were already rotten and by the third day they were giving off a heavy, sweet smell.

That was the day Thórarinn finally conquered Bókhlödustígur. He remembered San Francisco, where every street made Bókhlödustígur look like a joke in comparison. He lifted his bicycle on to its stand, looked down the slope and said out loud, 'How lucky I am to be an errand boy in Reykjavík.'

3

The four of them sat at a table in the Golden Ballroom at Hotel Borg, wearing their best clothes. Thórarinn was dressed in a suit and a bow-tie, his hair sleeked down with water and parted on the left. Sunneva wore a white gown cut low at the back. Vilborg's thick black hair made her dress look almost dazzlingly white. She was studying the menu and asked out loud, 'What's *consommé poulard*, Mother?'

'It's chicken soup.'

'And what's . . .'

'Let me see.' Sunneva reached for the menu on the invitation card.

'You've got one yourself, Mother.'

'No, you're the only one who brought your invitation with you.'

She took the card in her hands, opened it and read:

The Enterprise Construction Company
invites you to an
Autumn Celebration
at Hotel Borg
on 27 September 1953
from 10 p.m. until 2 a.m.

Dance Music by Björn R. Einarsson and His Band
Ballroom open at 6 p.m.

MENU
Consommé Poulard – chicken soup
Agneau en Brochette – kebab of lamb
Poires Belle Hélène – ice-cream with pears
Coffee, Liqueurs, Wines and Spirits included

About sixty people had been invited. Sunneva looked round for Ingirídur, but she was nowhere to be seen.

Sigurbjörn sat at the table in black and white evening dress. 'Lamb *en brochette*,' he said thoughtfully. 'Isn't that some kind of stew?'

'Who designed the Hotel Borg, Father?' asked Thórarinn.

'The City Architect, of course, do you need to ask?' said Vilborg.

'I know. I just find it a bit much that wherever one goes, whether it's a church or a school, a swimming pool or a restaurant, the place turns out to have been designed by Gudjón Samúelsson.'

'On this occasion, Thórarinn, we are celebrating a building that Father designed and built,' said Vilborg. 'It is not appropriate to discuss anything else.'

There was the gentle tinkle of piano music in the ballroom, and the waiters hurried to and fro. Aperitifs were served, and lemonade for the children. Thórarinn amused himself by watching the wives of the carpenters and hired labourers. He had tried to imagine what kind of wife each of them would have, but more often than not he had guessed wrong. A big fat man who had been taken on as an assistant to the carpenters during the final stretch of the work had talked for a long time in the coffee shelter about the benefits of having an ugly wife. Pretty wives did not know how to cook, the ugly ones were the best cooks. Now the fat man sat at a table not far from them with the ugliest wife Thórarinn had ever seen.

A waiter was opening a bottle of red wine at the table. He had cut away the seal round the neck of the bottle and put it on the tablecloth. Sunneva picked up the tattered ends and started to make a flower of them. Her head was tilted slightly to one side, as it always was whenever something was bothering her. The boy studied her oval cheeks, high forehead and curved nose. 'Is she still worrying?' he thought. 'Now, when nearly all the floor-space has been sold and we are rich?'

Sunneva had fallen asleep during the day and had been disturbed by her dreams. She dreamed that she was standing by the gate at Sjafnargata looking towards the house but that it was shrouded in black, so that its walls were hidden. She saw the big rowan tree wither. Then she dreamed of the new store. A dark hurricane came roaring in across the sea from Kjalarnes and broke over the building. The outer walls fell away all at once and she could see an inner wall and the spacious interior. The only furniture in one small room was a writing desk. The storm blew the papers off the table. What did the dream mean, she wondered anxiously. It had been unusually vivid. She looked at her parents. Geir Sveinsson was elegantly dressed and her mother was in Icelandic national costume, the silk braid brownish-yellow with large black tassels. Did the dream foretell a death? The old man looked around him like an angry goat, but Rósa was cheerfulness itself. No, that was not it. Sunneva had finished making a rose out of the seal from the bottle and she let it fall into the tall wine glass beside her daughter's plate and said, 'Look.'

Vilborg picked up the flower and examined it.

'Now don't go picking that to pieces,' said Sigurbjörn.

'It's priceless, then, is it?'

'Of course it is, girl, just like everything your mother makes. And,

Vilborg,' Sigurbjörn added when he saw that his daughter was beginning to sulk, 'Father will take you to the pictures tomorrow. What's the name of that ballet film you want to see so badly?'

'*The Red Shoes.*'

Sigurbjörn picked up his wallet and counted some notes out on to the table. 'Go to the cinema as soon as it opens, lass, and buy tickets for us.'

A waiter in a red jacket brought the soup. Vilborg picked up a soup spoon. She thought it was too large and was surprised to find that the bowl of the spoon had fine scratches on it. She pointed this out to her mother. 'Now, now, my love, just you concentrate on eating.'

'Yum yum,' said Thórarinn. 'Chicken soup.' And he made appreciative slurping noises.

'Tóti, don't do that,' said Vilborg. 'It's revolting.'

'Yes, stop it, child,' said his mother.

Gudbrandur went by in a tuxedo, his cheeks flushed and his eyes shining. He paused to say a few words to Sigurbjörn, his curly hair not moving even though he was bending over. He looked at Vilborg and said, 'Hello, my beauty.' Sigurbjörn listened, nodded his head, and broke a roll with his long fingers.

'Yum yum, that was good soup,' said Thórarinn. 'Slurp, slurp. Do we get second helpings?'

'Aren't you going to leave some room for the main course, Tóti?'

The waiter came and cleared their plates. Sunneva looked across to her older sons. Helgi had propped his elbows on the table and was gazing round him. She could see no sign of Ragnar. She glanced around. There was a flash from behind a palm tree at about the height of a man, and Ragnar came out of hiding with his camera. He smiled and said something to the people sitting at the table by the palm, and moved over to the next table to take a photograph. Recently Sunneva had found a photograph taken during their years in Copenhagen. They were on Gråbrødretorvet; she was holding Ragnar's hand and Christian had his arm round her shoulders. Ragnar had looked unhappy in the picture. Suddenly a flashbulb burst. Sunneva put a hand over her face.

'What's wrong, Mother?'

'I take such a bad photo, my dear.'

'Nonsense.' Ragnar took a picture of Vilborg and Sigurbjörn. Then it was Geir's turn to shield his eyes, but Rósa looked up cheerfully and adjusted the tassel on her headdress.

The waiter served the main course.

'Waiter,' said Sigurbjörn. 'Why are there no flowers on the tables?'

'I'm sorry,' said the waiter. 'We've tried it again and again, but the guests eat them.'

Sigurbjörn looked at him, wide-eyed. 'How's that? The people here tonight?'

'No, not these people, not so far. We would very much like to have flowers, but it's no use. I'm sorry.'

Thórarinn looked down at his plate, happy beneath his heavy brows. Sunneva studied her plate. Four thick crescent-shaped slices of meat lay one on top of another. Potatoes, red cabbage, beans, glistening brown gravy and a segment of orange. 'Good Lord. I can't eat all this. I'll burst.'

'Well, I'll help you out, Mother,' said Thórarinn, and immediately accepted a thick slice of meat from his sister.

'Don't spill gravy on the table,' said Sunneva. Another open bottle of red wine was brought for them. She sipped at her glass and the twilight encircling the white tablecloth grew darker and warmer. She felt better. After the ice-cream even Thórarinn had had his fill. By then the noise of voices in the hall was quite loud and steady. A young man had come to the table to speak to Sigurbjörn. His wide trousers could not conceal the fact that he was bow-legged. He placed a large hand on the table. A vein pulsed visibly in his neck. 'It's great to be here this evening, Sigurbjörn. The food's just great. It was a terrific idea to invite us all here.'

'Well, I didn't want to have a demonstration on my hands, Ostrich.' Sigurbjörn laughed his hollow laugh.

'And is this your wife?' Sunneva looked up. 'And here is your daughter and Tóti. I know Tóti,' he said, sounding important. 'He's been down at the site quite a lot. We're real pals.'

'What's your name, sir?' asked Sunneva.

134

'He's called Ostrich,' said Sigurbjörn, laughing so much his molars were visible.

The young man quickly straightened up from the table, went over to Sunneva and said, without appearing to be offended, 'My name is Reynir.' He gazed round the hall. 'But they call me Ostrich.'

'Oh, why? You don't have a long neck.'

'I know. Things like that are hard to explain.'

'Is your wife with you?' asked Sunneva.

'I'm not married yet. Sort of considering the possibilities. Maybe I can whisk one of them off to my little wooden hut at the weekend.' His gaze fell on Helgi. 'Is this your son Helgi?'

'Yes.'

'I felt really proud and patriotic that we managed to score against France this summer. My legs turned to jelly as I was listening to it on the radio at home.'

'You want to watch it. You don't want to be any more bow-legged than you are already, Ostrich,' said Sigurbjörn.

The band began to play 'All the Things You Are', and a few couples hurried on to the dance floor. For about an hour, one instrumental number followed another. Then Björn R. got to his feet, his hair and his trombone gleaming in the light on the rostrum, and began to sing in his soft, spellbinding voice, bringing the ballroom to life, 'Some enchanted evening you will see a stranger . . .'

Ragnar sat down beside his grandfather. Rósa had a glass of sherry and a cup of coffee in front of her. Geir had asked for brennivín and water. He held his drink well, but Ragnar could tell by his glassy eyes that he had drunk a fair amount. He put an arm round his grandfather's shoulders. 'Grandfather,' Ragnar said loudly, imitating the steel tape-recorder, 'Are you going to help me move into that bloody Vídimelur place tomorrow, Tóti? Or am I going to have a heart attack carrying out the radiogram?'

'How are you, Ragnar?' asked Geir.

Sigurbjörn bowed to Sunneva. He settled his cheek against her forehead and lifted her hands high in the air. They moved about the dance floor like the wind, and she began to remember her dream again.

4

Thórarinn woke first and watched the shadows of the rowan branches moving on the wall. The window was open and he could hear a boy in the house next door practising *Le cygne* by Saint-Saëns on the cello.

The celebration had gone wrong. Ostrich had sat down beside Grandmother and tried to pull off her headdress. He was thrown out. Thórarinn had gone out through the revolving door in the foyer. A whining wind tore at the low trees on Austurvöllur, and Ostrich walked in circles on the grass and howled at the pale moon, at the statue of President Jón Sigurdsson and at the Parliament Building. Thórarinn had gone back into the Golden Ballroom. Grown-ups looked at him and smiled. A red-cheeked woman with blond hair made him sit down at her table. 'Are you Sigurbjörn's son? You don't look like him at all. Well, let me look at you. You've got his heavy brows. Do you want some lemonade?'

A young plumber wanted to invite Sigurbjörn home. Sigurbjörn had got drunk and seized the man with both hands across the table, stared at him hard and shaken him about. The plumber got a bit scared. He did not realize that Sigurbjörn was trying to demonstrate to him that architects and craftsmen are brothers. Thórarinn had danced the last dance with his mother to the melancholy strains of the trombone. 'I'm getting sentimental over you' Sunneva had told him the song was called, kissing him on the cheek when the lights came on. Sigurbjörn became angry about something in the cloakroom and wanted to walk home on his own. Thórarinn went after him, although Sunneva told him not to. It was a pitch-black night. His father moved in semi-circles along the street. It was bitterly cold. The wind whistled in the trees on Hallargardur and the surface of Lake Tjörnin was ridged with the white crests of waves. He kept a close eye on his father all the way to their front door.

Thórarinn looked at his bedside table. There was a key there. He had been half asleep when he realized that someone was sitting by the bed in the dark. He switched on the light. It was Sigurbjörn. Thórarinn sat up. 'Yes, Father?'

For a long time his father had not said anything, but hung his head.

At last he jerked forward in his chair, seized Thórarinn's shoulders and looked hard at him.

'What's the matter, Father?' the boy had said, peevishly.

'Tóti! You and I, we're friends, aren't we, Tóti?'

'Yes, Father.'

'Don't dress like a tramp.' His father pulled a face. There was an unpleasant smell coming from him. 'Tóti, those new trousers your mother bought you. I don't want to be seen out with you in public dressed like that.'

'I won't wear them, Father.'

'For friendship's sake?'

'Yes.'

'The floor-space has been sold, Tóti. All of it.'

'I know.'

'They all said I would never amount to anything, Tóti. Tóti?' Sigurbjörn shook him.

'Yes, all right!'

His father had been at a loss for words, but all of a sudden his eyes filled with tears. He put a hand in his pocket and took out a bunch of keys. 'Do you see this key, Tóti? This is the master key. You must look after it, Tóti. We own that building together. You and me.' It took Sigurbjörn a while to get the key off the key ring.

'Tóti?' He shifted in the chair.

'Yes?'

'You should have known my brother Jóhannes.'

'You've told me about him, Father.'

The cello in the house next door grew louder. Thórarinn had intended to sleep late that last Saturday of summer. On Monday classes began again at school. He heard the telephone ring. It was half past nine.

Hjálmur had about a hundred orders that needed dealing with, and the shop was crammed full of customers. Sunneva stood in the doorway in her nightgown, and passed on the message.

Thórarinn raised a tousled head from the pillow and looked at his mother in utter disbelief.

'But I don't work there any more.'

'Come on now, shake a leg, Tóti. The old boy's in a lot of trouble.'

Thórarinn scrambled out of bed. 'This is the last real day of my holidays. I've been working there all summer. Are you all crazy?'

'I don't think you can refuse to help him, the way things are right now. He has spoken so well of you. I know it isn't fair, Tóti.'

Thórarinn got dressed, muttering. A sandwich was waiting for him on a plate. It was nearly ten o'clock. The shop closed at noon on Saturdays. It was a matter of either going at once or not going at all. He took the sports bag with him and put one of Helgi's footballs in it. He was going to go to the stadium after work to kick the ball about a bit, and then visit Grandfather and Grandmother at Vídimelur.

Winter was coming. What had happened to the trees? Solitary brown-yellow leaves hung here and there on the branches. The soft redcurrants hung limply on the bushes, and there were bunches of berries in the flowerbeds. Leaves stuck to the car. The dovecote was brown with damp. There was a biting autumn coldness in the air. He ate the sandwich on his way. He did not see a soul until he reached Barónstígur. Gudbrandur had come up behind him at the bar in Hotel Borg and whispered, 'Are you looking for someone new with a mole on her cheek, my lad?' He had liked the smell of some of the women and the rustling of their dresses had made him feel funny inside.

Hjálmur was alone. Neither of the women had shown up. This had thrown the old man off balance, as was only to be expected. Thórarinn took the bicycle, fixed the bag to the rear carrier, and put the packages in it. He left the football at Hjálmur's and set off. 'I'll make this up to you later, Tóti,' said Hjálmur. 'Didn't everything go well last night, and wasn't the dancing fun?' He strode to and fro behind the shop counter, though there were not all that many customers.

'Yes,' said the boy. 'It was OK.' His bad temper had more or less

138

evaporated. It did not take him long to deliver the packages. By the time he got to Ingólfsstræti the bag was empty. He dismounted and wheeled the bike beside him. It was a quarter past eleven. He had probably two or at most three houses still to do. He cycled up Skólavördustígur and managed it easily, though it was uphill all the way. On Monday he would get his full pay from Hjálmur. But should he spend it all on the model aeroplane? Or should he perhaps put his trust in his father? Even if he did not get the aeroplane for his birthday, perhaps he might get it for Christmas? He decided to wait for his birthday, that was not so far away. He had arrived at the toyshop. There it hung. Putting it together would be child's play. He had intended to fly it on the lawn at Austurbær School. It was flat and good for landing on. He leaned on the bike and looked at the treasure. The girl in the shop smiled at him.

He became aware that he was not the only person looking in the window. Beside him stood a big man in a brown and utterly thread-bare anorak. The man was fair-haired, with a crewcut. He was chewing on a match. His eyes were blue and watery, and his jaw was unshaven, with white patches of stubble. He looked stupid and lazy.

'Are you an errand boy?' asked the man. His voice was clear and slightly aggressive. Thórarinn had expected more of a drawl. He said yes, he was.

'And are you wasting time?'

'No, no,' Thórarinn said apologetically, as though he was answerable to this stranger. He was angry with himself for replying.

'She your friend?' asked the man, making it clear by a lift of his head that he meant the girl who worked in the shop.

'No, no.' Thórarinn was surprised at the question.

'She your tart then?' asked the man. But Thórarinn did not understand what he meant. 'My tart? It's not a cake shop. It's a toy shop.'

The man laughed. He said, 'Do you want to buy that aeroplane?' He looked at the aeroplane in the window and chewed on the matchstick, cheerfully.

'Yes,' said Thórarinn. 'I've saved up for it all summer.'

'And are you going to go in and buy it?'

'No. I can't make up my mind whether I should buy it on Monday when I get my wages or wait until it's my birthday and buy it then. I'm quite hopeful that I'll get it for my birthday. My father has half promised me it. Do you know my father? He's an architect. His name is Sigurbjörn Helgason and he used to work for the City Architect.'

The man shook his head. He looked at the aeroplane. His anorak was undone. He had a large belly and he did not restrain it in any way. He seemed to be pondering what Thórarinn had told him, weighing it up. He said, 'You're waiting for your birthday to arrive.' By the way he spoke it was clear that all this meant a great deal to him, and he added, 'But I have a better idea.'

'Oh, and what's that?' asked Thórarinn, wanting to be free of this conversation.

'I like you a lot,' said the man. 'And I'm going to tell you a secret. Did you see the news in the papers the other day? They found some gold sovereigns in a package in some timber down by the docks.'

Thórarinn nodded. He had read about this in the newspapers and had heard his grandfather talking about it. A dock labourer had found some treasure when timber was being unloaded from a ship.

'Well,' said the man. 'I was the one who found that treasure. And because I think you're a good boy, I'm going to give you one or two gold sovereigns. It makes no odds to me. I've got hundreds. And with just one of them you could buy two or three aeroplanes like that. Four even.'

Thórarinn was doubtful.

The man said, 'I'm only a short walk from here. I think you should come home with me.'

'But I haven't finished work yet.'

The man clicked his tongue. 'It won't take a moment. My place is on Grundarstígur. That's the next street along from here.'

'Yes, I know where it is,' said Thórarinn. Yet he was still doubtful. He could not really see that it would do any harm for him to accept this present. He had read about the gold sovereigns in the news-papers. This man was a dock labourer. His appearance was enough to quell any doubts about that. 'Why do you want to give them to me?'

'Because I was a boy myself once.' Something seemed to amuse the man. 'And I well remember how bad it feels to want toys and not be able to buy them.'

'No, thanks,' said Thórarinn. 'I'm not interested in presents.' He walked away, pushing the bicycle.

'Where are you going?'

'To put the bike away.'

'I'll walk with you.'

'That's not necessary.' But the man was still walking beside him. 'Where do you live?'

'On Sjafnargata. My father's an architect. He's been building a store.'

'Yes, you said that before.' The man was sullen. 'And where is the store?'

'It's that big new building on Vitatorg. Haven't you seen it?'

The man made no reply to this, but continued to chew on his matchstick.

'I own the store jointly with father.'

'Don't talk nonsense,' said the man.

Thórarinn slowly put his hand in his pocket and walked with the bicycle alongside him. He had put the key on a ring before leaving home, and he fished it out. 'Look, this is the key.'

The man eyed the key and snorted. 'You're lying.'

'No,' said the boy. 'There was a celebration at Hotel Borg last night. Father let me have this key.'

The man smiled. 'The big new building on Vitatorg?'

'Yes, that's what I was saying.'

'That key could open just about anything.' The man seemed preoccupied.

'No, it's for the store. It is the only key there is.'

'Bah, I don't believe it.'

'That's your problem,' said Thórarinn.

'Let's go and look at the place,' said the man.

They walked across Frakkastígur and turned off Grettisgata down Vitastígur. From the corner of Laugavegur they could see the store.

'It's a big place,' said the man.

'It's to be called the Reykjavík Department Store.'

'And you say you own it?'

'The key fits.'

'Show me,' said the man. He looked at Thórarinn, who noticed his eyes were not as dazed as they had seemed to him earlier. The pupils were hard dots. He remembered now that he had seen the man before. He had stood on the corner one day in late summer, gazing at the building for a long time. He was the husband of the redhaired trawlerman's wife who was always so frightened.

'You're a trawlerman, aren't you?'

'Eh?' The man seemed distracted. 'What are you on about? You shouldn't talk nonsense to grown-ups.'

Thórarinn wanted to go, but they walked down Vitastígur together. He put the cycle away and locked it, and they crossed the street.

'Does your father have all this sand here to stop people walking about?'

'Why don't you ask him?' said Thórarinn.

'Have you started eyeing up the girls yet?'

'No.'

'Don't talk rot. Of course you have.' The man walked splay-footed across the pile of sand and looked at the concrete-spattered timber door. 'Is your father pushed for a penny? Why hasn't he put a proper door in here? Do you own any of this place?'

'Yes, my father built it this summer with a friend of his. He's called Gudbrandur Jónsson and he's a master builder.' Gudbrandur's name had no effect.

'If you're telling the truth, if the key fits, then I'll give you one of the gold sovereigns.'

Thórarinn felt for the key at his side. It was a secret that his father had given him the key. But it could hardly do any harm were he to show that it fitted the lock. He took the key from his pocket, went to the timber door and unlocked it. The padlock fell open. The man took the lock off its hasp and opened the door. The spacious interior appeared, and a rough concrete staircase leading up to the second floor.

'Why is the building cut away in the middle like that?'

'There's to be a moving staircase.'

'A moving staircase, ha!' This information seemed to make the man annoyed for some reason. Under the space where the moving staircase was to be, there was timber and a pile of debris that had been thrown down from the upper floors.

The man walked up the stairs. It made Thórarinn uneasy that the man had got into the building. He followed him up. The second floor had been Hoovered, and in the middle of the floor stood a vacuum cleaner.

'We ought to go down and lock up. We're not supposed to be here. Father will be mad.'

'There's no hurry. It's warm and cosy in here.'

'Yes, they put in the heating last week,' said Thórarinn.

He went over to a window in the warmth from the radiators. He looked out. The sun was shining palely over the roofs. There were tiny splashes of cement on the window.

The bicycle was in its place by the wall. He grew anxious and turned round. Behind him the man stood with his legs wide apart, his arms outstretched.

WINTER

IV

1

'Our son was working as a delivery boy this summer.' Sunneva sat on the edge of her chair, the words coming out in a rush. 'When he hadn't come back to the shop by about three, the shopkeeper telephoned us. My husband answered. We'd been out the night before. It was the firm's dinner. I'd just gone to fetch the vacuum cleaner from the department store.'

'The new building at Vitatorg? Where he was found . . .?' The superintendent hammered on the typewriter.

'Yes, his father rang the boy's grandparents. They live in the west end of town. Then he rang the Melavöllur football stadium. Nothing bad has ever happened to any of our children.'

The policeman looked at Sigurbjörn. They knew each other slightly. Sunneva took out a cigarette. 'You're chainsmoking, girl,' muttered Sigurbjörn. He said he had walked down to Grundarstígur to look for the bicycle. He'd been there with the boy a few weeks back. 'Tóti had told me about some poor frightened woman who lived there with her husband, a trawlerman. It was the first place I thought of going. I've no idea why, Arnbjörn.' He thought for a moment. 'I had nowhere else to go. The door was open, there wasn't anyone there, and the place was in a terrible mess. I telephoned home from a nearby kiosk and our daughter told me that her mother was in casualty with the boy.'

'That was where we picked up the suspect this evening, on Grundarstígur.' The policeman carried on typing. 'He's the brother-in-law of the woman who used to live there. She moved out some time ago.'

Arnbjörn rummaged among his papers. Sunneva crossed her legs.

Arnbjörn read from a report: '"Police officers 46 and 40 were summoned to attend the incident. They arrived at 29b Grundarstígur at six twenty." When did you arrive at the new building?' He was looking at Sunneva.

'A minute or two before four.'

'Could you tell me what you found there?'

Sunneva looked out of the window. Arnbjörn waited, his hands poised over the typewriter.

'He was on the floor,' she said, almost harshly.

'Was the boy unconscious?'

'No, he was mumbling something.'

'Haven't you got the doctor's report?' asked Sigurbjörn. His face was puffy, and he was staring at the policeman.

'Yes, we do have a medical report, but as your wife was the first person to arrive on the scene, her statement is very important.' Arnbjörn looked at Sunneva and waited.

'One of his eyes was very bruised. His cheek was swollen, and he had a bruise at the corner of his mouth.'

'What about his clothes? Were they torn?'

'He wasn't wearing his trousers.' Sunneva did not dare look at Sigurbjörn, but could feel him staring at her.

The policeman typed briskly. 'I must ask you to excuse me.' He looked at his watch. 'I have to leave you for a moment.'

When they were alone Sunneva put her hand on the back of Sigurbjörn's. He got to his feet, picked up his cup of coffee and walked over to the window. In the garden below there was a small red pavilion with a green roof. The building they were in, 11 Fríkirkju-vegur, was very fine, the first real villa in Reykjavík, built by the business tycoon Thor Jensen in 1908. Sigurbjörn had often dreamed of seeing inside. The floor was constructed of matched planks, two inches thick. It had one of the most beautiful bay windows in town and Borgundholm granite up the staircases. Now its upper floors housed the Police Headquarters.

The clouds had cleared, and the waves on Lake Tjörnin were glittering in the sunlight. Outside Hljómskálinn some men were loading timber on to a truck, the wooden scaffolding that had blown down during the morning. By the bridge the northerly gale was driving the water up on to the shore of the lake. In spite of the fierce wind there was a strange stillness about the sky, as though it were a painted backdrop. He looked down at the windowsill and saw that a bubble of yellow resin had broken through the coat of white varnish. The wood was still alive after half a century. Sigurbjörn looked across at the cemetery on Sudurgata and could feel his father's presence. Helgi Vésteinsson had had a plot reserved for himself beside his parents, and sometimes he and Sigurbjörn had gone together to tend the grave. Helgi would stand there for a long time, looking at his own patch of earth with a sombre expression on his face. His son grinned mirthlessly at the memory. A swan rose up from Lake Tjörnin, beating its wings.

'Women always get their own way,' he said, watching the bird.

'What's that?' Arnbjörn looked at him, and sat down.

'You're not going to make her go through it all in detail, are you?' Sigurbjörn turned round.

'Only as much as she can bear to.'

There was not a great deal to add. She had dressed her son as best she could, run and called out to a stranger who had helped her carry Thórarinn downstairs. By then he had more or less regained consciousness. 'Then I tried to ring you, my dear, as soon as I came to myself,' she whispered to her husband. He was still standing at the window.

Sigurbjörn swung round and brought his fist down hard on the corner of the desk. 'Last spring I begged you to let the boy stay at home, woman. Are you out of your mind? Why didn't you tell me all this before?'

'You didn't want to know, Sigurbjörn,' she said quietly, her eyes lowered. 'Please sit down, for my sake.'

He sat down and looked at a large framed aerial photograph of the police station in Pósthússtræti on the wall behind the desk. The policeman watched him. 'May I?' Arnbjörn took a cigarette from Sunneva's packet on the corner of the desk.

'You've searched the building site?' Sigurbjörn asked, after a long pause.

'Yes, but we didn't find anything.'

'Nothing to go on?'

'Only a few drops of blood on the floor.'

'Yes, one of his ears was bleeding quite a lot,' said Sunneva, quickly. 'I was going to go and wash the floor there yesterday.'

'How did the boy get in? Wasn't the building locked?'

'No, I remember that I gave him a key the night before. I don't know what I was thinking of,' Sigurbjörn said, looking at his palms. 'I was drunk.' When Arnbjörn did not help him out, he looked up and said, 'It's not often I get drunk nowadays.'

'My husband hasn't taken a drink for ten years . . .' said Sunneva.

Arnbjörn interrupted her. 'This case will now be taken over by the state. That means that it'll be a public, not a private prosecution. If you want to make a claim for compensation at some later date, of course you have the right to.' He went on typing for a while.

'What's the man's name?' Sunneva asked as he took the sheet of paper out of the typewriter.

'Ketill Einarsson. But don't say I told you.'

'How did the police know they'd find him on Grundarstígur?' asked Sigurbjörn.

'It's the second time he's committed this sort of crime,' said Arnbjörn. 'He'd been watching the other boy for a long time too. I'm afraid it's been the same in this case.'

'And you let maniacs like him loose?'

'He'd served his sentence.' Arnbjörn looked at Sigurbjörn. 'There was no option but to set him free.'

'Eighteen months is no sentence at all for such a crime,' said Sunneva.

'You're probably not the only one to think so,' said Arnbjörn, checking over his report. 'However, that incident was not quite as serious as this one.'

'They're far too young to be allowed to start work, these boys,' said Sigurbjörn. 'Far too young.'

'May I read it over to you?'

Arnbjörn read them the report right through, and then placed it in front of Sunneva with a fountain pen. 'Sign at the bottom.'

Standing at the corner of the desk, Sunneva signed her name.

'He'll be inside a bit longer this time,' said Sigurbjörn. 'And when he gets out I'll kill him.'

The policeman did not look at him, and made no comment.

'Please, for God's sake, don't be like this, Sigurbjörn, I've got a headache, we've enough problems as it is.' Sunneva put the tip of a finger to one eye.

'I suspect the sentence will be heavier this time,' said Arnbjörn. 'I think that's on the cards.'

'Where's he being held?' asked Sunneva. 'We are safe, aren't we?'

'Safe? What are you talking about, woman?' Sigurbjörn muttered.

'Well, as a rule remand prisoners are kept in custody in the gaol on Skólavördustígur until they're convicted and sentenced. That'll probably be quite soon. Then most likely he'll be transferred to Litla-Hraun to serve his time.' Arnbjörn got to his feet and held out his hand. 'Thank you for coming. I'm very sorry about what's happened.'

Sigurbjörn handed the car keys to Sunneva and walked in the opposite direction from her away out of Hallargardur Gardens.

'Shouldn't we go together?' Sunneva said.

He shook his head without looking round.

2

When Sigurbjörn came home, there was a stranger waiting for him at the front door. He wanted Sigurbjörn to design a house for him. He was the first client to have called for months. Sigurbjörn invited him down to the basement, listened to his ideas and promised to give the matter his attention.

When they'd finished, he followed the man out. He had been listening to the man as if he was miles away. His mind was beginning to picture Thórarinn as he must have looked when Sunneva had found him.

He lay down on the bed without getting undressed and pulled Sunneva's quilt on top of his own. Gradually it got dark outside, the sky turned blue, and still he felt no warmer. On the way home he had been aware of a smell of decay from the gardens.

'Father, there's a man come to speak to you.' Vilborg was knocking at his door.

'Oh Lord, who is it?'

'I think it's a priest.'

Astonished, Sigurbjörn tumbled out of bed. A large young man with snow-white hair and a full black beard was standing looking at the Kjarval painting. The two men shook hands. The priest introduced himself and Sigurbjörn asked him to sit down at the parlour table. 'I was asked to call in on you,' said the priest.

'Oh? And who asked you to do that, my good man? My mother? I didn't say I wanted to see a priest,' Sigurbjörn grumbled.

'No, it was Arnbjörn of the Police.'

Vilborg was hovering by the spiral staircase, curious.

'Vilborg, my dear, go upstairs and do your homework. Leave us alone.'

He listened for the sound of Vilborg's footsteps on the staircase and said nothing until she had gone upstairs. The day's newspapers lay on the table, but he could not bring himself to read them. 'We don't need any help from anyone else,' he said. 'My mother may be a pillar of the Church but it's years since I lost my faith, if I ever had one. That's why I thought it was her who'd sent you.'

'Who is your mother?' asked the priest.

Sigurbjörn told the priest about his mother and Jóhannes. 'He was accounted a very clever man, my brother. He was a doctor of theology, but he died the summer before he was due to be ordained. The Heavenly Father made a big mistake there, in my opinion. He just withered away. Our doctor, Matthías Einarsson, thought he would have to have an operation. I took him to be examined at St Joseph's Hospital . . .' Sigurbjörn drew a deep breath. 'He couldn't walk any more, the poor old chap, so I had to carry him out to the car. Two old witches stopped and stared.' Sigurbjörn looked hard at the priest and said, with passion, 'And he never left the house from that day on. When I came home from my studies in the summer of 1929 I went to his graveside. I was thinking about that today at the police station, that there was no one there in the cemetery. The old woman had him buried beside my brother Jóhannes at Fossvogur.' He snorted bitterly. 'Women always get their own way.'

'What were you studying abroad?' The priest lit a cigarette, his fleshy cheek wrinkling as he brought the flame close.

'Architecture. My mother pushed me through secondary school. She was on the parish council of Hallgrímskirkja right from the beginning.' He laughed his mirthless laugh. 'Then, when I was in my first year studying architecture at Copenhagen Academy of Art, I got a letter from her. At that time I was with Professor Nyrop – he designed the Town Hall in Copenhagen. Bloody Nyrop, he certainly made Gudjón Samúelsson's life a misery,' he said morosely. 'There was a competition to design the Hallgrímskirkja and she wanted me to give it a go.' Sigurbjörn shook his head over his mother's ambition for him. 'And I did it,' he said. 'I designed a church. How ridiculous, a first-year student. But what a church it was! This was at about the same time I met my Sunna.' He fell silent and looked sorrowfully at his large hands. 'And what are you priests expected to say to a person?'

'Well, not much, but people often find it good to have someone to talk to.'

They were silent for a while. A gust of wind caught the house, making the leaves brush against the window. 'What does He want now?' asked Sigurbjörn.

'The Lord?' The priest looked at him and Sigurbjörn nodded. 'If people like that don't repent they'll probably get what's coming to them,' he said, exhaling smoke. 'Well, and a lot depends on whether the victim asks the Lord to forgive the person who's hurt him. That's probably what he means when he asks us to love our enemies.'

'Oh, is that right?' said Sigurbjörn, growing animated. 'Then it's all up to me.'

'Well, who's to say?' said the priest, doubtfully.

'You've got that right.' Sigurbjörn looked him up and down. The priest's bushy eyebrows were pitch black, even though his hair was snow-white. He was looking straight at Sigurbjörn, stroking the end of his black beard. This reminded the architect of an old painting of Mephistopheles he'd seen in an art gallery. Sigurbjörn laughed. 'Well, my friend,' he said. 'You ought to drop in on the wife. She's up at casualty with the boy. I'm sure she'll welcome you with open arms. She's a Christian. Not like me. And ask her to phone home.' He followed the priest to the door, laughing his dry laugh.

The satisfaction he had got from the conversation did not last long. Sunneva phoned a little later. The priest had come and gone. The boy was asleep. She was going to stay overnight at the hospital. An extra bed had been brought in for Thórarinn. She asked about Vilborg.

'The girl's fast asleep.'

'You left me alone in Hallargardur Gardens.'

'Sunneva, we are both tired and not feeling too good.'

'Try to eat something.'

'I've eaten enough for one day, thanks,' said her husband, now in a temper. 'How's the boy?'

'As well as can be expected. They've given him something to help him sleep.'

He went upstairs and opened the door of his daughter's room. She was sitting on the bed, reading a book. She looked at him solemnly, stroking the quilt with her fingertips. 'Tóti's worse than you said he was. Isn't he, Father?'

'Yes.'

'Is he going to die?'

'No, no. He'll be home in a day or so.'

'What happened?' she asked, hesitantly.

'I can't tell you now, Vilborg. Your father's worn out. Be a good lass and go to bed soon.'

'Shall I put the lights out downstairs?'

'No, Helgi'll take care of that when he comes home. Have you managed to eat anything?'

'Yes.'

Sigurbjörn went back to bed, fully clothed. A violent squall lashed the windows; he could hear the wind roaring in the trees. The telephone rang. Vilborg rushed downstairs and answered it. She spoke for a long time; it must be Gudbjörg, she almost seemed to have moved in with them now. A little later he heard a car and loud voices. One of the heroic sportsmen was bringing Helgi home. He came upstairs, opened the door and said, 'Father?' Sigurbjörn pretended to be asleep.

He heard Helgi opening and closing the refrigerator and walking from room to room. Then Helgi went to his own room, and gradually the house grew quiet. 'I should never have dragged him out of his den in the basement,' Sigurbjörn thought. 'Helgi's a bit too old to be up here with the rest of the children.' He looked at his alarm clock, it said half past ten. He lay there for a long time half asleep. The next time he looked at the clock, it said half past two. He clambered out of bed, went into the bathroom, poured a glass of water and rinsed his mouth. His face looked ugly in the mirror, and the harsh electric light in the bathroom hurt his eyes. Helgi had turned down the radiators and it was cold.

They're working round the clock on the plumbing down at the site, thought Sigurbjörn. The work mustn't be held up. It's just the same as any other bloody building. He had walked around the courtyard of the department store with Gudbrandur that morning. Gudbrandur had not asked him any questions, but Sigurbjörn thought he could sense pity in his manner. The men were tense and silent as he looked round the shelter door. Were they waiting to see if he would be man enough to go up to the second floor?

He went down into the basement to look over the designs to set his mind at rest. He spread one of them out on the table: basement, storage area, lift for up to eight people, ventilation system and electrical wiring, all agreed at a meeting of the Buildings and Works

Committee of the City Council on 29 August 1953. 'It would be easy enough for me to install the electricity myself,' he muttered, got to his feet, ran a finger along the bookshelf and took out Audel's *Handy Book of Practical Electricity*. Here was everything anyone would ever need to know about electrical wiring. He looked up the chapter on neon lighting. It would be good to have a neon sign over the entrance: THE REYKJAVÍK DEPARTMENT STORE. He heard a heavy book fall against its neighbour. He looked at its spine. It was the Bible.

He picked up the book, felt its weight, and opened it. Oslo 1924. The Norwegian Bible Society Press. He had written his name in very delicate handwriting at the foot of the page. He turned the pages with his thumb. Some verses were marked in red. He sat down at the writing desk. He had underlined passages where he had had difficulty in coming to terms with the text. He peered at some of these verses and read for a long time. 'For if ye forgive men their trespasses, your heavenly Father will also forgive you. But if ye forgive not men their trespasses, neither will your Father forgive your trespasses.'

'Is God not greater than me, then?' Sigurbjörn, full of fury, asked the room. 'Is God not greater than me?' he said loudly. 'Am I to kiss the hand that killed my child?'

He rushed upstairs, brought down his shotgun, and put some cartridges from the cupboard in his pocket. He put on a thick overcoat and his peaked cap and went out. Mist gleamed raw and wet in the streets. A cat crossed at the corner of Freyjagata without paying him the slightest attention.

There were lights on in the top floor of the gaol. Sigurbjörn stood on the other side of the street and looked at the building. A man came by the worse for drink. 'What, going fishing in the middle of the night?' Sigurbjörn looked at him blankly and then realized the man thought he had a fishing rod in the bag. He said, coarsely, 'Get the hell out of my way.'

'OK, OK. I didn't mean any harm,' the drunk said. Sigurbjörn watched him go. It was dark at the end of the street. How many times had he thought about the Hallgrímskirkja, which was still waiting to be built? There were plans to illuminate the church tower with electric light. All at once he realized who had assaulted the boy. It was the man who had been sitting under the statue of Leif Eiríksson that spring when he and Thórarinn were walking over the hill. 'He was looking at Thórarinn,' said Sigurbjörn out loud. 'He was looking at my boy.'

He eased the bag down below the magazine, took two cartridges out of his pocket and loaded them. Then he pulled the bag back up over the barrel but didn't draw up the cord. He walked purposefully over to the other side of the street and banged heavily on the door. After a while he heard the jingling of keys, and a tall thin man appeared in the gap.

The gaoler looked first at the man and then down at the gun bag. Then he looked him in the eye. The gaoler thought the man looked drunk. He asked drily, 'Have you lost your way, my friend?'

Sigurbjörn moved away from the door without saying a word and went home.

3

The snow was tumbling off the roofs, smothering Njardargata. The boy woke up and peeped out of the window. A car was stuck in a drift. Another was sounding its horn. There was frozen snow on the dovecote. The snowstorm blew about the street, graceful, dancing. He had stood by the window, looking at his bicycle, and heard the man's breathing. The snowstorm swirled across a drift on the pavement and then solidified in the garden like a hand. The man had stood behind him with outstretched arms as if he was herding sheep.

He lay back in bed and tried to go back to sleep, but he could not sleep any more. He heard his sister out in the passage. She had begun attending the Women's College as though nothing had happened. Her friend Gudbjörg came to the doorway and peeped in. 'Get the hell out of here and shut the door behind you!' he bellowed. 'Get out!'

Sunneva came running up the stairs.

Was it a bad man he had met? No, the man was his friend, and kind. They had met by chance in the street, old friends, and the man had wanted to give Thórarinn some gold sovereigns so he could buy anything he wanted in the shop, but Thórarinn was ungrateful and wanted more money. Was it any wonder the man got angry? Yesterday the man had come and apologized for having lost his temper, and had asked Sigurbjörn and Sunneva to forgive him for having hit Thórarinn. They had made it up with the man and called Thórarinn down, and he too had forgiven him. Sigurbjörn had made a big joke of the whole affair. It transpired that the man was a marvellous cook. It so fell out that a leg of lamb was thawing in the refrigerator. The man didn't hang about, but cooked it there and then, making a particularly fine sauce to go with it. They had all enjoyed themselves far into the evening, laughing like the best of friends. As it happened, Thórarinn had babbled some rubbish or other, and the man had looked at him kindly and said, 'Don't talk nonsense.' He said his name was Ketill. And Thórarinn bade him farewell at the door with these words: 'Goodbye for now, Ketill. Come and see us again soon.' Ketill kissed him on the cheek and ran the palm of one hand over the boy's chest.

He remembered the splashes of cement on the window. 'I must go downstairs! Someone might steal my bicycle!' he had shouted. There was a sour smell from the man's mouth. Thórarinn had been shouting for his father. 'I shouldn't have been wasting time like that looking at the aeroplane,' he thought. 'I got punished for it.' Then he sat up in bed. The rowan tree was bare. The veil of snow was trying to find its way out into the street. It swirled across the drift in the garden and spilled over the wall. The wind took its time, coiling itself around the street like a snake. 'I won't go to school,' Thórarinn thought. The Black List was in its place in the chest-of-drawers. Enemy of the State No. 1: Gudbrandur.

Everyone must know that something nasty had happened. So a few gold sovereigns had been found in a package in some timber down at the docks, had they? That was what it said in the newspapers. What was so terrible about that? Nothing had happened. It was nice to be in a pleasant room. It was warm and cosy.

'I can't go back to school. I want to go to another school, you saw how Gudbjörg stared at me.'

'But Reykjavík is such a small town.' Sunneva sat down on the bed. 'Reykjavík is such a small town, my darling Tóti.'

He woke up in the middle of the night to the sound of sleet on the windowpane, but it was not the weather that had woken him.

'Calm down, Father! I'm telling you to calm down, do you hear?' Helgi shouted. 'Don't touch her!'

Footsteps running up the stairs. A scream. Who was screaming? Had Helgi gone mad? Thórarinn rushed out of his room to help Sigurbjörn. Vilborg stood in the passage like a ghost. Sigurbjörn was sitting alone in the darkness of the parlour, staring in front of him, more drunk than when he had staggered along by Lake Tjörnin, not answering when anyone spoke to him. Sunneva was standing at the kitchen sink in a torn nightgown, weeping.

'You'll have to divorce the bloody man, Mother. You'll have to divorce him,' Helgi kept saying. 'That's the only thing you can do.'

When Thórarinn came back into the parlour, Sigurbjörn had gone, and the front door was open. A crescent moon lit up the frozen vista. There was snow on the trees. The light caught the crystalline icicle above the door.

Sigurbjörn vanished for two days. Sunneva thought of having a radio announcement put out for him. She telephoned Gudbrandur. She telephoned the police; he had spent one night in the cells. The day after, Helgi saw him with the drunks on Hafnarstræti. The falling snow wrapped itself around Thórarinn's window like a soft quilt.

Sigurbjörn suddenly appeared in the workmen's shelter looking the worse for wear. He drank brennivín from the bottle and chatted to the quiet group of men. His hands were bruised and torn and the men stared at their sandwiches and sipped their coffee nervously. Only Gudbrandur tried to keep the conversation going. Sigurbjörn looked out of the door. The sun was shining on the icy ground. The snow had swirled across a rusty bundle of metal rods and frozen solid. He looked at this for a long time, clenching and unclenching his fist. He vaguely remembered having hit the sharp, jagged surface of a seashell-covered wall in a terrible snowstorm in the middle of the night.

Around noon, Gudbrandur went to the state liquor store. Sigurbjörn waited in the shelter and dragged him off on a drunken binge. They took a taxi to Óldugata.

'We're both carpenters, Gudbrandur, working men. We've done our duty,' Sigurbjörn said, banging his hand down on the parlour table. 'A building like that has never been put up in Iceland in such a short time, and it's all because of you, my friend! You stood by me. You risked everything.'

The light faded from the window and with the darkness came cold and snow. Light, downy flakes blew against the pane, and Sigurbjörn's mood changed with the weather. Ingirídur came home with the children and cooked lamb cutlets, boiled potatoes, green peas. Sigurbjörn could not eat much, ran outside and threw up. He forced more brennivín down, and as the evening wore on he cursed Sunneva for having forced the boy to take a summer job against his, Sigurbjörn's, will. 'The damned woman can go to hell for all I care.' He confided to Gudbrandur that he was no damned architect at all. 'What does the Creator want?' he asked. 'What does he want? I must have sinned terribly, Gudbrandur,' he said sorrowfully.

They both got blind drunk and Ingirídur made up a bed for Sigurbjörn in the guest room. He refused to sleep there and went out into the blizzard, swaying on his feet.

She had taken a photograph of them, and was shocked when she got the film back from the developers. Gudbrandur was pouring whisky into his glass, smiling blissfully, but Sigurbjörn had hidden nothing from the camera. He was staring straight ahead, and the look in his eyes frightened Ingirídur.

'I'll have to help the man,' said Gudbrandur, when he saw the photograph. 'Old Sigurbjörn is my friend, Inga.'

Helgi lay awake night after night, listening to his parents rowing. Did neither of them notice what a bad way Thórarinn was in? Vilborg appeared in the doorway in her nightgown. 'Helgi, I'm afraid. That's a terrible sound.'

'I know all about that,' he muttered, sitting upright in his bed, remembering many a night from his boyhood. He had quite seriously considered killing the guilty party. He had the feeling that the people at the bank knew what had happened. The whole town knew it.

He was on his way to the bank when he noticed a stranger looking at him from a car window. 'He knows I'm Tóti's brother,' he thought, watching the car move off. 'That's why he was grinning.' The car stopped at a corner and Helgi very nearly ran to catch it up. 'I'm getting as crazy as Father,' he muttered. 'That chap has seen me at the stadium or read about me in the papers. It's not every day that Iceland scores a goal against the French.'

He went over the goal in his mind. He had been very disappointed that it had not attracted more attention from abroad. He still hoped that one of the directors of the Football Union would phone: 'We've had a letter. They want you to go to the Racing Club de Paris. Albert is going to pave your way in France.'

'A talent the like of this has not been seen since Albert Gudmunds-son was playing football here in France,' a major daily newspaper in Paris had said after the game, but that was as far as it went. Helgi was determined to follow in Albert's footsteps, even outdo him. 'I've got all it takes,' he thought, 'the technique and flair, the ability to kick hard, the stamina, the iron will. I can become the best, and I'm going to be the best. I'm good at heading and my tackling is strong. Helgi Solo, the White Pearl.'

He tried not to let the atmosphere at home have any effect on him. He dreamed of playing for Arsenal, Leeds or Liverpool, of lobbing a ball from midfield into the corner of the goal in the last minute of the Wembley Cup final, of becoming one of the best players in England, 'I can do anything with a ball. Football is my architecture,' he liked to think. 'Alex James, pack your bags.'

What could be better than scoring a goal, trotting off to the dressing room, having small boys flock around you, in ecstasy because they've actually managed to touch you? He thought of Thórarinn, and a shiver ran through him.

Ragnar came on Thórarinn's birthday, dandling his small daughter on his knee. Her name was Rúna. She was blond, like her mother, and wanted to touch everything. She got halfway into the crockery cupboard. 'Leave that alone, you wretched child!' Sunneva burst out. 'Oh, Ragnar, you'll have to forgive me, I don't know what's come over us all.'

He tried to comfort her and took her in his arms. 'How is he?'

She shook her head.

'I've just bought a van and started work as a driver.' He led her over to the window.

She looked at the blue-grey roof of the van. November was nearly over.

Thórarinn blew out twelve candles and was given some lavish presents. Sunneva would have to go along with his wish to change schools. It was her, wasn't it, who'd refused to let him have a holiday, against Sigurbjörn's wishes?

Freysteinn the shop assistant knocked on the door. There was snow on his shoulders and a parcel in his arms. There was all sorts of confectionery crammed into the box, a whole carton of chocolate wafers, a crate of Coca-cola. 'So you got the goodies and the bloody Coke, did you, little king?' said Geir on the telephone. 'Now mind you don't give yourself a tummy ache.'

'Try and make it last, Thórarinn,' said his mother.

'Oh, shut your trap,' the boy snarled.

Ragnar looked down in embarrassment, and Sigurbjörn flushed scarlet. They were all sitting at the birthday table. Vilborg looked superior, but she kept silent.

Thórarinn carried the box up to his room. His ear was ringing. The man had struck him on the head. 'Where do you think you're going?' the man had said, mocking him. 'There's no rush. It's warm and cosy here.'

'It'll end in murder,' muttered Sigurbjörn. 'It's the way it'll have to be, Sunna. It'll end in murder. I can't live with this. I can't breathe. I'll kill the man as soon as he gets out. No one's going to be allowed to live after doing something like that to my child.'

'Well, kill him then,' she said. 'But stop talking about it all the time.'

There was darkness outside the window, a sickle moon. A cat walked step by step across the frozen snow, its eyes glittering. Sigurbjörn drew the curtain.

'If anyone betrayed him you did, Sigurbjörn. You know it's true. You could have put your foot down, but you had to use me to get the land.'

'What are you talking about? I built this bloody department store for my family, didn't I?'

'But you never say who let him have the key.'

'Don't forget, Sunna, who dragged him out of bed on the last day of his summer holidays,' he said. 'Don't forget that.'

'I don't think I'll ever be allowed to forget it.' She went ceaselessly over the dream in her mind: Sjafnargata had been wrapped in a black shroud; that meant sorrow. The big rowan had withered; was that the boy? But how was she to interpret the rest of the dream? She had seen a storm break over the Reykjavík Department Store, the outer walls fall away and the wind blowing through the interior of the building, ripping everything apart.

'It blew through the interior, did you say, woman? The morning before the floor-space was sold there was the devil of a gale out in the bay. I was wandering about alone on the roof. But I don't believe in dreams; they're just nonsense,' Sigurbjörn said. Yet puzzling over the dream made him feel better. A black shroud! They most certainly hadn't had to wait long for the sorrow. He had himself had many dreams these last weeks, some of them of a kind that couldn't be discussed with anyone. Strange! What did it mean that the outer walls had fallen away? Did it mean all the shops would go bust?

Sigurbjörn roamed through the streets, his cheeks sunken, his hands in his pockets. When he noticed that curtains were twitching in the houses on the street, he stayed indoors and went out only when it was dark. He sat in the basement, turning the pages of old books. He stumbled on a quotation from Alexander the Great: 'To conquer the world is no great feat. But to conquer oneself! He that succeeds in doing that is divine.' 'I can handle this,' he muttered grimly, and tried to do a little work on the house he had been asked to design.

Gudbrandur came to discuss business. They were down in the basement. 'There are one or two things that have to be cleared through customs. You'll have to look after it, Sigurbjörn. I'm not used to taking care of things like that.'

'Let's wait. There's no hurry. Christmas is coming.' Sigurbjörn read aloud the words of Alexander the Great. Gudbrandur looked at him, surprised. 'Are you serious, Sigurbjörn? Do you think these things are important?'

'You ought to read Rousseau's *Confessions*, Brandsi. That book would open your eyes.' Sigurbjörn wore the same expression he had when the glass in the windows hadn't fitted.

'I can't be seen in public any more, Sunna,' he said. They were standing in the garden. She was sprinkling breadcrumbs on the frozen snow and snow buntings were cascading down from the trees.

'I don't want to listen to this,' she said angrily. 'The boy isn't dead.'

After all, it was she who had found Thórarinn . . . The new building open, the wooden door left ajar . . . Amazingly careless, she had thought, and felt cross. The padlock was lying in the sand. She had picked it up and hung it on the hasp. She looked around the first floor, the grey, chilly interiors, where the floors had not yet been cleaned. The expensive appliance would be ruined; no vacuum cleaner could tolerate such treatment; the man could be incredibly stupid . . . She had gone up to the second floor. She had stood over Thórarinn for a moment before taking off her coat and covering him with it.

4

Helgi had gone to sleep with his bedroom window open. He was woken by the sound of the wind at about three. He sat up in bed and lifted the curtain to see a blizzard raging outside. He went downstairs and put the telephone on a chair at the foot of the stairs. He expected Ragnar to phone early to say the trip was off, but when he woke at six the weather was dead calm. It was Sunday morning. They were going shooting grouse. Helgi had asked his father if he wanted to come with them, and was thoroughly relieved when Sigurbjörn said he did not feel up to it. He brewed some coffee, made a few sandwiches and got his shotgun from the gun cupboard. He moved about silently so as not to disturb anyone. He enjoyed being alone. On the dot of eight Ragnar sounded his horn.

He was reading a newspaper and had his back towards the house. Helgi opened the rear door, heard the sound of the car heater, and threw his bag on the floor. He settled the end of the barrel between the seat and the gearbox. His brother folded up the newspaper, stuffed it out of the way and looked up at the building. Helgi had a suspicion he was reckoning how much the Sjafnargata house might fetch.

'What's the news with SS?' asked Ragnar.

'Southern Slaughterers? Do you need to ask? They fight tooth and nail like mad dogs. If I wasn't there he'd have killed her by now.'

'Mother? What for?'

'He blames her for the whole thing.'

'What?'

'Poor Tóti doesn't get a look in,' said Helgi.

'How is Tóti?'

'The boy's unbearable. I don't know why they don't try to put a stop to his tantrums.'

'What?'

'He's making Mother's life a misery, and she fusses around him morning, noon and night. Oh, let's not talk about it. Can I have a look at the newspaper?'

Ragnar put the indicator on and pulled out into the street. Hringbraut was empty and black with dirty slush. The going got heavier when they reached Selás. As they drove over the ridge to Raudavatn, they could see the ice-covered lake gleaming in the moonlight. They turned east round the lake. Snow drifting off the ice made for difficult driving on the winding road, so Ragnar changed into a lower gear and kept the revs high. The Mercedes Benz slid to and fro. Helgi was hunched over the newspaper. Ragnar took his sunglasses out of the glove compartment. The hard-frozen field on their right sparkled. The yellow rim of daybreak illuminated Mount Vífilsfell in the east.

'Well, the world and his wife gets his picture in the paper,' said Helgi. 'This chap was at school with me.' He held the paper open and showed his brother. 'He's a lunatic. I remember him only too well.'

'Doesn't everyone want to be in the newspaper? You're in the papers every other day. "The only one whose talent approaches that of Albert Gudmundsson." "Our next great star to play overseas."'

'You've got to have the chance to show what you can do. Don't be an idiot, Ragnar. Can you see me running on the pitch for Nottingham Forest?'

'Why not? Isn't that what you want?' Ragnar looked at his brother. 'I'm just teasing you. Can't you take a joke? You can't say anything to these guys,' he murmured to himself as he squinted into the rear-view mirror.

The yellow rim above the mountain had turned gold. The sky against it was violet beneath a red sheen, the vault of heaven was black, the land a phosphorescent white.

'The sauce brings out the grouse's innermost essence,' Ragnar added. 'Once I was driving near here when I hit a patch of loose gravel. I went into a terrible sideways skid. A Land-Rover was coming towards me, and I crashed straight into it. The door flew open and I went sailing out and ended up on my arse by the side of the road. I was sitting there on my backside, not knowing where I was. When I looked up and who should come hopping towards me but the farmer from the jeep. His leg was broken, and the broken leg was dangling from the knee. He'd got a pack of cigars and kept shouting, as he hopped, "Do you want a cigar, friend? Do you want a cigar?"'

'You should be thankful you weren't killed that time, Ragnar,' Helgi said, cutting short the familiar story.

Ragnar bounced cheerfully in his seat. At the top of Hellisheidi a gentle wind was blowing a fine veil of snow across the glistening ice. It was nearly daylight.

As Ragnar drove down the Kambar cliffs, the sun was rising in the sky and the county of Árnes gleamed below it. 'I said the weather would be fine.' Ragnar pointed to the steam rising from the geysers.

'Now we'll simply massacre the grouse at Grímsnes,' said Helgi.

'You're a bastard, you are.'

'In the bastard stakes I don't even run Father close.'

'The architect with the terrifying eyes, Kjarval's bosom buddy,' said Ragnar, sniggering.

'Poor Father, that friendship meant so much to him,' Helgi said.

'Do you remember when that drunk staggered into the garden and broke the nose off the figurehead? The master builder's skilled hands tried to carve her a new nose, but he couldn't do it. He went and got Kjarval, who immediately carved this very fine nose, just like that. But Father had to make a joke of it. He said, "Maestro! I will see to it that, when we are both dead and the Kjarval Museum is open, there is a clause in my will instructing my sons to remove the nose from the figurehead, put it on a small velvet cushion, put the cushion in a glass case and take it as a gift to the Kjarval Museum with the condition that the glass case should stand on a pedestal in the entrance hall, with the following inscription: '*Nose*, by Jóhannes Kjarval'."' Ragnar smiled as he pushed his sunglasses up on to his forehead.

'And what did Kjarval make of that?'

'He just laughed.'

'Being ordinary was never quite good enough for Father,' said Helgi.

A lorry drove past on its way to Reykjavík, a few links of snow-chain hanging loose from a rear wheel, singing as it struck the road. Ragnar turned inland towards Ingólfsfjall. The rocks beneath the mountain were tipped with white. The rapid thaw of a few days earlier had melted much of the snow, and here and there on the meadows a tuft of grass could be seen. They drove across the bridge at Thrastarlund, the Sog below them sluggish and black. Helgi saw a grouse in the brushwood right by the side of the road. 'Stop! Grouse.'

Ragnar slowed the car. The grouse sat dead still under a birch sapling. It looked like a clay pigeon in a shop window. Helgi reached for the key and turned the engine off. Ragnar wound his window down very carefully. The silence flowed in, ice-cold. The grouse sat motionless.

Helgi reached for the shotgun case, undid the fastening and took out the warmly familiar gun. He loaded it, got out of the car, and slipped the safety catch off. He was raising the gun to aim when Ragnar suddenly tapped his fingers on the windscreen and whispered, 'Let me do it, I'm sure I can hit it.' Helgi lowered the shotgun. Ragnar moved behind the car. Still the grouse did not move. Ragnar took his gun out of its case, loaded it, leaned against the car and fired. He missed. The grouse flew away, first whirling its wings, then letting them droop, gliding in a wide semi-circle. Soon it began to beat its wings again, fast and heavily, and disappeared over the river in the direction of the mountain. It got smaller and smaller, and in a little while it could not be seen above the whiteness of the land.

Helgi got into the car with his shotgun across his knees. 'You're not the handiest of chaps when it comes to hunting, are you?'

'I hit a goose by the side of the road the other day. It raised its wings, screaming. We drove right at it and shot it in the breast out of the car window. It's a long time since I've been so unlucky.'

'Let's go on.' Helgi looked left and right and saw another bird sitting in philosophical calm in the red-brown heather by a sapling. The brothers saw the grouse fix them with its dark brown eyes.

'Its winter plumage isn't much use to it now,' said Helgi.

Ragnar carefully opened the car door, took the shotgun from behind the seat, smiled and put one foot on the road. 'I think it's my turn,' muttered Helgi, and nipped out of the van. Ragnar was still taking aim when Helgi fired over his shoulder. The bird flopped over, dead. Ragnar rammed an open palm up against his right ear, jumped to his feet and with one hand grabbed his brother by the collar and flung him against the car, his fist raised. 'Have you gone stark staring mad? Do you want to kill me?'

Helgi laughed and held the shotgun away from his body. Ragnar opened his mouth, lost for words, and let him go. Helgi went over to the knoll, put one foot on it and reached for the warm bird. The grouse's breast was bloodstained. He spread the wing out like a fan. It was unharmed. He remembered Ragnar's fiancée. There had been something wild about her. She slept around and Ragnar knew about it. Everybody knew about it. He couldn't work out why it should be such a crime for him to have gone to bed with her. She had said she was leaving Ragnar anyway. It had only been the once.

'You should be glad to be rid of that woman, Ragnar.' Helgi looked at the wing. 'She was crazy.'

'Glad to be rid of her!' said Ragnar, furious. 'We were going to get married. You could always have any woman you wanted. You could have left her alone.'

'It was three years ago.' said Helgi. 'I did you a favour. What's her husband do?'

'Hilmar? He's a lawyer. I don't want to talk about it. Let's go up to Kerid and park the van there,' said Ragnar, still pressing his hand against his ear.

Helgi looked at the brushwood on the way, but he didn't see anything moving.

Ragnar backed the car into a gravel car park and took out a sandwich box. He passed Helgi a meat-paste sandwich and Helgi raised his eyebrows in surprise. 'Want some?'

'I've brought some food of my own. I made a box of sandwiches and filled a thermos this morning.'

'Oh, shut up. I'm used to looking after you.' He gave Helgi the top from the flask, full to the brim with very sweet coffee, and a flatcake with smoked meat.

'It's obvious you've not got a woman living with you at the moment.' Helgi looked at his flatcake. 'No woman would be so lavish with the butter. I've got something for myself, but I'll eat this for you anyway.'

Ragnar gulped down the coffee, grinning sarcastically. 'Do you remember the lad you beat up that time down at Hotel Borg, and then spent the summer torturing when we were working as navvies on the road up here somewhere? You could be a real bastard, couldn't you? Sometimes you surprise me, Helgi. I remember the day the foreman brought you in the car. The expression on the poor lad's face when he saw you. You were waiting for another chance to beat him up,' Ragnar said. 'It was unforgivable.'

'That's all over now,' said Helgi.

'What had he ever done to you?'

'I can't remember any more.' Helgi drank the last of his coffee and got out of the car. There were frozen raindrops in the dead winter grass, the sun was high in the sky, the hard snow glistened.

He put on his spare sweater and tugged the anorak over his head, pulled on a woollen hat, fastened on the cartridge belt, found his gloves, and picked up the shotgun from the front seat. He saw his reflection with the weapon in the windscreen. He brought the gun up to his cheek. He could smell the powder in the magazine.

'Well, you're ready for anything.' Ragnar picked up a mutton-paste sandwich.

'I came here to shoot our Christmas dinner. Not for a picnic. Let's hurry up and get on with it before the place fills up with idiots blasting off in every direction all over the moors.' Helgi looked eastwards. 'You know, I'm certain we could do it.'

'What?'

'Break into Litla-Hraun and kill the bloody pervert.'

'How would you get past the guards?'

'A single knock-out punch, no bother. Haven't you seen me fight? Then you'd hold him down for me while I shot off his balls with this.' He jerked the shotgun at Ragnar. 'Then he'd sing a few octaves higher and no mistake.'

'And spend ten or twelve years in gaol?'

'No one's inside that long in Iceland,' said Helgi. 'I'd be given parole after three or four years, and you'd get off with a caution.'

'Father's the one to go for a crazy plan like that, not me.' Ragnar put the lid on the aluminium sandwich box. It was shaped like a half-moon.

'Let's split up,' said Helgi. 'I'll go that way.' He pointed towards Kerid.

'The forecast is for snow later.'

'It's still very early.' Helgi looked at his wristwatch. 'Let's meet here in two or three hours' time. We must get our Christmas dinner. Grouse is Tóti's favourite.'

When Helgi reached the rim of the crater, he felt a cold breeze blowing towards him from the east. He walked round Kerid. The water covering the bottom of the crater kept constantly changing colour as though light were fragmented down there. He saw one bird, and shot two in quick succession. An hour passed. Nowhere was a grouse to be seen. He heard gunfire in the distance. It sounded like planed pieces of wood being knocked together. He saw another bird. The weather had turned cold and grey. As he lifted the gun, a few flakes of snow fell on the barrel. He fired, but missed. The grouse flew up the side of the crater and stared at him. He fired again, from a distance of only a few yards.

The grouse fell over, its wings flapping frantically. They were still fluttering as he picked it up off the ground. A dark eye was watching him. It was calm, as if it was quite independent of the rest of the bird. He had meant to wring the grouse's neck, but made a mess of it. He put the bird on the ground, picked up a lump of lava and banged it down on the bird's head. The lava was rough and it was difficult to hit the bird with it. Its head was undamaged, the feathers on its throat were ruffled, but the eye still looked steadily at him. In the end he managed to knock the life out of it.

He sat down on a tussock and tied the grouse to his belt. It was out of the wind here, but he could hear it singing loudly down in Kerid crater. He was hot and breathless, shivering from the exertion. It was a long time since he had heard Ragnar's gun. Fear settled on him, and he looked around.

At the top of Kerid a fierce northerly gale was blowing. As Helgi made his way along, a raven came flying towards him, letting the high wind carry it over the rim of the crater. It turned its ragged tail towards him, its talons pressed up against its breast, and cawed. The water had turned black and the wind was lashing it into little eddies.

They met at the car. Ragnar had shot seven birds but had not seen anything move for almost two hours. A black storm was brewing in the east, and the brothers drove back to town.

He fetched the Black List from the chest-of-drawers and sat down at the writing desk that Sigurbjörn had bought new in the middle of September. He tore out the first page with the Enemies of the State on it and flung it into the wastepaper basket. He let the words on the cover remain as they were; anyone who opened the exercise book still did so on pain of death. He looked out of the window. There was a kite stuck in the gutter opposite, its tail fluttering in the wind.

23 November 1953
The weather is very good today. Helgi and Ragnar caught ten grouse yesterday. I have now won a great victory in the battle with my mother. She's got me into Laugarnes School. It would have been better if Father and I had stuck to the decisions we made this spring. I visited Grandfather today and got a very bad stomach ache, which surprised me, and that is why I am making a note of it here. He has some tins of Mackintosh chocolates in his windows and gave me a whole tin. Vilborg is being very kind to me.

1 December 1953
Today I listened to a play on the wireless. It was a bit depressing but very convincing and realistic. A woman killed herself. 'God, I have decided to return the gift you gave me. I do not want it. Here! Now take it back.' She slashed her wrists. Vilborg gave me two westerns she bought in a second-hand bookshop.

3 December 1953
My friend Bragi came to visit me. He has been helping out at a farm all summer, and I have not seen him since the spring. I had a feeling he was spying on me. He didn't stay long. I started to read one of the books V. gave me. A Red Indian stole a dog from a white man and treated the poor creature so badly it did not dare greet its old owner. I couldn't read any more. Gudbrandur has just called in and he and

Father went down to the basement. I think we are about to be poor again. I opened the door of my room and listened down the passage. 'Well, Brandsi, so it's the bank and the customs tomorrow,' I heard Father say. Mother was laughing and talking loudly. Helgi wants us to start training together. I said I wouldn't go to the stadium. He suggested we kick the ball about in the garden. He wants me to be nicer to my mother. Mother says I must try to live a normal life.

4 December 1953
Father did not go to work this morning. I don't understand how he can waste time like this. I went to see Grandfather. I walked over to the Department Store with him. No one was working there. There was a light on in the shelter. Gudbrandur was there on his own. I said goodbye and walked home, even though Grandfather wanted very much to drive me in his car. A man who lives in our street watched me as I passed. Vilborg and Gudbjörg are enemies now. V. says she hates her.

5 December 1953
Today Mother told me to make a list of things I want for Christmas. I looked at her with contempt. 'Why are you looking at me like that?' she asked. 'Because I don't love you any more,' I said. She thinks she can buy my affection. She doesn't realize she's dead to me utterly and for ever.

What I Want for Christmas
1 Electric train.
2 *Old Graves and Archaeologists*, a scientific treatise by C. V. Ceram.

6 December 1953
I went to Bjössi's shop for the first time today and stuttered. Bjössi gave me a Coke and a bar of chocolate. I wish he hadn't done what he did. God doesn't exist. It's a bloody lie.

10 December 1953

I had a bad dream the other night and haven't written anything down for a long time. It's true what Father said: 'There are some things a man has to have the sense to keep his trap shut about.' Father came and sat for a long time on my bed. His hair is almost grey now. Mother is always trying to get him to go to work. I went for a walk. In Grandfather's shop I had the feeling the men were talking about me when I came in. I had a bottle of orangeade. Grandfather was very pleased. 'So you're giving up that bloody Coke at last, are you, Tóti?' I love Grandfather. The estate agent came this evening. There is big trouble again.

11 December 1953

I walked to Hjálmur's today. Ragna went out and bought me Coke and chocolate. Hjálmur gave me five hundred krónur. They all said they had been very pleased with me this summer. Everyone is terribly kind to me. The heat in the office gave me a headache.

12 December 1953

Father is always in the basement. Yesterday Mother said that the man who wanted him to design a house for him had given up waiting. I asked her to forgive me for having been so rude to her and gave her the five hundred krónur and she kissed me on the cheek. Why did Sigurbjörn let her boss him around this spring? He said to me, 'It's not so easy to boss me about, Tóti.'

I've made up my mind to be an architect when I grow up. I hear that Laugarnes School is a far better educational institution than Austurbæ School. I have decided not to be so lazy over my schoolwork. After the final exams I will be better prepared for higher education. V. is angry with me.

20 December 1953

I went into town with Mother today to look at Christmas presents. I showed her an electric train in 'Liverpool'. On Laugavegur there was a little fellow shadow-boxing, looking into a kiosk, and shouting,

'What have I done?' He stopped for a moment and then began to box again. He was crying and drunk. There was quite a large crowd of people looking at him. I saw the man in the kiosk concentrating on his business and not get bothered. I thought of the meat thief, Gústi the finger. He'd've gone charging in there and laid him out with an upper cut.

23 December 1953

Mother and Vilborg bought a Christmas tree this morning and then took the car into town. It's Grandmother Sigurlaug's birthday. 'Is she getting a necklace?' Helgi asked. 'She could set up her own market stall on Lækjartorg.' Father laughed and the sound startled me.

The weather was good. We took a taxi. A sand-cake (a bit dry), coffee and Coke were waiting for us. Father rubbed his great big paws together and stared at the floor. It was warm and cosy in Grandmother's house. There were vases of flowers by the picture of Jóhannes. Jóhannes was a handsome man. In the parcel there was a tin of Mackintosh sweets in a cardboard box. I am looking forward to telling Helgi about it. He is in town with his friends.

I suggested we walk home. In the town, Father kept looking around him. I asked him why he was peering about like that. 'I don't want your mother to see us,' he said. 'I want to buy her a Christmas present.' He didn't find anything, and we walked up Laugavegur. On the corner of Vitastígur Father spent a long time looking down at the Department Store. He is going to start work again in the new year.

24 December 1953

Sigurbjörn decorated the Christmas tree. At five o'clock Helgi went to fetch Grandmother. By six, the grouse were on the table. Mother bought four extra. Helgi ate five. Ragnar came. We listened to the Evening Service on the radio. I got the lucky coin in the Christmas pudding and the electric train. Father's brother, bloody Jóhannes, was a halfwit. Anyone who has seen the picture of Father's brother knows I'm right.

1 January 1954
Father didn't go into town yesterday. R. bought some ship's flares. One of them fell away to one side and the children went running in all directions. It hit the garden wall and exploded. There was a smell of gunpowder in the air afterwards. We didn't go and see Grandmother and Grandfather. We had gammon steaks. This morning I picked up some rocket sticks from the snow in the garden. Now school will soon begin again.

4 January 1954
Pouring rain. Basements are being flooded, I'm told. Mother said, if this goes on, the trees will begin to come out. She is going to come with me in the bus for the first few days. V. always goes out to the shop nowadays. Mother and V. quarrelled.

12 January 1954
I have not been able to write anything for a whole week. I consider myself lucky with this school. In the hall there are glass cases with stuffed animals. In my form there is a boy they call the Tern. He lisps. Today he threw stones. 'Lisp, lisp, Tern!' they all shouted. Helgi has come with me for several days. He catches the bus down to the square and gets to work early. I see the way people look at him. He is famous now. Mother says she feels very frightened of people. Is it because of me?

16 January 1954
Now I'm going on my own. At the bus stop I can see down into a basement room. There is a lot of rubbish under the iron grating by the window. In the mornings a man lies there on a camp bed, smoking. There is no furniture in the room. Grandfather's shop is closed. It is snowing again. Two large windowpanes have been broken on the second floor of the Reykjavík Department Store. V. has moved to Grandmother and Grandfather's and is going to stay there for several weeks. I must be brave.

18 January 1954

I have lost a battle with my mother. She wants me to do gym and swimming and refuses to let me take a medical certificate. I cannot imagine going. Father is lying in bed.

19 January 1954

I did not go into the showers. Someone told on me. Mother was not waiting outside as she promised. The weather was very good, it was quite warm. I gave up waiting and walked to the bus stop. A man was standing there. 'Don't you feel well, my lad?' he asked. I decided to save the bus fare and walk home. Then it began to snow, big wet flakes. I remembered the night Sigurbjörn screamed, 'I'm going to kill you, Sunneva!' I imagined seeing Mother lying on the floor in her own blood. I tried to comfort myself, but it was no use. At last I got to Grandfather's. He comforted me. Mother had telephoned twice and asked after me. It had taken her so long to change a tyre, she had just had a puncture. Now she is sitting at the parlour table, I am writing this in Father's chair.

21 January 1954

Today is Sunday. Ragnar brought that boring bloody baby of his and a bag of sweets for me. Mother made waffles. Father took the brat in his arms. I sneaked out to the dovecote with the breadknife so I could slash my wrists. I sat there for a very long time. The snow has gone and it is as if the autumn has come back. I put the blade against an artery and said, 'I am going to return the gift. I think it's repulsive. I hate my father. I hate Sigurbjörn Helgason. I'm not going to go to San Francisco with him. I'm going to set fire to this horrible ugly bloody dovecote he made, and commit suicide. That religious brother of his was a halfwit.'

23 January 1954

They have found out who I am at school. I flew into a rage and threw a boy against a stuffed seal. The glass got broken and his hand got cut. Then I heard the tap-tap of the headmaster's feet coming down the stairs. I did not cut my wrists in the dovecote so I could take my revenge on them all instead.

2 February 1954
Everyone knows everything about me. I'm not me any more.

6

Gudbrandur boarded up the broken windows with plywood. He found cigarettes and empty soft drink bottles on the first floor. No work had been done since the turn of the year. He walked from floor to floor through the building. He liked being there alone and listening to the sound of the traffic. It was better than staying at home. He jumped every time the telephone rang. There was no peace from the men who were still owed their wages, firms with unpaid bills, lawyers and ultimatums. Gudbrandur opened the skylight and looked out across the roof, letting the rain fall on his face.

With the milder weather, the plywood buckled and blackened in the wet, the trees came into bud and the grass grew green. Gudbrandur went to see Sigurbjörn, determined to stand up to him. He rehearsed over to himself what he planned to say: 'I am not prepared to mort-gage the house on Öldugata, Sigurbjörn. Not unless some order is brought to the business.'

Sigurbjörn sat in his office, poring over documents. He looked pale, distracted and dishevelled. He'd grown a beard. It was flecked with grey.

The court had given its judgment. Ketill Einarsson had been sentenced to two and a half years' imprisonment, with a recommendation that he serve the full term. 'Listen to this, Gudbrandur, listen to his testimony: "The boy came with me of his own free will. He wanted me to reward him with sweets. He fell on the stairs and that was how he got injured. I covered him up the best I could and went to get help." I am going to pull down the building,

Brandsi. He's appealed to the Supreme Court. Don't you understand?'

'Is there no money, Sunna?' Gudbrandur asked at the front door. 'I'm standing surety for all this.'

'Not as far as I know, Gudbrandur. He's never let me in on any of the financial details.'

'But you keep sending everyone to me.' Gudbrandur was having difficulty restraining his anger.

'I can't take much more of this,' she said.

'We'll have to meet and talk,' he said.

They met at her parents' home. Sunneva took both her elder sons through into the parlour. 'Why do I feel like a thief?' thought Gudbrandur. 'Sigurbjörn is dumping all this bloody mess on me. They behave as though no one else exists.'

Helgi went over to the parlour table and greeted them. Gudbrandur had already noticed the change that came over Helgi when he was in the presence of his wife. He watched Ingiridur as she greeted Helgi with cool aloofness. That was how she had behaved when he had first met her. Helgi sat down at the table next to Gudbrandur and could not take his eyes off Ingiridur.

'How's your father?' asked Gudbrandur.

'Are you still messing about with all that sports nonsense, Helgi?' Geir chipped in.

'Of course, Grandfather. Didn't you used to swim in the old days?'

'Yes, well, I went to the baths now and then, but I didn't let it become an obsession.' Geir pulled a face and smiled sarcastically. 'You should have seen Bendedikt Waage standing in the main doorway of Kveldúlfur's Warehouse on Seamen's Day. He made a speech saying we all ought to be ashamed of ourselves, us cigarette-smoking, hands-in-pockets good-for-nothings. Then they swam in the sea off Skúlagata, Sigurjón from Alafoss and the others, puking up the sewage in the icy cold. They're all stone dead now, thank goodness. But I'm still alive and healthy as a horse.' Rósa put a plate of pancakes down on the table and Geir helped himself to one of them.

'Well,' said Helgi, now they were all settled round the table. 'What's the first item on the agenda?'

'The first item on the agenda is to make your father see reason,' said Geir. 'I wasn't exactly over the moon at having to sell the house and them putting up that dark and dreary monolith on the square.' He looked at Sunneva. 'I was tricked into it.'

'That's not true, Father,' said Sunneva angrily. 'You weren't tricked into anything. You got exactly what you wanted and more than we were reckoning on letting you have.'

'I remember it well. We were eating pancakes just like we are now. What did I say to you when you came in wafting that plate under my nose? That it would all end badly, and so it has.'

'And what do you want to do, Grandfather?' asked Helgi. 'Have the man locked up in the asylum?'

'I'm not saying that, Helgi,' said Geir, but his expression showed he thought the idea might not be so far-fetched. 'But he must try to understand that he can't just close down the business as though no one else exists. I never shut my shop all the times your grandmother broke her leg.'

'Then what do you want to happen, Father?' asked Sunneva, sharply.

'I want Sigurbjörn to get himself up out of bed and be of sound mind. Anyone can see that he isn't.'

'It's my opinion he ought to get help,' Gudbrandur said, carefully.

'And don't you think the same thing hasn't occurred to me, Gudbrandur?' asked Sunneva. 'Do you think I haven't tried to persuade him to get help?'

'The way it's going now, it could be that he doesn't have any say in the matter,' said Geir, firmly.

'Can't we leave it until the spring?' Helgi asked.

'Tóti looks so much better,' said Rósa. 'The boy's so brave.'

'Am I to tell people that Sigurbjörn won't let us touch the building?' Gudbrandur asked impatiently, scanning the faces round the table.

'So what's to be done, then?' Sunneva asked, looking at Gudbrandur. 'Have him certified?' She smiled sarcastically.

'No,' said her father. 'We'll just vote him off the board.'

A silence fell, and they all concentrated on their cups. Now the dream has come true, Sunneva thought. This is the storm that broke over the Department Store. She looked at the piano behind Ragnar and Ingirídur. Her father had given it to her as a present on her eighteenth birthday. Shortly after that she had told them that she was expecting a child.

'I can't pussyfoot around people like that,' said Geir. 'I've never done it and I've no patience with it. Sigurbjörn hasn't ever pussy-footed around me. I kept warning this would happen. But none of you paid any attention to me. And there's a lot of money at stake. That bloody building is worth a good 7 million all told.'

'You never were one for pussyfooting, Father,' said Sunneva.

'Are Ragnar and I supposed to kick Father out of the firm because we're on the board?' Helgi asked. He had hardly looked at the pancakes, but now he put two together and bit into the double thickness.

'You needn't look so shocked,' Geir said, rather angrily. 'As soon as he gets better he can pick up the reins of the whole damned business again, Helgi. We need to raise more capital. I may be able to arrange it, but not with things the way they are.'

'You've never liked Father.'

'I don't think he's that bad, Helgi. I just think he's always been so damn conceited. I make no apology for that.'

'We'll have to give it time,' said Helgi. 'I expect he'll soon be right as rain.'

Gudbrandur took an envelope out of a portfolio and put it on the table. He had witnessed a meeting in the basement office the previous winter. Sigurbjörn had screwed up his eyes at his client whenever there was any discussion. It was this stare that strangers did not like. They might be having the friendliest of conversations with the architect about how the rooms should be laid out, but Sigurbjörn would have about him an air that made people who did not know him very well think that he might lose control at any moment, jump to his feet, order them out and throw furniture about. Was it any wonder he found it hard to keep his architect's practice going? Working for the City Architect had suited him much better. He had been able to develop designs and polish individual elements under the guidance of others. The City Architect was a patient man and knew how to get the best out of him.

'Oh God, how I love this man,' he thought, surprised that he could put his feelings into words and admit it to himself. 'I'm glad I stood firm about having my child christened after him. That ought to have told him something. But what now? It doesn't make sense for everyone to lose everything. He's bound to understand that when he gets better. Then he'll thank me for averting this tragedy.' Gudbrandur took a letter out of the envelope and pushed it across to Geir.

Geir read aloud: '"The undersigned comprise the board of the Enterprise Construction Company. Chairman of the Board: Sigurbjörn Helgason." Well, no one here needs to be reminded of that,' the old man added. He read out the names of those present. 'A meeting of the board has been convened and it has been agreed, for special reasons, to relieve Sigurbjörn Helgason of his position for an unspecified period of time and to appoint Gudbrandur Jónsson in his place.'

Sunneva and her sons had yet to sign. Helgi pushed the letter across to Ragnar and he passed it to his mother. She counted the votes and mentally added them up. 'I don't need to vote,' she said. 'There's a majority here already.'

'Do you think that Father would neglect to vote, Mother?' Ragnar asked. 'It all rests on you. I agree with Helgi. Let's wait. We're all too fond of Sigurbjörn.' Sunneva noticed that Ingirídur glanced for a fraction of a second at Ragnar's profile and smiled faintly.

'I signed it,' Ingirídur said when she saw Sunneva looking at her. 'But I was opposed to it. I wanted to exhaust all the other possibilities first.'

'But everything's been tried, Inga.' Gudbrandur looked at his wife in surprise.

'Has it? Have you told him straight out that this is what will happen?'

'It's no use, Inga. The man's ill. It's the easiest thing in the world at this point to take the position you're doing.'

'No one is suggesting anything other than that Sigurbjörn will take over again once he's regained his health.' Rósa looked at her daughter with an imploring look.

'We have to be sensible, Sunna,' Gudbrandur said. 'What about Vilborg? What about the boy?'

'Yes, hasn't Tóti been through enough?' said Geir. 'You don't own a single brick of Sjafnargata, and the chap from Akureyri has gone crazy and is threatening to sue Gudbrandur. He'd've had his shop open a long time ago if Sigurbjörn still had his wits.'

'So it's all up to me?' Sunneva clasped her hands together on the table. Her cheeks were burning.

'So it seems,' Gudbrandur said.

'I'd rather try and talk to him.'

'And say what? That he's to be dropped from the board if he doesn't drag his arse out of bed?' Helgi looked mockingly around him. 'I know what Gudbrandur's driving at. There's no point in discussing it. Don't do it, Mother.'

'Mother, don't do it,' said Ragnar.

Sunneva looked away from them round the parlour. On the wall above the old sofa hung a photograph in a gilt frame. She and Sigurbjörn had spent their honeymoon in Italy and visited buildings in Rome, including St Peter's. While he was strolling about observing pillars and calculating bearing capacities, she had been admiring the sights. She remembered the women kneeling in prayer at the grave of the Apostle Peter, rosaries wound in their fingers. She had gone up to the *Pietà*, Michelangelo's sculpture of the Holy Virgin with her son lying dead in her lap. What softness and gentleness there was in the marble! People had gathered around it, some of them moved to tears. At a small kiosk she had bought this large photograph of the statue and sent it to her mother.

Gudbrandur cleared his throat.

'Don't do it,' Ragnar said again.

Sunneva picked up the pen and wrote her name.

V

1

She was drinking a cup of coffee and eating a slice of toast with her back to the parlour door. He came into the kitchen and, without saying a word, hit her hard on the nape of her neck.

He flung the piece of paper at her and said, 'Right, Sunneva, now you're on the floor, just like you were when I first laid eyes on you. The sooner you get out the better. Be grateful I'm not going to kill you, you whore.'

Sigurbjörn was sitting at the end of the table when Helgi came home. 'Where are Mother and the kids?'

'Gone.'

'Gone where?' Helgi felt uneasy.

'Away. And I'll thank you and Ragnar not to do the dirty on me, Helgi.' Sigurbjörn looked down at his bony hands.

'So you've had the letter?'

'Yes.'

'When are they coming home? Have they gone out for supper?'

'Don't be stupid, boy,' said his father, loudly. 'I hope she never sets foot in the place except to collect her rubbish. I'm asking you to go out to Vídimelur in a bit. I don't want her stealing my car.'

'You're not serious?'

His father stared at the table. 'How did it happen?' he asked, at last.

'Grandfather and Gudbrandur thought there was no other way.' Helgi began to feel embarrassed.

Sigurbjörn snorted. 'The bastards want my house.' He was silent for a while. 'I can't believe Brandsi would do this to me,' he said, in utter astonishment. 'The man's my friend.'

'Phone her, man.' Helgi sat down. 'It wasn't her decision.'

'Am I a dog, Helgi?' Sigurbjörn asked loudly. 'Or am I a man? Last spring I asked her as nicely as I could if Thórarinn could stay home for the summer, but she had to have things her own way.' He looked hard at his son. 'What do you think it's like to be treated like a child in front of a twelve year old? Eh? Answer me that.' He waited for a moment as though expecting a reply, and when it did not come he said, 'People can trample each other into the ground, Helgi. If he hadn't taken that summer job things would be different now . . .'

'You know the firm was going bust, Father,' Helgi pleaded with him. 'You know that. The Department Store was going to have to be auctioned off. There's a pile of distrainment orders down at the bank. I've asked them to hold off on them but they can't for ever.'

'I hardly think it would have gone bankrupt,' Sigurbjörn said, scornfully. 'They all own masses of property. Your grandfather owns five or six apartments at least. And Gudbrandur's got that place down in Austurstræti.' Sigurbjörn was quiet for a few moments and then added, angrily, 'I was going to go back to work after the weekend. I'd have got the whole damned business sorted out.'

'She'll probably phone,' said Helgi.

'Then you can speak to her,' Sigurbjörn said. 'I won't answer. I won't talk to her.'

Helgi looked in the refrigerator. His mother had been going to fry some fish for the evening meal. She had already coated the haddock with breadcrumbs. 'Who's going to eat all this?' he called.

His father laughed. 'I expect you'll be able to put it away, my friend.'

Sigurbjörn was lying on his bed still fully clothed, snoring, when Helgi came upstairs to tell him supper would soon be ready. He looked as if his sleep had been fitful and disturbed. He had thrown off his quilt, and Helgi could see his heart thumping through his shirt. It was something he had seen before. Sigurbjörn had come home half out of his mind because of some terrible insult at the City Architect's office, all set to take it out on his son. But Helgi was now bigger and stronger than he was. He had hurled Sigurbjörn into a chair and stood over him threatening him. Sigurbjörn had not fought back, and since then things had not been quite the same between them. Helgi looked at the shirt as it rose and fell. 'How could I have been so stupid?' he thought. 'Any battle with this man is never ending.'

He went into his room. The first mild low-pressure system of the season was hurtling across the country bringing the rain that was battering the trees in the gardens and thrashing against the roofs. The wind changed direction before his eyes and he saw the rain sweep away from the houses and whirl in a circle above the airport and the Tivoli Gardens. Everything fell into a dead calm.

Now spring was coming, and soon the amusement park would be open again. Sigurbjörn and Helgi had often gone to the circus when the family had been living abroad. Sunneva did not like that sort of thing. Helgi remembered his father looking up towards the dome where a woman in a glittering costume with bare thighs hung by her teeth from a length of rope, spinning round. 'That must take a lot of practice, Helgi,' Sigurbjörn had said, spellbound. 'Father's going to build a dome over the Tivoli Gardens in Iceland,' he had told his mother when they came home.

The eye of the storm turned clockwise over the airport and then struck the houses below Skólavörduhæd. Helgi went downstairs to phone his mother. 'Hello, Grandma, is Mother there?'

'Hello,' the old woman said, anxiously. 'What a terrible storm this is. Should we phone the police? He hit her.'

'Let me talk to Mum,' he said impatiently. He could hear his grandfather's loud voice in the background. Sunneva came to the phone.

'Well, Mother, what did I tell you?'

'Are you phoning to say "I told you so", Helgi? He hit me on the head. From behind.'

'He didn't tell me that,' Helgi said, embarrassed. 'I wanted to know how you were.'

'I feel numb.'

Helgi could hear his grandfather's voice rumbling on without pause, but he could not make out the words. 'Grandfather'll be happy now,' he said. 'I can hear it from here. This is what he's been predicting for over a quarter of a century.'

'Predicting what? I'm staying here with the children for a few days,' said Sunneva. 'Then we'll see.'

'He wants me to pick up the car.'

'Well, isn't it best that way? I don't want him coming over here to the west end of town.'

'I'll keep you informed,' Helgi said. 'Everything'll be all right, you wait and see.'

He fried a plateful of fish, boiled some potatoes and sat down at the table. The fish was rather dry and flavourless. He could not remember ever having partaken of such a sad meal.

Sunneva came the following Sunday and fetched her own and the children's clothes. Sigurbjörn waited in the basement. Helgi sat anxiously in the parlour. 'So you're not going to live at Grandfather's?' he asked.

'No, he's got us somewhere to live in Laugarnes. That'll soon be available. Then Thórarinn won't have far to go to school.'

'You're not coming home, then?'

'No, not for the moment. It doesn't do anyone any good living in this atmosphere – least of all the boy.'

'What about Vilborg?'

'She's so grown up now. I'm not worried about her having to take the bus into town.'

'Poor Vilborg. And what are you going to live on?'

'I'll get by,' said his mother. 'Don't you worry about that. I suppose I'll get some money out of that bloody building. If that isn't enough, I'll have to go out and get a job.'

'A job?' He bit off the words, stunned.

'Helgi, I went to Copenhagen on my own when I was eighteen and pregnant.'

'But that was a quarter of a century ago.'

'You'd be surprised how tough I am,' said Sunneva, firmly.

'What did I tell you?' Sigurbjörn laughed, when his son brought him the news. 'The bloody man owns flats all over town. How could she do that, take the firm away from me? We've gone through thick and thin together for a quarter of a century, Sunneva and me.'

'What firm, Father? You never had any intention of putting up another building once you'd got out of debt. All you wanted to do was to work on your designs in peace and quiet.'

'So Tóti would rather live with his mother,' Sigurbjörn said, bitterly, gazing morosely at the table. 'And Gudbrandur!' he shouted, looking round the room in bewilderment, as if he expected his friend to have hidden himself there. 'I've nursed a viper in my bosom, Helgi! And the legal system in this godforsaken country! Two and half years' imprisonment for a crime that's worse than murder! Helgi,' he added sadly, staring at his hands. 'You were the only one who stood by me. And Ragnar.'

'Ask her to come back and bring the children, man,' said Helgi, impatiently. 'It's not too late. You're still fond of each other.'

Sigurbjörn looked at him in amazement. 'I'd sooner blow my brains out, boy.'

Helgi waited for him to work his way round to Jóhannes Helgason, who had betrayed his brother by dying in Germany. 'Everything was over for me the day my brother Jóhannes died,' said Sigurbjörn, still staring down at his hands. 'What do you think it was like, knowing that he was all alone abroad? "It was the will of God,"' he wailed hoarsely, quoting his mother. '"Jesus took him, he alone knows when it is time to call them home."' Sigurbjörn looked around the parlour with hatred, as though he were searching there for the old days.

2

Early one autumn day in 1928 he arrived at the Café Skindbuksen before it had opened. He stood there alone and waited, watching the rain fall on the street until it seemed to him that the drops were raining upwards from the pavement. He had been drinking the night before and in his pocket was a letter from his mother, Sigurlaug, with the main items of news. His father was very ill. The Parish Council had decided to hold a design competition for the cathedral to be built on Skólavörduhæd in memory of the Icelandic national poet Hallgrímur Pétursson.

At half past nine the café opened. He sat down at the table at the far end and asked the waiter for a pick-me-up. Sigurbjörn was not the apple of his mother's eye; such passionate love she had reserved for Jóhannes. Her whole life had revolved around her eldest son, the parish priest-to-be, her passport to life. Now he was dead, and her younger son had not been able to put his mind to the catechism at a Norwegian school.

An old boxer, a regular visitor to the café, had come in unnoticed and was now sitting at a table by the window. Many years ago this boxer had lost a fight for the heavyweight championship and was consequently a man without honour. His hair was thick and tousled, and his beard might have been carved out of wood. He looked like an icon.

Sigurbjörn asked for pen and paper, and began to sketch. He had travelled all the way to Barcelona in the spring and had decided to become an architect as he stood in front of Cologne Cathedral. He had been ecstatic. What artisans and designers there had been in former times! What masterbuilders, what buildings! To have studied and worked in the presence of such men must have been a miracle. What must have been the feelings of an architect standing beneath a roof like that, knowing that the building was his own work?

Throughout the train journey to Rome he had been like a man possessed. The sense of wonder did not abate while he was in Italy. Then he had sailed to Barcelona on a ferry and walked up into the town to find a hotel room. The weather was glorious as he passed the redbrick warehouses on the quay, went through the Ciutadella Park where chimeras guarded a fountain and spewed water into a green pond, under the Victory Arch and up the San Joan Boulevard where old men were playing pelotta. Carrying all his luggage in a small travelling bag, he walked towards a church tower, entered a square and saw the Sagrada Familia. The Church of the Holy Family.

He sat down at a pavement café. It was late in the day. He studied the towers, which looked like stalactites with the sky as the roof of the cave. He asked the people at the café to looked after his bag and walked towards the front of the cathedral. Above the entrance, there was a statue of the Coronation of the Virgin Mary. He pictured a cave mouth in Iceland high up in the cliffs of Eyjafjöll. The façade of the church was like candlewax dripping down into the street. For a few pesetas one could climb the winding spiral staircase to the top of one of the towers. He looked out through the slits at the blue mist of the sea and far across Barcelona and the tree-covered hills. He looked down at the old chapel and the pavement café where his bag was.

It was terrifying walking down the staircase. He bought a tankard of beer at the café. A beggar asked him if he was an artist. 'No, no,' he replied, and explained to the man in mime that he was a carpenter. Then the other man said in stilted English, 'You knew my master Gaudí? All the time yes! I work at the Sagrada Familia with my hands,' and had shown him his large hands.

Sigurbjörn had never heard the architect's name, but was happy to meet a fellow craftsman. As the man had worked on the Cathedral he tried to tell him that in his opinion such a thing would not do. To *think* of building such a cathedral, that was all very well, but to put one's thought into execution: madness. No one would get away with anything like that back home in Iceland, and no one should be allowed to get away with it anywhere. 'Does my Spanish friend know what an icicle looks like?' That was what the towers put him in mind of. The Spaniard did not know what an icicle looked like, and a considerable amount of time and energy was expended in explanation. They became heavily inebriated in the quiet of the evening, and Sigurbjörn wanted to go and find the architect himself in order to give him his opinion, but his colleague put a hand on his heart and said, dolefully: '*Se ha muerto*. My master is dead.'

'That's good, my friend,' said Sigurbjörn Helgason. 'Then he can't get up to any more mischief. A church like that is enough to make one want to change profession.'

A man at the next table with a beard like the horns of a buffalo shook his head with good-natured tolerance. 'Don't listen to him,' he said to the traveller, waving a brown hand. 'He's of no consequence. He's never done an honest day's work in his life.'

And now Sigurbjörn sat in the Café Skindbuksen designing, for his mother, the cathedral, the holy Hallgrímskirkja, the Icelandic Sagrada Familia.

He got a Danish colleague of his to help him work out the details of the design. They sat by an open window as a woman in a blue dress with a white parasol passed along the yellow beach and the sea washed around the rotten struts of the pier. They sipped kirsch. Outside a warm darkness fell.

When the project was finished it looked as though the lava rock Hvítserkur on Húnaflói were sitting in the middle of Skólavörduhæd. The tower was to be over 900 feet high. He wrote a covering letter and made a considerable effort to couch it in the most appropriate language:

None of Europe's great ecclesiastical buildings can be described in a few words; often they are the work of more than one masterbuilder and are centuries in the making. Where do people go when they come to Rome? To St Peter's. What is the first thing people want to see in Paris? Notre Dame. Let us build a church on Skólavörduhæd that people will want to see in centuries to come. The idea is that it should appear to burst from the earth as a mountain range rises when two plates of the earth's crust overlap. On the interior walls there should be pictures of saints and above the main doorway there should of course be an image of the Holy Family: Joseph and Mary with their child.

3

The children had never been allowed to touch the letters Jóhannes had written from the Bible School in Norway. They were kept in a yellow wooden box, and Sigurbjörn pored over them for days on end. One evening when he was out for a walk the box was left on the sofa, and Helgi sat down with it on his lap, looked around him, and listened.

A picture of a middle-aged Sigurlaug was lying on top. She was sitting in a large chair in front of her bookcase. Jóhannes stood behind her and her younger son, looking boyish, by the arm of the chair. Sjafnargata during its construction, with some men beside the scaffolding, Sigurbjörn laughing in a roll-necked woollen sweater, holding a hammer. Booklets from the Bible School. A letter to Sigurbjörn from his mother, reminding him to pray to God and study hard. 'You never mention Professor Hart and his family, boy.' Sigurbjörn's and Sunneva's wedding photograph. The bridegroom ramrod-backed, the bride grandly elegant. Ragnar was holding his mother's hand. A small picture of Sunneva. The face had been scratched away with the point of a knife, a nail or something of the kind. A letter from Ragnar – he had been sent to Iceland to work on a farm one summer. Many things in this life had come more easily to Ragnar than spelling.

Dear mum and Sigurbjurn,
Her I am out in the country. I was sik on the way here three tims. Yesterday Granfather hit a hork that was trying to kill the hens. I help with milking the cows and cleaning the cowshd. If you want to send me a parsil, mum, please send me crayens. There is a litl puppy her I play with.

By by,
Ragnar

If only I could get some impression of what Jóhannes was like, thought Helgi. Perhaps then I could help my father? He picked up a letter and admired the delicate handwriting.

Leith, 1 November 1926
My dear Mother,
I hope that these lines, whenever they reach you, will find you fit and well. I have at times been concerned about you, but I hope that God

has given you strength when you have most needed it. I fear the hours will hang heavy until I receive a letter from you.

We have now put in at Leith, in a detour which I would least have expected the ship to make in its course. It adds at least two or three days to the voyage, and there is also the fact that it adds eight krónur in expenses a day for me. In other respects the voyage has gone well.

I stood on the deck for as long as I could make you out, and that must have been longer than you could see me, for I watched you and Sibbi walking back along the quay. I felt a little uneasy when I saw that, as was only to be expected. You looked somewhat lonely. But there was nothing to be done except to commit you to God's keeping, and that is what I did.

I slept very well in the night, was not really seasick, as the weather was excellent. At seven o'clock in the morning we reached the Westman Islands, and I rose from my bunk.

I did not go ashore in the Westman Islands; our stay there was too short. And in the Faroe Islands the ship did not put in to the harbour, so I could not go ashore there either.

On the voyage from the Faroes over here I was a little poorly, but even so I was up and about all day yesterday, and ate a little. The passengers are for the most part rather dull. I do not know any of them and have therefore remained silent most of the way so far. (For example, one of the trawler-owners on board is always either 'tipsy' or drunk.)

Oslo, 13 November 1926

Now I have arrived in Oslo. I went to see Professor Hart on Friday as planned but, alas, I got there half an hour late, and I am told that that is the worst thing one can do with him. But I apologized for this mistake, which was mainly caused by my not finding anyone to give me directions, so that it took me a long time to get to his house. He probably found this somewhat disconcerting, and I was in a frightful mood, so the conversation was both short and awkward.

When I was in Copenhagen there was another Icelander staying at the same hotel who had been on the ship with me. I was with him in his room on the first evening when a Danish girl came to visit him. She wore make-up in obedience to the latest fashion. (Though not according to Reykjavík fashion, for she had not daubed herself all over. If one were to dignify this terrible vain nonsense, one might say she was wearing admirably applied make-up.) I thought she was some kind of loose woman, and my suspicions were confirmed by the fact that the Icelander was drunk, so I quickly made myself scarce. However, the next day he told me that she was very hurt that I had left so quickly following her arrival, though I did not really believe this, and there the matter rested. But now I am of a different opinion, for I have discovered that she is a telephone operator. Then, on my last evening in Copenhagen, I was again in this man's room, together with several other Icelanders, when the same girl came in, wearing make-up as she had the day before, of course. But now I felt I could not just rush out at once, and in the end there were three of us left, this Icelander I have mentioned, the Danish girl and myself. She was smoking, of course, in order to be *à la mode*, and I employed all my politeness in order to keep the conversation going, talking mostly about the telephone, of course, but she did not appear to be at all interested in that, and so I changed the subject, but this seemed equally awkward, and so it continued, on and on. But even though I bore the YMCA badge on my chest, the gold cross on my tie, was a *cand. theol.*, had preached sixty or seventy times, led revival weeks and prayer meetings, been in Christian communions, had even been a board member, I was naturally very careful to avoid bringing religion into the conversation. I was, of course, affected by their view that it would be importunate, and I suppose that is what I am really, though I would not hold that against this young lady. But I learned a great deal that evening; I learned to be ashamed of myself. Somehow I blurted out something about Christianity, and thus was an appropriate subject for conversation arrived at! She seized on it gladly, as though it were a golden apple. Of course she tried to find fault with both priests and the Church, but I felt that her heart was afire with yearning for God. Indeed, I think I have never met anyone so smitten by hunger and thirst for righteousness. Of course she did not say so, but it could not be concealed. And never have I felt more keenly what a little way I have gone along the way of sanctity. At last tears came to her eyes, she was silent and listened to my unsatisfactory and, alas, ineffective words in bad Danish, and stared at me with a questioning look in her eyes, as though she wanted to say: 'Can this be true?'

And when we said goodbye, she thanked me for the time we had spent together – I think sincerely. And the Icelander said, 'We shall long remember the conversation we have had this evening.'

I shall probably never see that girl again, and only the Lord knows whether my words will have had any effect on her. I entrust it to him; he is able to use insignificant things in his service. But she was a sign to me, a sign that the children of the world yearn for light, life and peace, and yearn to meet the Apostles. Many of her accusations flew straight to my heart; they were true. When I went back up to my room I prayed to God for guidance, and I consulted the New Testament and found these words: 'I exhort therefore, that, first of all, supplications, prayers, intercessions, and giving of thanks, be made for all men.'

On Friday the 17th of this month I was invited to Oslo, where I gave a talk about Sunday Schools in Iceland, and asked those present not to forget that Iceland exists and to remember it in their prayers.

26 November 1926

I have not been anywhere this week and have mostly stayed indoors. But I get enough fresh air, because my unfamiliarity with the place and my shyness cause me to take a hundred steps where I need take only one. For example, the other day I went out to buy myself a clothes brush. I looked in every window, and I was never sure that in this shop or that a brush might be found and, though I quite expected to find one, I could not bring myself to go inside, because I was so afraid of making mistakes in my Norwegian. And so I walked street after street for two and a half hours and then went home without a brush. But here, right on the next corner, was a shop selling toiletries, of course!

If I let book and pen out of my hand, I cease to exist, and then the dejection comes over me. I am nearly always alone.

I enclose a few krónur, which you must use for Christmas, to buy some small thing for Sibbi. Please give my greetings to him, above all. I know that I may repose my trust in him.

16 January 1927

And now Christmas is past, my first Christmas away from home. This morning the Theological College began classes again. I have also decided to attend lectures in religious history, about Buddhism, Brahmanism, etc., for I greatly lack knowledge about them, and have often felt ashamed of it.

I grow increasingly fond of the dressing gown you sent me as a Christmas present! What a choice garment! I am like a new man since I received it, and am much more personable to behold.

I do not know why it should be, but now the homesickness has flared up in me again with redoubled force.

3 February 1927

In December I was often tired and low in spirit, and often wanted to lie still in my bed, but now, with the new year, the days have begun to lengthen again, and I have occasionally started to think about returning home, and then it is as if I had renewed strength. I find I have more energy than before, and I am interested in my studies.

Perhaps there will be a permanent improvement in my health. And it gives me so much courage and strength to know how brave you are

Now, with God's help, I shall use my time well. I have of course reconciled myself to the fact that I shall not be ordained and attain what I most desire. But is not that desire in itself vanity? The main thing is that I should be where God wants me to be.

I see no open road before me. God will have to open a road for me if he has called me to his work. He has at least a thousand ways of preventing a thing from happening if it is against his will.

Oslo, 9 February 1927

At the beginning of this week it looked as though you would have me home on the *Gullfoss*, because I have been very ill for several days. Most probably I got badly chilled, in spite of all my precautions, and have had a considerable fever. Friday was the first day I felt ill, but was up and about all day; on Saturday I was a little worse and stayed in bed almost until evening, but then I had promised to go on an outing with the Christian Students' Society. I felt remarkably well, but was of course very shaky.

Some evenings and nights, when I lay awake swimming in sweat, various dismal thoughts assailed me, as you can imagine. I did not really know what was wrong with me. And at last it was so bad that all the fight went out of me. Of course I had from the outset called upon God as best I was able, but at times I was so weak that I had difficulty doing so. But now I commended to God not only my health, but also my life. Why should I not be able to die young like so many others?

And of course he can do his work without me in my weakness; it would be laughable to place any hope in that. And perhaps he wanted to 'call me away' because he saw that he could not use me and wanted to prevent me doing harmful work. For that reason, I said, and asked for strength to stand fast: Thy will be done. Though I must confess that I have not yet learned how to pray without conditions. That will doubtless come to me. I had decided that if I was that ill when it came to the time for the *Gullfoss* to leave here, I would sail with her, for that was what we agreed if I were to be taken ill. And I asked God to give me an answer. It was clear to me what the trip home would cost; it would mean that I had lost hope. But so be it.

But, dear Mother! Now my heart is full of thanks to God for his mercy.

12 February 1927

Last Wednesday I had an invitation from Professor Hart, brought to me by his son, asking me to come and see him at his home at seven that evening. And even though I was not yet recovered from my infirmity, I felt I could not decline the invitation. First we had supper, and then we talked together, mostly about the situation at home and the work there. I told him about my brother Sigurbjörn, and discussed our worries on his account. Luke 12:35–48.

'Yes, in this struggle one gradually learns to be "thick-skinned",' said Hart. 'Do not preach with fever, Helgason, but with real fire!' He was very kind.

4

Helgi paused for a moment in his reading and opened the front door. The garden was deserted, dank and dark. The branches of the trees stirred.

He went down to the basement and looked along the bookcase. The Bible was lying on the desk. He looked up the New Testament reference, Luke 12:35–48, and read:

Let your loins be girded about, and your lights burning;

And ye yourselves like unto men that wait for their lord, when he will return from the wedding; that when he cometh and knocketh, they may open unto him immediately.

Blessed are those servants, whom the lord when he cometh shall find watching: verily I say unto you, that he shall gird himself, and make them to sit down to meat, and will come forth and serve them.

And if he shall come in the second watch, or come in the third watch, and find them so, blessed are those servants.

And this know, that if the goodman of the house had known what hour the thief would come, he would have watched, and not have suffered his house to be broken through.

Be ye therefore ready also: for the Son of man cometh at an hour when ye think not.

Then Peter said unto him, Lord, speakest thou this parable unto us, or even to all?

And the Lord said, Who then is that faithful and wise steward, whom his lord shall make ruler over his household, to give them their portion of meat in due season?

Blessed is that servant, whom his lord when he cometh shall find so doing.

Of a truth I say unto you, that he will make him ruler over all that he hath.

But and if that servant say in his heart, My lord delayeth his coming; and shall begin to beat the menservants and maidens, and to eat and drink, and to be drunken;

The lord of that servant will come in a day when he looketh not for him, and at an hour when he is not aware, and will cut him in sunder, and will appoint him his portion with the unbelievers.

And that servant, which knew his lord's will, and prepared not himself, neither did according to his will, shall be beaten with many stripes.

But he that knew not, and did commit things worthy of stripes, shall be beaten with few stripes. For unto whomsoever much is given, of him much shall be required: and to whom men have committed much, of him they will ask the more.

10 April 1927

On Friday evening a farewell gathering was held for me at the Bible School. It was an exceedingly convivial evening which I shall never forget as long as I live. Hart made a short speech. He began by saying something to the effect that it was sad I was leaving now, and though Helgason kept himself to himself, he had got to know him well, and now he wanted to thank him for his friendship, but most of all for his serious intent. He had interpreted the reality of the Gospels with enthusiasm and had lived according to them in our midst.

You can imagine how I felt during this. The bottomless sea of sin that God has concealed from men.

On Saturday I was invited to a farewell dinner at Holmenkollen Inn, and it was a large gathering. A barrister at the Supreme Court here in the city began to talk about how a Christian must make himself anew each day. How many people in his profession would stand up and be counted like that back home? After that there was a session of Christian witness, in which students, both men and women, took part. To end with, there were communal prayers. I think it must be a rare sight in that restaurant, as it would be in any other, to see a large group of young men and women kneeling down in prayer. And I cannot deny that it was a little strange to hear burningly ardent prayer in that room, while in the room next to it there was music and dancing.

I gave Hart a book in Danish to remember me by, but to his wife I gave the fur pelt that Father sent me for Christmas. I hope he will forgive me! And to a little girl who was visiting them I gave the little Father Christmas that Sibbi sent me. She told Hart that she wanted to marry me because I looked so solemn! Her father asked if he might tell me that. 'Ye–es, but then he'll be bound to smile!' she said.

A few of my close friends accompanied me to the railway station, and at 7 p.m. on the 8th of April the train pulled out of Oslo: my stay in Oslo, which has lasted nearly five months, was at an end.

Erlangen, 17 April 1927

I have now reached my destination. I arrived here at half-past six yesterday evening. More than that I cannot really say, because I am a a hotel. I had not intended to write to you until I knew my address, but in order to be certain that these lines catch the *Gullfoss* I do not dare delay. I went to the student accommodation bureau but it is not open until tomorrow. I have not met any of the professors yet, either. I want to get settled in first. This is a nice little town. It has been very hot here today, but they tell me it is cold compared to what will come later, and it made me a bit uneasy when I saw that all the windows have shutters with diagonal lattices for when the sun is at its hottest!

I saw quite a bit of Berlin, but really it is like an endless and bottomless sea, so that one can actually see very little in two days.

The journey has gone smoothly. My German is rusty, of course, but so far everything has gone passably well, though I don't know how it will be when I go and visit the professors and get myself a room.

I do much studying of timetables and dream of being with you. Every night now I dream that I am coming home. My mind is somewhat troubled, too. I do not know how long I shall be able to last out here. We shall see.

Please give Sigurbjörn my greetings. It is so strange – I feel I have never been so fond of him as I am now, and I know that God will hear my prayers that he will completely give his heart to Him.

5

'What would you have done in my place, brother Jóhannes?' Sigurbjörn asked out loud, alone in the parlour. 'Prayed for your enemy? I find the very idea repulsive. The God of the Old Testament is more to my liking.'

He stumbled around the house, exhausted and restless. 'There is something servile about Christ's teaching,' he muttered, snatches of biblical quotations coming into his mind: 'Vengeance is mine – an eye for an eye – he that rejects me rejects Him who sent me.' What if Christ really is the son of God? And what if there is eternal life? That would be horrible. And what if he says at the end of the world, 'I never knew you.' Because I have to go and kill this damned man, take my shotgun and shoot him in the face. I can wait until he gets out. I can wait. But will I then have to gnash my teeth in darkness until the end of the world if I kill him? Is revenge worth that much? But I can't live like this. And I can't kiss the hands that shamed my Tóti. Now this he-devil sits and drinks coffee as though it were the most natural thing in the world.

It had not occurred to Sigurbjörn until now that Ketill might do something so ordinary as have a cup of coffee. The thought shocked him to the core and he stood stock still in the parlour. Now he's reading the newspaper. He has no need to think about me. Perhaps he never thinks about me! But I have no choice; I can't stop thinking about him for a moment. My God, look what he's done! Doesn't he have to pay? Sigurbjörn pictured Thórarinn lying on the floor and, before he could stifle it, a howl of animal rage broke from him. It amazed him to hear it.

Afterwards he sat for a long time, prostrate with fatigue, and an almost pleasant drowsiness came over him. The table lamp with its ostentatious yellow shade cast its light over his brother's yellowed letters.

In the basement there were three old phone books he had not thrown away in case they came in useful for business. He found the name Ketill Einarsson. He looked it up in all the phone books. In all of them Ketill Einarsson was listed at the same address. Were his parents still alive? Sigurbjörn looked up the Einars and moved his finger down the page until he found Einar Kristjánsson also listed at Framnesvegur 22c. He stared at the name and felt a gratifying twinge of hatred. 'He lived in his father's house,' Sigurbjörn muttered. 'And ate at his brother's table. And laid his hands on his brother's wife, even when his brother was watching. That's what it said in the news-papers. They're bloody losers, the lot of them! An eye for an eye, saith the Lord. I'm going to go and harm that old man. What will his son think when he hears at Litla-Hraun that the old man's been beaten up? Won't he lie awake at nights, imagining his father with blood in his snow-white hair?' I'm not denied all comfort, Sigurbjörn though gladly. Even though it means staying with the damned in the kingdom of the dead until the end of the world. I can endure that. Yes, I can take it.

He went up to his room, lay down on the double bed and fell asleep. He dreamed he was walking down long corridors in a large building. All the rooms were empty until he opened a door and found his father sitting there at his writing desk with a cigar in his mouth. He felt in his jacket for his wallet and drawled in his kindly way, 'Oh, it's you, Sibbi, my lad. Come here and let your father give you something for chocolate and lemonade.'

He woke up. The branches of the trees criss-crossed the violet vault of the sky like a network of veins. He stretched out his arm for Sunneva, but then he remembered his wife had left him and he got up. He was stiff. It was Sunday morning. Helgi had gone to a dance, but had probably come home while Sigurbjörn was sleeping. I must get out of the house before the lad wakes up, he thought, as he sat on the edge of the bed. Helgi's getting on my nerves. I can't bear it. He went downstairs and heard a rustling in the kitchen. A girl with long, blond hair was standing at the kitchen sink with her back to him. She was naked except for her knickers. She had long legs and a slender waist. 'Are you with Helgi?'

'Oh,' she said, turning round with a glass in her hand. 'Yes. I just came in to get him some water. He's thirsty. I didn't realize there was anyone here. He told me his family had gone abroad.'

'I came home sooner than I had intended,' Sigurbjörn muttered under his breath, and sat down at the kitchen table. He smelt the girl's sweet scent as she walked past. He saw out of the corner of his eye that her breasts were large and beautiful, not so unlike Sunneva's breasts, the nipples puckered like mouths in a kiss, each holding a berry. Blessed be the women, he thought. What a long time it is since I saw a woman naked, apart from my wife Sunneva. He heard the girl go quickly up the stairs. And why did I go and hit her on the back of the head the other day? What a stupid thing to do!

He felt like jumping to his feet and driving Helgi and his bedmate out of the house. He ran upstairs but stopped at the top of the staircase and listened in surprise. Helgi was sobbing and the girl was trying to comfort him. Why is the lad crying? he wondered in astonishment, and tiptoed downstairs again.

'Perhaps God will make peace with me if I swallow everything I cannot accept' was the thought that flashed through his brain. The Lord's strong on mercy. Didn't God give Job back all his possessions? Sigurbjörn knelt at the kitchen table. Dear God, please spare this man Ketill. Do not let any harm befall him from this day forward. Just give me back my family and my life. Turn back time, and I'll see to it that the boy doesn't go out on the Saturday morning he met the man. He waited for a while on his knees. It was the first time the name Ketill had passed his lips. 'No,' he said hoarsely, and got to his feet. 'Let his flesh peel off him in hell.'

He went into the parlour. For the past few days rain and snow had alternated. There had been an incessant southerly wind and a steady stream of water had been driven into the house and lay on the windowsill. There was water on the floor. There was a time when he would have been glad to have something to while away the hours. He would have fetched putty and a ladder and replaced the windowpane. He was fascinated by the clear stream. It was as if it were a living serpent lying on the varnish.

He sat down by the telephone and looked up 'Einar Kristjánsson, Framnesvegur 22c'. After a while an old man answered and said, 'Hello.'

'Is Ketill there?'

'No, he's not in. Who is this?'

'My name's Bödvar. We were aboard the old *Gissur* together once during the winter fishing.'

'Oh, I see,' said the old man, sounding more friendly. 'Can I give him a message?'

'Yes, I've got a job on a trawler for him.'

'It's probably too late,' said the voice, after a silence. 'He's just got a good place.'

'Oh, is that so?' scoffed Sigurbjörn. 'A good place, eh? Then we can forget about that.'

'Who are you, if I might ask?'

Sigurbjörn hung up. 'So the old man's at home,' he thought, excited. 'And the old rogue's a bloody liar into the bargain. A good place on a trawler! His son'll get a shock when he hears at Litla-Hraun that his bloody father's been beaten within an inch of his life.'

He went out with the intention of finding Ketill's father and beating him up, even killing him. It was now quite light, and a strange sensation came over him. His surroundings suddenly seemed oddly unfamiliar. 'Perhaps I ought to get some shut-eye,' he muttered, and walked across Hringbraut. There was no snow on Vatnsmýrin. The whole of nature was strangely alive. There was a small puddle covered with a film of ice, dead grass; there was earth around it and a spring gushing down into a ditch. He felt these were bodily fluids, that the whole earth was like an old, sick carcase. At the beginning of time the earth had been healthy. For a while this comforted him, but then another thought struck: But it tore itself asunder with earthquakes. Lightning set fire to the land! Nature is no friend to man; it is the easiest thing in the world to freeze to death. There is no safety anywhere. Is it not outrageous that man has to die? From earth art thou come. And yet I have to thank God for everything. Thank you that I have a roof over my head. Thank you that I have food in my belly. And thank you that the body you created is not ill. But now, Creator, I declare war on you. On behalf of my brother Jóhannes and on behalf of Tóti. Have you any idea, God, who you've taken on? Sigurbjörn shook a fist at the sky and strode westward along Hringbraut.

He realized he was getting near to where Sunneva and the children were living. He suddenly had the idea of buying some Viennese pastries and crusty rolls, taking them in and offering them round, dropping in for morning coffee. He went into Hljómskáli Park to give himself time, to stop himself making such a momentous decision without thinking it through carefully. Not far from the shore there was a circular movement on the surface of the water, as though a hand from above were stirring it. Are you telling me something, Lord? He looked up at the sky. When he looked back at Lake Tjörnin he saw a swan a little way out. That early in the morning, no one had yet come to throw bread. The swan had seen the man and now swam over to him, full of curiosity, gently breasting the water, its yellow beak and shining white feathers were the happiest sight Sigurbjörn had seen for as long as he could remember.

He stood looking at the swan for a long time. Eventually it grew tired of waiting and swam away. I must turn to God, in spite of everything, the man thought. I have no other choice. I shall go to the west end of town and knock on the door and make peace with my wife. The poor soul had to sign. Of course I couldn't go on behaving like that. The people had to get into the store, and the workmen's salaries had to be paid. He felt for his wallet and decided to go into the baker's shop. 'I'm coming, Sunneva,' he said. 'Oh Lord, why did I hit her? She looked so wretched on the floor. My model. Now that's all ruined. It's all destroyed,' he said out loud.

As these words boomed from him, he passed a tent pitched over a ditch. Some telephone engineers were working on a cable. They were talking among themselves and laughing. Sigurbjörn had adopted an upright posture, so that he could retain his dignity as he walked past, but now it occurred to him that the men were laughing at him. They had read the newspapers. They knew what had happened to Thórarinn. They knew who his father was. And they thought it was funny. An anguished voice within him said, 'This is madness, man,' but even so he turned round and walked towards the ditch. One of the men looked at him nervously from inside the tent. He was in his teens, pallid and bespectacled. The earpieces of his glasses were thick and black. 'Are you laughing at me, young man?' asked Sigurbjörn. The young man looked at him in surprise, and shook his head.

'I would have you know, my good man, that I am a university graduate and one of the most respected citizens of this town. I am an architect and a natural son of the great Jóhannes Kjarval. I worked on the design of the National Theatre.'

'I was just telling him a joke. It had nothing to do with you,' said another young man, sitting at the far end of the tent, astride a thick cable on the bottom of the ditch.

'My, your father's a really fine painter,' the lad with glasses said, trying to calm Sigurbjörn down.

Sigurbjörn turned away, walked on and thanked God he had not mentioned Thórarinn. Why ever did I say I was an educated man and had worked on the National Theatre? A natural son of Jóhannes Kjarval! Well, my good, Christian mother must have had a serious lapse from grace. The nonsense he had talked to the workmen made him burst out laughing. But in an instant his mood had turned dark again. I'm on my way to the west end to beat up an old man. What a loser I am! Is it possible to stop caring for your child, when something like that's happened? Oh dear Lord, how wretched I am. Can a man stop loving his own son? Why do I not just put an end to it all and blow my brains out? he thought. Is not our every movement subject to the will of God? He could have put things right for me if he had wanted to. Tóti would not have met the man outside the shop. But he didn't do it. And why? Because he doesn't exist. And as for Sunna! How could she bring herself to let the boy take a job? Against my wishes. And how could she sign those papers?

Suddenly he remembered Sunneva had taken the children to Laugarnes. I've gone mad, he thought. He put a hand to his forehead and found he was burning up. At the end of Lækjargata he could see Mount Esja. But it was not the mountain he knew; it was another mountain pretending to be Mount Esja. He strode northward up Lækjargata the better to see the mountain. A few old, brown, rusty trawlers were moored in the harbour. It was much later when he heard the bells of the old Cathedral tolling mournfully.

He scarcely knew where he was going, or what time it was. He had stood beside a tree somewhere for a long time staring at a parasitical, mushroom-like growth on its trunk. He had had a hot dog at 'The Best Place in Town' and had been shocked by the colour of the mustard. He had sat on a park bench for ages, looking at his shoe.

All at once it had grown dark and he was at the Hotel Borg. He sat hunched over a table without ordering anything, and felt that the young people were smiling at him. 'Is your son dead?' Why did people think it funny that Thórarinn was dead? He had been in a backyard somewhere in the west end in the pitch dark looking for Gudbrandur, planning to kill him. 'Kill Gudbrandur,' he had kept saying hoarsely. 'Kill Gudbrandur.' When it was almost morning he had come upon an old man in a black hat with hard, white stubble on his chin, and had gone up to him threateningly with his fist raised. Was this Ketill's father? But it couldn't be, for this was the saintly old man who had walked Njardargata year after year with his milk-churn. 'God bless you, old man,' he had said, taking him by the shoulders. 'May the Lord smile upon you.'

He had met the postman at the gate and exchanged a few words with him. The postman had looked at him in surprise, and said, 'It's Monday morning.'

Fortunately, Helgi had already gone off to work. Sigurbjörn opened the post. A threatening letter from a lawyer. But in another envelope there was a cheque for twenty thousand krónur from Gudbrandur. It was wrapped in old carbon paper, and there was a note written in a clumsy hand:

27.3.1954

All the floor-space is now sold. I have done everything ahead of schedule. Ingvar Hjálmarsson has changed his mind. Everything is OK, partner. There are plans for the future. Enterprise is going to build next in Stigahlíd. A salary and profits from your shares. I look forward to seeing you at work soon.

Your friend, Gudbrandur

6

The gardens in the rest of the street were bursting into life. Sigurbjörn was surprised the season did not impinge on the black shroud engulfing Sjafnargata 1a. He had grown accustomed to thinking of the house as Sunneva had seen it in her dream.

The first ten days of June went by, and the good weather held. The rowan tree came into leaf and the parlour grew dark. The Icelandic football season began, and Helgi was seldom at home. One Saturday Sigurbjörn could no longer stand hanging round the house doing nothing. He put on jeans and a sweater, found a rake in the basement and forced himself out into the garden. It was warm, but the sky was heavily overcast. He raked the flowerbeds. The bulbs his wife had planted were in bloom. He did not know their names. He grew tired surprisingly quickly, and sat down, feeling shaky. The sun came out from behind a cloud and the scent from the flowers grew stronger. He sat there for a long time, enjoying the warmth. He lay back in the grass and watched the leaves change colour as the light filtered through them. The insects were buzzing and, as he sat up, a bluebottle flew in an arc over the lawn. He moved to the warm steps leading up to the house.

He had been in the habit of thinking of Sunneva and himself as a single entity. He felt that everything he was doing they were doing together. But now it dawned on him that he had not worked in the garden since he was a young man; it was Sunneva who had looked after it. He studied the rake lying on the lawn where he had left it. He was relieved when the car's red nose appeared at the gate a little later. Helgi came up the garden path with the trusty sports bag. When he was quite close, his father smiled at him and said, 'Did you give Valur a good thrashing?'

'Not today, Father.' Helgi sat down on the steps. 'We were playing KR.'

'How did it go?'

'They won 3–2.'

'That's a shame.'

'Win some, lose some.'

'And who deposited the goals?'

'Deposited? What do you mean?'

'In the opposing goal?'

'Oh, I see. I scored one.'

'God dammit, you're good.'

'One tries to do one's best.'

Helgi glanced at his father. He had never shown any interest in football before.

'How about going to the pictures with your old man this evening? I'll treat you.' Sigurbjörn placed a large hand on his son's knee.

'You're too late,' said Helgi.

'Is it the blonde?'

'No. Her sister.'

'What are you saying, boy?' Sigurbjörn almost fell over.

Helgi laughed. 'No, I must go and see Mother.'

'Can't you put it off?'

'No, I can't.'

'Well, how about some time during the week, or next weekend?'

'Next weekend I'm going to Laugarvatn to relax before the match with the Finns.'

'Why the devil can't they bring in a team you have some business playing?' Sigurbjörn asked. He sounded irritated and released his grip on Helgi's knee.

'Well may you ask.' Helgi looked at his toes. The answer surprised Sigurbjörn. It would have been more like the boy to get angry. He studied Helgi. He was so like Sunneva it was almost as though her face were hidden in his profile. He had the feeling his son had something to tell him. 'Is there any news of your mother and the children?'

'No, not to speak of.'

'What do you mean?'

'Oh, nothing.'

'I think you're hiding something.'

'Why don't you go there or phone, Father?'

'She never phones.'

'Why don't you take the children out to the pictures? Vilborg told me the other day that last year you promised to go to the pictures with her.'

Sigurbjörn now remembered he'd arranged to take his daughter to the pictures the previous autumn. He could not remember what it was she had wanted to see. 'Well, I'll just come in to Laugarnes with you when we've eaten,' he said. 'Can't you send both the children down here, and I'll take them to the pictures?'

'Won't you come up and see Mother?'

'No, I will not,' Sigurbjörn said, firmly. 'Phone them for me and say I'll be coming to fetch them for the nine o'clock film.'

'I suppose you want me to buy the tickets in advance,' said Helgi. 'You're as bad as Grandmother. There has to be an Icelandic tasselled bonnet, a brass band and a red carpet before you'll show yourselves at the cinema.'

Sigurbjörn laughed drily. 'You're a funny one, Helgi, I like that about you. But I know you've got something up your sleeve. I can read you like an open book, my lad.'

'I must let you into a secret. What do you think I found the other day when I moved into Vilborg's room? When I was moving the chest-of-drawers, I found there was something fixed to one of the back legs. So I tipped the chest up, and there was a matchbox, wound round and round with tape. I got it loose, and what do you think was inside?'

'I've no idea.'

'The earrings there was all that fuss about last summer.'

'Well, I'll be damned,' Sigurbjörn said, in surprise.

'Why do kids do things like that?'

'She couldn't get used to us being broke,' said Sigurbjörn, gravely. '"Death and the glacier" as *Faust* has it. She realized, bless her, just how much we'd been relying on Gudbrandur, and she couldn't bear it. Please don't tell your mother.'

'What do you think I am?' said his son.

'Was that all you were going to tell me?' asked Sigurbjörn. 'Kids do things like that all the time. Did you get a newspaper?'

'No, as it happened today I forgot. Was there something in particular?'

'No, I just need to know what's on at the pictures.'

The gate squeaked and they both looked down the path. A man was walking towards them, apparently in no hurry. He had a leather briefcase under his arm. 'Good afternoon,' said the man. 'I'm from the Electricity Board. I've come to disconnect the supply.'

'There must be some mistake.' Sigurbjörn peered around angrily. 'My wife said she'd pay the bill. Are you sure you've got the right house, man?'

'It's your name on the bill,' said the disconnector. 'Sigurbjörn Helgason, Sjafnargata 1a. I've been here before.'

'I don't owe anybody anything,' thundered Sigurbjörn, ignoring the bill the man was handing him. 'Check the figures on the bill against the meter in the basement. Then you'll know if you're in the right house.'

'A mistake like that is impossible,' said the man. 'Your name is logged with all the figures on the meters. It's been like that for years.'

This news made Sigurbjörn both angry and surprised, and he motioned to Helgi to get up. 'Helgi, stand up, my lad, and take the man down to the basement. Both of you check the figures.'

'I really don't think there's any point, Father.'

'Look here, take the man down to the basement, my lad,' said Sigurbjörn. 'I don't owe anybody anything.' He turned to address the disconnector. 'Check the figures in the basement, my friend, like I told you to, and then you'll know where you are. Now Helgi, get to your feet, and take the man downstairs.'

'He's a big chap, isn't he?' said Sigurbjörn, indicating his son with an outstretched hand as Helgi stood up.

The man from the Electricity Board agreed, and asked, 'Isn't he the famous footballer?'

'One of the tallest of men,' said Sigurbjörn, not listening. 'His name is Helgi, he's my son, and he scored the goal against the French last year.'

'I've heard the name.'

'Have you ever seen a bigger, more handsome man?'

'I doubt it,' said the man from the Electricity Board.

'Pull me up, Helgi, my boy,' said Sigurbjörn. 'What clammy hands you've got,' he said when he was on his feet. 'Were you out drinking last night?'

'They broke the mould with him,' said the disconnector, as they stood by the meters. 'There's really no point in us standing down here in the basement,' he added. 'It's ridiculous. There's no question about who's got to pay the bill.'

'Can it wait until after the weekend? I work at the Fisheries Bank I'll get some money on Monday.'

'Well,' said the disconnector, 'do you think we'll beat the Finns?'

'I should think so,' Helgi said. 'I'll trample them into the ground. When I see them in possession of the ball something'll snap inside me.'

'Well, I think we can let this wait,' said the disconnector. 'One would like to do all one can for such a famous man.'

Helgi put some potatoes on to boil and waited in the kitchen. He heard his father clear his throat on the sofa. After twenty minutes he took the pan of potatoes, drained off the hot water and began to peel them. 'What would my mates say,' he muttered, 'if they saw me now in an apron. Are you going to eat or not, man? I've finished cooking,' he shouted.

'I'm dog tired,' said Sigurbjörn. 'I dozed off for a while.' He sat down at the table and hunched over his plate. Helgi had made meatballs with cabbage, a dish he knew his father liked. Sigurbjörn's thoughts seemed to be elsewhere, and he ate almost nothing. The lapel of his jacket was caked with mustard and dandruff.

'Father, you should take your clothes to the cleaners.'

Sigurbjörn pulled himself up and his eyes flashed. 'Listen, my boy. Do you want to give me a bath as well or are there some things I'm allowed to do for myself?'

'Have a bath when you want,' the son replied. He stood up to get some milk, towering over his father.

After a while, Sigurbjörn put down his knife and fork and pushed his plate to one side. 'I'm awfully sorry,' he said. 'The food is fine but I've got no appetite.' He gazed morosely out of the kitchen window at the old stone wall between the houses. A tree in the garden next door was in blossom.

'If the opportunity presented itself, couldn't he be given a good seeing to?'

'Who?'

'The bloody pervert.'

'Who's going to do it?' asked Sigurbjörn. 'Are we about to break into a state prison?'

'Well, sooner or later he'll be out,' said Helgi.

'Are you prepared to spend years in prison for manslaughter? Would you make such a sacrifice, my boy?'

'Maybe he could be fixed for good and all? Crippled?'

Sigurbjörn laughed harshly. 'That would be too good for him. He'd be getting off too lightly.'

'Would you be prepared to go to prison?'

'I could handle it. But there's something else I'm afraid of.'

'Something else?'

'The Creator,' Sigurbjörn muttered, sheepishly. 'What will He say if I take matters into my own hands like that, Helgi?'

'I didn't think you were religious.'

'You think my mother's upbringing left no mark on me?' Sigurbjörn said, pulling himself up erect at the table. 'Your grandmother wanted me to be a Salvation Army missionary. Sergeant Sigurbjörn Helgason. How would you have liked to see me selling the *War Cry* on Laugavegur, my boy?' His laugh sounded hollow. 'If there's anything I'm afraid of, it's Eternal Life. Are you a believer, son?'

'I still have to make up my mind.'

'I can't agree with that Jesus of yours,' Sigurbjörn said morosely. 'Why should I forgive?' He looked at Helgi angrily. 'I've never known a soul who's ever forgiven anyone else a damned thing.'

'I don't think you're expected to forgive, Father, any more than the next man.'

'Ah, but that Jesus of yours. He expects it. We're to love our enemies and pray for them. Am I to pray for a man who shames my boy? Am I to kiss the hands that killed my son?' Sigurbjörn looked at his eldest son sharply. 'No, Helgi. I'll go and kill the man. I'll kill him!'

Helgi was startled by the look of insane fury in his father's eyes. Sigurbjörn had raised a clenched fist in order to demonstrate what would happen on the day of his wrath. Helgi unconsciously put up a hand to protect himself, but immediately let it fall.

'Don't be like that, man,' he said, embarrassed. 'It scares me to death.'

'Ah, forgive me, boy.' Sigurbjörn suddenly looked tired, the energy drained from his face, and he became old and haggard. 'If I had your strength, Helgi my lad,' he said, growing animated again, 'I could do such things.'

'Thank the Lord you don't have my strength.'

'You're a good boy, Helgi,' said Sigurbjörn. 'You tried to talk some sense into them when they took the firm away from me.'

'For God's sake let's not get on to that.'

'All the same, you're a good boy, son. You stood by me.'

'So did Ragnar.'

'Yes, and Ragnar too.'

'I'll help you beat the man up, Father.'

'That won't be necessary yet awhile.' Sigurbjörn took a long time to stand up, stumbled as he let go of the chair, and waited, bowed over, for a moment. The potatoes, meat and cabbage remained almost untouched on his plate, swimming in congealed butter.

'Damn it, I've no strength at all.' And he laughed again.

'Well, you're not eating anything, man.'

'You must excuse my poor appetite, boy. I'm going to lie down for a while.'

'That's OK,' said Helgi, helping himself to the rest of the food from the tray. He heard his father running a bath.

It was getting on for nine when they set off for Laugarnes. Helgi leapt up the stairs in two large bounds. Sunneva and the children lived on the upper floor of a two-storey house at Kirkjuteigur.

7

Vilborg came tiptoeing downstairs with her purse. She was wearing a skirt and her red moccasins. The lace trim showed beneath the hem of her cape. Her long hair was curled and kept off her forehead by a slide. There was a string of pearls at her throat. She had put bath salts in the water, and lain for a long time in the tub, enjoying the sensations as she moved her body. She was a woman now.

What pleased her most of all was that Thórarinn was sulking and did not want to come with them. At last she could have her father all to herself. She did not like living at Kirkjuteigur. This weekend had promised to be as awful as the last.

They were living in a three-roomed flat. The furniture was borrowed from Grandfather and Grandmother. Sunneva had bought divans for the children and herself to sleep on at a jumble sale. There were two very ugly landscape paintings in the parlour. At Kirkjuteigur there was no handcarved grandfather clock, no Kjarval painting, no cupboard containing fine crockery and ornaments. Vilborg had asked her mother, 'Mother, why don't you fetch some of our things?'

'Because your father's become dangerous.'

'That's silly. Father isn't dangerous.'

'I know him much better than you do, Vilborg,' Sunneva had replied.

Sigurbjörn had grown a handsome beard that half concealed the scars on his cheeks. Vilborg opened the door, jumped into the car, kissed him on the cheek and pulled up her white socks.

'Doesn't Thórarinn want to sit in front?' asked Sigurbjörn.

'He's not coming.'

'Really?'

'He's ill.'

'Really?'

'Father, look, Mother is standing at the door waving to you.'

Sunneva stood on the front steps. She did not smile but raised her hand and waved. The gentle evening breeze stirred her hair.

He looked away and did not acknowledge the greeting.

'Aren't you going to wave?' Vilborg asked, horrified.

He changed his mind, but the door had closed.

'What's wrong with Thórarinn?' Sigurbjörn asked, as they drove off.

'I don't know. He's become a real stay-at-home.'

'Really?'

'You keep saying "really" all the time.'

'What film are we going to see?'

'I expect you saw that *The Red Shoes* was given a single extra showing this spring,' Vilborg said. 'I got all the girls at the school to

216

sign a petition to the Tjarnarbío asking for the film to be shown again, and then I took it to the cinema manager and he agreed to show it, but what do you think happened then?'

Sigurbjörn shook his head and gave his daughter a long look. 'No one turned up except me and my friend Gudbjörg. There were only two of us in the whole place. Can you believe that, Father?'

Sigurbjörn laughed. 'So you're friends again, are you?'

'Yes, auld acquaintance shouldn't be forgot,' the girl said sheepishly.

'What film do you want to see, lass?'

'*High Noon* at the Tripolibío.'

'But that's a cowboy film, girl.'

'Yes. I've been going to them ever since I was little. What kind of films do you think Helgi and Ragnar used to take me to? Love stories?'

Gary Cooper played a sheriff who got into a lot of trouble. Some outlaws were on their way into town to kill him. Cooper needed help, but no one dared give it. Sigurbjörn had seen the film the previous year and remembered that he had found the sheriff's isolation and the townspeople's cowardice a bit unlikely, but this time the plot seemed to ring true and caught his attention. Every now and then they passed each other chocolate-covered raisins and sweets.

'The townsfolk's cowardice is disgusting. They're all waiting to see the man killed,' Sigurbjörn muttered, his eyes on the screen.

'Hush, Father,' Vilborg whispered. 'People'll hear us.'

'The rabble at the church are the worst of the lot!' Sigurbjörn mumbled, as he ate a cupped palmful of chocolate raisins.

Cooper walked out of the church alone and killed the outlaws. When the townsfolk wanted to make it up with the champion, he looked from man to man very quietly and then drove off out of town in a horse and buggy with his fiancée.

Sigurbjörn laughed loudly. 'The bloody devils got what was coming to them.'

'Father!' Vilborg said anxiously.

'Ah, forgive me, lass,' her father said, and kissed her on the cheek. Toward the end of the film Vilborg slipped her hand into his.

They drove home along by the harbour, and Sigurbjörn plied his daughter with questions, but took care not to mention Sunneva. 'Did you get good marks in the spring exams?'

The girl said she had.

'Does Helgi come and see you often?'

'Yes, he sometimes eats with us.'

'So the boy gets two dinners, does he? And what does he talk about?'

She was silent.

'About me?'

'I don't think he much likes being your butler.'

'What are you saying, Vilborg? Is that really how he sees it?'

'There's some trouble because of Tóti just now,' Vilborg said. 'Something in the papers. Some mistake.'

'Mistake?'

'I don't know any more about it, Father. Buy the *Morgunbladid*.'

Sigurbjörn drove along Hverfisgata. Gudbjartur had changed the name of the department store to 'Magasin Reykjavík'. He saw that they had painted it white, and put up flags, four of them on the roof over the main entrance. There were fully dressed dummies in the windows. The yellow flags hung in the calm weather, the letter 's' of 'MAGASIN' was visible.

'They've made it look nice, haven't they?' said Vilborg.

'And then some. Have you visited Gudbrandur and Ingirídur at all?'

'No, I'll never go there again,' his daughter said, haughtily. 'They tried to call me a thief.'

'Well, just between you and me, Vilborg,' her Father said, 'I found the matchbox taped to the foot of the chest-of-drawers.'

'Heigh-ho,' sang his daughter, turning as red as a peony.

'I was tidying up.'

'And you opened the box.'

'I had to. I was curious.'

'Father, you're a complete Rasputin. I would have believed it of Helgi, but not of you.'

'Don't take it to heart, lass,' said her father, and patted the back of her hand. 'I used to pinch odd things like that when I was a kid too.'

'Well, all right then,' she breathed in relief. 'Will you swear to tell absolutely no one about this, and especially not Helgi? Mother mustn't get to hear about it.'

He nodded.

'What do you suppose happened last weekend?'

'Well, I don't know.'

'I was invited to Thingvellir with the head teacher and another girl, because the two of us had won the knitting prize. The lady said to me, 'Vilborg! You are from a wealthy family, but Elín here is poor. She made me clean the whole of the summer cottage from top to bottom. Would you believe it, Father? She had me scrubbing the floors, beating the carpets, taking out the mattresses and bringing in firewood, while she went off for a walk with Elín.'

'What kind of a witch is she?' Sigurbjörn asked angrily.

'Well, some people are like that, Father. Are you coming in?' Vilborg opened the door and waited. The redness in her cheeks had faded.

'No, I'm too tired. I think I'll be off home, lass.'

'You never telephone, Father.'

'Neither do you. And neither does Thórarinn. It's Tóti I'm most surprised at not ringing,' Sigurbjörn muttered, looking wounded. 'And your mother doesn't get in touch.'

The girl offered him her cheek to kiss, and Sigurbjörn drove off to look for a newspaper vendor. He did not see any, and the only place he could remember where he might buy a newspaper was the kiosk at Arnarhóll. The man offered him the Sunday paper.

'No thanks, today's paper.' Sigurbjörn flicked through it quickly, but found no picture of Thórarinn, or even any mention of his name. He flicked through again, but found nothing. He went back to the kiosk and bought some other newspapers in case the girl had remembered it wrong, but nowhere was there any mention of Thórarinn. He went home and sat down at the coffee table and scanned through the *Morgunbladid* again. He had in fact let his eyes run twice across the headlines, but it had not occurred to him to look there.

Amnesty Declared for Many Criminals
to Mark the Tenth Anniversary of the Republic
on 17 June 1954

The President has signed statutes pardoning a large number of prisoners on the occasion of the tenth anniversary of the Republic. Many people will doubtless be surprised to learn that among them is a man who was sentenced only seven months ago for a vicious assault on a twelve-year-old boy. This newspaper contacted the Ministry of Justice shortly before it went to press. To a reporter's question as to whether a terrible mistake was being made in this instance, since the newspaper has it on good authority that the others involved are only petty criminals, the official concerned replied that it is not customary to discuss individual cases. It should, however, be noted that the procedure is such that official pardons signed by the President cannot be revoked.

8

He sat for a long time, his mind a blank. Then he read the item again slowly and calmly. Then his head fell forward and he slept peacefully. He woke up with pins and needles and stumbled downstairs. 'He got seven months,' he whispered softly. 'He got seven months.'

He fetched the Bible from the basement, and walked along the corridor but then stopped halfway up the stairs. 'Now he's just had his evening coffee. And he's eaten a meal at his old father's as though it were the most natural thing in the world.' He stood motionless and listened for a long time to the words he had spoken and then quoted from the statement to the court: 'The boy came with me of his own free will. He wanted me to reward him with sweets. As the girl assistant in the toy shop can bear witness, everything was fine between us.'

'I don't want to live like this any more!' Sigurbjörn howled, his throat hoarse. 'I don't want to live like this any more!'

He put the Bible down on the staircase, dashed upstairs and took the weapon out of the cupboard. The gun was heavy and it felt good in his hands. He found some cartridges and rammed two into the magazine. I'll shoot his head off as soon as he opens the door. No, that won't do, he thought. He'll see me on the steps from the upstairs window. 'I know those houses. They're built like old farmhouses,' he said aloud. 'Gudjón designed them in 1922.'

Sigurbjörn put the shotgun on the parlour table and ran down to the basement. There was a hammer, an axe and other tools in a small room behind the laundry. He picked up a long, razor-sharp awl and looked at it.

In a flash God's purpose was clear to him. I must go and meet the man and make peace with him in Christian love, whatever it costs, he thought. I have never done anything for God, but now that shall come to pass! I'll make peace with the man. The salvation of my soul, indeed, of both our souls, depends on my getting him to kneel and pray with me. Then God will reward me as he rewarded Job, and will give me twenty thousand camels and all that is mine back again. '"For I say unto you," said the patriarch Abraham' – Sigurbjörn threw out his arm – '"that the Lord can make people rise up from those stones." I am no longer in my right mind,' he said in a deep voice, and shook his head in wonder. 'I am no longer in my right mind . . .'

He went upstairs, put on his overcoat and shoes. The clock in the parlour said half past two. Has so much time passed since we were at the cinema? Why doesn't Helgi come home? He looked in his pockets for the car keys, but could not find them, and sat down at the dining-room table. Outside it was so quiet it was strange to think that anyone lived in the city. On the other hand it was clear to him that the trees in the garden were living beings and that knowledge caused both anxiety and dread. The crystal-bright night cast its light on the parlour table and the old familiar knots became clear in the shining wood. He felt as though the past would return to the house again if he looked long and hard enough at the knots.

After a while he went through into the kitchen and took the car keys out of the drawer where they were usually kept, went outside, sat down in the driver's seat and wound down the window. It was quiet on the street, leafy treetops stood out against a cloudy grey sky. 'Now I will make peace,' he whispered. 'Now this matter will end happily for all of us.' He drove off.

On Hringbraut he pulled up at the side of the road and let the door stand half open for a while. One of the 'Faxes' aeroplanes was parked with its large nose outside the hangar. Perhaps nothing really happened, he thought. For a moment he almost felt cheerful, then the happiness changed quickly to first rage then sadness. This business has been blown up out of all proportion. All sorts of things happen to people on this earth. Yet they grow from grass and learn to live their lives all the same. I must make peace with the man. There is no other way.

'I gather the rents on those houses are quite high,' he muttered, as he parked on Framnesvegur and looked at the terrace. 'Maybe I can help this man get on his feet financially. After all, I was an employer of men before that fiend Brandsi took the firm away from me.'

He switched off the engine. A young, slender birch tree was growing near the wall of the house. So graceful was it, its bark so unusually white, that in his mind he gave it his daughter's name. The windows looked kindly in the dusk. Now the man was sleeping in his bed, completely exhausted, the poor fellow. The garden was small and neat with an iron gate low enough to be climbed over. Steep stone steps with a rusty handrail led up to the front door. Under the roof gable there was a diamond-shaped window.

Sigurbjörn examined himself in the rear-view mirror. He was without his hat, and his cheeks were brown and deathly-looking. While he had been waiting and watching, cold had seeped into his bones. He started the engine and looked at the house. The clock on the dashboard said seven minutes past three. He turned on the radio.

There was dance music from the station at Keflavík, but he was not in any mood to listen. He began to think about the holy prophets of the Old Testament. They would not have been afraid to approach a wayfarer in order to speak to him or to demonstrate to a soul that had gone astray the peril it was in. What men of courage! They stood in the marketplaces barefoot and dressed in rags, aflame with the word of the Lord, declaiming it to the people. Those were real men, worthy of the name, like old Jeremiah, for example, Sigurbjörn thought. 'Then the word of the Lord came unto me, saying: Before I formed thee in the belly I knew thee; and before thou camest forth out of the womb I sanctified thee, and I ordained thee a prophet unto all nations.'

He opened the door and got out. An icy gust blew down Framnesvegur and through his thin woollen jacket. He buttoned it up to the neck and walked towards the house, climbed over the little gate and ran up the front steps. On the door there was a small window and an iron knocker, which he lifted and then rapped vigorously.

There was no movement in the house, in spite of the knocking. What if the street were on fire? he thought impatiently. Then there would be no way of waking the man. The whole row of houses would blaze, just as it was, and this devil, whatever his name was . . . would sleep on and fall victim to the fire. Sigurbjörn grasped the knocker and rapped on the door in a frenzy. Inside, there was deathly silence. Then there was movement at a window on the upper floor. The man was struggling to open the window, but the window was stuck, although eventually it did come loose a bit at the top.

Sigurbjörn could see feet coming down the stairs. The man came up to the window in the front door and looked at him with an evil, questioning stare. He was wearing a vest, and was rather fat, his arms pale.

'I want a word with you,' Sigurbjörn called, in a voice he himself did not recognize, beckoning to the man with one finger. The man had not yet opened his mouth. He looked at his visitor aggressively. Sigurbjörn pointed first to himself and then to the front door. The man opened the door.

Ketill was wearing black trousers and had put on a pair of slippers. He was holding up his braces with his right hand. The skin of his arms was white and freckled. The freckles had not been visible from the steps. There was the impression of breasts. He had a crewcut, and his stomach was a mass of soft flesh. He looked suspicious, now that the door was ajar. His nose came to a sharp point and his blue eyes were shining. There was a flabbiness in his cheeks. Ketill pulled the door towards him and asked, 'Yes, what do you want?' He sounded irritated.

Sigurbjörn's voice carried great authority: 'There's a fire down by the sea. In Ánanaust. I'm an officer of the Fire Department. We want to wake people up and warn them, see how well equipped they would be if it became necessary to tackle the fire directly. The wind might change, the sea of fire is unbelievable. People still remember when the centre of Reykjavík went up in flames in April 1915. The situation is not unlike what it was then. This is a crisis!'

'Everything should be all right here,' said Ketill, his face taking on an inquisitive and relieved expression at the news.

'Well, let me in, my good man, if you would be so kind. There are several more houses in this street, and I have a lot to do.'

Ketill opened the door and let Sigurbjörn pass. Sigurbjörn was conscious of Ketill's body as he strode by, and thought of Thórarinn.

Ketill closed the door again and went on ahead into the kitchen. His ankles were snow-white and his voice seemed to come from a long way away: 'I don't have anything to put fire out with. Is a wet rug any good in minor emergencies?' The slippers slapped on the kitchen floor. He looked outside and drew his braces over his shoulders, turned round suspiciously and said, 'But I don't see any fire.'

'It's along at the west end of the street,' Sigurbjörn muttered. 'Down at Ánanaust, that's where the fire is.' There was a big round table in the kitchen. He sat down without being asked.

A slice of white bread and cheese lay on the table, unusually thick at one end. The cheese had turned pale yellow and was hard and wet, the red wax still on it. Strangle the man, Sigurbjörn said quietly inside himself, looking at his hands.

'We've got to deal with the fire ourselves?' asked Ketill. 'That's odd.' He was shuffling his feet by the window, leaning his face against the pane and peering southward, as though hoping to see a glimmer of fire. A few long, white hairs sprouted from his shoulders. 'There's something fishy about this,' he said, looking at Sigurbjörn.

'There's nothing fishy about it,' Sigurbjörn said, harshly. 'Are there any flammable liquids in the house?'

'No, not really,' Ketill replied. 'Maybe some old painting stuff. And, yes,' – he gave the matter some thought – 'half a can of petrol down in the basement. The old man bought it to put some life into my brother Binni's car in the terrible cold last winter.' Ketill rubbed his hands together and seemed to shiver at the memory.

'Well, you'd better get it, and be quick about it.'

'I'll go and look into it. I'd better wake up Father too.'

'No, that's not necessary,' said Sigurbjörn.

'Don't you think I ought to wake him?' Ketill vanished downstairs.

Does he keep his father in the basement? wondered Sigurbjörn. There shouldn't be anything down there apart from a laundry. And he beat up his brother's wife at Grundarstígur with his brother looking on! Damn layabouts they are!

A book was lying on the kitchen table. He opened it and was astounded to read his mother's name. He had not realized he had brought the Bible with him.

He read on the title page: 'Bible. This is Holy Writ. Revised Version.' At the bottom of the page was the following: 'Printed at Spottiswoode's Printing Works, London, at the Expense of the British and Foreign Bible Society, 1866.' The book had not been read much, and that made him laugh.

He turned the page and found a gross printing error: 'Contents of the Bibel.'

'The Bib–el,' he said out loud, irritated by the carelessness of the printer, who had typeset the book almost a century ago. 'The British and Foreign Bible Society,' he read slowly. 'Bibel,' he thought sadly. I must bring this to the attention of the proper authorities. Funny that mother never mentioned it . . . He heard Ketill in the basement and remembered where he was. Now my brother Jóhannes would be proud of me, he thought. I would have risen and borne witness on Holmenkollen for him and the flock of old women would have howled with rapture.

'What's that book you've got there, my friend?' Ketill asked.

'The Reykjavík Street Directory.'

Ketill had a can of petrol and a little turpentine in a bottle. A piece of cork had been stuffed into its neck. He looked at Sigurbjörn, inquiringly. 'Here's the petrol and the other flammable stuff I could find. Haven't we met? You seem familiar.'

'Not as far as I remember. May I use your telephone?'

Ketill went into the parlour and Sigurbjörn waited a second in order to avoid being too close to him. 'Help yourself,' Ketill called.

Ketill had pulled out a telephone table, and moved the coffee table away from an upholstered chair, so that his guest would find it more convenient to sit down.

The parlour looked old-fashioned. It was quite different from what Sigurbjörn had imagined. A black cupboard stood against one wall. In the middle of the wall there was a clock, a green water nymph made of copper rose up out of a scallop shell, holding a pendulum that moved across her arm with the clockface above it. The clock said half past three.

Ketill brought the telephone over to the coffee table and motioned to Sigurbjörn to sit down. The gesture made Sigurbjörn angry. He looked at Ketill for a moment, then sat down. On the wall opposite there were photographs of relatives, there was scarcely an empty space to be seen.

'You're not exactly short on family. All these old chaps with long beards and plump women in Icelandic national dress.'

'Well, I don't think I'm any different from other Icelanders. We're all related.' Ketill sat down opposite him.

'No, that's wrong,' Sigurbjörn said with heavy emphasis. 'I don't count you among my relations.' He picked up the telephone receiver.

He let it ring for a while, and Ketill looked on intently. It would take seven to ten rings to bring Helgi downstairs if he were at home. Sigurbjörn looked Ketill in the eye and listened to the phone ringing.

He put his hand in his pocket. Ketill's gaze swerved, and he ran his eyes over the cornices from one angle to the other. Sigurbjörn hung up.

'Don't you need to make some more calls?' Ketill offered. There was a note of suspicion in his voice.

'I'm really here on false pretences,' said Sigurbjörn. 'There isn't any fire. I've come here to talk to you about God.'

Ketill looked at him coldly and replied, 'I'm not prepared to discuss God with you, my good man.'

'It may be that you need to.' Sigurbjörn sat forward on the edge of the chair. He struck the coffee table and his voice broke as he shouted, 'You had the cheek to say that my small son told lies.'

'You're that bloody architect,' Ketill said, surprised. 'The bloke who was pestering me the spring before last. I thought I recognized you. Have you gone mad?' He brought his fist down in a mighty blow on the table and shouted, 'Will you get out of here this instant? This is my home!'

'Is this your home?' Sigurbjörn echoed. He leaned back in the chair again, and studied Ketill. There was something close to affection in his voice as he said, 'That never occurred to me. But it's true.' A kindly look came to his face. 'And that is why it's so important to save you. The judgment of God hangs over you and you need His and my forgiveness.'

An old man with bare legs like a stork's came through the door. He was wearing a long nightshirt. He hadn't a tooth in his head and his hair was snow-white. 'Are you from the Salvation Army? I must ask you to leave,' the old man requested, doddering. 'You mustn't make him angry. He has had to put up with so much. Ketill, go up to your room.'

'Go downstairs, Father,' said Ketill firmly, and made as if to move towards the guest.

Sigurbjörn rose from his seat and thundered, 'Jesus Christ is the Lord. And no one comes to the Father except by him.' He felt in his pocket. 'I could have killed you, but I didn't do it.' He picked up the owl and rasped, 'Jesus said: "Be not afraid of them that kill the body, and after that have no more that they can do. But I will forewarn you whom ye shall fear: Fear him, which after he hath killed hath power to cast into hell."' He looked at Ketill for a moment, and then said quietly: 'And that is where you will end up.'

9

Sigurbjörn sat behind the steering wheel and took some time to recover his equilibrium. It was now broad daylight, and thrushes were singing from the rooftops. No movement was visible in the house. In the rear-view mirror he saw a man with a stoop walking along Framnesvegur towards the car, going from door to door. Sigurbjörn was startled when the man tapped on the window and offered him a newspaper. Sigurbjörn refused, and watched him go. Just as the newspaper vendor disappeared, a police car came along. Sigurbjörn wound down the window and the policemen touched their caps. 'Yes, good morning, we've had a complaint from an old man that there was some disturbance here. Are you drunk? Please be so good as to get out of your car.'

'I haven't touched a drop of alcohol for months, my good man,' said Sigurbjörn.

After he had got out, one of the policemen smelled his breath. 'No, I don't think you've been drinking.'

His colleague had got out of the car, and was studying the house. Still no movement was visible. 'Have you been in there?' he asked.

'Yes.'

'Ketill Einarsson lives there, doesn't he?'

'Yes.'

The one who had smelled his breath gave him a hard look. 'Are you on drugs?'

'No.'

'Are you a relative? We've been asked to keep an eye on the house.'

'No.'

'Where do you live?'

'Sjafnargata 1a.'

'And you've been in there?' he asked, surprised.

'Yes.'

Both policemen fell silent. The first to have spoken, a big, tall man, said, 'Don't you think we ought to drive you home in your car, Sigurbjörn? You are Sigurbjörn Helgason, aren't you?'

'Yes, I answer to that name. No, thank you. I'll get there myself.'

'Well, we'd prefer it if we could see you back to Sjafnargata. You understand.'

'I'll sit on the woman's side, then,' said Sigurbjörn.

He expected the man to make excuses for the official pardon on the way back, but that did not happen. Instead, the policeman asked, 'He's your son, isn't he? Our famous footballer? It's not so long to wait now for the game against the Finns.'

Sigurbjörn acknowledged the question with pride, and said, 'The boy intends to score against them.'

The policeman chatted about football on the way. They followed him up to the front door, and the bigger one said, 'I'm sorry to say this, but we'll have to ask you not to cause any further disturbances over there in the west end of town.'

'It won't happen again.'

He woke up at noon, and heard Helgi in the kitchen. His son had made coffee and cooked bacon and eggs. He poured a cup for his father. Sigurbjörn had not eaten for a long time, and had an excellent appetite. 'Thank you for all the good food you've been buying, Helgi my boy,' he said with his mouth full. 'I'll be more help around the place than I have been up till now.' His large eyes looked at his son.

'The police were here half an hour ago,' said Helgi.

'And what did they want?'

'To return Grandmother's Bible. It's on the parlour table. They said they drove you home last night.'

'Well, yes,' Sigurbjörn said sheepishly.

'They told me where you went. Are you going a bit funny in the head, or something?'

'I'm not surprised you ask, Helgi my boy.' And Sigurbjörn's dry laugh filled the room.

'What were you thinking of?' Helgi asked, flabbergasted. 'Were you planning to turn him into a Christian?'

'I think I went temporarily insane when I saw that story in the *Morgunbladid*,' Sigurbjörn said. 'I've not been too well recently.'

'Yes, but to go charging in there in the middle of the night with the Bible, man. It's sheer lunacy. You're not even a Christian. What's going on? You ought to have waited until I got home. Then we could have gone together and killed him. That would have been a far more sensible thing to do.'

'Yes, you're right,' Sigurbjörn said, and smiled broadly, revealing his teeth.

'You never know, you might have got the better of the bloody man,' Helgi said thoughtfully. 'I've heard you were a real mean bastard in the old days.'

When Helgi came back from the bank on Monday evening, Sigurbjörn was sitting at the parlour table with his chin propped on his hand.

'Mother phoned me today and said she had had a strange dream on Friday night,' Helgi said, sitting down. His father raised his head from his knuckles and looked at him questioningly.

'She dreamt she walked through to the hall. Then she felt that there was a horribly frightening atmosphere outside. She screamed with fear in her sleep, but did not wake up. She opened the hall door and then caught the back view of a tall man who had gone beyond the stairs and was on his way down to the gate.'

'The woman was dreaming about the man who came to disconnect the electricity,' Sigurbjörn said, grinning.

'No, she thought the tall man had his head on one side and was walking in a strange way.'

'Then it was my brother Jóhannes,' Sigurbjörn said in surprise. 'He used to put his head on one side like that when he was concentrating on something. I've often told Sunneva that.'

'Well, listen to the dream,' said Helgi. 'The man disappeared from sight for a moment, but when she saw him again a bit further down the path, he was dressed in your overcoat, so it wasn't Jóhannes. It was you. You looked over your shoulder, and where your face should have been there was darkness, so thick one could touch it. Then she woke up.'

'Is this a premonition of my death, Helgi?' Sigurbjörn asked, peering round the room.

'No, I don't think so. I thought you didn't take any notice of dreams.'

'I didn't use to, but now I'm not sure what to think any more. Especially as my Sunna had dreams that predicted all those terrible things last autumn.' Sigurbjörn let his gaze stray about the table, worried. 'What disaster is about to befall us now, Helgi my boy? How did your mother interpret the dream?'

'Why a disaster? She looked at it like any other omen or warning.'

'Warning?'

'Yes. The meaning is plain for all to see. You are knocking on doors but walking in darkness.'

'Am I walking in darkness, Helgi?' Sigurbjörn was taken aback.

'Yes, that's almost certainly the meaning. When I told her about this escapade of yours the night before last, she felt the dream had come true.'

'And why was it your mother who had this dream?'

'She seems to be the one with the second sight in the family. Please don't go talking about this. She told me the dream in confidence. She doesn't want to cause you any worry, and she'd be angry with me if she knew I'd said anything.'

VI

1

The yellow flags above the entrance to the Department Store were flapping in the rain, their poles ringing as the ropes whipped against them. Gudbrandur hurried in through the main door.

It was nearly ten o'clock. Not many customers were there yet. The Department Store had opened on the eighth of June. Gudbrandur heard the gentle humming of the empty escalator and walked over to it.

He had not been able to bring himself to invite Sigurbjörn to the opening ceremony.

'Phone the man,' Ingirídur had said.

'No, I can't,' he had replied. 'Sigurbjörn will come on his own when he's well enough, and then everything will be fine.'

'You're such a fool,' said Ingirídur. 'Can't you get it into your head that a man like Sigurbjörn never forgets anything and never forgives anyone?'

He thought of his father. When Gudbrandur was a boy, father and son had made a trip east of the mountains to shoot geese. Gudbrandur's father was a master plumber and had had a keen eye for horseflesh. Some years earlier he had handed over a pedigree horse with an ulcerated hoof to be slaughtered for meat at a farm in Flói. They had had no luck with the geese that Sunday morning long ago, because they had arrived too late and the birds were wary of them. Gudbrandur's father had suddenly decided to drop in on the farm. They recognized the horse from a long way away. It was harnessed to a cart. The hoof had healed. Without a word, his father unharnessed the horse, led it up to the homefield fence and killed it No one said a word. Gudbrandur had never been sure if he liked this intransigence or not.

232

He chose a step for his foot, supported himself with both hands on the handrails, and leaned sideways a little as the moving staircase bore him aloft. He heard little María give a shriek of joy as her mother helped her on to the bottom step. Ingirídur was carrying the little boy in her arms. Perhaps I should have phoned him, thought Gudbrandur. From the escalator he could look down on the copper saucepans on the top shelf in the household appliances department. Ingirídur had admired them the day before, and he decided to take one home as a surprise.

He waited for María, helped her off the staircase and then took little Sigurbjörn in his arms. 'Well, now for the stairs, Inga.'

'Are you going to be here long?' asked Ingirídur.

'No, I just need to check some bills.'

'Can I have another five hundred krónur? There're so many things I have to buy.'

'Yes, of course. But you realize you can have credit on every floor.'

'I don't like buying things here,' she said, embarrassed. 'A person feels as if the store's swallowing them up.'

'What do you think Sigurbjörn would say to that?' asked Gudbrandur.

Women's wear was on the second floor. At the east end a staircase led up to the higher floors. Gudbrandur had opened an office for Enterprise on the sixth floor. He had had to sell the house at Ánanaust in the autumn. And their home on Öldugata at the beginning of April. The firm was getting by. He had taken out a loan to meet the worst of the debts and sent Sigurbjörn twenty thousand from his own pocket on the quiet. That was the first step towards reconciliation.

'Hold the boy,' said Gudbrandur and took his daughter in his arms. On the third floor stood rows of washing machines and refrigerators. Some of the refrigerators were open at the top so the customers could see inside the freezing compartment. On the fourth floor there was an area partitioned off for a dressmaker. The fifth floor was still being fitted out.

'It'll make a difference when the lift's working,' puffed Ingirídur. Her voice echoed down the passage.

'Really, Inga? Are you so tired?' asked Gudbrandur, concerned. 'There's only a little way to go now.' He looked up and saw Sigurbjörn sitting on the top step of the stairs leading up to the sixth floor. His head hung forward and his fists were clenched between his knees. Gudbrandur could see that the roots of his hair at the centre parting were now growing snow white. He's gone completely white, he thought, shocked, and looked down at the grey steps to give himself time to take a few deep breaths before coming face to face with his friend.

Sigurbjörn had become aware of them.

'Is that you, Sigurbjörn?' said Gudbrandur.

'I think I know what this dream of Sunneva's is all about,' Sigurbjörn boomed. 'Jesus is not the son of God.'

Gudbrandur reached the top step and put María down. Ingirídur was halfway up, looking at them. Sigurbjörn had risen to his feet. They shook hands.

'Well, how do you like the store?'

'It's all right, Brandsi,' Sigurbjörn thundered. 'Everything's been painted from top to bottom, and the work on the fifth floor's going well.'

'Did you know we'd opened?'

'No.'

'Really? It was in all the papers.'

'I never see the papers.'

'Come and look at the office. This way.'

'Yes, they told me downstairs.'

'Hello,' said Ingirídur, shaking Sigurbjörn's hand. 'And welcome. What do you make of your namesake?'

Sigurbjörn stroked the boy gently on the cheek with the back of his index finger. 'He's a fine-looking boy.' Young Sigurbjörn tried to grab Old Sigurbjörn's finger.

They walked down a corridor with many doors leading off it. A gilded plate said INGVAR HJÁLMARSSON LTD. Gudbrandur opened a light oak door with a similar plate: ENTERPRISE LTD. There was a writing desk, a pile of papers on the desktop, and two chairs.

'Well,' said Gudbrandur, 'what do you think of the office?'

'It's not bad.' Sigurbjörn looked around.

Gudbrandur sat down and took María into his arms. She waggled her legs energetically. With one hand he reached into the drawer of the writing desk, took out two 500-króna notes and handed them to his wife. The little girl wailed, 'I want to go home to ours!'

'Father will meet you later, and then we'll "go home to ours",' Gudbrandur said. He put the girl down on the floor, walked over to the window and looked down at the car park. Just at that moment a car drove in, the rain beating on the roof like a drum. All four doors opened and people ran for cover. From a rear door emerged a pole, like a tent pole, then an umbrella sprang open and an old woman got out.

Sigurbjörn laughed his hollow laugh. 'I should have designed a steel-framed roof here and put corrugated iron over it so people could come in without getting wet. Look at the old lady. Grandmothers are the same the world over.'

'Well, I'll say goodbye for now,' Ingirídur said, hovering by the door.

'Yes. I'll see you at the café in town, my dear.'

'Goodbye, Sigurbjörn.'

'Yes, goodbye, Ingirídur.' Sigurbjörn did not look over his shoulder. 'What happened to the beard?'

'I shaved it off,' Sigurbjörn said, drily.

'Didn't someone come and ask you to design a house for him?' Gudbrandur said, when Ingirídur had closed the door behind her.

'Yes, did that have something to do with you?' Sigurbjörn looked out across at the bay.

'No, he came here and asked about it. Did you do the designs?'

'No, it never came to anything.'

'Can I do anything for you? Have you been looking round the store?'

'I need some money. I was thinking of taking all the children out to Naustid on the evening of the seventeenth if Helgi hoiks the bladder through the Finns' goal.'

'I don't have a bean on me.'

'But I must have something coming to me for this place,' Sigurbjörn said, glaring angrily at the windowsill.

'Yes, certainly, but I don't have any ready cash.'

'Two or three thousand?'

'Drop round my place at midday on the seventeenth. Maybe I'll have it for you then. But at the moment I don't have a krónur to my name. Did you hear we had to sell Öldugata and Ánanaust?'

'No,' said Sigurbjörn. 'Why was that?' He seemed surprised.

'Because things were very tight.'

'Where are you living now?'

'In a flat I still own in Mother's house in Austurstræti. We're all right there.'

'And now you're a director, Brandsi,' Sigurbjörn said with an evil grin.

'It's more or less just a formality.' Gudbrandur raised his voice. 'You can have my position any time you want it. Today if you like.'

Sigurbjörn did not answer, but looked at the roof of Bjarnaborg. An old person was putting a flowerpot in a dormer window.

'Show up for work on Monday and take all this over again,' said Gudbrandur. 'Next I want to build a big block of flats in Stigahlídin. There's nothing the City Council won't do for us now.'

'Yes, maybe that would be a good idea.'

'Would you be willing to design it?'

'I can try,' said Sigurbjörn. He turned away from the window. 'I'm not blaming you for signing, Gudbrandur,' he said. 'I know who was behind it.'

'Who?'

'My father-in-law.'

'Well, I think it was me who started the ball rolling,' said Gudbrandur. 'I felt everything was slipping out of my hands.' He was afraid Sigurbjörn would want to start talking about Sunneva, and he asked, 'How's Tóti?'

But Sigurbjörn did not answer. 'So you want me to come and get the money at midday tomorrow?'

'Yes, and show up for work on the dot on the nineteenth.' Gudbrandur smiled.

'Very well,' said Sigurbjörn. 'But I'd've preferred to have the office at Ánanaust.' He felt in his pocket, took out his peaked cap and walked to the door without shaking Gudbrandur's hand. In the doorway he looked over his shoulder and nodded quickly as he closed the door. Gudbrandur sat down at the table and heaved a sigh of relief. But the idea of Sigurbjörn taking over the firm the following week was deeply troubling.

2

Helgi arrived from Laugarvatn on the morning of the seventeenth. The national team had been relaxing there for a few days before the game. The weather was at its best in Reykjavík, cloudless and warm, and there was a festive mood in the town.

'And now the great day has arrived,' said Sigurbjörn.

'Yes, aren't you going to the stadium?'

'No.' Sigurbjörn shifted his weight in his chair.

'You promised to come, Father. You've never seen me play,' Helgi said, taken aback.

'Don't take it so much to heart, my boy. Thórarinn and I are going to Thingvellir.' Sigurbjörn looked at the clock.

'But he was dead keen to see the match. I don't like this. I wanted you both to come.'

'Oh, I've never been much of a one for football, Helgi my boy,' Sigurbjörn muttered. 'I phoned him. He wants to come east with me. It's a long time since Tóti and I have been anywhere together.'

'The Finns will be slaughtered,' Helgi said. 'I'll show you, I'm going to score at least two goals. I'll drive them into the ground.'

'Two goals! ' His father clapped his hands and laughed.

'Why are you so surprised?' Helgi cleared his throat. 'You know our coach is a Scot. The lads' English isn't too good, so I've been interpreting for them. Last night he had a word with me in private.'

Helgi paused a moment and took a deep breath.

'And?'

'He was an assistant coach with Glasgow Rangers and used to play for them in the old days. He asked me how I felt about playing professionally.'

'And leave Iceland?' Sigurbjörn asked. 'It's going to be lonely here at Sjafnargata.'

'Nothing's settled. I'd have to do a trial period. If it goes well, maybe I'd get a contract. And it will go well,' he said, sounding determined.

'You're a cracking forward, you'll show them,' said Sigurbjörn, still laughing drily. 'Can you "forward" me a thousand krónur?'

'Are you sure that's all you need?'

Sigurbjörn was silent for a moment, then replied, 'That's all for the time being. Perhaps you can top up the loan this evening. I'm thinking of starting work next week.'

'That's good news. Have you seen Gudbrandur?'

'We had a chat yesterday. I want to take you kids out for a meal this evening. That's why I need the money.'

'Where are we going?'

'To Naustid.'

'What about taking Mother, too?'

'Your mother?' Sigurbjörn said, looking at his son in surprise. 'What's the news with her?'

'She went and talked to the people at the Ministry of Justice. But she didn't get much joy.'

Sigurbjörn stared at the dining-room table and beat his clenched fist on its surface a few times in a steady rhythm. 'Please bring both the children at about seven,' he said. 'If you score,' he added, with a smile.

Thórarinn was waiting outside. Sunneva stepped forward. 'Mother wants to talk to you, Father.'

Sunneva smiled and walked round in front of the bonnet. He rolled down the window. 'When will you be back?' She leaned forward, holding her hair back off her face with her hand.

'This afternoon.'

'Ragnar is coming for a meal. Then I'm going with Mother to Kópavogur for a while. We'll be back about six.'

'We'll be back by then, too, Tóti and me,' Sigurbjörn said.

'Aren't you taking anything to eat with you on the trip?' She looked around the inside of the car.

'No, of course not, woman, we'll have a coffee at Valhöll like gentlemen do.'

'Well, Sigurbjörn, then perhaps we'll see each other this evening.'

'That wouldn't be a bad idea, Sunna.'

'Enjoy yourself, Thórarinn.' She looked at her son.

'Well, Tóti, my man. It's been a year and a day since we've gone off on a trip together,' Sigurbjörn said, and drove off.

'"My man"! You've never called me that before,' said Thórarinn.

'Shame on me. But it's a long, long time, all the same.'

'Yes, a very long one,' the boy said in a deep voice.

In Mosfellsdalur the sky was overcast and it was drizzling. On the moor it came on to rain. Thórarinn looked out of the window. At the side of the road the sheep were soaking wet. A row of electricity pylons came into view one by one. It looked as though a schooner had been stranded on the moor.

'Helgi's lucky with the weather in Reykjavík,' said Thórarinn.

'Yes,' said Sigurbjörn. 'Is Ragnar going?'

'Yes, and Grandfather, too. Grandfather hasn't been to the stadium since 1912.'

'How come he's going now?'

'Helgi said he was going to win the match all by himself, and Grandfather's going to see him make a bloody fool of himself.'

Sigurbjörn laughed.

'There won't be many people at the Old Parliament today,' said Thórarinn. 'Father, don't you find Thingvellir always takes you a bit by surprise?'

'How do you mean?'

'Well, here we are driving along and everything's as flat as a pancake. Then we drive down Almannagjá and everything's completely different.'

'But first you see the lake in all its glory, my boy,' said Sigurbjörn.

'Yes, that's true.'

They drove down into the ravine and let the car glide slowly past the cliffs. A glittering stream of water ran in all directions across the road. There was heather-flecked moss on rocky ledges, and a young birch high on a ridge. As the slope gave way to flatness again they saw a man on the grass at the right-hand side of the road with a painter's easel before him.

'Well, there's the maestro himself, and the painting looks quite something,' said Sigurbjörn, opening his eyes wide. 'Would you like to meet Kjarval?'

'No, I'd rather not. Men like him always seem a bit odd to me.'

'Don't you remember him in the old days? He often used to visit us.'

'No, I was too young then. But once I saw him on a school outing. He came out of the ski chalet at Hveradalur wearing pyjamas and a hat, and gave a speech.'

'And what was the speech about?' Sigurbjörn had parked the car.

'It was complete nonsense, I think. I can't remember a word of it. Yes, it was something about the mountains.'

'And do you call that nonsense, talking about the mountains, boy? Don't let anyone hear you saying things like that.' Sigurbjörn was whispering in mock horror.

'No, but people thought it was nonsense,' Thórarinn reflected. 'But some of them took photographs all the same.'

'Let's go and say hello to him.' Sigurbjörn opened the door slightly. It had stopped raining.

'No, I don't want to, Father. I'm too shy.'

'That's enough of that cowardy-cowardy stuff, Tóti.'

There was dead calm in the ravine. Kjarval was dressed in a waxed sackcloth coat with a rope tied around his waist. On his head he wore a bowler hat with the brim cut off.

'Hello, Kjarval,' Sigurbjörn boomed, walking towards him with large strides and an outstretched hand. His son lagged behind. Kjarval completely ignored them. Sigurbjörn took his time and refrained from offering his hand.

In the grass at the painter's side lay an open trunk. Kjarval dropped his paintbrush and palette into it and flipped the lid of the trunk shut with the toe of his boot. The battered old trunk was bound with iron hoops.

'Well, maestro,' Sigurbjörn said. He put his hand on his son's shoulder and studied the painting. 'So you've just been painting Ármannsfell and the ravine. My son and I wanted to say hello to you.'

Instead of replying, Kjarval took some sailcloth and covered the easel with it.

'Are we disturbing you?' Sigurbjörn grew anxious. Kjarval stood beside the easel with his feet wide apart and his arms crossed on his chest, and gave Sigurbjörn a sharp look.

'It's good that Thingvellir's on the canvas,' said Sigurbjörn. Then he began to tell an anecdote about a painter whom they both knew called Óskar who churned out paintings of Thingvellir by the dozen. 'Well, it so happened, Kjarval, that a good friend of mine was driving along Mosfellsdalur, and who should he see there but old Óskar going at it like mad with his brush in the brilliant sunshine. He stopped his car, flabbergasted. The last thing he would have expected was to find Óskar painting there. He hurried out on to the moor to take a look at the painting, but he needn't have worried – it was Almannagjá at Thingvellir on the canvas after all. The chap was painting it from memory. He said he didn't feel like going any further, and the weather forecast for Thingvellir had been bad.

Kjarval glowered angrily at the visitors and said nothing.

'Well, Thórarinn,' Sigurbjörn said. 'I can see we're disturbing him. Let's be on our way.'

'I didn't mind, even if he was so boring,' Thórarinn said in the car. 'I don't think his pictures are of much importance, actually.'

Kjarval had removed the cloth from the easel and was stooping over the trunk.

'Well, now it's coffee and cakes, as much as we can stuff inside ourselves,' said Sigurbjörn.

He stopped the car on the forecourt outside Hotel Valhöll. The higher face of the Almannagjá ravine was black and dreary-looking.

The wind blew in off the lake, rippling the Öxará river by the boat shelter. Lake Thingvellir was grey and rough, and the waves were lashing the shore in a regular pulse. Two other cars were parked on the forecourt.

They went inside, and Sigurbjörn ordered coffee and cakes. He rubbed his hands. 'They might heat this place a bit better,' he said to his son.

'Father?'

'Yes.'

'I didn't mean what I wrote in my diary about your brother Jóhannes. I am sure he was a good man. I saw someone had looked at the Black List. Was it you? And I didn't mean any of the other nasty things I wrote.'

'No, of course you didn't mean them, Tóti. Did you write something bad? It doesn't matter. Here's the waitress now.'

The waitress, who was a little plump, wore a black dress trimmed with white lace, and bade them good day. Thórarinn asked for orangeade. The cakes looked delicious but turned out to be dry, and he needed the fizzy drink to swallow them down. He mentioned this, but his father did not call the waitress, just peered towards the door into the kitchen.

The waitress peeped out. Then another one came to the doorway to look at them.

After a short while, the owner of the restaurant came to the door to look. Sigurbjörn stared at a half-eaten jam tart on his plate, and then gazed forlornly round the room. Tiny drops of sweat had erupted on his forehead. 'There aren't many people here today,' he said.

'Those cars on the forecourt probably belong to the staff. I think most people are at the match,' said Thórarinn.

'I have to leave the room for a moment, Tóti,' Sigurbjörn said.

'The toilets are at the back,' said Thórarinn.

Sigurbjörn got to his feet and put his wallet on the table.

Thórarinn waited. After a long time he began to wonder where his father had got to and went through to the toilets, but there was no one there. He looked out at the forecourt and saw that the car was gone

He remembered having heard a car. There must be a telephone here. He would wait calmly and then call his mother if his father did not come back. Perhaps he had gone to tell that Kjarval what for. Thórarinn sat down and finished his orangeade. He ordered a Coke and tried the cakes, polishing off the whole plateful. A car pulled up. It was not Sigurbjörn. It was getting on for five o'clock. Now the first half of the game would be halfway through. Sunneva would be home around six. He looked in the wallet. A driving licence. A picture of his father as a young man. A few hundred krónur. He laid the notes out on the table and counted them. Then he raised his hand, and the waitress came.

'Father left and asked me to pay,' said Thórarinn.

'Your father's an architect, isn't he?'

'Yes.'

'Will you tell him when he comes back that it would be a real pleasure for us if he would accept the coffee on the house?'

'Yes, but why?'

'Didn't he used to work at the City Architect's office?'

'Yes.'

'The restaurant owner wants to show his respect and gratitude. The City Architect designed Hotel Valhöll.'

Thórarinn began to sob, to the consternation of both the waitress and himself.

3

It was one evening in spring when she first saw the flock of geese at Laugardalur. They had been carried across by a fierce trough of low pressure. The gale had blown for two days and nights, loosening the roofs of houses far and wide, and the geese had drifted in on the southern Scottish wind in the space of a few hours.

Sunneva cooked salmon for Ragnar after father and son had gone to Thingvellir. The previous evening she had baked a chocolate cake. Salmon and chocolate cake: his favourites.

She had woken early in the morning and walked down into the valley in the morning sunshine when no one was about except the geese and she had picked some flowers – buttercups, meadowsweet, wood geranium and dandelion.

'You spoil me,' he said after coffee and cake.

She looked at him and saw he was suntanned and smiling. She suggested they go for a walk together, but Ragnar was going to the big match and had to go somewhere else first.

'Is it a girl?'

'Yes.'

'And what does she do?'

'She's a student.'

Sunneva raised her eyebrows, questioningly. 'A student? What's she studying?'

'Three guesses.'

'No!' she said in disbelief, and clapped her hands together. 'Architecture.'

He laughed.

'God help you, Ragnar.'

'She's going abroad again this autumn,' he said. 'She has a three-year-old daughter. Have you been in touch with Snjólaug's husband?'

'The lawyer? Yes. Apparently, no one takes the government to court without good reason. We'd just stir the whole thing up. None of us can take it. I called the Ministry of Justice direct, but all they said was it's the President's constitutional right.'

They went outside together. 'Are you sure you won't come to the match?' he asked. 'The boy's taken a solemn vow that he'll score.'

'No, I'll listen to it on the radio. I like being on my own.'

She walked down Kirkjuteigur and thought about this son of hers who was so handsome and so like his father. The streets were deserted. All at once she saw a tall man in an anorak walking towards her. Was it Ketill? She turned round and quickly walked halfway up the front steps, and pretended to open the door.

The man walked past the house. His cheeks were hollow and he was wearing glasses. His black hair was so dirty it looked as though it had been smeared with oil.

At Laugadalur they were building a sports stadium. The valley was crisscrossed by ditches, but she knew her way over the wooden planks scattered here and there.

The flock of geese was keeping to the tall grass. Sometimes she had tried to creep up on them, but they always spotted her and rose up in flight, cackling. She liked to see how close she could get and then watch them go hurtling up into the sky and gather in a V.

She saw a graceful head above tall couch grass. The gander was on guard, waiting quietly. Sunneva also stood dead still. That morning she had written Sigurbjörn a letter and asked him to forgive her for having signed the document. She had asked him to bury the past.

She listened for the sounds of the valley. A sluggish wind sang in the grasses, a stream purled in a ditch. She turned round calmly. She saw dandelion heads dancing here and there in the grass in time to the breeze. The gander looked at her and stretched out its neck.

She had thought of handing the letter to Sigurbjörn when he brought Thórarinn back in the car. Suddenly she saw her husband before her: 'What do you think it feels like to be nineteen, Sunneva, and know that your brother is dying in Germany?'

She remembered taking the newborn Ragnar into her arms. He had lain awake all night at the hospital and prattled to her. She had seen him smile, though no one believed it. 'Sigurbjörn made me betray my eldest son,' she thought, and drove the flock of geese up into the air as she took a step forward. She watched the geese ascend angrily one by one out of the grass. All of a sudden through her mind shot the thought: 'He showed me the door. I am alone. And that is how I want to be.'

He rang the doorbell. When no one answered, Sigurbjörn put his face to the frosted yellow glass. He could see the outline of the corridor. The door into a parlour was standing open, and a clear ray of the late-afternoon sun glowed gently in the window.

He sat down on the stairs leading up to the loft. On the next landing there was an door opening on to a balcony. A corridor window stretched the full length of the building, and a narrow passage ran along by the window on all the floors. Outside the house at Austurstræti there was an iron manhole cover that clanked when the cars drove over it. Sigurbjörn could hear by the frequency of the noise, *clank*, *clank*, that not many cars were driving by. There was a courtyard at the back, and the echoing sound of the children playing in the underpass. It was nearly seven o'clock.

He had gone over and over in his mind everything he wanted to discuss with Gudbrandur. One of things he wanted to say was: 'What did you mean by asking, "How is Tóti?" What were you getting at?'

Twice doors had opened on the floors below. People had gone out but no one had come in.

He heard the front door. Sigurbjörn took a deep breath and listened. Someone had come into the hallway. On the doorjamb there was a steel arm to pull the door to. When it closed, he could hear the person coming up the stairs. If it was Gudbrandur he was going terribly slowly, dragging his feet on the steps and pausing to rest on the second and third floors. Sigurbjörn could hear breathing. He looked down the stairwell but could see nothing. Now a gloved hand was placed on the dark-brown mahogany bannister. A woollen coat, a wrist, a woman's watch. A ginger-haired girl, with freckles and red cheeks, appeared. She put down a suitcase, looked at Sigurbjörn in surprise, and bade him good evening.

Sigurbjörn returned the greeting. 'Good evening.'

'Are you waiting for someone?' The girl was quite out of breath.

'Gudbrandur Jónsson.'

'Isn't he home?' The girl glanced at the door. 'Have you rung the bell? It sometimes sticks.' She rang. *Brrr*. A hoarse murmur was heard from within. 'There doesn't seem to be anyone in,' she said.

'I'm going to wait a bit,' said Sigurbjörn. 'I need to talk to him. That's why I'm sitting on the stairs.'

'I'll have to ask you to move,' she said, and laughed. 'I need to get past.'

'Upstairs?' he asked, inquisitively. 'There's only the drying loft up there.'

'My room's up there,' the girl said, and smiled. She picked up the suitcase and the redness of her hair gleamed in the light from the corridor window. 'I rent it,' she said.

He got to his feet and had to hunch over under the eaves. 'In the loft?' he asked, looking at the door like a simpleton. 'That can't be so, my dear. There isn't a room in the loft. I've seen the plans for this house.'

She took a long time finding a key in her handbag. There was a room there, she said. She had been renting it since early in the spring. She was studying nursing at Landakot and was from Reydarfjördur. He could hardly believe his ears and waited impatiently for her to open the door. 'My father knows Gudbrandur,' she said.

Sigurbjörn went in first, and saw that a corner of the loft was partitioned off. 'Cheek,' he muttered. 'I'm an architect, you see.'

'Did you design this house?'

'No, but it's all the same. No one's allowed to make changes without asking the architect. There's the matter of copyright. You must respect it. It makes no difference who the architect is.'

'I knew there wasn't planning permission for the room. Brandur told me. But does it matter so terribly?' She looked at him with hope in her eyes.

'Gudbrandur and I were friends,' Sigurbjörn said loudly. 'Yes, friends! But recently the man's done all these things without consulting me.' He peered around the drying loft, angrily. 'He took my firm away from me. Had me dropped from the board of directors and informed of it by registered letter. How do you think it feels to have something like that thrown in your face? He made my wife sign and tried to get my sons to put their names to it as well.' Sigurbjörn had gone red in the face. 'We've been married for a quarter of a century. Something happened to my youngest son, and I've found it hard to accept. I got a bad shock, you see. I've not been in the best of health. Perhaps you've heard something about it?'

The girl shook her head.

'I'm going to take it up with Gudbrandur,' said Sigurbjörn. 'Try to get that man to see things the way I do. I've kept my feelings under control for a long time. I've been reasonable. But I cannot allow myself to be treated like this for ever. I think you can understand that.'

He looked at the girl with his large eyes. She looked at him rather nervously. Rays of light fell obliquely on the wooden floor through four skylights. Without being asked, he picked up her suitcase and carried it into her room. The room was partitioned by sheets of chipboard, which gave off a sour smell.

'Bloody chipboard,' Sigurbjörn muttered. 'How can you live with the damned stuff?'

'Yes, it's awful,' she said, and laughed anxiously. 'I have to keep the windows open a lot of the time.'

'What's the rent?'

'Three hundred.'

'Three hundred krónur!' Sigurbjörn exclaimed, scandalized. 'The man's a thief,' he said loudly and laughed. He put the suitcase down in the small room and looked around him. 'An unadulterated thief.'

'I'm told it's quite cheap,' the girl said. 'I look on it rather as a favour.'

There was a bed and a chest-of-drawers, a writing desk under a skylight, an old door in a frame. The room was painted white and there were pictures hanging on the walls or stuck up with glue.

'I think that's an awfully nice picture,' she said, pointing to a framed photograph of a house by a duckpond. 'But it would look better higher up.'

'Then why not move it?' asked Sigurbjörn.

'I'm afraid of heights. If I stand on a chair I can see right down to the courtyard, and I get so scared.'

'Have you got a hammer?' Sigurbjörn pulled a chair up to the skylight.

The girl went out into the loft space, could not find a hammer but brought back a large crowbar and handed it to him. They positioned the picture on the wall together, Sigurbjörn standing on the chair. He held the nail to the wall and drove it in with the back of the crowbar, looking down at the concrete courtyard. Over the roofs of the houses he could see Mount Esja, the shadows in its cliffs, and the black-backed gulls hovering over the harbour.

'Well,' she said. 'Thank you very much for your help, but you must excuse me. I'm tired after the journey. I'd like to be alone. I have to be on duty at midnight.'

'Oh yes, I do beg your pardon,' he said, and got down. 'But that rent is far too high. Far too high. Take my word for it, my dear.'

They heard sounds from below. He went out to the top of the stairs. The door of Gudbrandur's apartment was standing open. Gudbrandur was bareheaded, wearing a light grey overcoat, stooping over a pram on the landing. 'Let's go "home to ours",' Sigurbjörn said.

'What?' Gudbrandur looked over his shoulder. 'Oh, is that you, Sigurbjörn? You never came to collect your money. What did you say?'

'What you said to your little one in the office yesterday. "We'll go home to ours."'

'What do you mean by that?' Gudbrandur looked at him in surprise.

Sigurbjörn leapt downstairs brandishing the crowbar. Gudbrandur put his hands up in front of his face. The first blow missed and landed in the corner by the door frame. The second blow landed on Gudbrandur's temple, and he fell over backwards and crashed into the door. He stumbled in through the hall, put his hands out in front of him and sank to the floor.

The third blow fell straight on to his head. Gudbrandur shouted, 'What are you doing, Sigurbjörn? God help you.'

Sigurbjörn gave a yell and grabbed the crowbar with both hands, the iron spikes turned downwards and he smashed them into the crown of Gudbrandur's head. Gudbrandur rolled on the floor with his eyes closed. Sigurbjörn sat down on a wooden chest and looked at him in astonishment.

He was facing a white panelled door. It was not quite shut. He looked into the parlour. There was a square of sunlight on the broad floorboards. He heard footsteps on the stairs, leaned forward and saw the lodger peep in. She ran back upstairs. He stepped over Gudbrandur and closed the door.

Sigurbjörn washed his hands in the bathroom. He heard Gudbrandur give a long drawn-out death-rattle.

He looked at the white panelled door. It had been closed. He heard a quiet cough. He picked up the crowbar from the floor and opened the door.

Vilborg was sitting on a couch. María, red-faced, was asleep on a cushion. Vilborg was stroking her petticoat and the blue checked bedspread by turns. She said, not looking at him, 'I'm looking after little María.'

Sigurbjörn was silent.

'We took Young Sigurbjörn to the Outpatients' Clinic. María got restless. Ingirídur sent us home.'

'Have you started babysitting here again, child?' her father asked, in a thick voice.

'Yes. Mother and Ingirídur are friends again. Helgi scored two goals, Father. Iceland won 3–2. I was listening to it on the wireless,' the girl said quickly. She looked up. Then she looked at the crowbar.

Sigurbjörn closed the door, put the crowbar down. With his legs wide apart, he took hold of Gudbrandur under the armpits and dragged his corpse into the corridor. Blood was oozing from the head and left a trail across the floor. He dragged Gudbrandur into the bedroom. In the corner there was a child's cot. The quilt had been pulled back from the embroidered pillow. On the pillow there was an needlework picture of an angel blowing a trumpet. Beneath the angel stitched in fancy lettering, was: SIGURBJÖRN.

He dragged Gudbrandur up to the foot of the bed, wetted a towe in the bathroom and bent down to mop up the blood, but the towel was too thick and wet and there was too much blood. A wet pink sheen remained in the corridor. He could not bring himself to wring out the towel, nor to do anything more about cleaning up. He threw the towel into the bath and took a key out of the parlour door. The key fitted the children's room, and he locked it. In the parlour he found a bedspread and wrapped it round the crowbar. He went out into the corridor with the roll under his arm and locked the door behind him.

5

At Geithals, about ten miles from Reykjavík, there was a single-storey corrugated-iron inn with a low roof. The inn was quite large and rested on loose stone foundations. Many of the windows looked out on to the gravel forecourt. There were a lot of horsemen gathered there chatting, downing schnapps and offering each other snuff. There were a few women and some children playing. Some of the horses were grazing down by the river. A few men were standing together in a group. One of them was holding the reins of two horses. They hung their heads behind him and waited patiently with large, gentle eyes. It was warm outside and midges were biting both horses and men. Sigurbjörn walked briskly over to this group and asked, 'Can you get a coffee here, lads?'

'Yes, yes,' said one of the men, pointing to the inn with his whip. The others looked at Sigurbjörn rather distantly. Sigurbjörn had a burning desire to talk to them. 'And maybe a schnapps?' he asked.

They were silent and looked at one another. One of them had been telling a story, the most cheerful one in the group, a man with a flat cap on his head and a boxer's nose. 'Give the man a schnapps,' he said. A long-faced, foolish-looking man handed a silver flask to Sigurbjörn. He took a swig.

He thanked them and walked into the restaurant. There were some men were sitting at tables, making a considerable noise. Children were

251

running to and fro. There was a smell of horses and pancakes. There were patches of wet sand and dry sand on the floor and the window-sills needed painting. It was obvious that the inn was not kept open through the winter. The cracked green-lacquered canvas had parted company from the ceiling here and there and sagged over the room. Now the landlord himself emerged. He was short, wearing black trousers and a white shirt that was not quite buttoned up. He had black, close-clipped sideburns and grey hair combed straight back from his forehead. Grey hairs peeped round the edge of his collar. He was listening to one of the horsemen standing opposite him in a dirty, greasy anorak and shiny riding boots. They were deep in a discussion of some new building project they both seemed suspicious of. The horseman was drunk and was saying loudly, 'Yes, that's it, they just want to put that place up to get their hands on public money . . .'

'I'd never set foot in a restaurant like that,' the landlord said. 'It's a brothel.' He had very thick purple lips, and he put his hand on his hip and stood with his legs wide apart.

The landlord had been aware of Sigurbjörn's presence but had not paid him the slightest attention. Now he walked over to him. Sigurbjörn ordered coffee and a pancake with jam and cream. On the way up out of town in the car he had been frozen to the bone.

A girl, perhaps about eighteen, wearing a black dress and with long blond hair, came in and stood in the middle of the floor, looking for someone. Sigurbjörn watched her. He began to weep without realizing it. He found his cheeks were wet and wiped them with the back of his hand.

The coffee was hot and good and the pancake tasty. Though he had drunk only a little schnapps, he was burning hot and the sweat flowed from him. He felt much better for something inside him.

A group of men came in. They were a bit tipsy, had a bottle of brennivín between them, seemed to know the landlord and were eager to give him a drink. He declined. 'No, not this evening, lads.'

'Come on, what's this, Steini, have a drink.'

'No, I tell you, not this evening.'

Three drunken lads came in soon after, and behaved badly. One of

252

them exposed himself. The landlord strode swiftly across the floor. He was built like a boxing coach. He pushed the young men out of the door. He did not even give the offender a chance to do up his flies.

This made Sigurbjörn enormously happy as he drank his coffee. Laughter burst from him.

'The bastards come in here exposing themselves,' said the landlord. He was in a filthy temper.

'They're thugs,' Sigurbjörn agreed. He took a swig of coffee, but now it was tepid and tasted foul. He looked down at his trousers. They were stained with blood. He felt in his breast pocket, he had three hundred krónur there. He got to his feet and the landlord came over to him. The landlord felt in a black leather bag hanging on his belt and counted out some small change. His expression was now more cordial.

Sigurbjörn went out to the forecourt. In the meadow beside the road he saw the river Hólmsá bend sharply. The water level was surprisingly high. The river was singing by its banks as it did in the spring, splashing them. The light had not yet begun to fail. He walked over to the horsemen who had offered him a drink from the flask. The man with the boxer's nose had disappeared, but the others were still standing there talking. A little way from the road, in a meadow, there were the foundations of an outhouse. The men were silent and looked at Sigurbjörn. 'Do you see those foundations over there, lads?' he asked.

The men looked in that direction. The one with the hook nose and the lower eyelids sagging so much that pink skin was visible beneath the eyeball, replied. 'Yes. So what?'

'Sometimes I think Icelanders aren't ambitious enough when it comes to buildings.'

'But those are foundations the British Army left behind . . .'

'I know.' Sigurbjörn laid a friendly hand on the man's leather sleeve. 'But all the same, lads' – the word 'lads' felt somehow stiff in his mouth – 'we ought to think big . . . we are all Icelanders together, we are descended from Norse chieftains and kings and we're second to none, lads, the devil we are. We should be putting up big buildings, none of this mediocre stuff. We should build large, solid buildings, and then future generations will remember us with pride.'

'What with?' asked one of the men. 'There's a ban on imports and wherever you look there's all kinds of rules and regulations. You can scarcely get the timber to make a door.' The man scuffed the toe of his rubber boot in the red gravel of the forecourt. His horse slowly closed its eyes and trembled slightly. Its hindquarters were black and wet, and the sweat shone with a metallic gleam.

'Yes, that's right, of course,' said another. 'We ought to build big. Everyone remembers the pyramids.'

'Yes, precisely,' said Sigurbjörn, eagerly, raising a finger in the air and nodded in agreement. 'Everyone remembers the pyramids. Never a truer word, my friend.'

'We're the sons of slaves,' said the third man, sneering. He was looking for something out across the river. 'They say there were sixty thousand slaves in Iceland. Do you think they didn't have any descendants?'

'No, what your colleague says is right,' said Sigurbjörn. 'Everyone remembers the pyramids.' He was silent. 'Take me, for example,' he said. 'I'm an architect. I was educated in France.'

'And how was life in France?'

'Why, bless you, it was all just one long *parlez-vous*.'

The men all smiled at this and Sigurbjörn was quite beside himself with mirth. 'My dream was to design a church,' he said happily. 'Not a traditional church; no one would take any notice of that. No, something magnificent. Something peculiarly Icelandic. It was to be inspired by the cliff formations at Almannagjá. I was going to study the geology closely and make the structure of the tower exactly the same.' He raised both hands in the air. 'Erect Thingvellir on Skólavörduhæd in all its terrible beauty, if I may put it like that. A church to put Iceland on the map. A church that would be a glory to the land. Then ever afterwards people would say, yes, St Peter's, that's in Rome, but the new Thingvellir Church, that's in Reykjavík. The public money would be used for something lasting that would make us a true member of the family of nations.'

'Have you designed it, this church of yours?' asked one of the men.

'I have, yes.'

'And what did they say about it?'

'They didn't like it.'

There was a silence and one of the men said, roughly, 'Yes, that's it in a nutshell, bloody arseholes. The only time that someone in this country comes up with a good idea it's stifled at birth. I think this sounds good. Of course money should be spent on such things. That's the crux of the matter. Instead of lavishing public funds on all kinds of things, yes, as the man put it himself: bottomless mediocrity.'

The others nodded their heads gravely.

Sigurbjörn looked at the men, one after the other. He walked round them and shook hands with them one by one in farewell. For some reason they bowed to him. He noticed the horse was still trembling. 'Tell me, lads, what's the matter with the animal?'

'I think it's afraid of your car,' said the one who had appeared to have the least faith in the building of the church.

'Well, then, it's best I went.'

He parked the car at the turning to Heidmörk. A brook was babbling by the side of the road, couch grass rose up from the green moss at the edge of the water. The clear water flowed over water-cotton, a plover pretending its wing was broken ran this way and that, trying to decoy the man. Sigurbjörn scooped up water from the brook and lifted it to his face. The dampness of the moss seeped through the seams of his leather shoes. He drove into Heidmörk, parked the car, walked some way across the lavafield from hollow to hollow. He had never been there before, and was surprised at how deep the hollows were. In some places there were almost small valley formations in the lava. Moss alternated with grass and here and there wood geraniums were growing. It was warm, and completely still.

He stood at the top of a ridge of lava and looked at the red roof of the car in the distance. While he had been wandering about it had grown darker. Now there were patches of mist here and there at ground level, and the lava rose up out of it like a mountain ridge. The fog was following the line of the river in the valley, creeping along it in graceful coils. He lay on his back and looked up at the sky. The clouds were strangely bright, and looked like paintings. He remembered that he had driven out here to hide the roll containing the crowbar, but he was too tired to fetch it and fell asleep among the bluebells.

Thórarinn woke up late that night and heard his mother sobbing. It sounded strange, different, wrong. He had never heard her weeping in such a high and hollow voice. He grew afraid and tried to go back to sleep again, but the sobbing would not let him. He crept to the door. Who was being so nasty to her? He grasped the door handle cautiously, it freed itself with a click, and the door opened of its own accord.

It was not his mother who was crying. His father sat at the parlour table, with both hands covering his face. Grandmother Sigurlaug was staying with them and was standing behind her son's chair with her hands on his shoulders. Sunneva stood a little way away, looking quite out of place.

VII

1

One morning in the spring of 1955, Sunneva packed a picnic lunch for Thórarinn to take on the school outing. He needed a new anorak, and they went into town as soon as the shops opened. The bus was due to leave the school no later than half-past ten. The day before she had seen a reasonably priced anorak in Egill Jacobsen's shop on Austurstræti.

Thórarinn grumbled in the shop. He did not want a hooded anorak so early in the spring. His mother reminded him that he had applied for a gardening job with the City Council for the summer, and she and the shopkeeper were agreed that the anorak would stand him in good stead if the summer were to be a cold one.

'But it was you who applied for the job, not me. You're always doing that,' said the boy.

The shopkeeper showed them a black leather jacket with a gold zip, and Sunneva bought it to sweeten the pill. Everyone was happy.

In the street there was a mixture of spring and winter, there was clear air and sunshine, but it was cold in the lanes between the houses. The Easter snows had not yet melted on Mount Esja. It was a bit too warm in the shop, and they had stayed there longer than they planned. Sunneva sauntered along Austurstræti with her coat undone. They were walking towards a young man who kept staring at her breasts. She stopped, held her coat open, and looked at her jumper with revulsion as though she had found a gravy stain. She stood like that until he had passed.

They had moved back into Sjafnargata. She had thought of selling the place, but could not bring herself to raise the matter with Sigurbjörn.

257

During the winter she had tried to visit him in prison once a week. The visits had passed in silence. He never said so much as a word about what Vilborg had seen.

Thórarinn had wanted to go and see his father on the day of his confirmation. She had forbidden it, not wanting the visit to be what he would remember of that day.

The bus was parked on the forecourt. The children were waiting with their bags and rucksacks. Some were already sitting on the bus. Thórarinn got a window seat. She waved and he nodded. She had promised not to wait until the bus left the school.

She had confused dreams and felt ill in the mornings when she woke up. She dreamed that she had returned to her childhood home on Vitatorg. The corrugated iron was as dry and brittle as paper and turned to powder in her hand. The wooden cladding on the inside was black and crumbling with old dry rot. She stretched her hand further and the rafters disintegrated. She dreamed that a fair-haired, grim-looking man handed her a sheet of paper folded twice. She opened it out and read a name on it: Gudbrandur Jónsson. She had to get into the house! She felt she knew that her grandfather from Búdardalur was in there, in terrible danger. The floors cracked under her feet. And in the chair where she had expected to find her grandfather there sat Sigurbjörn. Then she woke up and lay in bed exhausted.

She found a safe corner in her mind to live in. She was in Búdardalur during the great frosty winter of 1918. She was six years old, and the ceiling was coated with frost that glittered yellow and blue in the light from the oil lamp. Her grandfather came to kiss her good night. He blew into the lamp glass and extinguished the flame. And to bring him back to her she shouted, 'Grandfather! Grandfather! It's smoking! It's smoking!' She did not want to take this memory any further, because the next thing she heard would be her grandmother, old and sick, dragging her feet along the passage.

'What's that?' Grandfather asked, peering around in the darkness. 'Is the lamp smoking, Sunna? Are you pulling my leg?'

A few weeks later Sigurbjörn was to be transferred to Litla-Hraun, the state prison at Eyrarbakki, to serve his sentence. A tall, haggard man opened the door of the gaol on Skólavördustig. His name was Vilhjálmur. 'Good day to you.'

'How has he been?'

'A lot more cheerful. A lot more cheerful. He's begun designing again, the dear man. Asked me to buy paper and pencils for him last Wednesday.' She followed the warder along the corridor and Vilhjálmur picked up the bunch of keys.

Sigurbjörn was lying on the bed and it took him a long time to get up. He had wasted away almost to nothing. His handshake was cold. 'Good day, Sunneva.'

She kissed him on the forehead. The little room was narrow and the walls were thick. There was a checked counterpane on the bed. There were books and magazines lying scattered on the floor. From the street came the hum of traffic and the sound of people walking past. 'You've got wrinkles under your eyes,' he said harshly.

'You're nothing but skin and bone.'

'But I'm still the same old lady-killer, wouldn't you say?' And he laughed.

She was pleased to hear him laugh. 'Of course you are. You're much better looking than when we first met. All the same, you're an old bugger.'

He motioned to her to sit down and asked for news.

'Thórarinn went on a school outing this morning in a new leather jacket looking as smart as you please.'

'That's my Tóti. Will he be away long?'

'No, no, he's coming back this evening.'

'And what's the news of Helgi?'

'He rang on Friday evening to say that he'd got an offer from an English football club.'

'What's the name of the club?'

'Arsenal. My, was he happy!'

'Arsenal, you say, woman. That's a great honour. Ah Helgi, that's my boy!' Sigurbjörn said proudly, and then asked for news of Vilborg.

'She grows and grows. She's stopped looking like me and gets more like you with every day that passes.'

'Oh, poor girl. And Ragnar?'

'He's fine. He drives around in that van of his and has a new girl-friend. She's got a little daughter, by the way. There'll be a wedding soon. They have a son, you know.'

He nodded. 'And you? Have you enough to get by on, my dear?'

'Yes, the rent gets paid.'

He sat down on the bed. 'Look.' He took some sketches from the table by the head of the bed. 'This is the church. The Icelandic Sagrada Familia.' He ran his finger around the sketch and showed her the towers that the wind was supposed to have carved. 'Don't you think it will be something to see the seagulls wheeling around up there? The highest tower will be nearly a thousand feet high.'

'But will you be able to see them on cloudy days, Sigurbjörn?'

'Then the rock pillars will vanish into mist and reappear above the clouds. The beauty of it will be terrifying. I admire the black-backed gull,' he said fondly. 'It has always been my bird.'

'Most people think of it as a bird of prey,' she said.

'But it is so completely fearless. Look, this is where the bells will be in the belfry. The music'll ring out over the town when the raging blizzards blow, won't it?' And he laughed again.

'It'll be a real trolls' cathedral,' she said.

He stared at her and she was not sure whether he liked the name she had given it. But when he saw she was not joking, he continued to explain it to her.

'Sigurbjörn,' she said, in sudden and genuine surprise. 'You've begun to remind me of Kjarval.'

'Well, I'm glad to hear it.' He got up and edgily shifted his weight from one foot to the other, raising his arms in the air. 'The Spanish poet García Lorca said that when he looked at the towers of the church in Barcelona they rose into the sky before his eyes until the blowing of the angels' trumpets could be heard in a glorious tumult that he could not bear to listen to for more than a moment.' Sigurbjörn let his arms fall. 'They know how to put it into words.

those arty chaps. The poet explained to me what I feel like inside when I'm at Thingvellir.' He looked at the sketch. 'This is the holy church of Hallgrímur.'

'But what's this?' she asked, pointing to a tiny, familiar-seeming annexe beneath the enormous cliffs.

He bent down to look. 'That's the chancel already standing on the hill. There is no reason why it shouldn't be allowed to stay. It's a strange coincidence that Gaudí incorporated another man's work in the same way,' he said in a deep voice. 'That's fate for you, Sunneva,' he whispered. 'Gaudi was only thirty-one when the work was entrusted to him. By then a chancel in traditional Gothic style had already been built.'

He sat down and picked up the sketch. 'Well, now the thing is to draw some very simple plans to show to the authorities. Perhaps you can take them to members of parliament and the City Architect if they can't be talked into visiting me.' He put the sketch on the table, clasped his hands together and stared at the floor. 'I ought to be able to take charge of the building work, even though I'm locked up. Don't you think?'

There was nothing she could say.

'Well,' he said. 'I mustn't keep you.'

He pushed a bell push on the door-frame. She kissed him on the cheek and he put his arm round her shoulders.

When she got to the car, she looked up Skólavördustígur. Suddenly it seemed to her she could see the façade of the trolls' cathedral with its soaring towers. The belfries reminded her of the dark mouths of caves high in cliffs.

She had to queue at the petrol station at Klöpp. At last she reached the pump. 'Fill it up,' she said to the attendant, and went in to pay. 'The service is terribly slow,' she said to the man at the cash desk.

He did not reply.

'I wonder if they'd check the oil.'

'Ketill,' the man at the cash desk called loudly. 'Check the oil for he lady, will you?' Sunneva looked out. A man in an Álafoss anorak was filling the car with petrol. His hood was up and he had turned his back to the cold wind. He shifted his feet, chewed on a matchstick and looked awkwardly at the car wash. She felt weak. Ketill finished filling the tank and put the nozzle back on the pump. He opened the bonnet and looked at the dipstick. He closed the bonnet again. He began to observe some totally unremarkable incident in the street. A lorry loaded with concrete sewage piping had stopped and the driver was tending to the ropes. Some people were hooting their horns. Then she heard Sigurbjörn's voice: 'Can you imagine, Sunneva, the fierce, evil expression that came to his face the first time he looked at Tóti and me? I think he envied me the boy. Do you hear that, Sunneva? He envied me the boy.'

'The oil's OK,' Ketill called.

'It's all right for oil. That'll be seventy-five krónur,' said the man at the cash desk.

What if he comes in here and speaks to me? she thought. I'll scream.

Ketill came in the door and said, 'Excuse me, ma'am. Could you move your car?'

She did not scream, and went outside. Water was cascading from a brush in the car wash.

She fumbled with the ignition before managing to start the engine. She caught sight of the brown anorak at the edge of her field of vision. Thórarinn had turned into a silent ghost, and Sigurbjörn had lost his mind . . . How could the man stand here chewing on a matchstick as though nothing had happened? She started the car but was too quick with the clutch. The car jerked and the engine stalled. The man in the anorak looked at her.

She had to use all the self-control she could muster to get out on to Skúlagata. Her legs trembled beneath her. She drove up Vitastígur and down Laugavegur, frantic, beside herself. I'll go to the police, she thought. No, there's no one I can turn to for help. She drove slowly past the petrol station. Ketill was not outside. I must get Ragnar, she thought. Kill him!

Sigurbjörn went back to bed after her visit and dreamed he was in Barcelona on a fine, warm day, sitting at the pavement café and looking at the Sagrada Familia, which was even more magnificent than he had remembered it. He saw the church shimmering white in the heat. The haggard Spaniard who had said that Gaudí was dead was there, too, performing bizarre dance steps in and out of the tables. Sigurbjörn saw his father sitting morosely by the pavement. There was some jollity amd high jinks at the tables. Gudbrandur was sitting on his own, in a typical pose, looking sadly at Sigurbjörn. The drunken Spaniard appeared to command little respect; the other customers were laughing at him. Sigurbjörn began to feel bad in the dream, and woke up.

2

The first time Helgi ran through the dark tunnel out on to the pitch at Highbury with the Arsenal team he felt terrified. What am I doing here with the likes of Tommy Lawton and Alex Forbes? he thought. They ran out on to the turf, and he was overwhelmed by the roaring of the crowd.

In the first half he felt he was doing everything wrong. At half-time he was sitting on a bench in the changing room in despair when a chubby man in glasses came up to him, patted him on the shoulder and said: 'Very good, son. Very good.' It was the team manager, Tom Whittaker.

'He likes you,' said the man sitting next to Helgi. 'He's never said that to me.'

I could do it against the Finns, thought Helgi. I can do it against Newcastle, too.

In the second half he played like a man possessed. 'Very good, son,' he muttered to himself. 'Very good.' He did not remember how he scored the first two goals, he just knew that everything he did worked perfectly, that he was in complete control of his body. Instead of growing tired he found greater reserves of energy and skill as the game went on. It was as though the sonorous roaring of the spectators were a refreshing sleep and the game itself a light and happy dream. The score was 2–2.

They got a penalty. Helgi jumped in the air, took the ball on his chest, and rammed it into the throng of players, his foot like a cannon.

He did not hear the noise from the grandstands; he felt the stand and terraces envelop him like a black circle. After the game, Tom Whittaker came up to him and said, 'You're very good, son, almost too good to be true.'

Around the middle of June he came home for ten days with presents in his suitcase for the family. He had brought scent for Grandmother Sigurlaug. She received him in her best dress. 'Well, Grandma, this will make a change from the wretched necklaces,' he said.

'What have you got for an old lady, Helgi?' She unwrapped the present. 'Eau de cologne.'

He asked her to open the bottle and put some on, but she was reluctant to waste it. 'Come now, look on top of the cabinet, boy.' She took his hand and tugged him towards her.

There, in a frame, was a postcard he had sent her. When he looked at the players around him, men he admired, names he knew from the newspapers, it seemed incredible to him that he was sitting there among them with his arms folded across his chest. 'You're quite incorrigible,' he laughed. 'You framed the postcard. The lads'll have something to say when they hear about that.'

She made him sit down in the easy chair and put cakes and coffee before him. He spied a half-empty bottle of sherry by the curtains, picked it up and said, 'Well, someone has tipple when there's no one looking.' He told her about the family he had digs with, his train journey in the morning, the pubs and the hot-dog sellers at the football ground. He went on and on, but then he noticed that she seemed abstracted, and fell silent.

'Things would have been different for him if Jóhannes had lived,' she said.

One of the panes in the kitchen window was broken. Ingirídur gathered up the broken glass and found the stone in the parlour. She toured the house, examining household objects, opening kitchen cupboards and looking at the cups and plates they had decided to make do with at Eyrarbakki. She felt chilled and lay down under the quilt, but the bed was cold and clammy. She had touched Gudbrandur before the coffin was sealed. She had never felt such cold on any corpse before, even though she was a nurse. She felt it was as if it came from deep inside a glacier.

She went down to the shore and sat down. There was a breeze off the sea from the south. Out on the horizon a cargo vessel sailed by. She walked along the seaweed-strewn shoreline, there were pools here and there, the seaweed was black.

Sunneva could scarcely conceal her surprise when Ingirídur said she wanted to talk to her eldest son. Helgi took the receiver, clearly concerned. 'She's going to burn everything in the house,' he said to his mother, when the conversation was over. 'She wants me to help her to carry the furniture and other stuff down to the shore, says she can't manage the heaviest things. I can't possibly refuse.'

She arrived early the following morning in a little Morris, having gathered together all of Gudbrandur's clothes she could find and stuffed them into four sacks. A fifth sack was half filled with shoes.

'How are you coping?' he asked when he had told her about his time in England.

'Oh, fine, I have a full-time job and I get the rent from that bloody building, like your mother.'

'What are you going to do with the summer house?' he asked quickly.

'Sell it. I can hardly bear to go there.'

The air in the house was heavy with the smell of sewage. The night before she had stuffed a rag into the hole in the kitchen window. The toilet cistern leaked constantly. Helgi went out to the petrol station to ask about a wheelbarrow. The man knew where he had come from and thought he was Gudbrandur's son.

'He was a fine man, that father of yours,' he said. 'Think of it, boy, a full-grown man like that, going off to sea when there wasn't much carpentry work to be had. There's not many would have done that. You have my condolences, lad.'

'Gudbrandur wasn't my father,' Helgi said, drily.

'Hey,' said the man. 'Aren't you the famous footballer?' Helgi shook his head.

He fetched the wheelbarrow. She had carried the mattresses outside and taken the bed to pieces. He put the base and the bed heads crosswise on the wheelbarrow. She followed him along the beach and showed him where she wanted them piled up. A Chesterfield sofa and chairs, and an escritoire. Kitchen stools and a large writing desk. It was easy for him to move them, even though the wheel of the barrow sank into the sand. The writing desk was the heaviest. 'Are you sure you want to throw all this away?' he asked.

'Yes, quite sure.'

The lyme grass bent in the wind. He looked at the sad pile on the yellow-brown shore and began to gather things together. The bonfire seemed to him untidy and graceless. He found a large white log half buried in the sand. The log was narrow at one end. He gripped it from beneath and was surprised at how heavy it was. The wood was coal black on its lower side. He pushed it away from him with his foot. He felt the strain in his thigh muscles. He made an effort and rolled it alternately with first one foot, then with the other. There was a mass of small dead crabs lying in the sand and the shells cracked as the log rolled over them. On with the log, over molluscs, seaweed and sea anemones – *very good, son!* He gripped the narrower end and the log skidded, wet and slippery in his hands. *Too good to be true!* He let it crash on top of the sofa and sat down and stretched his legs. A wind was blowing up.

He walked westwards and the terns came to greet him. He found a lot of wooden floats lying here and there. He began to bring them to the bonfire, carrying two in each arm, walking on tiptoe, strengthening the calf muscles.

There were few people about in the village. She had gone to

266

Laugabúd and bought food, rye bread, cheese, meat paste and flatcakes, milk. He felt uneasy about sitting down to eat with her. He had always felt large and awkward in the presence of this slender woman with the black, graceful mole on her cheek. She did not eat much. He had the lion's share and felt like a peasant.

'Well,' she said. 'I'm ready.'

She collected some clothes from the wardrobe and dumped them in his arms in one bundle. He put the kitchen table on the roof-rack of the car. They drove a little way along the track where the lyme-grass dunes blocked the view of the beach and parked the car. She had found half a bottle of cognac in the kitchen cabinet, and offered it to him. He accepted the bottle and took a good swig from it, then had another. He felt a pleasant spasm round his eyes.

He carried all the sacks in one go, running across the sand, and felt a few raindrops fall on his forehead. A swarm of sandpipers flew in, the storm of birds plunged below a ridge, they reappeared one by one and whirled in an arc above their heads, making for the shore in a long curve. Some settled on the sea while others ran in the seaweed, trying to avoid the waves. Helgi put the sacks down. 'That's some bonfire you've made,' she said.

He fetched a long piece of electrical tubing he had found on the shore.

She tossed petrol from a can over the floats and the sofa and lit it. The fire cast itself over the pile like an orange quilt being torn away from above.

She gathered an armful of shirts and underwear and let the wind help her throw the clothes on to the bonfire. A hat landed beyond the fire. She tried to run towards it but had to back off because of the heat. Helgi went close and poked the fire with his iron tubing. He managed to fish the hat up and dropped it into the flames.

The fire burst out of a clear, yellow opening and split apart into tongues on the sand at the bottom. She ran towards it and emptied the contents of the whole of one sack. For a while the flames damped down, as the drizzle turned into a light rain. The sea turned black. The driftwood log blazed. The sofa burned. She went over to the clothes from the summer house, every scrap went into the flames, item by item.

He felt it was taking too long, and went as close with the iron tubing as he could bear, but had to turn his face away, his cheek burning hot. A few black-backed gulls had settled on the waves. The tubing was bent and tended to slip in his hands. Ingirídur was holding a grey smoking jacket.

'Father has a jacket like that,' said Helgi.

'This is his jacket,' said Ingirídur. 'He left it here when Young Sigurbjörn was christened. I couldn't bear the thought that he was to be his namesake.' She studied the jacket as she held it.

'I'll take it with me into town,' said Helgi.

She flung it on to the bonfire. He tried to catch hold of the jacket and lifted it out of the fire. The wind raised the burning arms.

She looked at it, and smiled.

He threw tube and jacket into the fire and sat down on the sand. The rain had stopped. A white shirt of Gudbrandur's was melting into a black resin.

She picked up the half-full sack of shoes and flung it into a hollow under the wooden floats. Now everything was on the fire. She moved away and sat down.

The thin sack round the shoes burned up quickly. Helgi watched them roll out. Suddenly there was an explosion. Ingirídur had forgotten a half-used canister of lamp oil.

The wind changed direction and shreds of clothes and half-burned rags blew out of the burning pile. She walked about the sand and inspected the beach until she had found every bit of clothing that the eddying squalls had whirled out of the fire.

The flames soon died down and at once it grew colder. 'Shouldn't we go now?' he asked.

She shook her head and turned her back to the embers, hunched over in sorrow. She stood like this for a long time. Then she picked up the tubing and poked about until she was sure that everything had burned. She left a few shoe-heels red and yellow in the embers.

He waited for her in the car. She joined him, stooping and tired, got in and started the engine.

'Is there anything else you need taken from the house?' he asked.

'Yes, cups and odds and ends. And the girls' mattresses.'

'Is there any cognac left?'

She felt in her pocket and gave him the bottle.

He sat down on the mattresses in the empty bedroom and swigged the cognac while she gathered the bits and pieces together. Outside the wind was singing in the long grass. She stood in the doorway. He handed her the bottle. 'Where will you put the mattresses?'

'Can't we just roll them up and put them in the boot?'

She sat down against the wall and did not refuse the cognac.

'I have always longed for you, ever since I first saw you, Ingirídur,' he said after they had exchanged a few sips. She did not reply, but when he touched her hair she did not move away. She smiled.

Afterwards, she ran out with her clothes. He heard her in the shower, then she came back fully dressed, cool and distant.

He got up and dressed and she watched.

'You mustn't tell your mother about this,' she said. 'That you've slept with a woman so much older than you.'

'No,' he said. 'You don't need to worry. I won't tell Mother anything.'

In the doorway he took some earrings out of his pocket and showed them to her. 'Look,' he said. 'I found these in the rubbish.'

3

The white marquees shone in the sun. They were offering cakes, sweets and balloons. At Arnarhóll there was a children's entertainment on a wooden stage. It was a few scenes from *The Wizard of Oz*, with the Wicked Witch of the West eager to get her hands on Toto the dog. The weeping Dorothy clutched him tightly in her arms. A small child in the audience began to cry on his father's shoulder, and the father snorted, 'You call that entertainment?'

An aeroplane showered Lækjargata with caramel sweets. Helgi heard an older man say to his son, 'They're going to drop them on Kalkofnsvegur next. Let's go there.'

Helgi walked over to a column outside the Cabinet Office and saw the boy a little later standing between his parents some distance away down the nearly empty street. The aeroplane passed over Lækjargata for a second time scattering its sweets and then flew off to the south.

He picked his way through the human sea to Idnó Theatre and caught sight of Ragnar. His hair was thinning, and his bald patch was sunburned and freckled. Ragnar was pushing a pram backwards and forwards. Helgi had a bottle of whisky in his pocket.

They embraced, and slapped each other on the back and shoulders. Helgi handed him the present and glanced into the pram. In the pram was Ragnar's son.

Ragnar looked in the bag. 'Aha,' he said, laughing. 'So it's like that. Cutty Sark?'

'It would do the boy no harm to take after you a bit less.' Helgi squeezed his shoulder. 'Congratulations.'

'Thanks. Have you seen Father?'

'No, I'll go later today. And where's the wife?'

Ragnar nodded in the direction of a blond-haired woman who had her back turned to them. She was standing on the bank of Lake Tjörnin leading a little girl by the hand. The girl was pointing at a swan.

'She's going to study architecture. We're going abroad in the autumn.'

'Introduce me to her then, mate.'

Helgi was wearing a black raincoat with wide lapels and a belt. The tip of his black umbrella rested on the pavement. He knew what a fine figure he was cutting.

'We've already packed and sent our stuff overseas,' Ragnar said. 'We'll be in Dresden next winter. Gréta!' he called. The woman standing on the bank of Lake Tjörnin looked over her shoulder. 'Do you think my German will be up to it?' He gave Helgi a gentle nudge with his elbow. 'Just now we're living in the summer cottage at

270

Grímsnes that father-in-law owns. You ought to look us up some time.'

'Where is this house at Grímsnes?'

'First on the right as you turn on to the Thingvellir road. We could come and collect you. You'd enjoy spending a weekend with us.'

'I'm not here for long. We're playing in Belgium next week. I could use the Plymouth.'

'All the better, man. Come this evening. Gréta!' Ragnar called. 'Come here a minute.' She came. 'I want to introduce you to my brother. The famous sports champion and ladykiller. I'd just ask you not to shake his hand for too long.'

Ragnar's wife shook hands. Her hand was small and soft. She introduced herself, 'Hello, I'm Gréta Thorkelsdóttir.' She was very shy, small and round-faced. She picked the little boy up out of the pram. He had a blond curl in the middle of his forehead.

The little girl's ice-cream was melting, and Ragnar wiped her face with his handkerchief. 'I call him Woody Woodpecker,' he said.

'His name is Thorkell,' said his mother.

It took him the better part of an hour to drive east that evening, and he found the house at once. The delivery van stood in the drive. An excitable dog welcomed him, a black bitch that went hurtling round and round him in circles over the gravel. He told the dog to shut up in a sharp voice. It had no effect. Ragnar and Gréta were both astounded to see him. They showed him over the house and the land. There was a kitchen garden and a forcing frame with broken panes. The grass under the splinters was pale yellow. A birch thicket grew on grassy mounds around the fence. Some trees had been planted in the grounds, poplar and fir. By the gate there was a heap of sand, and another of manure.

Helgi had intended to go straight back to town again, but Ragnar eventually persuaded him to stay the night. They were going to drive down to Selfoss to buy soda and chocolate, and Helgi offered to spread some manure round the trees while they were away. They refused the offer, but Helgi would not rest until Ragnar's wife had found jeans and boots large enough to fit him. They left the little girl behind and he found a wheelbarrow and a shovel the right size and filled one barrow after another. He felt good. The little girl prattled about everything under the sun. The family dog was constantly getting in the way and took not the least notice when rebuked. The guest seemed to make her anxious, fearful. Helgi wanted to go into the house for a glass of water and had to kick her out of the way, sending her skidding and howling over his boot. She sat up with her front paws on the sill, glaring in at the window.

He turned to the heap of sand for the kitchen garden. There were some large clumps of rhubarb. The little girl would not leave his side, but kept up a constant stream of questions.

'Can all the horses in the world beat all the dogs in the world?'

'I've haven't the faintest idea, child.'

'Well, how many giraffes would it take to beat one polar bear?'

'Where do you get such silly ideas?'

'Did God make the rhubarb?'

'Yes.'

'And what about the trees?'

'Yes, he made the trees, too.'

'And the spiders?'

'Yes, he made the spiders, too. He made everything.' Helgi shovelled energetically. He was sweating now, and the physical exertion felt good after a few days' rest.

'Everything,' said the child, looking around her, perplexed, and her gaze fell on the house. 'Even Grandfather's house?'

It began to drizzle, the damp glistening on the waterproof coat and trousers her mother had had the foresight to make her wear. The wet grass brushed against her boots. All at once the dog disappeared with a yelp. A stretch of peaty land lay barren within the birch thicket. Something white crossed the peat, vanishing now and then in the tussocks. It was a black-backed gull. The bird had a broken wing, and headed straight for them, puffing out its breast, with the same jizz as a large goose, while smaller birds hopped fearlessly around it. Helgi saw that the bird was dragging its wing behind it upside down, the ball joint shining white. The gull came straight towards the man and the little girl, and Helgi was startled. Did the bird expect help? Curlews attacked it from the air. Now and then they landed and hopped around it, screeching.

'What's wrong with the bird?' the little girl asked.

'Its wing's broken.'

'Why?'

'It flew into a wire.'

Helgi went closer and told the dog to be quiet. She turned slowly in a wide circle but then came back to them at full speed, skimming across the peat moor like a flat stone, slithering on her belly with wild enthusiasm and falling on the seagull cowering in the tussocks.

'Get away from the bird!' Helgi bawled. He ran over and drove the dog away. The seagull vanished into a thicketed area with the whole mob of wildlife on its tail. A moment later, it emerged from the thicket. Helgi grabbed a potato fork. 'I want to go home,' the little girl said.

'Yes, off you go home.'

The child began to walk towards the house without looking over her shoulder. Helgi was afraid the little girl would wake her brother. He stuck the fork in the earth and followed her into the house, then turned to look for the bird, but could not see it. He saw the female bird stand gracefully for a while on a patch of ground stripped of turf, and then unfold her large wings and fly off into the moorland.

Just at that moment Ragnar drove up. Gréta admired how much Helgi had done.

'You've saved my life, mate,' Ragnar said.

'You wouldn't believe', said Gréta, 'how he has fretted over this. We only got the house on condition that he'd keep the trees manured.'

'We saw a bird with a broken wing, Mummy,' the little girl said.

'Oh, what was it?'

'A seagull.'

'You should have taken a shot at it, mate.'

'What, you have the shotgun here?'

They went inside and Ragnar pointed to the wall. The shotgun was hanging there. 'I've been practising in a dell a little way off. We didn't exactly notch up the highest score of the season, if you remember.'

Gréta made some open sandwiches for their guest, and Ragnar fetched a flask of cognac, which they finished. Gréta drank the soda and ate the chocolate with her daughter. Helgi was relieved that she did not discuss architecture. A nasty thought crept into his mind as the cognac took effect. He realized how easy it would be for him to take advantage of his superior strength, knock out his brother and take his wife. He made a great effort to avoid thinking about this idea. Gréta fetched the little girl who came through in her pyjamas and kissed them both good night. At about midnight Gréta went off to bed. By that time Ragnar had got them each a glass of whisky. He was mildly drunk now, and looked at Helgi, his big cheeks a fiery red.

'She's awfully like Snjólaug,' Helgi whispered. 'You always go for the same type, don't you? Though this one isn't so wild.'

'Why don't you make a pass at her, get her into bed, like you did Snjólaug?' Ragnar was looking at him, his eyes narrowed and evil. 'You're a mean bastard, Helgi. I was going to marry her. We had a little girl.' Suddenly his face broke into a grin.

'What are you grinning at, Ragnar?'

'You.'

'What's so funny about me?'

'What were you saying to that father of ours back in that spring?'

'Eh?'

'Mother told me he was obsessed by some dream. That he was walking in darkness. That his brother Jóhannes had walked in darkness. The most awful guff. She was supposed to have dreamed this. But she didn't remember having the dream.'

'She mentioned it to me too,' Helgi said. 'I said that he must have dreamed it himself.' He turned the glass in his fingers, confused. ' made up the dream, Ragnar. She didn't dream it. I'd seen some of i at the pictures, and the rest I just imagined. I even had a look in th Bible. In the first bit of it there are some terrifying dreams. I couldn' bear to think he was making a fool of himself all over the place.

hoped the dream would be strong enough to keep him home. I meant it for the best.'

'It seems to have worked better than you thought.'

Ragnar changed the subject. 'I went to the funeral. I've seldom seen a more dignified affair. She put her hand on the coffin to guide it into the grave. She's a tough cookie. Have you still got her on the brain?'

'Yes.'

Ragnar showed his brother to the small guest bedroom. Helgi put his hand on the bed. The bunk was hard and narrow. 'Well, I hope you can squeeze yourself in there, mate.'

'I'll just take the mattress and put it on the floor.'

He lay on the floor and listened to the sounds of the house. He heard the couple chatting together for a good while, but could not make out what they were saying. Little by little, he was overcome by drowsiness. He dreamed that he was out walking over a heather moor and came across the severed head of a troll. When he looked at the head, its face came to life and the troll blew down its nose and opened an eye. In the dream, Helgi took fright and ran away.

He woke with a start, and realized that he had slept for only half an hour. He was wide awake. He put his clothes on and went outside. The wind had died down somewhat. It was still quite light, but there was a dark bank of cloud over Ingólfsfjall. He fetched the shotgun, found some shot in a cupboard in the parlour, and walked out on to the moor to look for the bird with the broken wing. He hunted for the gull for a long time, but could not find it anywhere. When he came to Kerid, the sky had turned grey and the clouds were white. He walked up to the rim of the crater, there was mist in it. He went down into the heather where he had shot the grouse. The mist rolled at his feet and the land disappeared. He could hear plovers and curlews. He knew that the breeze was blowing from the east. He decided to walk further down the slope and make a long detour around Kerid, so there would be no risk of losing his footing and falling in. He held on to lava rocks and moved gingerly, step by step, but he could not find any heather to hold on to. He sat on a stone and waited for a long time, with no idea where he was.

The mist cleared suddenly. A black disc of water appeared through the vapour straight ahead of him. The mist swept up the walls of the ravine and the blue sky was revealed. He had clambered down nearly all the way to the foot of Kerid, to the surface of the lake. The wind must have changed direction. Now it became overcast again. A vortex of cold air made the water tremble, its colour that of crude oil, and on the rockface a birch sapling tossed its leafy crown.

Ragnar awoke to the dawn chorus from the roof and the sun on his face. He tumbled out of bed and went over to the door. He saw at once that the shotgun was not hanging on the wall. Helgi was sitting on the steps of the veranda, his broad back turned to him. The gun lay across his knees.

'What are you doing, boy?'

Helgi turned round very calmly. 'I was just making up my mind to shoot my bloody head off.'

'Why?'

'Two guesses,' he said, mocking his brother.

Ragnar went calmly out to the veranda. Helgi stood up on the steps and walked backwards out on to the lawn. He was holding the shotgun in both hands, letting it rest against his thighs.

'Give me the gun, Helgi.'

'Go inside, Ragnar, you're annoying me.'

'It isn't loaded, is it, you idiot?'

'Yes.'

'Give it to me.' Ragnar went down the steps.

'No.'

'It could go off.' Ragnar went up to him and took hold of the handle and the barrel. Helgi felt the barrel on his biceps like a pipe pressing against his flesh. The gun fired, ripping off his arm.

EPILOGUE

1

That very morning Thórarinn was woken early by the sound of pebbles being thrown up at his window. He had been aware of the tapping in his sleep for some time. He knelt up in bed. His father was standing in the garden, bareheaded and with a finger to his lips. Now the boy understood why, at about midnight, a police car had driven past the house three times.

The police had knocked at the door and asked to speak to his mother. It all sounded very official. He had thought it was because of 'the man' and found it hard to get back to sleep. He heard Sunneva moving around the house for a long time.

Thórarinn looked at the alarm clock on his bedside table. It said half past four. He quickly got out of bed, crept down to the hallway and opened the front door. Sigurbjörn strode up the stairs. He had a sweater on under his jacket. 'Draw the curtains in the parlour and the dining room, Tóti.'

Thórarinn drew the curtains. Sigurbjörn went straight over to the glass cupboard where the shotgun was kept. He took the gun out and felt in the small drawer where he usually kept his shot, but found it empty.

'Helgi has some cartridges in his room upstairs.'

'Then be quick and get them.' Sigurbjörn dropped the shotgun into its bag. 'And get dressed as quickly as you can. Don't wake Mother. I've come to get you.'

'Where are we going?'

'Abroad.'

'But why do you need the shotgun?'

'To threaten the buggers if they try to arrest me.'

Thórarinn got the cartridges. He took about ten from the packet and quickly went into his room. He put on trousers and a sweater but could not find his socks and so put a pair of plimsolls on his bare feet. He hesitated at the top of the stairs, but decided against waking his mother. His father had taken off his jacket, and put on an overcoat and his peaked cap. He was standing watchfully by the sofa as Thórarinn came downstairs. Sigurbjörn took the cartridges and slipped them into his pocket. Thórarinn put on his anorak. They tiptoed down the stairs to the basement. The grey morning light fell though a window on to the enamel boiler in the laundry. Sigurbjörn carefully lifted the latch on the door. He grimaced with concentration.

Thórarinn looked at the thinning silver hair. He had not seen his father since they had gone to Thingvellir the year before. They went out to the basement stairs and Sigurbjörn put his head on one side and listened. Then he carefully closed the door. A cat was sitting on a dustbin by the wall. Sigurbjörn let his son walk ahead of him up to the bin and whispered hoarsely, 'Get over.' The cat did not move.

Now Thórarinn was alone, and the idea of running away flickered through his mind. Sigurbjörn sat astride the wall, letting the shotgun bag slither down to his son. Then he jumped down, stiff and heavy.

They walked quickly through the neighbours' backyard and out through the gate. The street was empty. The weather was mild, and it was light. The town was deserted. They walked quickly over Skólavörduhæd and down Frakkastígur without meeting a living soul. On the corner of Grettisgata Sigurbjörn stopped and listened. They walked across Hverfisgata. The flags on the Department Store hung limply on their poles in the still air. The sea looked dense in the fine morning weather. Nowhere was there anyone about. It was as though Reykjavík had been evacuated.

They walked along Skúlagata and trod the worn wooden planks of the pier at Faxagardur, the oily sea swaying beneath them through the slats. There was a bar across the door of a warehouse, a coal crane towered above the harbour. Sigurbjörn headed for the lighthouse. Thórarinn felt the morning breeze on his face. His plimsolls were rubbing his feet. They sat on the side facing the sea, where they could not be seen. Sigurbjörn propped the shotgun bag up against the wall. 'Don't you think we ought to just go home?' said Thórarinn.

'No, let's go to San Francisco, Tóti,' said Sigurbjörn. 'We always planned to go there, the two of us, and trudge up and down those hills.'

'But how will we get there, Father? We haven't any money.'

'I'll borrow some. Let's rest here. There aren't many people about.'

'How did you get out?' asked Thórarinn.

'Some of the lads wanted to go to a dance.' Sigurbjörn laughed. 'They asked me if I knew anything about buildings. I said I might well do, but no one could just jump through the walls of old stone buildings. "Do you have something up your sleeve?" they asked. I did have something up my sleeve.'

'Well, what was it?'

'The window frames were rotten. It took nothing to rip the bars out.'

As the morning wore on a wind got up, and the sea slackened and tautened like a rug being pulled between two men; the waves bunched up and then released cascades of folds. The seagulls coasted with the wind, rocking on their wings and gliding on currents of air. Sigurbjörn put his face on his knees and appeared to be asleep. Thórarinn started to feel the cold. A ship's siren sounded. The sea lapped the stones of Faxagardur. A black carpet of seaweed billowed on the foreshore. An old trawler was sailing out of the harbour, a man on deck was coiling a rope. Thórarinn heard the sound of sawing. He stood up to ease his stiffness. The machinery in Völundur sawmill had been started up. He nudged his father. 'It's nearly eight o' clock, Father.'

As they walked up Klappastígur, men were moving about in the buzz of saws over on the sunbaked street between the factory buildings at Völundur. They went into the courtyard of a small house. There were large, whitewashed stones in its foundation wall, and its roof was black. Sigurbjörn knocked on a basement door. After a while, it opened. A man appeared in the doorway. He was wearing trousers but his feet and torso were bare. You could see the bones through his flesh, his belly was flat, his arms pale and sinewy. Thórarinn recognized the plumber who had invited his father home at the celebration dinner almost two years ago.

'Is that you, Sigurbjörn?' said the plumber.

'Aren't you up yet, lad?'

'No, I'm on my summer holidays. I thought you were . . .' He studied Sigurbjörn with a mixture of suspicion and concern.

'In gaol? No, I got a pardon, my good chap. But, say, could you lend me and the boy a few thousand? We're flat broke. We're going abroad.'

'Not a few thousand. But perhaps a few hundred. That would be a real pleasure for me, my friend.' The plumber was looking at Thórarinn, uncertain what to make of it all.

'Well, the boy and I will just have to go trout-fishing instead,' Sigurbjörn laughed.

The plumber went inside and came back some time later with four hundred krónur. Sigurbjörn thanked him and shook his hand.

'Don't you think we'd better be going home?' said Thórarinn.

His father took his hand tightly in his, and did not reply. They walked along Lindargata towards Arnarhóll.

2

People were standing by a bus near a Jugendstil transformer station. Sigurbjörn found out that the first bus out of town would leave in twenty minutes for Vík in Mýrdal. 'Absolutely splendid,' he said, loudly. 'It's simply ages since the boy and I have been to Vík.'

He bought himself a ticket, and another, half-price, for Thórarinn. The woman in the ticket office looked at Thórarinn suspiciously, but was not confident enough to question whether he was under twelve.

Thórarinn let it pass. They sat down outside in the sunshine and waited. People were gathering with their suitcases, bags, and cardboard boxes tied up with string, and the the driver was arranging them on the roof rack. Thórarinn wanted to get on the bus so they could have seats right at the back, but his father could not be persuaded to embark until the very last moment.

They sat at the front. Sigurbjörn put the shotgun bag down by a window. The driver collected the tickets. The bus was full now. He turned on the engine and the bus shook from stem to stern. It moved off out of the town with a screeching of gears.

A foreigner was sitting on the other side of the aisle. Sigurbjörn was in an expansive mood and kept asking in Icelandic, 'Where are you from, my good man? Where are you from?' When the man was unable to answer, he laughed. The driver looked quickly over his shoulder and eyed Sigurbjörn.

The bus drove through the slum housing of Selás. At Raudavatn there was a column on the right by the lake. Sigurbjörn told Thórarinn that it had been been put up as an experiment before the church at Landakot was built. 'You told me that already, Father,' said Thórarinn.

A man in grey trousers and a white shirt stood outside the inn at Baldurshagi in the fine weather. They drove past Geitháls, over Hólmsárbrú and past the farm at Gunnarshólmi, the roofs dark red in the morning sun. Hens were scuttling away from a dog. The dog turned its attention to the bus with great gusto. Sigurbjörn watched it all with extreme satisfaction and chatted freely with people. There was an empty seat beside the driver, and Thórarinn moved to it. The bus began to climb the moor. It crawled over the sandy ridge, sighing and groaning, nearly expiring on its way up Hveradalur. 'Didn't an army truck fall off Kambar during the war with soldiers on board?' Thórarinn asked as they crossed the moor.

'Yes, yes,' the bus driver replied. 'I remember hearing about that. In the mist. Ten or a dozen men. Many things happened here during the war years, but they were very quick to hush it all up.' The driver changed to a lower gear and stepped on the brakes out of respect for the mountain road.

They stopped at Hveragerdi and a few people got out. A farmer needed to go and buy some black bread. Thórarinn got out, but his father stayed on the bus, with his peaked cap pulled down over his forehead. Then they moved off again. At Ingolfsfjall Thórarinn pointed to the polished stones on the hillside, and asked, 'Why do the stones look like that?' The bus driver shook his head.

'It's probably because a long time ago this was the sea bed,' an old man said. 'Then the land rose out of the sea and the cliffs that once stood by the shore for thousands if not millions of years are now in the middle of the rock face. If you go for a walk on the mountain you can find seashells here and there.'

'My friends the ravens drop molluscs on the rocks so they can get at the flesh inside. Then people find the shells and think they've made some great discovery,' said Sigurbjörn.

The bus made its way along the road below Ingólfsfjall. There was a stop at Tryggvaskáli and some more people got off. Two girls got on the bus. Thórarinn asked one of them what time it was. The girl had a watch with a red leather wristband and read from it proudly, 'Ten.'

'Look, there's old Hekla.' The bus driver pointed Thórarinn towards the volcano which had rags of cloud around its summit.

'And there's Grandfather's old house,' said Thórarinn. The rusty shack was still standing on oildrums. A piece of corrugated iron hung loose and swayed from a gable.

There were patches of sunlight on the ground, as they drove past Hella to Hvolsvöllur. There father and son left the bus. Sigurbjörn sent his son to buy a litre bottle of milk at the Rangæingar Co-op. Thórarinn bought mutton paste and black bread, and had a few slices cut in the shop. They walked into Fljótshlídin in sweltering heat and ate their breakfast on the way. Sigurbjörn opened the packet of paste and spread it on the bread for them both. They walked past a freshly painted church, where there was a clump of rowan trees in their summer finery. They passed the bottle of milk to and fro between them. They finished the paste and most of the milk, but a good bit of the loaf was left over. Sigurbjörn sent his son to give the bread to a bored-looking horse which was peering at them, large-eyed, from behind a ramshackle fence. They had to cross a ditch, thick with clay soil at the bottom, the trembling water shimmering in the sunlight. The couch grass at the edge of the ditch was at its tallest. Thórarinn tried to jump across, but did not quite manage it. A fence staggered, splay-footed, up a gravel road to a farm. The fence posts were white with age and reinforced with pieces of old wooden boxes. The horse ate the bread and livened up a little. Thórarinn succeeded in jumping across the stream without having to take a run up and without getting his feet wet. His father praised him for his athletic prowess. Suddenly Sigurbjörn wanted to practise his shooting, using the milk bottle as a target. Thórarinn ran on to the road and set it up.

'Step aside, Tóti.' Sigurbjörn took careful aim, but the shots did little more than raise clouds of sand. The reports crashed and echoed around them. There was no movement at the farms. No one passed along the road.

'Put it on top of a fence post.'

'But what about the milk?' Thórarinn thought it was a pity to waste it.

'Oh, they'll invite us in for some at one of the farms,' his father said.

They had to walk several hundred yards before they reached a post that was sufficiently thick and flat on top for the bottle to stand steady. At last they found one. The shots whined in the air. Sigurbjörn loaded and fired again. Smoke came from the magazine. The cartridges fell on the road. One shot hit the top of the post and the bottle fell into the dusty grass and rolled over to the the edge of the road. It came to rest by some pebbles and some of the milk trickled into the sand.

'You've really lost your aim, Father,' said Thórarinn, stretching out for the bottle, but his father shot it away from the road. 'That nearly hit me,' said the boy.

Sigurbjörn held the shotgun in his arms and looked at him, silently.

'Shall I try and find another bottle?' asked Thórarinn.

But his father was not interested in shooting any more. 'I must keep some cartridges,' he said, counting them.

They walked up to a gloomy, rust-brown corrugated-iron house on a small hill, with a cowshed some way away, tall trees on a little fenced-off plot by the front of the house, dandelions by the road and expanses of buttercups on the meadows. A dog came flying towards them, spoiling for a fight. Sigurbjörn squatted down on his heels and calmed the dog down.

No human soul was to be seen. An enormous stone stood in front of the door. Sigurbjörn knocked heavily several times. At last a woman came out. Her face was twisted into a grimace that seemed to have become habitual to her. She stepped out on to the stone with reluctance and answered every question absently, all the time gazing out towards the glacier. No, the farmer was not at home. Yes, they owned cows. How many? Two. Was the man a vet?

'Yes, I have to go round the farms and inspect the general condition of the cattle,' Sigurbjörn said in an official tone of voice.

'We look after our animals well here,' said the woman. 'They get the best.' Thórarinn thought her grimace seemed to relax. She had to keep wiping her watery eyes. She was about to invite them into the parlour, but Sigurbjörn said he would feel more at home in the kitchen. She showed them into a large kitchen in the basement. It was spotlessly clean. Its walls were painted pink, and the table was large.

'Will the man have coffee? Will the boy have milk to drink?'

Sigurbjörn thanked the woman kindly. Thórarinn was given lukewarm milk from a jug and the woman set before him a slice of extremely sweet cake. A window was open and a hen passed it, pecking at the ground. When it had gone, a bluebottle could be heard buzzing loudly. Thórarinn's stomach was full after all the bread he had eaten but a glance from Sigurbjörn decided him to polish off everything on the plate. Sigurbjörn and the woman were discussing the welfare and needs of the country. It soon became apparent that the public veterinary health inspector had a distinctly limited knowledge of cattle. The conversation took a turn towards architecture. 'The structural forms in this kitchen,' he said, with a wave of his arm, 'they bear witness to a grandeur of vision. The man who builds a kitchen like this beneath his house knows what time of day it is

What's that you say? Your husband helped in the building of the church at Stóra Núpur, did he? Ah, there you are, then, you see. I know a thing or two about these matters. My name is Sigurbjörn Helgason. I'm a well-known architect. I ran a building firm with my colleague, the master carpenter Gudbrandur Jónsson.'

At this assertion an enormous smile broke out on the woman's face, and Thórarinn began to have had enough of being indoors. He thanked the woman and went outside. The dog greeted him most warmly. He walked down towards the cowshed along the cattle track that led to it, ending in a slippery mess of mud by the door. A large rusty rear axle lay at the western end of the shed in the shade by the concrete wall. Thórarinn walked round the cowshed, and returned to the house once again. He found a dead plover under the parlour window. It had flown against the windowpane, been slightly flattened by the impact, and had stiffened in that shape. He threw the bird on to the grass, and said, 'Here, doggy doggy.' The dog merely sniffed at the bird.

He peeped through the window and could see into the passage and out to the gravel forecourt through the open door. In the parlour there were photographs of the family on top of a cabinet. There was a small table on thick, bevelled legs, a green crystal bowl with some postcards in it.

A large painting of a swan hung on the wall. A small stream ran through the grass at the eastern end of the house, washing up stones from the sandy soil.

Thórarinn walked in front of the house. He seemed to conjure up a mirage of a village in the hot air, through the haze of blowing sand. When he came back down into the kitchen, he asked, 'Why have you got a picture of a swan in the parlour?'

'Well, it was like this,' said the woman. 'We fostered a baby swan here, and the creature became a bit of a household pet. Then a travelling painter came here and was eager to paint something for us and we asked him to paint the full-grown swan.'

Sigurbjörn became extraordinarily interested and wanted to be allowed to see the picture. They went through to the parlour. There the swan sat, gigantic, in the foreground of the painting with the farm in the distance behind it. Sigurbjörn read the name of the painter. He said that today was a joyful, red-letter day. This was the artist, Óskar, who had spent his entire life painting Thingvellir over and over again. Never had he, Sigurbjörn, expected to see such a beautiful painting; it was a masterpiece. He did not have the words to give the picture the praise it deserved. The woman was surprised to learn that she owned such a remarkable painting. 'But it was an unusual swan too,' she said.

Sigurbjörn had walked over to the window. 'We're going to walk into Raudaskridur later, the boy and me,' he said, looking towards Stóri-Dímon. 'But I'm terribly tired.'

There was a bed against the wall at the end of the parlour, which was lined with blue panelling. Sigurbjörn pulled up a chair and sat down at the table. He was shivering rather, and complained of feeling cold. The woman was surprised by this, for the house was oppressively hot. She fetched a thick woollen blanket. 'I'm still cold,' he said when he had pulled the blanket round his shoulders. The woman was grimacing again. She fetched another blanket, but the man was still cold. Then she produced a large, black fur cloak. Sigurbjörn sat down on the bed with his legs under him and the fur cloak over his shoulders. He had the shotgun with him in the corner. He dozed off immediately. 'Is this man your father?' the woman asked in a low voice.

'Yes,' said Thórarinn.

'Is there something wrong with him?'

'Not as far as I know,' said Thórarinn.

'Where are you from?'

'Reykjavík.'

'Can you phone home?' asked the woman.

'No, unfortunately not. We haven't got a telephone.' Thórarinn saw that there was a communal telephone in the passage.

'Are you having me on?'

'No,' replied Thórarinn. 'I want to stay with father as long as I can.'

Then the woman went out. He sat down at the table. Sigurbjörn had put two cartridges on the corner of the table. Thórarinn took the cartridges and put them on top of the postcards in the bowl. Through the window he saw Stóri-Dímon in the hot sandy air. Raudaskridur shone red in the sun. The river Markarfljót was rising from its bed. Claps of thunder broke across the sands.

The woman had almost closed the door when she went out, but Thórarinn let it stand slightly ajar. He went over to the window, a breeze was ruffling the buttercups in the field. After a while he heard her on the telephone. 'Is that the Selfoss police? There's a man from Reykjavík sitting on the bed. He's got a shotgun which he refuses to let go of and he's spread a fur cloak over himself. He's got a boy with him.'

Thórarinn could not quite make out what else she said. He sat down on the bed right up against his father. He could no longer hear the woman talking. Sigurbjörn appeared to listen, without a muscle in his face moving. 'Sunna!' he said suddenly in a loud voice. There was surprise in his voice and on his face. He hung his head and strained to catch any sound from the passage.

Father and son sat like this for a long time in silence and did not move. It was as though a sculptor were at work in the room, creating a bas-relief to adorn the holy church of Hallgrímur, the Icelandic Sagrada Familia, to be placed above its west door. Thórarinn looked at his father.

Sigurbjörn had leaned back into the corner and was looking at him angrily as though he were surprised to see him there. 'What do they want of me?' he thundered, full of fury. 'Can no one understand that I have to be allowed a little dignity in my life?'

Some time later there was the sound of a car being driven up the gravel road. Thórarinn, who knew it was the police, moved slightly.

'Where are you going, Tóti?' asked Sigurbjörn.

'Nowhere, Father,' Thórarinn replied. 'I was just making room. If mother's coming, she may want to sit between us.'

MARE'S NEST

Mare's Nest brings the best in international contemporary fiction to an English-language readership, together with associated non-fiction works. As yet, it has concentrated on the flourishing literature of Iceland, which appears under the Shad Thames imprint. The list includes the three Icelandic Nordic Prize-winning novels.

The poetic tradition in Iceland reaches back over a thousand years. The relatively unchanging language allows the great Sagas to be read and enjoyed by all Icelandic speakers. Contemporary writing in Iceland, while vivid and highly idiosyncratic, is coloured and liberated by this Saga background. Closely observed social nuance can exist comfortably within the most exuberant and inventive magic realism.

Epilogue of the Raindrops

Einar Már Gudmundsson
Translated by Bernard Scudder
160 pp.   £7.95   pbk

'A fascinating and distinctive new voice from an unexpected quarter'
Ian McEwan

Magic realism in Iceland is as old as the Sagas. Described by its translator as 'about the creatures in Iceland who don't show up in population surveys', *Epilogue of the Raindrops* recounts the construction (and deconstruction) of a suburb, the spiritual quest of a mouth-organ-playing minister, the havoc wreaked by long-drowned sailors, and an ale-oiled tale told beneath a whale skeleton, while the rain falls and falls and falls.

Justice Undone

Thor Vilhjálmsson
Translated by Bernard Scudder
Nordic Prize 1988
232 pp.   £8.95   pbk

'Thor Vilhjálmsson's hallucinatory imagination creates an eerily beautiful vision of things, Icelandic in far-seeing clarity, precision, strangeness. Unique and unforgettable.'
Ted Hughes

Based on a true story of incest and infanticide and set in the remote hinterland of nineteenth-century Iceland, *Justice Undone* is a compelling novel of obsession and aversion. An idealistic young magistrate (a figure inspired by the Whitmanesque Icelandic writer Einar Benediktsson) undertakes his first case. His geographical and emotional journey into bleak, unknown territory, where dream mingles sensuously with the world of the Sagas, tests him to the limit.

Angels of the Universe

Einar Már Gudmundsson
Translated by Bernard Scudder
Nordic Prize 1995
176 pp.   £7.95   pbk

*'I'm one of those invisible citizens that the wind sweeps along . . .
I only make myself known when the volcanoes start rumbling
within my soul.'*

With humane and imaginative insight, Gudmundsson charts Paul's
mental disintegration. The novel's tragic undertow is illuminated
by the writer's characteristic humour and the quirkiness of his
exuberant array of characters whose inner worlds are
gloriously at odds with conventional reality.

Night Watch

Frída Á. Sigurdardóttir
Translated by Katjana Edwardsen
Nordic Prize 1992
176 pp.   £7.95   pbk

'We all dangle from umbilical cords . . .'

Who is Nina? The capable, self-possessed, independent,
advertising executive, the thoroughly modern Reykjavík woman?
Or is she the sum total of the lives of the women of her family,
whose stories of yearning, loss, challenge and chance absorb her
as she watches by the bed of her dying mother?

William Morris

Icelandic Journals

The Icelandic Journals are pivotal in Morris's aesthetic, political
and literary development. He was fascinated by Iceland and his
experiences there helped to clarify his ideas of the relationships
between function and beauty in design and between art and labour.
His translations of the Sagas and the vocabulary he evolved for them
influenced his late fairy tales.
The Journals were last published in England in 1969.

The volume has a foreword by William Morris's biographer,
Fiona MacCarthy, and an introductory essay by Magnus Magnusson.
The illustrations include facsimile pages from the original edition and
endpaper maps of Morris's routes.

£15.99   hard cover